The Silent Sister

ALSO BY JAN BAYNHAM

The Greek Island Secret
The Sicilian Promise
The French Affair
The Secret Sister
The Silent Sister

THE
SILENT
SISTER

Jan Baynham

Choc Lit

A JOFFE BOOKS COMPANY

Choc Lit, London
A Joffe Books company
www.choc-lit.com

First published in Great Britain in 2025

© Jan Baynham 2025

Cover art by Jarmila Takač

ISBN: 978-1781898956

For Jo, with much love.

PROLOGUE

Kefalonia, 1948

Manolis Lucatos burst into the taverna, his eyes blazing.

'Where is she?' He spotted his eldest daughter in the corner by the bar, deep in conversation with the man he hated most. Nikos Makris. 'So, the rumours are true, then?'

Cassia looked in horror as her father approached. She grasped her boyfriend's hand. Complete silence descended on the bar as her father marched over to where she sat. Grabbing her arm, he dragged her from her seat.

'You're hurting me. Get off!'

Nikos came between father and daughter, but was pushed away by Manolis's free arm and fell to the floor.

'I'll deal with you later, Makris.' He turned back to his daughter. 'And as for you, you're coming home with me.' Her father's voice rose to a bellow. 'No daughter of mine is going to be a plaything for a commie bastard.'

Cassia looked back at Nikos, who was being helped up from the floor. 'You can't make me! I love him and there's nothing you can do to stop me seeing him. He's worth ten of you and your fascist friends.'

Audible gasps reverberated around the bar. No one argued with the generally well-respected village doctor, especially when it came to politics. He raised a hand as if to strike his daughter, loosening his hold on her arm. Cassia ran back to Nikos.

'You come home with me now! If you choose that communist over your family, you are dead to me! You will never show your face in my house again.' Manolis's face was red and blotchy, his stance defiant. 'Well? What's it going to be?'

Cassia's eyes burned with tears. '*Antío*, Baba. I'm going nowhere.'

Her father turned and strode out of the taverna to the sound of applause from everyone present.

CHAPTER ONE

CASSIA

Kefalonia, 12 August 1953

The air was thick as Cassia walked back from the centre of Argostoli. The place was silent, wearing a cloak of fear, with a real sense of foreboding. The pewter-grey sky resembled one threatening a thunderstorm at dusk rather than one approaching midday when the sun was at its highest in the sky. Despite being drenched in perspiration, Cassia shivered. Something was very wrong. Glad to have reached her house, sitting halfway along the street leading out of Argostoli, Cassia dismissed the ominous feeling by making herself busy. First, she unpacked her shopping. She went to put the vegetables away in the small outhouse when the whole building shook. Crockery, pots and pans fell with a crash to the floor. The shaking and shuddering increased in intensity before there was an almighty deafening bang. A huge gaping crack tore from floor to ceiling down the opposite wall. Cassia screamed. The floor underneath her continued to move violently. She grabbed onto a kitchen chair that toppled over and took her with it. The chair shielded her head as another crack above dropped large chunks of masonry on top of her. She yelled out in pain. Coughing and spluttering, Cassia found it hard to breathe as the room filled with grey dust. She struggled to free herself when a wooden rafter crashed from the ceiling, pinning her to the floor. Excruciating pain shot through her whole body. She tried to push herself free. Outside she heard shouting, yelling, haunting cries. The sound of crumbling masonry, wood snapping. It was the last thing she remembered.

* * *

'She's in here. She's alive. I need help to free her.'

There was urgency and panic in the voice. To Cassia, it seemed distant, yet the man was close. Another person scrambled over the rubble blocking the doorway to join him. Together, they lifted the heavy wooden beam off her. Cassia tried to open her eyes and became aware of a stabbing pain in her lower leg. She cried out.

'You're safe now.' The older of the two men, neither of whom she'd seen before, smiled at her. 'We're going to lift you out. Is it just your leg that hurts?'

Cassia nodded. She looked down to the source of her pain and saw a wound encrusted with dried blood and grey dust.

Once outside, the two men placed Cassia down to sit on the ground. 'It looks nasty, but I think it's just superficial,' the man said. 'Are you all right if we leave you to go and help some of your neighbours? This street is one of the worst affected.'

'Yes, please go! *Efcharistó*. Thank you to you both.'

Cassia had not been prepared for the devastation she saw in front of her. Not one of the houses stood unscathed. A gaping crack zigzagged the length of the street. Some buildings were completely flattened, while others had single walls intact. Some people wandered around aimlessly, while others held loved ones in their arms as they sobbed or dug through heaps

4

of stones to get to the people buried underneath. Cassia knew she was lucky. The pain in her leg was already easing, now it was free from the weight of the ceiling rafter. It was then the tears fell. Bereft and alone, her whole body wracked with sobs. If only Nikos were still alive.

A soft voice she knew so well interrupted her thoughts.

'Oh, Cassia. Are you hurt? I'm so pleased to see you are safe.' Cassia looked up at the weathered, wrinkled face of her dear neighbour, Sophia. 'Your house was so badly hit, I was afraid . . .' — she stifled a sob — 'it had taken you, too.'

Cassia managed to get to her feet without putting too much weight on her injured leg and flung her arms around the old woman who had been so caring when the news of Nikos's death had come. 'I'm all right. Oh, Sophia. Isn't it terrible? We knew it was coming, but not as awful as this. It's a bad one. What about you?' Cassia looked across at Sophia's house. The roof and one side of the house had completely disintegrated.

Tears streamed down the old woman's face. 'Everything's gone. My photographs of dear Vasilis, the children, the grand-children. All buried in a heap of rubble. I don't know what to do, I don't know where to go.' Sophia paced up and down the road in front of her house, confused and disorientated. Cassia begged her to stop. Eventually her neighbour fell to her knees, letting out a piercing wail.

Cassia crouched down beside her. 'It will be all right.' She took Sophia's hand in hers, stroking the papery skin and look-ing into her frightened eyes. 'We'll get through this, Sophia. We're both lucky. Let's see if we can find out what's going on. It's been hours since it happened. Someone will know where we can get shelter from this awful heat. I'll go and find out.'

Cassia helped Sophia to her feet and in spite of being in pain, moved along the street to find someone to ask. By this time, crowds of people were milling around the end of the street where piles of rubble and large blocks of masonry were the only remnants of the houses. Some of the men were digging through the chaos with their bare hands.

'They've got someone out!' shouted a woman, pushing through the crowd trying to see who it was.

The man carrying a body shook his head, his face ashen behind the grime of the earthquake dust. 'He's gone.' A howl from someone who was watching and waiting broke the grim silence that had descended on the crowd. The man walked over to where a pile of bodies lay and placed the latest victim down. Cassia looked away.

'Where is everyone going?' she asked anyone who would listen.

'They're setting up shelters in the park. The Red Cross has arrived, so anyone who is injured should go to Maitland Square, where they're erecting tents,' Demosthenes, another of Cassia's neighbours, answered her. Just as he'd finished speaking, a loud crash from the last wall to collapse made everyone jump and hide their heads in their hands. 'It isn't safe here. Go to the open space of the park.'

Cassia thanked him and hung her head as another body was recovered, alongside one more wail of recognition from a bystander. She went back to get Sophia and led her up the street. It was now full of people, all walking in the same direction. Some carried crying children, others items of bedding, even chairs. Many clutched icons of Mary Theotokos, the mother of Jesus, retrieved from the ruins of their homes, all making their way in the direction of the park. When they approached the house where the desperate rescue was happening, another body was carried out. This time it was a woman dressed in a blue floral dress, caked in dust. Strands of long black hair obscured part of her face, but Sophia grabbed Cassia's arm, her face distorted. 'I know her. She's got a little girl.'

She broke loose from Cassia and rushed up to one of the rescuers. 'A little girl. About three. That's her mother. Please, have you brought her out?' She pulled on the man's arm. 'Please. Tell me.'

The man shook his head.

Sophia became hysterical. 'She must still be in there. Her name is Eléni.'

CHAPTER TWO

Cassia eventually persuaded Sophia they had to get away to safety. Large chunks of masonry fell around them as the tremors continued beneath their feet.

'We can't do anything, Sophia. They know about Eléni now, thanks to you.' Cassia took her friend's arm, and they joined the others trudging along the road. Some walked in silence, in shock; others shouted at each other as if to mask their panic. The town looked like a warzone. The elegant town hall had been flattened as if it had been bombed. The library had just one wall still standing, revealing empty, broken shelves and scattered books, whereas the other side was a heap of debris. The opposite end of the park was edged with evenly spaced oleander trees. Once standing perfectly upright, they were now at precarious angles where deep splits in the earth had uprooted many of them. The open space in the centre had been transformed into a place of shelter for those whose houses had been destroyed. Large tarpaulin sheets suspended on wooden poles covered makeshift beds, and these were to become their homes. Some people had managed to bring mattresses and chairs, but Cassia had nothing. Crowds of people wandered around looking for people they recognised.

Cassia found room for her and Sophia with a young family. The woman gave Sophia a blanket and helped Cassia settle the old lady onto a makeshift bed. Now clear of the pink-grey dust that had filled the air earlier, the night sky above them was inky black, dotted with stars and a full moon.

* * *

After tossing and turning on the thin mattress she'd been given for most of the night, aware of activity all around her, Cassie had finally drifted off to sleep. In the morning, she was awoken with a start by the sound of shouting: 'There's a ship in the bay. British. Help has arrived.'

Cassia looked across at the tear-stained face of the woman lying on another mattress close to her. 'Sophia? Did you hear that? We're going to be all right.'

Sophia's eyes were closed, but she nodded her head and began to sob.

Cassia patted her neighbour's arm and persuaded her to sit up. 'It's good news. We'll get help now.'

Once Cassia had settled Sophia and accepted water from the family sharing the shelter, she became restless and knew she had to do something. She made her way to the harbour where the ship was anchored in the bay. Walking along the quayside was treacherous, and she took care to avoid the large cracks in the slabs of concrete. Tugboats were travelling back and forth from the ship, HMS *Daring*. Its white ensign flag with the Union Jack in one corner fluttered in the breeze. The ship was piled high with boxes. Two lines of islanders snaked from the harbour wall to several waiting donkeys and carts. The sailors handed over boxes and these were passed along each line. Cassia joined the end of one, starting to pass each box as it arrived with her to one of the cart owners.

'It is not too heavy for you, eh?' One of the sailors from the ship checked the boxes onto the cart. He smiled at her. His Greek was halting with a heavy accent. 'Here, I like to help you.'

She realised she was the solitary woman in a line of men. The sailor's broken Greek suggested he did not have a full grasp of the language yet, so she answered him in English, grateful that her father had ensured she and her sister had a good command of the language. 'I thank you. No, my arms are very strong.' She laughed for the first time. 'What is in them?'

The young man reverted to his own language. 'These boxes contain medical supplies. That line has the food.' He pointed to the second line where the boxes were much larger, and now sacks of grain were being handed along the men. 'You picked the right line. Our ship was based in Malta, and we were commanded to get here as soon as the captain heard about the earthquake. I am Thomas Beynon. Tom.'

'Cassia. Cassia Makris.'

She stepped back from the line, her arms and shoulders aching from the lifting. Once she stopped, she realised her arms were not as strong as she had boasted about to the handsome man standing in front of her.

Once the cart was full of boxes, he directed the cart owner to the Red Cross base.

Speaking slowly in Greek, Tom said, 'Please, you go to find tents. They are in park. They are next to shelters. You must be very fast. They need this soon.'

The cart owner looked at Cassia for her to translate his Greek, which she did so. He nodded at the British man and left very quickly.

Cassia turned to Tom. '*Efcharistó.* Thank you.' She spoke to him in his own language again. 'Perhaps I will be of more help to the injured at the Red Cross centre than here. You are right. For a woman, the boxes get too heavy.'

Tom's smile reached his eyes and little wrinkles radiated out from each corner. 'You did well. But I can see you as a nurse. You will have to prepare yourself. I've heard some of the injuries you will see there may be pretty horrific.'

Cassia looked puzzled. 'How can something be pretty and, how you say ho-rri-fic — does it mean horrible? It is not possible, eh?'

9

'I mean really bad. Some of the people are terribly injured from the earthquake,' said Tom.

Cassia became serious. 'I know. But I must do something to help. They are my neighbours, my friends. I say goodbye now.'

Tom shook her hand. 'Goodbye. We are here for as long as we are needed so I am sure we will see each other again.'

'I hope so.'

As she walked away from the tall, handsome sailor, she realised she did mean it. There was something about Tom Beynon that made her think he would make a good and caring friend. It was what she needed right now. Without warning, her eyes misted with tears. What did the future hold for her and the inhabitants of this island?

* * *

Her walk to the park was full of obstacles. The whole town seemed to be on the move. People blocked her path, scrambling to avoid the unsafe buildings lining every street. Children cried as they hung on to their mothers' skirts for fear of getting lost in the chaos; women dragged bags of bedding; men with spades shovelled rubble at every house she passed. In the town, large bulldozers attacked the piles of debris in order for the carts of medical supplies to get through to Maitland Square and the Red Cross centre. The cacophony of noise unsettled Cassia. She thought of Sophia and how the chaos would be affecting the old woman. She decided to check on her first before offering her services to the Red Cross.

The shelters now teemed with more people than when she'd left earlier, and for a moment, Cassia was disorientated, not remembering where their shelter was. She knew it was next to a row of cypress trees edging the side next to the road and rushed in that direction. She found the family who'd been kind to them. But Sophia was nowhere to be seen. Cassia's heart raced.

'Have you seen my friend?' she asked. 'I told her I'd be back. She's too frail. She won't cope on her own. Please.' Cassia heard the panic in her voice.

The mother looked up from trying to occupy her children. 'She left. I told her to wait for you, but she insisted she had to go. Something about an Eléni?'

'Oh, no.'

After thanking the woman, Cassia turned and hurried away. She knew exactly where she'd find her friend. Some of the streets had been cleared of a lot of the rubble, but groups of men were tackling piles of debris in front of houses where it was suspected there were people still trapped. Cassia passed through the hordes congregated around them and reached the street where her home had once stood. A large crowd still stood in front of the house Sophia had told her belonged to Eléni's family. Further along the street was a donkey and cart on which two bodies wrapped in sheets were laid. Cassia's heart sank, but she thanked God there was no tiny body among them. She searched for Sophia in the crowd. Standing on tiptoe, she could see her at the front, wringing her hands and quietly sobbing.

Pushing through the rows of bystanders, Cassia reached the old lady and pulled her into her arms. 'Sophia. What are you doing here? I was so afraid you were lost or injured. You should have stayed where it was safe.'

'I couldn't stay. I needed to see for myself they hadn't given up on her.'

Cassia knew to whom she referred.

'They've found two more bodies this morning. So it means Eléni is the last one to find. Her mamá, baba, yiayiá and pappoú are all dead.' Sophia began crying. 'I'm praying for her. She's an orphan now.'

As Cassia comforted her friend, she looked up at the men desperately digging away the debris. Their white vests were grimy with dirt and dust, and their skin glistened with sweat. One stood out from the rest with his thick blond hair and fair skin. It was Tom Beynon. He and his fellow sailors were part of the rescue teams here to relieve the local men who had been working all night. He walked over to her.

'Cassia, I thought you were going to help with the Red Cross.'

'I was, but I check on my friend first. She is missing. I find her here. She waits for Eléni.'

Sophia looked puzzled, unable to understand what they were saying.

'Sophia, this is Tom. He is from the ship and he's here to help us.' Cassia smiled. She turned back to Tom. 'She does not leave. She waits for you to find the little girl who lives in the house. Everyone is dead, I think. I do not want Sophia to see.'

Tom nodded. 'If there is anyone alive in there, we are digging very carefully. We will get her out if we can. Now I must get back to my mates.'

'Mates?'

'My friends. The other sailors.'

'Silence!' One of the men stopped digging. 'I heard something.'

A hush descended on the crowd. People strained to see what was happening.

'There it is again,' said Tom. 'It's faint, but it sounds like a cry.'

Sophia grabbed Cassia. 'Perhaps it's Eléni. She's alive.'

'We mustn't build our hopes up, Sophia. If Eléni is buried in there, it's been over twenty-four hours now. I'm afraid you must prepare yourself for the worst. Why don't we go back to the shelter?'

Sophia drew her mouth into a straight line, shaking her head. 'No. Her mother would want me to stay. Poor little thing — she has no one now. She has no other family here, her mamá told me. I'm staying to the end.'

Cassia knew there was no persuading Sophia to leave until the men brought the little girl out . . . dead or alive. She would have to stay too. She would forgo registering with the

Red Cross until this was all over. She squeezed her eyes tight to prevent tears from rolling down her cheeks. She prayed to St Gerasimos to keep them all safe from future tremors and for Eléni to be brought out alive.

Together, the sailors lifted each piece of masonry and heavy wooden joists with care. Something jumped out at them with a screech and scattered dust as it fled the scene.

Tom stepped back. 'What was that? Oh, a ruddy cat! The noise wasn't a child then.'

People started to drift away as the hours passed. It was over seven hours since the last two bodies had been retrieved. The pile of rubble diminished as the men filled barrows with what remained of the demolished house. Cassia noticed a smartly dressed man with a notepad in hand across the street from where she and Sophia were standing. He stopped people as they moved away, talking to them and writing down what they had to say. *A reporter! How dare he come here to our town, our island, cashing in on our catastrophe!* She clenched her fists so hard her broken nails dug into her palms. He crossed to stand by Cassia.

'*Kaliméra*, I'm Rhodri Jones, chief reporter from the *Celtic Chronicle* in Wales. And you are?' Before the question was out of his mouth, Cassia glared at him.

'You have no right to be here, watching our suffering! Watching our misery! I have nothing to say to you. Go away! Or better still, put your notepad down and get in there and help those sailors who are looking for a little girl buried under hundreds of tons of rubble.' She surprised herself at the force of her voice.

Rhodri Jones stood back from her and put up his hands in front of him. 'Hey, hey, stop. I'm just doing a job I was sent to do. It's far from invading your privacy. The more the rest of the world knows about this catastrophe and the devastation on the island, the more help and aid will be sent here. And I *will* help if I can.' He spoke in perfect Greek with a mere hint of an accent. He put out his hand. 'Can we call a truce, Miss . . . ?'

Warmth travelled along Cassia's neck. She took his hand. 'It's Mrs Cassia Makris. I'm sorry. I hadn't thought of it like that.'

Tom came over to them. 'What was all that about?' He looked at the notepad in Rhodri Jones's hand. 'Oh, a reporter.'

'I thought the same as you. But Mr Jones insists the more the rest of the world knows about us, the more help we'll get.'

Tom didn't look convinced. 'If you say so. Sorry, I came to tell you I think we're going to have to call it a day. There's nothing left in there. Will you explain to your friend?'

How am I going to tell Sophia? thought Cassia.

Rhodri Jones handed Cassia his notepad and took off his jacket. 'One more try, eh, old boy?'

Tom looked exhausted. He and his fellow sailors had been digging non-stop all day.

'Right. One more.'

The two men left them and began tackling the heap of stones.

It was just Cassia and Sophia left waiting. Time dragged. It was silent apart from the occasional talk of the men working to clear the house.

'Over here!' It was the cultured voice of the reporter. 'We'll have to be very careful as we lift this piece of wood from under those blocks of masonry. It looks like a door has fallen and then part of a wall.'

'What have you got?' shouted Tom.

'I can see a tiny hand. A child's hand. Poor little mite.'

CHAPTER THREE

Cassia hugged Sophia, who looked confused. The two men were speaking in English, so she had no idea what they were saying.

'They've found her, Sophia. They've found her.'

The old lady let out a scream of pure delight.

Looking at the expression on Sophia's face, Cassia wondered if she'd been premature in telling her friend the news. What if it was the child's body they'd found, not the living little girl of whom Sophia spoke so fondly? How was she going to deal with it? She put her fingers to her lips so she could hear what the men were saying.

'That's it. You hold her head while my mate and I lift this door away from her chest,' said Tom. 'It looks bad, bless her. The wood has splintered and cut deep into her arm. I don't think there's any wood left in the wound, though. After three — one, two, three.'

Cassia heard a child's whimper. Her heart raced as she imagined how frightened the little girl must be.

'There, there, *agápi mou*. We've got you now.' It was the reporter's voice soothing the young victim.

Cassia called out to them. 'Is there anything we can do?'

'We're bringing her out now.'

Soon, he emerged with a small child flopped in his arms. Dried blood covered her head and her pallor resembled the colour of milk. Her limbs were covered in blue-black bruises, and one of her arms hung at an odd angle below the elbow. Cassia gasped.

Sophia wailed, 'My poor, poor Eléni.' She rushed to Tom and the little girl. Tom shielded her from being touched by the old lady. 'Cassia, tell her she's in a very bad way. We need help immediately.'

By now, Rhodri Jones was at his side with the other sailor. 'Go to the Red Cross centre and get a stretcher. She needs to be lying flat. And warm,' Tom told them. His eyes were brimming with tears.

The two men raced off to get help. Cassia comforted Sophia. 'At least she's alive after all this time. She must be a strong little girl.'

Sophia sat down on the ground, exhausted. She looked up into the sky as if searching for her God. '*Efcharistó. Efcharistó.*'

'There's a long way to go yet, I'm afraid. Her pulse is very weak. I wish they'd hurry up.' The strain on Tom's face showed.

Cassia went to the end of the street and shouted back to them. 'I can see a Jeep with a red cross on its side weaving its way through the debris.'

When Cassia returned to wait with the others, Eléni whimpered. Tom was doing his best to keep her still. For a second, her eyelids fluttered as she opened her eyes. Then she lost consciousness again.

'She's waking up,' said Sophia. 'She's going to be all right. My prayers have been answered.'

Tom caught Cassia's eye and shook his head. They both knew there was a distinct possibility the little girl would not survive and would be joining the rest of her family before very long.

The Jeep stopped in front of them. Two Red Cross personnel jumped out and went straight to Eléni.

'You've done the right thing keeping the patient as still as possible, sir. Before we put her onto a stretcher, we need to get her arm in some sort of splint.' The medic handed Tom a blanket. 'Can you wrap her in this to help get her body temperature back up to normal? We are all sweltering in this heat, but the little one feels icy cold.' He looked at Sophia. 'Could we use your walking stick, *parakaló?*'

Happy to help, Sophia handed over the stick, which the men laid along Eléni's arm before binding it tightly with a bandage. Next, they laid out a stretcher on the ground next to Tom and lifted the little girl onto it.

Putting Eléni into the back of the Jeep, the driver looked at Cassia and Sophia. 'I think the little one would like her mamá and yiayiá to come with her. It's quite bumpy out there, and it would be good if you could help keep her as still as possible until we can get her to the base. If only the town's hospital hadn't been razed to the ground. But we'll do our best.' He turned to Tom. 'Thank you, sir. I think you saved the little one's life.' He nodded at Rhodri Jones. 'Make sure you put that in your report.' No one else had noticed that the journalist had retrieved his notepad from Cassia and was busily scribbling away.

Sitting either side of Eléni in the back of the Jeep, making sure she was as still as possible, Cassia reflected on what the Red Cross man had said. Eléni didn't have a mamá or a yiayiá anymore. If she survived, what would happen to her? She had no one. Cassia didn't know anything about her and had seen her for the first time as she'd been brought out from the rubble by Tom. Sophia knew the child, but she was too old and frail to look after a three-year-old. A wave of emotion washed over her. She closed her eyes. The handsome face of Tom Beynon entered her mind. Tom would know what to do. *Aren't you getting ahead of yourself? Eléni isn't out of the woods yet! She has a lot of healing to do.*

Sophia must have been having the same thoughts. 'Who is going to look after her now? She can't go to one of those homes. She can't.'

Eléni whimpered as the Jeep hit a bump in the road. Cassia reached across to stroke the little girl's face, then patted Sophia's hand. 'That's a long way off yet. We have to get her better first. We'll let the Red Cross do their job. We're almost there.'

Large grey bell tents had been erected to fill the empty space in Maitland Square. Men and women wearing white uniforms with large red crosses were busy seeing to patients. There was a queue at every tent with people having head wounds cleaned and bandaged, gashes on legs and arms stitched, and breakages splinted and cast in plaster.

The Jeep stopped outside a larger oblong tent housing a ward of seriously injured patients, where Eléni was rushed to a waiting bed. After giving as much information as they could between them, Cassia and Sophia were asked to leave. Both said their goodbyes, and as Cassia leaned over the little girl to kiss her, Eléni opened her eyes for the first time. She didn't make a sound but reached out with her uninjured arm, gripping Cassia's arm like a vice. The terror in her large brown eyes told her everything she needed to know. That little girl was not going into a children's home. If there was no one to look after Eléni, Cassia was determined to do it herself. She didn't know how, but if anyone could help her, she knew who it would be.

Before leaving, she did what she'd intended to do that morning. She told Sophia of her plans and that the old lady was to make her way back to their shelter alone.

'If they take me on, I'll be able to look out for Eléni. Sit with her at times. I'll come and check on you, and let you know how she is.'

'Thank you, Cassia. It would mean everything to me. I'm hoping my daughter will come from Athens once she's allowed to get in. All I want is for that little girl to get better and for you to look after her.'

Cassia kissed her friend and dismissed the idea of taking in Eléni herself. For now.

She found the tent where volunteers were registering to help. She reckoned if she worked at the base, she'd be able to see Eléni every day and observe the progress she was making.

'Name? Have you any nursing experience?' asked one of the men in charge.

'Cassia Makris. No, but I'm willing to learn. I must do something. I just want to help.' How she wished she'd done what her sister, Eugenia, had done and trained as a nurse, much to her father's approval. Instead, she'd learned lacemaking and embroidery from her mother. When she and Nikos had fled south after the argument, she'd had a stall in the market and had enjoyed seeing her beautiful tablecloths and antimacassars snapped up by admiring customers. All that was of no use now.

New casualties were arriving every minute, and they were short-staffed.

'Here, put these on.' The man handed Cassia a uniform and told her to do what she could. 'Watch the trained staff and follow their instructions to the letter. Do you understand?'

Cassia nodded and put on her uniform over her clothes. A nurse who introduced herself as Athina rushed into the tent. 'Are you free? We need an extra pair of hands.'

The two women broke into a run and entered another tent, where a man clutched his head and had blood streaming down his face.

'Wash your hands there,' Athina told Cassia, pointing at an enamel bowl of warm water on a table in the corner of the tent. 'Then press this on the wound to stem the bleeding.' The cold pad was wet and, from the smell, had been soaked in some form of antiseptic, judging by the yell the man made when she held the pad on the wound.

'Sorry.'

'It will stop an infection,' said Athina, taking over from Cassia and checking that the wound was clean. 'It looks worse than it is. I don't think it will need stitching. Watch me do this first one and then it can be your job as the casualties arrive. There's a queue already. Press a clean pad on and then bandage firmly round his head. You'll need to secure the ends by tucking them in like this.' She turned to the man, asking what had caused his injury. 'All done. Try to keep the dressing clean. Impossible, I know, in this mess. And you should try to rest. You've had a nasty bang to the head.' She walked away to bring in the next patient.

'*Efcharistó*,' called the man after her. He turned to Cassia. 'I have to get back to my street. They're still pulling people out alive.' Tears formed in his eyes. 'My mother is still missing. I can't rest while I could be helping the rescuers. I should go.'

A spot of blood had appeared on the man's bandage.

'You must take care.' Cassia was concerned for him. 'You want to be there when your mother is pulled out alive, don't you? Don't resume the digging yet. Wait for your wound to stop—' The man got up and left. 'Bleeding.' She wondered how soon it would be before he had to return to the centre for more treatment.

Cassia spent the next few hours cleaning and bandaging wounds, passing on any that were too serious for her to deal with. The queue seemed never-ending. Her back and legs ached from standing, but the feeling of doing something to help outweighed the tiredness and any discomfort. Through the doors of the tent that were tied back, she'd seen the sky change through a whole spectrum of oranges and corals as the sun had set. It was now pitch-black out there and the tent was lit by oil lamps.

Athina came to her. 'You can take a break now. You've done a great job. I should've asked you your name?'

'Cassia. I'm glad I could help. *Efcharistó*, I just need to check on my neighbour who's under one of the shelters. And I'll be back here at first light if you can use me.'

'That's good to hear, Cassia. I'll show you where to leave your uniform.'

She didn't mention there was someone else she wanted to check in on, too.

CHAPTER FOUR

Not knowing if she would be allowed in, Cassia made her way to the tent where she'd left Eléni. Her heart thumped as she wondered what condition the little girl would be in.

'I've come to check on a little girl who was brought in earlier. Eléni.'

After agreeing to let her see Eléni, they directed her to a bed at the far end of the ward. A flimsy screen separated it from the rest. Cassia took a deep breath and pulled back the screen.

'Tom! What are you doing here?'

'I could ask you the same thing. I wanted to see how our little girl was doing.'

Without warning, tears formed in Cassia's eyes. She'd only just met this kind man, but every time she was with him, she warmed to him more. She wanted to take him in her arms and give him a hug.

'That is kind of you. You must be — how do you say? — exhausted.'

'She's been sleeping the whole time I've been here. The nurses are checking her every half hour and they say sleep will help her heal.'

Cassia looked at Eléni. She appeared even more tiny in the bed than Cassia remembered. Helpless, vulnerable and alone in the world. She had a little more colour in her cheeks than when she'd been brought in, and she had a drip of clear liquid being pumped into her right arm. Her eyes were closed, but when Cassia sat beside her, she could hear her soft, regular breathing. Perhaps she was going to pull through. As Cassia leaned across and kissed Eléni on the forehead, the little girl opened her eyes and they widened. It was the same panic Cassia had seen in her eyes when she'd been rescued from the house. The little girl still didn't make a sound, but she moved her head from side to side in distress.

Tom got up from his seat and whispered to her. 'Do not worry, *cariad*. We look after you.'

Eléni screwed up her eyes so she didn't have to see either of them.

'I think we should go, don't you?' said Cassia. 'Let's see if we can ask a nurse or a doctor about her progress. You called her *cari* something. What is that?'

Tom smiled. '*Cariad*. It is a Welsh word. It means "love" or "darling". A bit like *agápi mou* that you Greeks say. Yes, let us find someone. She does not know either of us. Do you think it would help her if Sophia came and sat by her in the morning? She seems to be the only person left who she knows.'

It was true. With all her family dead, Sophia might be a welcome face for the little girl. Sophia had known Eléni's mother, and if it wasn't for her, the digging may have stopped, and the little girl would have perished alongside her parents. 'That's a good idea. Sophia will feel useful and I won't feel guilty when I leave her to do my shifts at the centre.'

The two of them managed to find a nurse sitting at a table, checking the details of the patients on her ward.

Cassia spoke to her in Greek. 'I wonder if you can tell us how Eléni is doing.' She realised she didn't even know the little girl's surname. She gave her own to save explaining who she and Tom were. 'We're worried that she gets upset and does not utter a word.'

'Ah, you are her parents, eh?'

Just as Tom was about to correct the nurse, Cassia nodded. It would help if they could see Eléni whenever they wanted. Who else would be there by her bedside? Could she persuade Sophia to take on the role of yiayiá? *It was just until Eléni was out of danger*, Cassia told herself. It didn't seem right for the child to be fighting to survive without a soul there to support her.

'Physically, she's making progress. It's very early days. But she is traumatised. That recovery is going to take much longer. The more you can visit the better. Just talk to her, sing her favourite songs. I expect she had a favourite toy, but I presume it was destroyed in the earthquake. I have to go. There is another casualty coming in and I need to be ready for her.'

'*Efcharistó.*'

Once outside, Cassia turned to Tom. 'Thank you for not correcting her. If they know we are not her parents, Eléni will have no one. Are you willing to be Kýrios Makris for a short while? Just until she's better.'

Tom took her hand. 'You're very persuasive, Kýria Makris. You're starting to fall in love with that little girl, aren't you?'

Was her feeling for Eléni love, pity or concern for her future as an orphan? Whatever it was, it triggered such painful memories of another little girl who would be the same age as Eléni now.

* * *

'All I want is for her to get better and she needs someone to be there for her. I cannot get those terrified eyes out of my mind,' said Cassia, as the two of them walked to the shelter. 'I think your idea of asking Sophia to sit with her is a good one.'

The sky was an inky indigo dotted with stars and a full moon to light their way. Cassia thought back to the murky atmosphere of the previous day. The dust had now settled and the air had cleared. She took in a deep breath as if to prove she could do so without spluttering. There was no acrid taste at the back of her mouth. The familiar sound of cicadas was back. For the first time since the earthquake had struck, she allowed herself to feel a glimmer of hope.

'Our shelter is the one on the right. Thank you for walking me home.' She looked at Tom and laughed a hollow laugh. 'Home. Why did I say that? My home is a heap of stones. I have no home. Thank you for walking with me to the shelter.'

Tom grasped her hand and kissed it. Cassia knew his gesture was one of a new friend, a friend who she needed more than ever before at this awful time, but it didn't stop the warm feeling she felt as his lips touched her skin. 'It will get better. More ships are in the bay now, and aid is coming through. Perhaps our reporter friend was right. The more the rest of the world knows, the more help will get to the island.'

Cassia thought of the handsome man who spoke perfect Greek. Rhodri Jones. She remembered how she had yelled at him. If it wasn't for him insisting the sailors should carry on digging, her lovely Eléni would never have been found.

Sophia was wide awake when they arrived. Since Cassia had left that morning, there were now two chairs and some wooden boxes used as a table, on which there was food and water.

'How is Eléni? Did you manage to see her? What did the doctors say?'

Cassia turned to Tom. 'Did you understand all that?'

He smiled at the urgency of the old woman's questions. 'Yes, we both have. She is very ill. The doctors, they say she gets better. Long time.'

Cassia continued, speaking slowly so Tom could understand. 'Eléni looks better now. The doctors and nurses say her injuries will heal, but when she's awake she seems frightened. When Tom or I try to talk to her, she gets agitated and scared. She doesn't know us, of course. Would you be willing to sit by her and talk to her? She knows you, doesn't she?'

Cassia and Tom knew Sophia's answer before she uttered any words. 'Oh, Cassia, I would love to. I have been thinking about her all day. She must be about the same age as the little girl sleeping over there. She has a mother to look after her, and now her yiayiá has been found and has joined the family. I'll be Eléni's yiayiá.'

Tom winked at Cassia. 'And we didn't even have to ask.'

* * *

The next morning, Sophia and Cassia left the shelter for the Red Cross centre. They arrived at the ward where the nurse receiving the casualties spotted them.

'Ah, the little girl's yiayiá, too.'

Neither of them corrected her. They walked the length of the ward to Eléni's bed. She was propped up on two pillows, and the drip had been removed from her uninjured arm. Cassia held back as Sophia stopped and inhaled deeply before approaching. She then bent over and kissed the child on her cheek.

'*Agápi mou*, I'm so pleased to see you looking better.'

The little girl looked up at the old lady, and a wide smile lit up her face. It was the first time Cassia had seen her look happy. Tom's idea had been right: it was only Sophia she would recognise.

Cassia approached the bed. '*Kaliméra*, Eléni. I can see you're pleased I've brought your friend to see you.' Cassia smiled at her. But it was as if a veil had been drawn across the little girl's face. Eléni turned her head away and squeezed her eyes tight.

Sophia took Eléni's hand. 'This is Cassia. She's a friend who has been concerned about you, too.' The old lady looked up at Cassia. 'Why don't you go to your shift and come back later? I'll try talking to her.'

Cassia agreed and made her way to the tent. She knew she would soon be so busy helping more injured survivors that she wouldn't have time to think about why Eléni was so afraid of her. She found her uniform and joined Athina, who was stitching a nasty, deep head wound on a young woman. Even though there were fewer patients needing medical attention each day, stories of people being pulled from underneath collapsed buildings were still coming through. Many were dehydrated and had breathing problems from inhaling so much dust. Others needed reassurance they were going to be all right. Cassia sat with them and listened to harrowing stories of loss, of children buried under rubble and taking their last breaths as they held their hands. When it was time for a break, she visited Eléni and Sophia. Approaching the bed, she heard giggling and saw Sophia making silly faces. Eléni's eyes sparkled in delight. So different from the wide-eyed terror Cassia had seen earlier.

'Look who's come to see you, *agápi mou*. It's Cassia.'

The little girl's expression changed, but she didn't turn away. Instead, she looked directly at Cassia.

'You two look as if you're having fun.'

The little girl nodded.

Sophia grabbed Cassia's hand and squeezed it. 'Still no words,' she whispered.

* * *

Eléni continued to improve over the next few weeks. The bruises faded and the splint was taken off her arm. But she'd still not uttered a word. All communication on Eléni's part was carried out by miming actions, a nodding and shaking of the head, and her facial expressions. Sophia spent the days at her bedside, making up stories about animals for her to enjoy. Whenever she was not needed at the centre, Cassia sat with Sophia and Eléni. They both talked to Eléni even though she couldn't answer them. Instead, Cassia learned to know Eléni's emotions and needs by reading what the little girl's eyes told her. She realised it would only be a matter of time before the doctors said the little girl was well enough to leave, now that her physical injuries were healing and she was out of danger. *But where would she go? Where would any of them go?* Still, no family member had claimed her, and Sophia was sure no one would.

Tom visited Eléni each night and marvelled at the progress she had made with Sophia's help. The child welcomed him with smiles now, too. But still, she didn't speak. One night, he brought her some paper and a pencil from the ship.

'The ship — it is where I live.' Tom drew a simple boat shape, surrounded by wavy lines representing the sea. He handed her the pile of paper. 'Now, you.'

Eléni smiled and began to draw four stick figures. Holding up the paper, she pointed first at each figure in turn and then at the person the drawing represented.

Tom beamed at her. 'Good girl. That is very good. Here.' He took the sketch from her and pointed to the first figure. 'Sophia?' The little girl nodded. Tom wrote the name underneath. 'Me?' He labelled the second figure. 'Tom.' The drawing was completed once he'd written *Cassia* and *Eléni*. He handed the paper back to her. She held it up for the others to admire.

Cassia looked at Tom. 'How do you say — genius, I think?'

CHAPTER FIVE

The three of them stood to leave Eléni for the night when they were approached by a doctor they hadn't seen before. 'Can you call in to see me before you go, *parakaló*?'

'*Kalinýchta, agápi mou.*' Sophia kissed Eléni. 'I will see you tomorrow.'

The little girl waved as they left.

The doctor waited for them as they walked the length of the ward.

'*Efcharistó*, I'm sure you can see your daughter and your granddaughter has now recovered from her injuries. We can do no more for her here. We must use her bed if someone comes in who needs it.'

Tom looked to Cassia before she began speaking. 'Her body, it is healed, yes. But she does not speak. There must be something more you can do for her. We do not have a home. We live under a shelter. It is not good for her, eh?' Panic sounded in her voice. It was the day she had dreaded.

The doctor shook his head. 'She is clearly not deaf. She has suffered a trauma from the earthquake. She chooses not to speak. Did she ever speak before? She isn't very old. Two or three, maybe?'

Sophia spoke for them. 'She's three. Yes, she could speak before this awful tragedy happened. She must have seen . . .'

Before she could finish her sentence, Cassia butted in. 'Isn't there a medical person who could help?'

'Normally, there would be, but times are not normal. They would have been able to help with the night terrors, too.'

'What do you mean? Night terrors?'

'You are not here in the night. You must prepare yourself. Eléni wakes up screaming most nights. But they are getting less. She is soaked in sweat. Her eyes show she is terrified, and she covers her head. If you say you cannot manage her, I can arrange for her to have a place with the authorities who are taking all the orphans. Otherwise, you must take her home tomorrow.'

Once outside the tent, Cassia began to cry. 'We cannot let that happen. We can't.'

Tom placed an arm around her shoulders. 'We think of something, eh?'

But *what* she didn't know.

Sophia was silent.

* * *

Cassia and Sophia watched Eléni drawing a picture. They had now been living back at the shelter for over a month. Cassia had given up her work at the centre to concentrate on getting the little girl settled and happy.

To start with, the screams had been recurrent and although Cassia had warned the family living next to them, it had been a shock to everyone how upsetting they'd been. The terrified eyes had come back, reminding Cassia of Eléni drifting in and out of consciousness in the hospital ward. Slowly, the night terrors had become less frequent and, in the end, had disappeared altogether.

It was all down to one person. Arianna. Eléni had made friends with the little girl from the other family living in the shelter and they enjoyed playing games together. Her days were once again filled with fun.

Although Eléni still didn't speak, Arianna consistently knew what her silent friend wanted and was feeling. They didn't need words.

Eléni's drawings were becoming more detailed too. The little girl had drawn a picture of a house, only to straightaway scratch it out, pressing so hard with the pencil that the lead snapped. She began to cry.

'Whatever's wrong?' said Cassia.

Eléni stabbed her index finger at the drawing.

'It's all right. Have you drawn your house and you're upset because the earthquake has destroyed it?'

The little girl nodded. She wiped her eyes and took another sheet of paper. Her next drawing was a sketch of the same house, but this time, a small stick figure lay with a large oval shape on the middle of the body. She grabbed Cassia's hand. She pointed at the figure and then at herself.

'Is that you, *Elenáki mou*?'

Eléni nodded. Sophia pulled the little girl into a big hug.

That evening, Tom stopped by. They hadn't seen him for a few days and Cassia had missed him. Eléni ran up to him when she saw him approaching.

'How is my favourite girl, then?'

Eléni grinned at him and, taking his hand, pulled him to where she and Arianna were playing a form of marbles with small stones. He bent down and joined in the game. His stone hit some of the others out of the way. Arianna squealed, and Eléni clapped her hands.

'I go to talk to Cassia. Later I play,' he told the girls.

Cassia was kneading dough to make bread. A bag of flour lay on the makeshift table to the side of her. Every time he visited the area they called home, there were new additions that made living there more comfortable. Colourful blankets covered the beds, and soft cushions now provided padding on the wooden chairs. 'Did I hear my name mentioned?'

Tom rewarded her with a wide smile.

He turned to Sophia. 'Do you mind keeping an eye on Eléni for the moment? I need to talk to Cassia.'

He led Cassia to a space where there was room to sit down. She wondered what was so important that Tom wanted her to be away from Sophia.

'We've been summoned back to Malta and my ship leaves next week. Our work here is done. There are no more survivors to rescue and nothing else for us to do now. There are other ships sailing in to help. I just wanted you to know.'

Cassia looked down. She had a sense of unease that once HMS *Daring* sailed out of Argostoli harbour, she would never see this lovely man again. He was right. Food, water and supplies had arrived on the island. There was an urgency for temporary buildings to be erected for the homeless as areas were cleared by bulldozers and cranes. 'I always knew you'd have to leave sometime. We're all going to miss you, especially Eléni.'

Tom took her hand. 'I still have next week. I've been making enquiries and thinking . . .'

Cassia looked puzzled and waited for him to continue.

'You can't stay here with Eléni. There are no permanent places to stay yet. Don't you think someone will mention they know Eléni? It can't only be Sophia who recognises her.'

'But if there is, they won't be family! Sophia is adamant she has no one else.'

Cassia's heart thumped. She knew what it would mean if Sophia had got it wrong. If found out, implying they were Eléni's parents would prevent any hope of her staying with them. Soon, Sophia's daughter would arrive to take her mother back to Athens to stay with her, and Eléni would be taken in by the authorities. How could she lose her just as the little girl was starting to trust her? When working at the centre, there'd been speculation about having to build an orphanage to accommodate the hundreds of children who had survived but had lost their parents and families. When she'd checked with Sophia, the old lady had reassured her that

Eléni's mother had never mentioned any other family. There was such chaos in Argostoli at the time, where would the authorities start looking for any other relatives of orphaned children? She had to take Sophia's word for it. She knew she was doing the right thing.

'Cassia, are you listening? There is one part of the island that escaped the devastation. It's the area around Fiscardo. All the buildings and houses are still standing. Many of the men came down to help with the rescue. Didn't you say it's where you're from?'

Cassia thought of the pastel-pink house her parents owned, untouched by the tremors and still intact opposite the pretty harbour. Her sister, Eugenia, lived on a smallholding with an olive grove stretching down to the beautiful, white-shingled cove.

'But I left to be with Nikos. Even though my father is dead now, they won't want anything to do with me if that's what you're thinking.'

'They wouldn't be so heartless as to turn you and your "daughter" away. Remember the driver with the donkey and cart delivering the medical supplies the first time we met? Well, he asked about you. I enquired if he knew anyone who had a horse and trap that could take us to Fiscardo. Guess what? *He* has. His farm is several kilometres out of Argostoli — he came in that day to see if he could be of help — and is almost untouched by the quake. Just a few of the outhouses suffered and the animals were spooked, but that's all. The best news is he's offered to take us . . . first thing in the morning!'

Cassia's mouth gaped open. 'Tomorrow? Tom, we can't just up and leave. I can't take Eléni away from Sophia. It will break her heart.'

Tom took both of her hands. 'Sophia will want what's best for Eléni. And I know deep down, you do too. It's your only chance, Cassia.'

She knew he spoke sense. She owed it to the little girl who had survived against the odds. It could work. If the little girl was too young to remember her parents and grandparents, would she come to think of Cassia as her mother? A vision of a tiny cherub-like baby lying swaddled in a finely crocheted shawl entered her head. Her baby. The baby who'd arrived sleeping. Angelika would have been the same age as Eléni had she lived. *Wouldn't I have wished for a new start for her if I'd been killed like Eléni's mother?*

Cassia knew what she had to do. She had to try. Not just for Eléni's mother's sake. For Angelika too.

CHAPTER SIX

'No! You can't take her away! This town is all she knows. What about Arianna? The two are inseparable. I shall miss my little girl. She'll miss me!'

Telling Sophia of their plans was harder than Cassia had thought. Her elderly friend voiced all the reasons why it was a bad idea, becoming distraught.

'When things improve in Argostoli, the doctors will help Eléni talk again. I know they will. I could take her back to Athens with me. Thousands of others are leaving the island.'

Cassia looked to Tom for help, glad his Greek had improved in the weeks she'd known him. He took Sophia's hand. 'It is hard to say goodbye. We want the best for Eléni, eh? I know you want that too.'

With his gentle persuasion, she reluctantly agreed that it was in the little girl's best interests to go to Fiscardo and live in a real home. Tears trickled down her cheeks. She brushed them away. 'On one condition. You leave me your sister's address.'

Cassia didn't want to tell her that she and Eléni might not be welcome at Eugenia's house. She quickly dismissed the unwanted thought.

'*Efcharistó*, Sophia. Eléni won't forget you. Once you get to Athens, please write and we will tell you how Eléni is doing. I will continue to tell her stories like you do and let her do lots of drawing. Last night I heard you singing a lovely lullaby soothing her to sleep. I'm going to rename it "Sophia's Song". She won't forget you. I promise. We'll talk about you all the time.'

The two women hugged, both with tears in their eyes. Sophia called Eléni to her and they sat down as her surrogate yiayiá explained what was going to happen. At first, Eléni shook her head and squeezed her eyes tightly shut.

Tom intervened and explained they were going to a beautiful place where there were no broken houses, no rubble, no cracks in the ground.

'You go to the beach and swim in the sea. Who knows? You find another friend like Arianna.'

At the sound of her friend's name, Eléni burst into tears and rushed to where Arianna was sat drawing. She tugged on her sleeve and mimed she was going away. She pointed to her chest and then kept brushing her hand away. Cassia followed her and explained to Arianna's mother that they were leaving.

When Arianna heard this, she started to cry too. The two little girls hugged each other tightly and eventually had to be peeled away from one another. Cassia wondered if she was doing the right thing. What if they got all the way to Fiscardo for nothing? Again, she speculated that Eugenia could reject her after the hurt she'd caused their family. But her biggest worry was whether Eléni would shrink back into her shell after all the progress she'd made.

That night, Cassia hardly slept. Every time she closed her eyes, she saw Eléni's distraught face and Sophia's expression as she tried so hard to be brave. At daybreak, the sun crept up into a sky brushed with bright shades of lemon and pale coral, almost as if it were willing her to have hope.

After gathering the few possessions they had — and eating a meagre breakfast prepared by Sophia — Tom, Cassia and Eléni left the park and walked to the harbour, where they found Stavros, the driver, waiting for them.

'We're off to Fiscardo, then. You will see a different scene, there,' he said.

Just as he helped Eléni into the horse's trap, a voice Cassia recognised called out to them. 'Off anywhere in particular? Did I hear Fiscardo? I haven't seen any of you for weeks now.' She turned to face Rhodri Jones.

Oh, no. The last thing she wanted was for a reporter to know where they were going. She began to stumble over her words. 'Umm . . .'

Not for the first time, Tom saved the day. 'I hear you've been reporting on the good job us British sailors have been doing. Thank you.'

'A pleasure, old chap. Folks back home should know how much these poor Kefalonians owe to you all.'

While Tom and Rhodri chatted, Cassia joined Eléni in the back of the trap where Stavros had placed cushions and blankets to make their ride more comfortable. Her heart racing, she strained to hear what the two Welshmen were saying, hoping Tom had continued to avoid divulging the exact details of their journey.

Stavros gave a loud whistle. 'Time to go,' he shouted.

The two men shook hands and Tom raced over to the waiting trap.

'Efcharistó, Stavros. Let us go.' Tom stepped up into the trap and sat on the other side of Eléni. *The perfect family*, thought Cassia. *But they weren't, were they? And Rhodri Jones knew it.*

As if reading her thoughts, Tom said, 'It's all right. I told him we were taking Eléni to see the donkeys on Stavros's farm as a treat after she had been so ill. I said it's on the road to Fiscardo.'

Cassia wondered if Rhodri Jones would have been fobbed off with the story, but there was nothing they could do about it now. The main thing was that they were on their way to the part of the island where no one would know Eléni. Cassia had to hope Eugenia would help her. There was no point in arriving at her family home. Her father had made it clear she was, in his own words, no daughter of his. Although he was now dead, she knew her mother would still agree with him.

As they set off from the harbour, Cassia was shocked to see how far the devastation extended. They were soon leaving the built-up areas and travelling along the open road. The smell of thyme filled the air, so different from the dry dust they'd left behind. The rhythmic clip-clopping of the horse on the rough road was soothing and lifted Cassia's mood. The weight filling her chest lightened the further they travelled from Argostoli. She admired the colours of the landscape again. The pines, the mountains on one side, the teals and turquoise of the sea below them on the other, stretching out in front of creamy limestone cliffs.

'Look at that beach, Eléni. The sand is almost white. Wouldn't it be good to play there and go in the sea?'

Ignoring her, the little girl looked straight ahead. It was going to take time to regain the progress she and Tom had made with her. Cassia had to keep hold of her conviction that what she was doing was right. Tom ran his hand along the top of the carriage seat and patted her shoulder, mouthing words of comfort. 'It'll be all right.'

'We're over halfway,' said Stavros. 'Do you want to stop and stretch your legs or carry on?'

'Please, can we go? The sooner we get there the better. *Efcharistó*, Stavros.'

There was still no reaction from Eléni.

* * *

The journey continued without incident. Nearing the beautiful village with its Venetian architecture caused feelings of nostalgia to flood through Cassia. She had called this place home for over twenty years of her life. Memories of a happy childhood all came flooding back — helping her mother with her embroidery-and-lace business, learning to cook her favourite moussaka and spanakopita, joining the partisans during wartime and meeting her beloved Nikos.

Stavros manoeuvred the horse and trap down through a narrow street that led to the harbour. On either side were pristine houses rendered in every pastel hue imaginable. There were more oleander trees with their pink-and-white blooms than Cassia remembered. The last in the row was where Nikos had lived and where they used to meet, before life had become impossible, living in the same town as her father, who'd had so much influence there. Her eyes misted when she thought of how happy they'd been when they'd moved to Argostoli, and of Angelika, the baby daughter they'd lost. Nikos had been overjoyed when he'd found out they had a baby on the way.

Tom interrupted her thoughts. 'Are you all right, Cassia?'

She nodded. 'Just memories. That house is where Nikos and I used to meet before . . .' She stifled a sob. 'So many painful things happened after the awful row with my father.'

One day soon she would tell Tom everything, including what had caused them to be estranged from her family. But not yet. He seemed to sense that she didn't want to talk about it and reached across Eléni's lap to squeeze her hand.

They stopped at the quayside. Fishing boats filled with nets and large pots were lined up along the harbour wall. Facing the water was a ship chandler's where a man with snow-white hair mended large ropes. Cassia recognised him as a friend of her late father's and hoped he wouldn't look up from what he was doing. She didn't want her mother to know she was in Fiscardo. Not yet.

'Where shall I take you?' Stavros said.

'My sister's place, *parakaló*. You carry on this road past the harbour and up the hill. Then you will see her smallholding overlooking a tiny bay. *Efcharistó*.'

Tom turned to Eléni. 'It is not a long time now, *cariad*. We'll soon go to the beach.'

Eléni didn't change her expression. Cassia wondered what she was thinking, and yet again doubts filled her mind. Turning up with a child her sister knew nothing about could be a huge mistake. The horse slowed as the incline steepened.

'We'll have to get out and walk, I think.' Tom's joke brought a tiny flicker of a smile to Eléni's face.

The little girl didn't make eye contact with Cassia, but looked down at her hands resting on her lap. She nodded.

CHAPTER SEVEN

Once they got to the top of the hill, they were rewarded with the most wonderful view. Through the pine trees, the sea was a vivid aquamarine, streaked with varying shades of turquoise and azure. Tiny frills of white foam edged the little beach. Eugenia's house was crystalline white and glowed in the bright sun.

'What a view!' Tom turned to Cassia. 'Your sister is so lucky to look out on that every day.'

Cassia's stomach churned the nearer they got to the house. To the side was an olive grove casting shade on the sandy soil underneath. White sheets billowed in the breeze on a washing line that stretched from the opposite side of the house to a tall pole hammered into the ground.

'It's the first time I've seen it,' said Cassia. 'When I left Fiscardo, Eugenia still lived with my parents. She hadn't met Georgios then. When she got married, a friend let me know her address but I didn't think I'd ever need it . . .' She lowered her voice. 'She sided with my parents. Believed what they said about Nikos.'

'Oh, I am sorry.'

Cassia got down from the trap and walked to the front door that was set back under the overhang that ran the whole

40

length of the house. She knocked on the door and waited, her heart thumping. How would her sister react?

The door opened. Eugenia's mouth dropped open when she recognised who it was.

'Hello, Eugenia.'

'Cassia! I don't believe it! What are you doing here? I've been so worried. I had no address for you and I heard most of Argostoli has been flattened.'

Her face drained of colour. She pulled Cassia into her arms and both sisters dissolved into tears.

'It's been terrible. I came to you. I have nowhere else to go. My house was destroyed along with others in Argostoli. You wouldn't recognise it. Our beautiful town has been reduced to a pile of rubble.'

Her sister looked past her as Tom and Eléni walked to join them. 'And who are these people with you?'

Stavros still stood by the horse and trap.

'These are my friends, Tom and Eléni. I will tell you more later. And this is Stavros, who was kind enough to bring us here. Please can we come in?'

'Hello. Of course, follow me.'

Relief that Eugenia had not rebuffed her surged through Cassia. All she had to do now was convince her sister that taking Eléni without the authorities' knowledge was the right thing to do.

Eugenia opened the door wide and led them into a large kitchen-cum-living-room. Dark wood panelling clad the walls and a long table took pride of place in the centre. It was good to finally be out of the sun and in a cool, shaded room.

'You must all be exhausted after your journey. Can I offer you some iced water or lemonade? Or perhaps you men would prefer a beer?'

'Lemonade for me. Eléni?' The little girl didn't respond. 'And one for my young friend.'

Eugenia looked puzzled. 'She's shy, is she?' Cassia just nodded her head, trying to be discreet.

41

'Two beers for us, *parakaló*,' said Tom.

'Why don't you go and sit under the awning outside, and I'll bring the drinks out to you. I'll call Maia to come and play with Eléni. She's down on the beach.'

They all walked outside while Eugenia went to the front of the house to call her daughter.

'Eugenia is very welcoming. You are safe here from prying eyes. No Welsh reporters, eh?' Tom smiled and Cassia relaxed. He was right. But she knew that if her sister's fisherman husband had been there, the reception would have been more frosty. Georgios had never approved of her relationship with Nikos even though they'd been a couple for some time when he came on the scene. Nikos would never say, but Cassia suspected Georgios had a dark secret he didn't want Eugenia or her father to know about. Now, Nikos was dead, and she would never know if Georgios had been involved in his death.

A little girl with crinkly black ringlets raced around the corner of the house, followed by an out-of-breath Eugenia.

Before going back into the house to get the drinks, Eugenia introduced her daughter. 'This is Maia, everyone.'

When she was around three, Eugenia had been identical to this little bundle of energy who introduced herself to everyone. How had Cassia not known her sister had a child?

'Hello, Maia. I'm your theía, Cassia. This is Eléni.'

'Do you want to come and play?' Maia took Eléni's hand, but she pulled it away and shook her head.

'Maybe later.' Cassia smiled at her niece. 'I'm going to help your mamá get the drinks now.'

Eugenia was waiting for her. 'What's going on? Friends?' She raised her hands, palms open.

'I'll tell you, but you must swear you will tell no one. Eléni's house was destroyed in the earthquake. She was buried under the rubble for two days, and Tom, one of the British sailors drafted in to help with the rescue, was the one who got her out, barely alive. Everyone else in her family died. She has no one.'

Eugenia's expression was one of shock. 'Poor little mite. Look, I'll take these drinks out and I'll come back for you to tell me more.'

On her return, Cassia continued to tell her the story. 'She has been nursed back to health by the Red Cross, and both Tom and I visited her every day. We've both become very fond of her and we can't let her go into a home for orphans — we can't.' Tears pricked her eyes.

'Oh. Come here.' Eugenia pulled her into a tight hug.

'It was Tom's idea. He suggested Fiscardo. There's no structural damage from the earthquake and no one to remember Eléni had a family who died. He thinks people will assume she is my daughter.' Tears then fell and her voice became a sob. 'I did have a daughter once. Angelika would be three now, just like her.' She looked up at Eugenia's puzzled face. 'Nikos and I had a baby who was stillborn. I keep thinking that if she had lived and I had died in the earthquake, I would want someone to look after her and become her new mamá.'

'Oh, I'm so sorry. That's awful. We must have been pregnant at the same time and neither of us knew. Damned stupid family row over politics. I'll never forgive Father! Come on, let's join the others. Tom's obviously fallen head over heels in love with you.'

Cassia stopped in her tracks. 'No! You've got the wrong idea. We're friends. We've only just met.'

Eugenia gave her a knowing look. All the years they'd spent apart disappeared and the two sisters reverted back to the teenage girls they had once been, always looking out for each other.

'If you say so. Surely you've noticed the way he looks at you . . . or you must be in denial.' Eugenia hugged her sister again. 'I'm so pleased you're back. I've missed you.'

Cassia thought about her sister's words as they rejoined everyone outside. Tom's eyes focused on her alone. She had been so moved by his kindness and his concern for Eléni that she hadn't thought of it as anything other than friendship.

Warmth spread along her skin. What if her sister was right and she'd missed all the signs?

'Mamá, Eléni won't answer me.' Maia looked disappointed.

Tom intervened. 'She is tired. The journey is long. That is right, eh, Eléni? She plays later.' Eléni got up from her seat and sat beside Tom on the bench. Smiling, he put his arm around her.

It was the first time Eléni had shown any reaction since leaving Sophia, Arianna and Argostoli. Tom had the knack of getting Eléni to respond that Cassia didn't. *What am I going to do when he returns to his ship?* She was going to miss the support he'd given her every day since that awful day back in August. But she realised it was more than that. Her heart skipped a beat.

'We should leave soon, Tom,' said Stavros. 'I must not be away from the farm for another day. My wife, she needs help with the animals, I think.'

Eléni grabbed Tom's arm. Panic returned to her eyes. 'It is all right, *cariad*. You are safe here. You have Cassia, Eugenia and Maia.' The little girl's eyes filled with tears.

'But not yet,' Eugenia said. 'I will make Stavros and Tom something to eat on the journey. Do you and Maia want to help?' Surprisingly, Eléni took Eugenia's hand and disappeared into the house.

'Stavros, I like to speak with Cassia alone. *Parakaló*, excuse us.'

Cassia and Tom walked in the direction of the little cove.

He turned to her, taking her hand. 'It is very hard for me to leave you and Eléni, but I have to go back to my ship. You know that already. Your sister will look after you and you will make a new home here.'

A wave of emotion washed over Cassia. She was never going to see this lovely man again. Tears trickled down her cheeks as she pulled him into a tight hug. 'I can't thank you enough for what you've done for us.'

Tom stood back and looked at her. 'It sounds as if you think this is the end. If it is all right with you, I will write to this address and you can reply telling me all about how Eléni is getting on . . . and you, of course. I hope even when the ship leaves Malta, we can still be penfriends.'

'Friends of the pen?' Cassia hadn't heard the word before.

'We will stay friends by writing. Wherever I go in the world, I can write to you and Eléni. I will never forget you . . . or her.'

Cassia heard a catch in his voice. They hugged again and walked back to the house. Stavros had gone to get the horse and trap from the olive grove, where it had been left in the shade.

Eugenia handed Tom a basket full of bread, feta and tomatoes. The two girls held a bottle of water each.

'We grow the tomatoes ourselves,' she said. 'More than we can eat. I take them to the small market in Fiscardo to sell. The olives are not ready yet. Girls, give the men their water.'

Stavros got down from his seat.

'*Efcharistó*, Maia.'

Eléni handed hers to Tom, who put the basket down and crouched down to the little girl's level. '*Efcharistó*. You are good for Mamá. You have fun playing with Maia.' Eléni nodded and grabbed his legs as he stood up.

Cassia's mouth fell open. It was the first time he'd referred to her as Eléni's mother. But wasn't that what she was going to imply to the people of Fiscardo? Eugenia alone would know the truth, and she'd been sworn to secrecy.

Tom shook Eugenia's hand. 'Goodbye and *efcharistó*. Look after them. I know you will help these two get over what's happened. I have a feeling little Maia will soon get Eléni talking. Now we must get back.'

He embraced Cassia. The warmth of his body against hers made her heartbeat quicken. 'Goodbye, *cariad*. I hope it all works out for you and Eléni. Remember, she's your daughter now.' His eyes full of unshed tears, he lingered no longer and picked up Eléni, swinging her round.

'Bye-bye, little one.'

As they watched the horse and trap disappear along the lane from the house, Cassia's chest filled with sadness. It was the last time Tom Beynon would be part of their lives. Letters would not be the same. She was on her own now. It was up to her to make a success of it.

Turning to go into the house, she saw the glaring face of a tearful little girl. Would Eléni ever accept her as her mother?

CHAPTER EIGHT

Cassia helped Eugenia prepare the evening meal, realising how life had carried on almost as normal there in Fiscardo. Back in Argostoli, she'd had to make do with meagre meals, which had to be shared between hundreds of homeless people, and she remembered how desperate they'd been until food supplies had finally got through.

'Did you notice Tom referred to you as Eléni's mamá. She didn't react, did she? I'll carry on doing the same, shall I?'

Cassia started on the Greek salad. She cut a slab of feta and placed it over the wedges of tomatoes, black olives preserved from last year and thick chunks of cucumber, before drizzling olive oil over the large serving bowl.

'But it doesn't seem right, does it? I'll never be her mamá. Yet, we can't stay hidden here forever — I need to get a place of my own in Fiscardo — so perhaps it would make it easier to be accepted. Is that being very disrespectful to Eléni's mother? What if, when Eléni eventually speaks, she remembers her mamá and knows it's a lie? She'd never forgive me. There's enough of a barrier there already. It was Tom she trusted and now he's gone.' Cassia placed the bowl down, her body wracked with sobs.

Eugenia put her arm around her sister. 'I'll do whatever you want, but you're not going anywhere yet. You can stay as long as you want. If you do decide to carry on with what Tom called you, we have to start now. There can be no switching from Cassia to Mamá. Isn't that what children who are adopted call their new mothers? Dry your eyes and let's enjoy our meal. A glass of retsina to celebrate our reunion?'

Through the tears, Cassia whispered, '*Nai, parakaló*.'

Cassia had been proud to be considered an independent, resourceful woman since Nikos had died, but the events of the twelfth of August had changed everything. She'd relied heavily on Tom's support and now her little sister was taking charge. Because Eléni did not — could not — speak to her, Cassia had no idea what the little girl remembered. Could a trauma steal your memories? What if Eléni not reacting to Tom calling Cassia her mother meant she didn't remember the woman lying motionless beside her under the rubble? Her real mother. Surely, the harrowing nightmares she'd suffered from when the quake had just happened had been her reliving the tragedy.

Cassia carried out the bowl of salad and placed it on a long table in the shade of a wooden construction covered with a vine in full leaf and laden with clusters of black grapes. Eugenia laid the table and brought out bread and the bottle of wine.

'Can you call the girls while I get their drinks?' Eugenia went back inside.

Cassia found them playing with two little stray kittens at the front of the house. For a moment, she watched them. Eléni held the tabby ball of fluff in the crook of her arm while she gently stroked the tiny creature with her other hand. When Maia chatted about her little grey kitten, Eléni smiled and nodded. Occasionally, she stopped stroking the little cat and used her hand to point and communicate.

'Time to eat, girls,' Cassia called. Before she could say any more, Eléni placed the kitten down and replaced her smile with a scowl.

'Theía Cassia, do you like the kittens? I'm calling mine Calix because he's very handsome. Can you help Eléni name hers? Mamá says hers is a girl.'

Eléni put her kitten down and walked back to the house.

'They're both lovely. Thank you for giving one to Eléni. I'll think of some names for her. Now let's go back and eat our meal.'

By the time they got to the table, Eléni was already eating.

'Someone's hungry and couldn't wait.' Eugenia laughed. 'It's good, eh?'

The little girl nodded her approval.

Once the meal was over and cleared away, Eugenia made up beds for Cassia and Eléni in the spare room with a view over the pretty cove below.

'*Efcharistó*. I wasn't sure if you'd turn me away after what happened. I can't thank you enough.'

'Why would I turn you away? You're my sister.'

'But what is Georgios going to say? He hated me, and certainly he hated Nikos, remember.'

An image of a large, swarthy man ranting at her and attacking Nikos for his political principles came into her head. She wasn't looking forward to seeing him again.

Eugenia looked serious. 'You've no need to worry about him.' There was a sharpness to her words. 'He left when Maia was two. He hasn't seen her since. *Bástardos!* Seems his fishing trips involved a different type of catch. In the form of a young girl in Ithaca. I'm running this place on my own and barely making ends meet. It's just me and Maia now.'

'Oh, that's awful. I'm so sorry.' Although incredibly sad for Eugenia and Maia, Cassia couldn't help feeling a little relieved.

'Don't be. It wasn't the first time.'

Cassia sensed it was the end of the topic as far as her sister was concerned. She stood and looked across to the faint shape of Ithaca in the distance. Word had come through that the earthquake had left havoc there too. What if Georgios was one

49

of those who'd perished? Maia would never know her father just as Eléni wouldn't. It was as if this part of the island was a different world, a haven of safety. She made up her mind there and then. She would become Eléni's mother and bring her up like Eugenia was doing with Maia. Alone.

* * *

Although Eléni wasn't as responsive with Cassia as she'd been before leaving Argostoli, the scowl disappeared. Together they'd all watched the sun sink and disappear into the horizon, a fiery orb in an orange-and-deep-coral sky. Eléni had pointed and smiled. They walked back to the house and found the two kittens playing in the doorway.

Maia squealed, 'Calix!' She scooped the ball of grey fluff into her arms. When Eléni saw her pretty kitten, she picked her up too.

'Shall we give her a name before we go to bed?' said Cassia.

The little girl smiled and nodded. Cassia, Eugenia and Maia came up with a list and Eléni shook her head at each one offered.

'Maia's little cat is Calix, meaning *handsome*, so what about yours being Callista? It means *beautiful*, doesn't it? And she is very beautiful.' Eugenia's suggestion was met with approval — Eléni beamed and nodded. Her new friend was Callista.

The first night sleeping in an enclosed room for many weeks seemed strange. Eléni was allowed to let Callista sleep in with them and seemed very relaxed and happy, falling asleep almost immediately. But Cassia lay awake, her mind swirling. As she'd done for months, she looked out at the clear night sky dotted with stars, but that night it was through an open window and not from under a tarpaulin shelter. She thought of Sophia, hoping it wouldn't be long before her daughter joined her. She thought of Arianna missing her little friend. She thought of Eugenia and Maia. While she tossed and turned, one face kept surfacing as the others faded into the background. The lightly bronzed face of a sailor with fair hair and hazel-green eyes.

A loud scream shattered her thoughts. The kitten shot out of Eléni's bed as the little girl sat upright, with her hands held over her ears and her eyes wide with terror.

Cassia rushed over, and Eléni's body shook as she held her tightly, whispering soothing words. 'Shh, shh, *agápi mou*. You're safe now. Mamá's got you.'

Gradually, Cassia felt the little girl's heartbeat slow down against her own chest. Eléni was soaked in perspiration. She stroked her forehead and held her until the little girl became calm again. By this time, Eugenia had appeared at the door.

'Is she all right?' she whispered.

Cassia laid Eléni back in her bed and the child shut her eyes straight away. Cassia went to talk to her sister.

'Yes. I should have warned you. Sorry. She often has these nightmares, but they are getting less frequent. When the quake first happened, it was a couple of times a night. It's as if she's not fully awake, but there is real fear in her eyes. I think she is reliving the horror of what happened to her. I suppose it has been a long and difficult day for her. Saying goodbye to Sophia and Arianna.'

'And to Tom.'

'Yes, and to Tom.' It had been difficult for Cassia, too.

By this time, Maia had joined them. 'What was that noise?'

Her mother picked her up. 'Poor Eléni's had a nasty dream, but she's all right now. Let me take you back to bed.'

CHAPTER NINE

'It's so good the way Eléni has settled. No more nightmares, eh? She and Maia have become great friends, haven't they? When you see them miming and signing now, it doesn't matter that Eléni doesn't speak. She will one day, I'm sure of it.'

Cassia smiled at her sister, thinking back over the progress Eléni had made since the day they'd arrived. 'I hope so. And it's all down to you letting us stay here.'

'It's lovely hearing those two having fun, especially with Calix and Callista.' Cassia and Eugenia were watching the girls play while they enjoyed a well-earned cup of iced coffee. They'd spent the morning collecting the zucchinis, which had ripened well over the last month.

'It's good for Maia. Living here, she had no one of her own age to play with, and now she's learning to share, too. I'd always hoped she'd have a brother or sister one day, but the siren in Ithaca put paid to that.' Eugenia became quiet.

What about the awful Georgios? Surely, he was to blame, too. Cassia kept her thoughts to herself and hoped her sister wasn't still hankering after a reconciliation with her husband. 'You may meet someone. You're still young and very attractive.'

Eugenia shook her head. 'Pah! No, I have finished with men.'

Cassia had declared the same thing when Nikos had died, but for a different reason. She could never love anyone as much as she had her dear husband, whereas Eugenia's reason was that she had been betrayed by a womaniser. She changed the subject.

'I've been thinking. Does Maia like drawing? The girls are doing so well pointing and miming, but I wondered if it would help if we let them draw what they want to say. It's what we did back in Argostoli and it seemed to work. I'm convinced Eléni will talk one day.'

While Eugenia was in the house getting paper and pencils, Cassia heard Maia shouting from the other side of the house. When she turned the corner, she witnessed Eléni push Maia to the ground and stamp on her hand. Maia screamed in pain.

'Eléni, stop! That's very naughty. What's going on? Maia, come here.' She placed her arm around her niece.

Both girls were crying. Eléni got more and more upset. She pointed at Maia and then at her leg, where there was an angry red mark. She picked up a small rock, pointed at Maia again and mimed throwing the rock at her leg.

'Are you saying Maia threw the rock at your leg?'

Eléni nodded and glared at Maia.

Cassia dropped her arm. Her niece wouldn't make eye contact.

'She wouldn't play. Anyway, she's not my friend anymore. She can't talk.'

Eléni ran to Cassia and grabbed her thighs, burying her head in her skirt.

'You mustn't shout at her, Maia, and you certainly shouldn't throw rocks at her. Eléni will talk when she's ready, won't you, *agápi mou*?'

Sad brown eyes looked at Cassia and Eléni nodded. Cassia took her hand and they returned to where her sister had set out paper and pencils on the table outside. Eugenia took one look at Maia's red-rimmed eyes and hugged her. 'What on earth's happened? Did I hear shouting?' The little girl remained silent.

'They've had a bit of a falling out. It's all dealt with now, isn't it girls?'

Cassia had a bad feeling it wasn't and this was just the start of Eléni being rejected because she couldn't speak. It had all started off with so much promise but of late, she could sense Maia's frustration that their communication was one sided and had overheard her niece becoming annoyed with Eléni. If she didn't do what she wanted, Maia would raise her voice as if Eléni couldn't hear her. They were starting to spend more time alone, each playing with their kittens in different areas of the yard.

'I notice it's happening more and more,' said Eugenia. 'I hope it's just a phase.'

* * *

The days started getting colder and they all spent more time indoors. Cassia was glad her sister had enough of a woodpile for them to burn logs on the open fire and dry their washing on two wooden clothes horses. It was time to collect the olives.

'In Greece, they say a man's worth can be gauged by how many olive trees he owns. I don't think it can apply to a woman's wealth. We may have many trees out there in our olive grove, but it doesn't bring in many drachmae.'

Cassia was conscious that having two extra mouths to feed must be making it even harder for her sister. Although she helped with all the household chores, the cooking and the chickens and the goats, she contributed no actual money.

'Have you ever thought of going back to nursing, Eugenia? I could look after Maia for you. I like to think I could make money by selling my tablecloths in the market, but when money is short I think that would be something people would cut back on.'

'I could, I suppose. Georgios didn't want any wife of his working. Her place was in the home, he said, so I haven't worked since we got married. Over four years ago. I think I would need some training. But I'll think about it, thank you. Now there's such a shortage of imported food, it's getting harder and harder.'

The girls played in the olive grove as the two women collected the ripe green fruit from the trees. They filled wicker basket after wicker basket and stored them under the covered slabbed area next to the outbuilding.

'I've asked Savvas, a friend who owns an olive press, to collect them in his truck in the morning,' Eugenia said. 'We can all go, and you can see how we make the olive oil. All this lot will merely make enough for our own use. There's not enough to sell.'

The sole income Eugenia seemed to get was from selling the hens' eggs and bottles of the goats' milk. These were collected each day and left at the top of the olive grove that opened onto the road that Stavros had come down from Fiscardo. A butcher who lived there travelled out each day and left money in the honesty box. Eugenia was still well known as Georgios's girl in the town. No one would take advantage of her, certainly not the butcher who'd known the family for years. With such a small amount of money coming in, and the fresh food from the garden and orchard becoming less now that winter approached, Cassia didn't know how her sister fed them all as well as she did. In the summer months, Eugenia had a small stall in Fiscardo market where she sold the excess fruit and vegetables. But she'd only travelled there a handful of times since Cassia and Eléni had arrived.

'Not worth the fuel it takes to get there,' she'd said on one occasion as she unpacked the box containing her craftwork.

* * *

Savvas arrived bright and early the next morning. He loaded the baskets of olives onto the back of the truck, then invited Eugenia to sit next to them while Cassia and the two girls sat up front with him.

'I don't suppose you remember me from school, do you, Cassia? I was in the year above you. Knew your Nikos. Bad show that. The reason I'm helping your little sister now is because that *maláka* has left.'

'What's a *maláka*?' asked Maia.

'A bad man, an idiot, *agápi mou*.'

Cassia hoped her niece didn't associate a *bad man* with her father or repeat the word. She'd been so young when he'd left, so she hoped she would have no memory of him. Eléni had also lost her father. Whether she would ever remember her parents was always niggling at the back of Cassia's mind.

The journey to the pretty fishing town was a lot quicker by truck than the one they'd taken by horse and cart to get to Eugenia's. Cassia hadn't left her sister's smallholding in all that time and had relied on her to get provisions for the family. She often wondered what reaction she'd get if she saw her mother again. She just wasn't ready to face her yet. Not ready to be rejected again, even though the cause of the rejection was no longer with her. Memories of the night when her father had hurled abuse at her would remain with her until her dying days. Nikos had been an undercover partisan fighting the Germans throughout the war. When it ended and he returned to her unharmed, she never thought for a moment there would be another war, a civil war, where family members fought each other. Fascists versus communists.

Savvas turned the truck into a yard behind his house just a kilometre out of Fiscardo. The gleam of the sun caused the sea to form a silver band in the distance. A large dog that looked like a German shepherd mix to Cassia came bounding over to welcome Savvas. Both little girls grasped Cassia's legs, too afraid to go nearer.

'Carina! Sit.' The dog did as Savvas told her and he took a leash from his trouser pocket. 'She won't hurt you, girls, but she's a bit excitable so I'll take her inside.'

'*Efcharistó*, Savvas,' Eugenia shouted after him as she dismounted from the back of the truck.

Cassia and Eugenia helped Savvas take the baskets of olives into a stone building at the top end of the yard, away from the house. Inside were shelves stacked with bottles of olive oil in different shades, from rich golden yellow to those with a greenish tinge.

'I've never seen so many bottles of olive oil, Savvas. How come they are all different colours?'

He smiled at her and told her about the different varieties of fruit. 'It also depends on how ripe the olives are.'

Cassia remembered being taken to watch the same process when she was a child and being just as mesmerised as Eléni and Maia were now. Everything was done by hand, from washing and sieving the fruit to grinding the olives between two millstones.

'It doesn't look like oil.' Maia watched the thick green pulp Stavros was spreading onto circular hemp mats, stacking one on top of the other, ready for pressing.

'You just wait,' he said. Once the pile was high enough, a press squeezed the oil from the stack. Vibrant green liquid flowed through to a container, from where it would be syphoned off into bottles. 'There you are. That's what you and Eléni will have drizzled over your salads and what Mamá will use to cook your favourite foods.'

'Not yet, though. When we get back, we'll have to put the bottles in the dark in the cellar and wait for about six weeks. Isn't that right, Savvas?'

Cassia reflected on how all the hours spent raking the olives from the trees to fill five large baskets the previous day had produced just a few bottles of olive oil. Still, being able to use olives from your own trees must be satisfying. Eugenia's face confirmed it as she handled the large bottles glowing with her very own *liquid gold*, as she called it.

'*Efcharistó*, Savvas. Not just for this, but collecting us too. Like I told you, I'm out of fuel now, so these olives would have gone over too far if I'd had to wait to be able to afford to fill the truck up.' Eugenia reddened.

Cassia was shocked. Things were worse than she'd thought.

CHAPTER TEN

Since finding out how much Eugenia was struggling financially, Cassia was determined to find a way to bring in money. Every evening, she worked on her embroidery and lace. She spent her days baking as much as she could with the ingredients she could find. She made large amounts of filo pastry, which was used to make spanakopita, her favourite spinach-and-feta pie, as well as her own versions of sweet honey baklavá with a few crunchy nuts as they were in short supply. The long walk into Fiscardo was slow going, and her arms ached by the time she reached the market. Eugenia had directed Cassia to the owner to tell her which was her sister's stall. It was the first time she'd left Eléni with Eugenia and Maia, so she hoped there wouldn't be a repeat of the upsetting row between the girls. The drawings were helping. Eléni answered everything with a detailed sketch Maia could understand. Although Eléni was only three, her drawings were particularly sophisticated. She had moved on from the simple stick figures she had drawn at the shelter in Argostoli.

On one half of the table, Cassia arranged the items of embroidery and lace. On the other, she displayed the baked produce. She had no idea how many drachmae to charge. It was when she was writing up the labels that she heard a voice that made her go cold. She looked up to find herself facing her mother.

'So, the rumours were right. And you have a child now.'

Cassia's heartbeat raced. Her mother's hair, now snow white, was pulled back into a tight chignon that made her already sharp features even more severe. The two had never been close and the glower on her mother's face oozed disapproval.

'*Kaliméra*, Mamá.'

It had been five years since she'd left, and in that time her mother had aged. It wasn't just the colour of her hair. It was her bent posture, her skin, the fact she wore black from head to toe. She looked like an old woman.

'I wondered when you'd show up again. I heard that husband of yours was gone.'

Her mother made it sound as if Nikos had just left her like Georgios had left her sister. *No, Mamá, he was murdered. I was the one who found him soaked in blood, down by the harbour.*

'His name was Nikos, Mamá. He didn't go. He was killed. They still haven't found the person who did it.'

Her mother's lips formed a thin straight line. 'If you say so.'

The older woman picked up one of Cassia's hand-embroidered duchess sets. 'At least you learned something from me. Your needlework was always the best.'

Did I hear right? thought Cassia. '*Efcharistó.*'

Her mother moved on to the next stall. No asking how she'd survived the earthquake in Argostoli, no enquiring after *her child*, as she'd called her, no finding out where she was staying in Fiscardo.

By the time the other stallholders were packing up, Cassia had sold out of the spanakopita and only a few baklavá remained. But it was as she feared — none of the lace or embroidery had sold. She counted the drachmae in her pot. When she allowed for the cost of the ingredients, there would not be much to hand over to Eugenia, but she felt better trying her best to contribute to the household.

Before leaving Fiscardo, she called into the little post office. She didn't recognise the elderly woman behind the counter, but it was clear from her expression that she knew who Cassia was.

'Your mother said you were back.' The woman's frown formed two deep lines in her forehead.

'My home in Argostoli was destroyed in the earthquake. I had nowhere else to go. With the state of the towns in the south of the island, I wondered if there was any post for me, *parakaló*. Cassia Makris.'

The woman looked under the counter and brought out an envelope addressed to Cassia and Eléni, care of Eugenia, and handed it to her.

'*Efcharistó.*'

It was from Sophia, she was sure of it. She placed it in her pocket, eager to get back. She would open it and read it to Eléni later.

***

As Cassia neared her sister's house, Eléni came running out to meet her. At first, she worried something had happened in her absence, but when she saw the smile on the little girl's face, she realised Eléni was just pleased to see her. How different she was now from the little girl who it had once seemed would never forgive her for taking her away from Sophia and Arianna. Cassia hoped those days were firmly behind them. The two girls still rowed sometimes, but her worries about Maia's frustration and unkindness towards Eléni's inability to speak seemed to be unfounded. They were settled now, and this had to be good for Eléni's recovery after what she had been through.

Eugenia was in the kitchen putting the finishing touches to the moussaka she was preparing. 'How did you get on?'

Cassia counted out the money, placing it by Eugenia. 'Our contribution. I'm sorry it's not much. The pie was popular and most of the baklavá went. But not one of the lace and embroidered items. I didn't think they would be essential for people who are hard up.'

'Thank you for trying. It's getting harder, isn't it? I suppose we are luckier than most. We have eggs and milk. And I can make feta from the goat's milk. We just have to try to be more economical.'

Cassia changed the subject. 'How have the girls been today? They seem happy enough playing now.' She looked across at Eléni and Maia playing with Maia's dolls. A lump formed in her throat. Eléni had no toys of her own. Everything she had would have been buried in the rubble of her house. Cassia didn't even know what toys she had or what she liked to play with. When things got better, she vowed she would buy the little girl whatever toys she wanted. She would have her own possessions.

While her sister made the sauce for the moussaka, Cassia made coffee. She watched as the thick brown liquid boiled in its copper *briki* on the stove. She remembered her mother teaching her to make Greek coffee and how to pour it into cups, leaving behind the sticky sludge formed at the bottom.

'I saw Mamá at the stall.' Cassia carried the two coffees over to the table. 'She knew I was in Fiscardo, but didn't ask where. I expect the woman in the post office will tell her, though. There was a letter for me there. I couldn't get over how she'd aged. She looks just like Yiayiá.'

Happy memories of time spent with her grandmother as a girl came flooding back.

What her sister said next surprised her. 'Mamá hasn't been the same since the awful row when you left. Father dying so soon afterwards was a shock and she's never got over it. I try to visit her when I can, but there's always something to do at home and . . .' She paused. 'And I hate saying this, but Mamá isn't the easiest of women, is she? She may appear not to care, but the number of times she says, "I wonder what Cassia's doing now", I've lost count. You were always her favourite — the one she wanted to carry on her embroidery business.'

'I never knew. She seemed to want me and Nikos gone.'

'We all missed you. Even Baba. The thing we didn't miss were the rows between him and Nikos. Then, of course, it was Georgios they hated. The main difference was that he was on the same side as them in his politics. Neither Nikos nor Georgios was good enough for his daughters. He'd have been happy with the old way of selecting a nice boy from a good Greek family of their choosing. And neither of them fitted the bill.'

Eugenia placed the earthenware dish in the oven and sat down next to Cassia to drink her coffee. There were tears in her eyes.

Cassia reached over and patted her sister's arm. 'You miss Georgios, don't you? But if he's betrayed you once — more than once — he'll do it again. You must see that.'

'I know you're right but I still love him, in spite of everything.' She stood to lay the table. 'There's no likelihood of him coming back anyway. The siren will see to it.'

'Perhaps it's for the best. Then you and Maia can move on with your lives.' Cassia could see her sister was upset and looked to change the topic. She fumbled in her pocket to take out the letter.

'Eléni. I have a surprise for you.'

The little girl came and stood by her.

'I've got a letter and it's addressed to both of us.' Eléni pointed at her chest. 'Yes, you.' Cassia smiled at the little girl's delight.

She slid her nail under the seal and took out the letter. The handwriting was neat and even, resembling her yiayiá's.

23 Davaki Street
Athens
Greece
12 October 1953

Agapití *Cassia and Eléni,*
    I hope you are both settled living with your sister. It is the address you gave me, so I hope this finds you safe and

62

well. It broke my heart to see you both go, especially when my lovely Eléni got so upset. But it was for the best. The nights are very cold now and with no place to stay apart from under the shelters.

I am one of the lucky ones. My daughter arrived and took me back to Athens to live with her. There is nothing left for me in Kefalonia now. Everything I had was buried in the rubble of my house. Whatever time I have left, I know I will be looked after by my daughter. But the earthquake couldn't take away my memories. I will never forget your kindness to me, Cassia, and how you never gave up searching for little Eléni. If you are in touch with Tom and the Welsh reporter who got her out alive, please remember me to them. If you are ever in Athens, please call to see me.

Your friend,
Sophia

Eléni smiled. She pointed at herself and mimed drawing. 'Yes, I think Sophia would love a drawing from you.' Eléni grinned and rushed to start a picture for Sophia.

CHAPTER ELEVEN

Cassia continued to travel to Fiscardo selling whatever food-stuffs she could, together with her lace and embroidered items. Sometimes she would take Eléni with her and the little girl would practise drawing while Cassia worked hard to try to sell her goods. On one occasion, they visited the post office on the way.

'Shall we send your beautiful drawing to Sophia?' said Cassia. The previous evening, Eléni had taken great care over a drawing of Cassia, Eugenia, Maia and herself that she'd got Cassia to label. Cassia signed it *From Eléni, with love* and the little girl had drawn kisses underneath.

Eléni beamed and held her hand to her heart.

'Sophia is going to love it,' said Cassia.

The woman in the post office was interested in Eléni and Cassia knew in a small village like Fiscardo, every detail, especially the fact Eléni didn't speak, would be relayed back to her mother.

'Wave goodbye to the lady, Eléni,' said Cassia as they went to leave. The little girl gave the woman a big smile and waved her hand as she was told. 'She's just shy.'

It had been a good day and all the goods Cassia had taken to the market had sold. She couldn't wait to give Eugenia the money she'd made. It had been her best day ever. She'd run out of spanakopita in the first hour. Perhaps all the comments that hers was the best around meant her reputation was spreading. Hand in hand, she and Eléni walked along the road to the place they now called home. Cassia felt more positive about the future than she had done for weeks. Eléni was more settled, sleeping through every night with Callista at the foot of her bed.

'Did you enjoy today?' Cassia asked. Eléni dropped her hand to place it on her heart and mime a smiley face.

As they walked, Cassia looked out across the bay. The sun was lower in the sky at this time of year, but the effect of the sunshine reflecting on the water still made the sea glow like an aquamarine jewel. It never failed to lift her spirits. Even though the talk in the market was all about the mass exodus of islanders leaving for America or Canada, she couldn't imagine living anywhere else. Things were going to get better. She was sure of it. They just had to get through the winter months. Eugenia was going back to the hospital as a nurse the next week, so it would bring in more money.

As Eugenia's house came into sight, Cassia noticed another vehicle parked alongside the old truck. Eugenia had a visitor. She heard laughter coming from the living room as she and Eléni entered the house.

Maia rushed out to greet them. 'My baba's here. And look what he brought me.' She held up a doll dressed in Greek traditional dress. 'Come and play.' The girls left Cassia reeling in shock as the implications of Georgios's return sank in.

Cassia's heartbeat raced and goosebumps prickled along her arms. Surely her sister wasn't stupid enough to have him back after all the heartache he'd caused. Cassia knew what it meant for her and her little girl. He would never let them stay. She entered the kitchen and unpacked the few shopping items she'd bought in Fiscardo.

Eugenia came into the room, shutting the door behind her. Before she could say a word, Cassia turned to face her.

'You must be mad! After all you said! I thought you swore you'd never take him back. So, he just turns up and all his dalliances are forgotten.'

Eugenia's eyes filled with tears. 'But I still love him. He's promised he will never leave again. You should have seen Maia's face. I've got to give it a try.'

Yes, the sight of a new doll was what my niece was reacting to, not a father she could never have recognised after he left her at two years of age.

'And you believe him? That means me and Eléni are out of here then, doesn't it? He's never going to let us stay. Have you even told him about us yet?'

At that moment, all Cassia could think about was what she was going to do. Panic raced along her veins. Where would they go? Where could they live? What would another upset do to Eléni?

'I've told him you're staying until you can find somewhere.' As she spoke, Eugenia didn't look at her sister.

The door opened. Georgios went to his wife's side, placing an arm around her.

'That's right. The sooner we're back together as a family, the better. It's time you stood on your own two feet instead of sponging off my gorgeous Genia.' He kissed Eugenia on her cheek.

Cassia didn't sleep that night. Images of her and Eléni huddled under a thin blanket in the cold, lying down by the quayside in Fiscardo, flooded her mind, interrupted only by the noises coming from her sister's bedroom. To make it worse, Eléni had the first nightmare she'd had since the one when they'd first arrived. The scream was piercing, the bedroom walls reverberating with the sound. Georgios burst into the room.

'What the hell was that? Can't you control the brat? The freak may not be able to talk but she can bloody scream, though. Shut her up, will you?'

He left as quickly as he arrived, slamming the door behind him. Cassia's heart hammered with rage.

'How dare you?' she shouted after him. She turned to Eléni. 'Come here, *agápi mou*.'

She settled the little girl in her bed and held her in her arms, comforting her until she stopped shaking. There was no way she'd stay under the same roof as that bully of a man. It was then she feared for her sister, too. Blinded by what she thought was love, Eugenia would live to regret taking her husband back; she was sure of it. But Cassia knew there was nothing she could do to change Eugenia's mind. She had to put Eléni first.

* * *

The next morning, there was no sign of Georgios. Eugenia was making breakfast when Cassia and Eléni came down.

'Are you all right this morning, *agápi mou*?' Eléni nodded. 'I'm sorry about Georgios, Cassia. He should never have said what he did. It was such a shock for him. He didn't know what it was.'

How can she stand there and defend him? How would she feel if someone called Maia a freak?

'Can you take me into Fiscardo this morning, please? We can't stay another day in this house now he's back.'

Eugenia's eyes filled with tears. 'Please don't be like that. Stay until you find somewhere. Georgios is back at sea fishing for the next few days, so you won't have to see each other.'

So that's your solution, is it? Just avoid him.

But Cassia's mind was made up. There must be somewhere in town where she could rent a room. How she would pay for it was another matter. Now Georgios was back, money would not be a problem, so Eugenia suggested her market-stall pitch should be transferred into Cassia's name.

'You can't do that. What if you need to make money for yourself and Maia again? And what's happened to your plans to go back to nursing?'

'You're thinking, "What will I do if my husband strays again?" Well, he won't. I know he means to stay this time. I'll go back to nursing when Maia goes to school.'

Cassia knew it was her sister's way of saying Georgios had forbidden her to work outside the home. He already controlled her again.

When Eugenia insisted on driving Cassia and Eléni into Fiscardo, she didn't object. They had very little to take with them. Because the atmosphere was cool between the two sisters, saying goodbye was brief. Maia got upset.

'Why can't Theía Cassia and Eléni stay, Mamá? I won't have a friend anymore.' Her eyes welled with tears as she clung to Cassia. 'I want Eléni to have this.' She handed over a well-worn teddy bear.

Eléni smiled and put her arms out to hug her friend. Cassia bent down beside her niece. 'It's very kind of you. Eléni won't forget you. Who knows, once we find somewhere to live, perhaps your mamá and baba will let you come and see us. We're not going to be far away, are we?'

It was for Maia's benefit. While Georgios was back living with her niece and Eugenia, it was never going to happen. Afraid of breaking down in front of the little ones, Cassia turned and walked away in the direction of the market.

Although Cassia didn't have any baked goods to sell that day, she used her stall as a base while she asked around for lodgings. The stall next to hers was run by a woman who sold a range of traditional Greek breads. She was about the same age as Cassia and they'd become quite friendly, chatting and swapping recipes.

'Old Kýria Galanos has a room. Her son has decided to leave the island to find work. She says she is too old to go with him, but he's going to send money home for her. She lives on Antipata Street, number fourteen. Say Rhea sent you.'

'*Efcharistó*, I will try there.'

Taking Eléni by the hand, Cassia walked away from the market and up a slight incline until they found Antipata

Street. The Venetian-style houses were painted in various pastel colours, typical of Fiscardo as a whole. Two-storeyed with wooden shutters, the houses had an air of being well kept and ordinary without being opulent or suggesting wealth as her parents' home did.

They arrived outside number fourteen. Cassia took a deep breath as they walked up to the front door. 'Here goes.' She knocked on the door and waited. A white-haired woman opened the door a fraction.

'*Nai*?'

'Kýria Galanos? Rhea sent me. I understand you have a room to rent.'

The old woman looked Cassia up and down, and then rested her eyes on Eléni. She narrowed her eyes and looked intently back at Cassia.

'No. I know who you are. You are trouble! What with your communist views. Your mother told me all about you and how you split her family by going off with Nikos Makris. I do not want a child in my house either. Especially his child. I am too old.' She slammed the door and left Cassia openmouthed, standing on the step with Eléni.

She wanted to ask when her mother had spoken to her. Recently, or when the row with Nikos had happened. What if everyone in Fiscardo thought of her that way? She'd been selling at the market for just a few months, and everyone had seemed friendly towards her. What if behind the smiles they looked down on her as the old woman did?

CHAPTER TWELVE

They walked back into the centre of Fiscardo. Cassia felt desolate. She looked down at the little girl walking beside her. What right did she have to take Eléni from the only place she'd ever known as home? If they'd stayed, at least the authorities would have given Eléni somewhere to stay with the other earthquake orphans, even if it would have been temporary. Instead, the two of them were homeless, and the thought terrified Cassia. Tears burned along her eyelids as she berated herself for thinking she could manage on her own. The last time she'd felt like this was back in Argostoli just after the earthquake. Then, someone had come to her rescue. But the person who'd calmed her, reassured her that things would turn out all right in the end, was back at sea. *Oh, Tom. How I wish you were here to tell me what I should do.*

As they passed the post office, Cassia looked at the notices in the window. One jumped out at her. *Vacant Room in return for help in Taverna Zervas. No children.* The taverna that held so many memories for her! Both good and bad. Her heart sank. It would have been perfect. It was the only advertisement there, so she plucked up courage to walk to the street where she knew the taverna was situated. She'd enquire anyway. Overlooking the harbour, it was the bar she and Nikos had frequented. It was where, much to the disgust of her parents, the partisans had openly met in the years during and after the war, and where her father had disowned her. After the meetings, she and Nikos used to cross the narrow street and walk down the steps to sit on the bench under the large pine tree.

Cassia entered the taverna. It was gloomy inside. A shaft of light from the open doorway illuminated her way to the bar. There was no one there, so she pressed the brass bell on the polished surface. A strong smell of tobacco, garlic and cooking came from what Cassia assumed to be the kitchen behind. Portraits of famous partisans lined the walls, the centre of which was a large black-and-white, head-and-shoulder portrait of Colonel Napoleon Zervas after whom the taverna was named.

She called out, '*Kaliméra.*'

A balding, florid man, as wide as he was tall and with a snow-white drooping moustache, came through from the back. '*Naí?*'

'I see you have a vacant room. I'd like to apply to work in the taverna.'

He peered over the bar to look at Eléni. 'No children.'

'I know, but my daughter is very quiet. You won't know she's here.' Cassia sounded as desperate as she felt. What she said was true . . . apart from the nightmares.

'No. No children.' He turned to go back into the kitchen.

'I'm Nikos Makris's widow. Do you remember him? We used to come here for meetings.'

The man stopped at the mention of Nikos's name. He walked back around the bar to face Cassia and Eléni. 'Ah, Nikos. One of the best. It was tragic he died fighting for what we all believed in, eh? And this is his daughter? She is very like him.'

Cassia didn't correct him. How Nikos would have been amused at his comment. She knew her husband would approve of what she was doing for Eléni.

The old man smiled down on the little girl who was looking up at him with her large brown eyes. He tousled her hair. 'Your baba was a good man. You will not disturb your mamá when she is working for me, is that right? You will be very quiet like your mamá says?'

Eléni nodded.

The man agreed for them to have the room 'because of Nikos'. He and Cassia agreed the terms. She would clean the taverna and make food each evening. Eléni could be with her as long as she didn't get in the way. She would help out in the bar when it got busy. 'But there's no fear of that at the moment. It's getting harder for everyone here on the island to find an extra drachma or two for their ouzos. Even the old men come less often.'

They shook hands. 'Michaíl Pavlis.'

'*Efcharistó*, Kýrios Pavlis. I came to Fiscardo because everything where we lived in Argostoli was destroyed in the earthquake. We were homeless. We've been staying with my sister until now. She has a place in the next bay. Her husband came back and I could not stay there a moment longer. I think you will know him. Georgios Papadatos.'

The old man's mouth gaped open. He banged the bar with his fist. 'Pah! Fascist pig! He caused so much trouble for Nikos.'

'Shh!' Cassia made it clear she didn't want Eléni to hear. Michaíl raised his hand.

It was as Cassia thought. Opposite political views, completely different men. Georgios gets to live, but poor Nikos lost his life because of what he believed in.

Cassia told Michaíl about her stall in the market and he agreed to let her use the kitchen to bake her signature spinach-and-feta pies.

'And in return, you leave some for me, eh?' He laughed and patted his large stomach.

Cassia laughed, too. She had a feeling she was going to like this man.

72

While the adults talked, Eléni was distracted by a pretty grey-and-black cat that had entered the bar and wound itself around her legs. She tugged on Cassia's skirt.

'Ah, he is so pretty. What is its name?' asked Cassia.

'Kynigós. He is the best hunter of mice I've ever had. Let me show you the room.'

Michaíl led Cassia and Eléni up to the room that was to become their new home. In contrast to the darkness of the bar downstairs, this room was light and airy, with a wonderful view of the harbour and Ithaca in the distance. There was a large double bed in the centre of the room, draped with a hand-embroidered white coverlet. A bowl of dried lavender had been placed on the chest of drawers to the side of the window. A light breeze wafted the smell towards Cassia. It reminded her of her mother's bedroom when she was young.

'Is this all right? It was all my wife Cora's doing. She embroidered the bedspread before we got married, so it is very old now. I'll get the small fold-up bed for the little one,' said Michaíl. He hurried out of the room, but not before Cassia noticed how his rheumy eyes had filled with tears.

She walked to the window and watched the fishermen as they mended their nets by the quayside, their hauls of fish from early-morning expeditions all sold. Some stood and chatted while they smoked their cigarettes. Life went on as normal for some of the inhabitants of this most northerly part of the island, yet in Argostoli, life would never be the same again. Her thoughts were interrupted by Michaíl struggling through the door with Eléni's bed.

'I'll put it in this corner for you, *agápi mou*. Your mamá will put the sheets on for you.'

Eléni pointed at the door and mimed stroking her arm, then pointed at her bed.

'You want Kynigós to sleep on your bed like Callista did?' asked Cassia. Eléni nodded, her eyes wide. 'I think Kynigós sleeps outside in the yard. He goes out at night and catches all the mice for Michaíl. You can play with her once you're downstairs. Callista was a kitten and hadn't learned to do that yet.'

The little girl looked disappointed, but nodded as if she understood.

'Thank you for taking me on. I will work hard for you. The room is lovely — the bedcover especially. Your wife is very clever.'

The old man took Cassia's hand. 'She died seven years ago. I still cannot sleep in this room without her. She did all the cooking and the cleaning. I just served in the bar. I tried, but I cannot do it. So, it is me who should thank you. Nikos's wife, eh?'

Later that afternoon, Cassia and Eléni went back to the stall in the market. Rhea was still there, but was packing away for the day.

'Any luck with Kýria Galanos?'

'No, she turned me away by just looking at me. My mother had told her I was trouble, apparently. And on no account did she want a child in her house.'

Rhea sighed. 'I'm sorry. I don't know where else to suggest. We haven't got the room or else I'd say you could come to us. What are you going to do?'

Cassia told her about being taken on by Michaíl Pavlis. 'He seems nice. And the best bit is once I've finished the cleaning, I can cook for the stall and continue to earn some money. I'll see you tomorrow. I must get to the butcher. I've promised Michaíl moussaka tonight so I need some lamb to mince.'

* * *

This is our life now, Elenáki mou. Cassia watched Eléni as she slept. *I know you miss being with Maia, but I had no choice.* She missed Eugenia's company too, but, because Georgios had given her no other option, she was back to fending for herself and relying on no one. Michaíl seemed to revel in having company again and fell into the role of an adoring *pappoú* figure

74

for Eléni. While Cassia went about the household chores, she would often find them playing a game of Tavlí.

'Remember, she's only three, Michaíl.' Cassia heard him explain the rules for the umpteenth time or gently scold her for throwing the dice down too hard.

'She learns very fast, this daughter of Nikos.' The old man rewarded Eléni with a huge smile.

Cassia realised she had no idea about Eléni's actual age. She'd taken Sophia's word for it. She didn't know when her birthday was either.

The cold weather meant they were staying indoors more frequently, and when Cassia left to take her spanakopita pies to the market, Eléni would often stay behind with Michaíl and spend her time drawing. Often, she would come home to find Eléni playing with Kynigós, rolling a ball of wool to him from Kýria Pavlis's work basket, given to her by Michaíl.

Christmas was just a month away when she received a visit from Eugenia. Her face was drawn and she appeared to have lost weight.

'*Kaliméra.* What brings you here?'

'I didn't know where to look for you but Rhea at the market told me where you were living. I used to follow you and Nikos here, you know. I was always scared Baba would find out. He always said he didn't see what you saw in "the communist" and how you were throwing your life away.'

Some of their father's last words came back to Cassia. "If you choose that communist over your family, you are dead to me." And now *he* was dead, and she would never hear his voice again.

'I came to give you this . . . and to tell you that me and Maia miss you and Eléni.' Her sister handed over an envelope addressed to her at Eugenia's house.

'What's this?' It didn't look like Sophia's handwriting, but she hoped it was. She put it in her overall pocket to read when she was alone.

'It arrived with overseas mail at the post office.' Appearing uninterested in anything else, Eugenia said, 'Please come back.' Tears welled in her eyes and without warning, she grabbed Cassia and hugged her tight.

'He's left again, hasn't he? Who for this time?' Cassia knew she sounded harsh, but it was what she'd thought would happen.

Eugenia didn't answer her. 'I'm afraid I need my stall back. I have to make a living on my own now he's gone. If you come back, we can share it and split the money we make.'

Colour drained from Cassia's face. She now had a roof over her head, Eléni was settled and she was starting to put aside some money. It was due to the growing number of customers and the fact that her prices were what people could afford.

'No, no. I can't let Eléni be uprooted again. She's settled now, happy too. All her drawings are of people with smiley faces. She adores Michaíl and it's good for her to have another person apart from me in her life. I can't risk it. What if Georgios comes back yet again? Will you accept his profound apologies and believe him when he says he will never do it again? I'll come to visit, yes. It will be nice for the girls, but I can't move back to live with you. I'm sorry. My life is here now.'

Her sister began to cry.

'You can have your stall back,' added Cassia. 'I'll have to ask if there is another one going vacant.'

Michaíl and Eléni joined them in the bar as Eugenia wiped her eyes. The little girl rushed to hug her theía and Eugenia swung her around. The little girl squealed as she circled the room.

Eugenia offered Michaíl her hand. 'Kýrios Pavlis. I've been hearing all about you from Cassia. My sister and niece seem very happy here with you.'

Cassia saw her sister to the door. 'If you need the stall back, will you go and speak to the owner today? I'll ask him to keep me in mind when there's a new stall available.'

They embraced and all seemed well, but Cassia couldn't help thinking her days at the market were numbered. She enjoyed Rhea's company and would miss her.

CHAPTER THIRTEEN

Once Eléni was settled in bed, Cassia returned to the sitting room downstairs. She remembered the envelope in her pocket. Having been so wrapped up in the conversation with Eugenia and the prospect of losing her income, she'd momentarily forgotten about it.

She looked again at the handwriting. She still didn't recognise it. As she unfolded the letter inside, her heart skipped a beat when she saw the words HMS *Daring* on the top right-hand side. Tom hadn't forgotten them after all! Her hands shook as she read.

> Agapití *Cassia and Eléni,*
>
> *I hope life, it is good for you at the house of Eugenia and you enjoy the goats and the chickens, Eléni. The sea, it is cold now, and you do not swim but you paddle, I think. If no, you look at the beautiful sea and cove. It helps you forget the awful sights we left at Argostoli.*
>
> *I write to tell you we move from the ship here in Malta. After some weeks, they send us to other ships.*

Tom had written the next part of the letter in English:

I would like to visit you both again before my posting. I will arrive on the island at the beginning of December and we could spend Christmas together if you'd like that. I'll find somewhere to stay and call to see you each day. There isn't time for you to send a reply so I just hope you will both like to see me.

I think about you both every day. I can't wait to see you. How are your drawings coming on Eléni, my little artist? Perhaps by now you have started to talk to your mamá.

Your friend,
Tom xx

Cassia sat back in the chair, placing the letter on her lap. Her stomach somersaulted. Tom Beynon was coming back to the island, and she couldn't wait. Nowadays, she thought of Michaíl as a friend she could confide in, but, when she remembered the days after the earthquake in Argostoli, their new friendship was nothing compared to the closeness she'd come to appreciate with Tom. Without making her feel inadequate, Tom always appeared to know the right thing to do when decisions needed to be made, helping her rather than taking over. She thought of his soft lilting voice and the halting way he attempted to speak in Greek to her, and encouraged and praised her as she did the same when she spoke English. It was as if they'd known each other for years. Was that all it was? She quickly dismissed the idea that the two of them could be anything other than friends. She couldn't wait to see Eléni's face when she told her in the morning.

Later, up in the bedroom she shared with Eléni, Cassia looked out over the harbour. She wondered if Tom's ferry would be docking in the larger bay of Argostoli, where tons of earthquake rubble had been bulldozed into the harbour. Could ships and ferries even get into the once-busy port any more? Perhaps he'd get a smaller boat and arrive in Fiscardo itself. She imagined taking Eléni down to the quayside and watching the fair-haired sailor's face break into one of his heart-warming grins when he spotted his little girl.

She failed to get much sleep that night, thinking of all the things she wanted to tell Tom. She hoped he'd be proud of her for standing up to Georgios, for building up her business at the market and trying to make a happy, settled home for Eléni. She was sure he'd like Michaíl. She tossed and turned, worrying about her sister and her niece now that they were on their own again. *Damn Georgios Papadatos!*

* * *

Daylight filtered into the bedroom, causing Eléni to stir before she turned over and fell back to sleep. Cassia lay watching her, marvelling at how she had blossomed since arriving in Fiscardo. Gone was the grey, tired pallor from the lack of sleep and frequent nightmares. Although it was getting harder to get a full range of foods, Cassia made sure Eléni still ate well even if it meant going without herself. Their stay with Eugenia had ensured they'd had an abundance of fresh fruit and vegetables to eat. Eléni's glossy black hair, spreading out like a shiny fan on the white pillow, had grown enough so each morning, Cassia enjoyed plaiting it into two pigtails. It made her look older than three. *Perhaps you are older. All we want now is for you to talk to us.*

Eléni stretched and opened her eyes.

'*Kaliméra.* I have a surprise for you.' Cassia held up the letter and unfolded it.

The little girl sat up, eager to hear what was in it.

'It's from Tom. Remember him?'

Eléni squealed and clapped her hands. A wide smile spread across her face. Cassia read the letter to her and when it came to the part where Tom said he was going to arrive in Fiscardo to see them, she jumped out of her bed and hugged Cassia.

Cassia's eyes blurred with tears. 'Isn't it good news? You'll have to do lots of drawings to give him when he arrives.'

Eléni immediately reached for her paper and pencils and began drawing straight away. It then dawned on Cassia that Eléni might not have any recollection of what Christmas was if she had been only two the year before. A lump formed in her throat. She imagined Eléni's parents and grandparents celebrating with their beautiful toddler, unwrapping little gifts and imagining the Christmases to come. Now it was up to her to make the first Christmas they'd spend together a memorable one for her. And Tom would be there too. The thought of sharing time with him made her heart beat a little faster. She remembered her sister's words when they'd first arrived from Argostoli. *Tom's obviously fallen head over heels in love with you.* Could she be doing the same thing? She pushed the thought to the back of her mind.

'*Elenáki mou*, do you know what happens at Christmas?'

Cassia explained that on 25 December everyone would celebrate the birth of Jesus. 'We will go to the church on the hill with Michaíl, and we may see Eugenia and Maia there. I hope Tom will come with us, too.'

The little girl listened intently.

'Weeks before, all the boats in the harbour will be decorated with twinkling lights. The best bit is that we eat special Christmas foods. And then a few days later, on St Basil's Day, we give presents to each other.'

Cassia remembered the magic of festive times spent when she was a child, but stopped herself from saying any more. This year would be nothing like those Christmases. Afraid to promise too much and let Eléni's excitement build, Cassia had no idea what to expect. There would be lots of prayer mainly from the older people, but she'd heard so many others question how God could have allowed such a terrible disaster to happen. Would people waste money on decorating boats when they had very little to spend on food? She'd noticed sales for her pies were a lot fewer, and she had to eke out what ingredients she could when cooking meals, serving smaller portions for herself.

Downstairs, they found Michaíl on his knees, trying to light a fire with pinecones and an old newspaper. On the floor beside him were thin strands of olive tree branches he must have stripped from the solitary tree in the corner of the yard. The house was bitterly cold. Cassia shivered, rubbing her arms with her hands to try to keep warm. She knew it would not be good for the old man's joints. 'Michaíl, please get up. Here, put this round you and sit down.'

Groaning, he struggled to stand. 'These ancient bones of mine have stiffened up down there. *Efcharistó.*' Cassia took a rug from the back of his chair and placed it over Michaíl's knees. 'We'll have to get some logs from somewhere. Once those cones and twigs have burned, the fire will go out. Back to nothing.'

The previous night, they had burned the last of the logs from the stack outside in the yard. Cassia remembered the outhouse at Eugenia's place, piled high with logs. At the time they'd never needed a fire, but she was sure they would be burning logs now. But surely they wouldn't have all been used. Could she swallow her pride and ask for help? She'd done it once so it was worth trying again.

'I've got an idea,' she said. 'I'm going to call on my sister and see if she has any spare. Eléni, you stay here and keep Michaíl company. Look, there's Kynigós, too.'

The little girl sat down on the floor to play with her feline friend.

* * *

When she reached Eugenia's house, Cassia saw the outhouse pile of wood had been started on, and a curl of smoke corkscrewed up into the clear November sky. The sweet smell of wood burning wafted in her direction. She knocked on the door, her stomach churning as she waited for her sister to open it.

'*Kaliméra*. Can I come in?'

'Eléni not with you?' Eugenia led the way into the kitchen where Maia played with her Greek doll.

'No, I left her with Michaíl.'

'*Theía* Cassia.' Her niece got up and rushed to hug her. 'I've called my doll Eléni now you don't live with us.'

'Oh, that's lovely, *agápi mou*. I'll tell her.' Cassia turned to her sister. 'I'm sorry about how we left things. I came to tell you the letter was from Tom.' She didn't know why, but warmth crept along her throat. 'He's coming to see us and he'll be here in time for Christmas.'

Eugenia smiled. 'That's good news. I know how much you've missed him since he went back to his ship.'

'This will be the last time we see him. He's being posted to another ship, goodness knows where.' She heard the catch in her voice. 'Do you think people will celebrate Christmas this year? I'd like him to see how we do things here in Kefalonia, but it doesn't seem right with all the suffering elsewhere on the island.'

Eugenia looked at her daughter. 'I know what you mean, but I think we should try. Even if it's just for the little ones. We can all cut back, can't we? Come and look at this.'

She beckoned Cassia to follow her into the living room, where she brought out a bag of fabrics. Inside were two cloth dolls with beautifully embroidered clothes.

'They are not finished. One for Maia and one for Eléni. They cost me nothing.'

Cassia was touched by the fact that her sister included Eléni. 'They're beautiful. They're going to love them. *Efcharistó*.'

'Quick! Hand it here, she's coming in.' Maia arrived in the room just as her mother managed to hide the bag away.

'I've come to ask you a big favour. Michaíl is out of wood for the fire. I don't suppose you could let us have some, could you, *parakaló*? Just until we can get some money to buy from the farm on the way here. He wants to go out into the woods behind Fiscardo and cut some down himself, but he's too old to be doing that. Once I can sell some of my spanakopita and people are buying some tablecloths and duchess sets again, we can buy more wood. This is the worst winter I've known — the house is freezing. And I worry about him and Eléni.'

Eugenia agreed to help and offered to take Cassia back to Fiscardo before it got dark. The two sisters sat and talked. Georgios's name never came up in the conversation. Instead, they talked about what preparations would be needed for Christmas. Jointly, they decided to revert to sharing the stall and split the money made.

'I don't know how I would manage without my sister,' said Cassia. 'I've been feeling guilty about reacting the way I did. It's natural you need the stall now you and Maia are back on your own.' She leaned across and patted her sister's arm. 'I am genuinely sorry about Georgios leaving, you know.'

'Even though you were proved right?' Eugenia smiled at her.

CHAPTER FOURTEEN

Over the next two weeks, Cassia worked harder than ever. Sharing the market stall with Eugenia, she cooked during the day and made small, inexpensive embroidered items for the local inhabitants of Fiscardo to buy as Christmas gifts. The money earned meant Michaíl could restock the logs, and she could start to collect the ingredients for the traditional Christmas treats she was looking forward to making. As it got closer to the first of December, she looked out to sea every day, hoping each ferry arriving would be the one reuniting her and Eléni with Tom. It got closer to 6 December, but there was still no sign of him. She worried he would miss the lighting of the boats in the bay. Even though it would be much more subdued than normal, the people of Fiscardo had decided the feast day should still be celebrated in some way.

It wasn't Tom who arrived at the taverna early one morning, but Eugenia holding Maia's hand. She'd parked the truck on the quayside.

'Can you and Eléni come outside? I've got someone there I think you'd like to see.'

Cassia ran upstairs to wake Eléni and get them both dressed. She looked out of the bedroom window. The truck was empty and the only person she could see was Eugenia herself walking back to her vehicle. *Where was Maia? And who was looking after her?*

'Ready?'

Eléni nodded and held her arms wide, as if to ask what was going on. Michaíl, coming out of his bedroom, asked the same thing.

'I don't know myself. It was Eugenia hammering on the door. I'll tell you later.'

Cassia and Eléni walked towards the truck. She could still only see her sister.

'*Kaliméra*, Kýria Makris.'

The voice she had been longing to hear! She spun around and Tom Beynon walked up behind her. Eléni ran towards him and jumped up into his arms. Placing the little girl back on the ground, he embraced Cassia. Her heartbeat raced. She'd told herself she wouldn't cry when she saw him but tears spilled over, trickling down her cheeks.

'I didn't know when you'd be arriving,' she said. 'And how come Eugenia brought you here?'

Eugenia got out of the driver's seat. Together with little Maia, who got out of the back of the truck, she joined them. 'Did you enjoy your surprise? Mine wasn't a surprise, more of a shock. A banging on the door after we'd gone to bed last night.'

Of course. It dawned on Cassia. Eugenia's house was where he knew she and Eléni had last been living. It was where he'd addressed his letter.

'I'm sorry if I scared you. I thought if I asked to sleep on your sofa last night, I could work out lodgings in Fiscardo today. I didn't realise how late it was.'

Cassia couldn't stop smiling. She had so much to tell her Welsh hero.

* * *

'At six o'clock tonight, the boats will be lit for the first time.' Cassia nodded her head towards the quayside. 'I can't wait for you to see them in the dark.' She and Tom were sitting outside Taverna Zervas while Eléni played inside with the doll dressed in Maltese costume that he'd brought for her. Michaíl had offered to look after her while they talked. He'd winked at Cassia and whispered, 'I think he wants you to himself.'

She explained to Tom about the long-held tradition of decorating boats as part of the Greek Christmas activities and how she wasn't sure if it would be done this year.

'It's because Kefalonia is an island and Greece is a maritime country. Decorating boats is important for them. More important than decorating Christmas trees. It's quite new here.'

'But why December sixth?' Tom asked.

'Today is the feast of Agios Nikolaos, the patron saint of sailors and fishermen. They say he worked hard to save sailors from the angry seas. Nikos and I always celebrated his saint's day, and we joked that the boats all being lit up were just for him. You arrived on the right day.'

'But I don't think there's a Tom Day.' They both laughed.

As they talked, Cassia relaxed. She didn't think about money, or lack of it, or the dire state of the island once. Instead, she enjoyed being in the company of someone who was interested in *her*. It was obvious he was pleased to see her again. He kept looking at her, smiling with his eyes, and every now and then when they remembered something from the early days when they'd met in Argostoli, he would give her hand a gentle squeeze. Sophia and Eugenia's words about him being in love with her entered her head for a second, but she dismissed the thought. He told her about his work aboard HMS *Daring* and how it was coming to an end. When Tom told her, her skin prickled.

He took her hand. 'Not for a time yet, though, but it's what I do, Cassia. I signed up to join the Royal Navy and if it means going to an area of the world to protect my country, I have to do it. But let's not talk about me leaving. I've only just arrived.'

They walked along the quayside watching the fishermen fix the lights for the evening and position their boats in a row. Larger vessels with masts were anchored further out in the bay.

'Show me where you found a room to stay,' said Cassia.

They left the harbour and walked up a narrow street to a house Cassia recognised. It was the one belonging to Kýria Galanos, the woman who had refused to let a room to her and Eléni.

'I asked at a bar along from Michaíl's and they sent me here. The old lady doesn't speak a word of English. I don't think she understands my feeble attempts at Greek when I try to speak with her, either. She seems very nice, but she could be swearing at me and I wouldn't know!'

They both laughed.

'You'd better not let her know you're a friend of mine.'

Tom looked puzzled. Cassia explained how she'd been rejected and how Kýria Galanos had treated her with such disdain. 'That was before I answered Michaíl's notice. He, on the other hand, took us in *because* of Nikos. Fellow partisans.'

She and Tom had been in each other's company for a short time and already, Cassia had laughed more in that hour than she had in weeks. Carrying on with their walk, Cassia pointed out places of interest, including where she had played as a child, and pointed in the direction of her parents' house.

'Do you want to tell me about why you don't have anything to do with them anymore, Cassia? I know it was something to do with them not approving of Nikos.'

Cassia linked her arm with Tom's as they walked. He deserved to know. She took a deep breath.

'After the war ended, Greece was a divided country. Families were split, with some members on the side of the fascists and others were communists. My father was a typical Greek man whose word was law in the family. He fought in the war and was a very proud Greek. He supported the far right, but Nikos had played an important part as a partisan in the war and could not agree with my father. He and his partisan friends were communists wanting the best for the poor people who had nothing. Secretly, I began meeting him, and we fell in love. Once my father found out, he forbade me to see him. He made me choose between my family or Nikos. Said I was dead to him. In the end, we fled to Argostoli where we would not be noticed in a big town. We married in secret. Then one night, he did not come home to me. He'd been to a communist meeting and was killed on the way home.' Her voice cracked. 'To this day, we do not know who did it. I still wonder if Georgios Papadatos was involved, but I have no proof. No one has ever been caught.'

Tom pulled her towards him and placed his arms around her. 'That's terrible. I'm so sorry.' He kissed the top of her head. 'Thank you for telling me.'

They walked on, the mood now sombre.

'Come on, let's talk about *Christoúgenna*. Christmas.' Cassia broke the silence, lightening the mood. 'I've tried to explain what it's all about to Eléni. She won't remember last year, will she? Michaíl has been making some little wooden toys for her and a spinning top for Maia, carving and whittling them when she's in bed, and I've made her some cloth teddies and teddy clothes. Tell me about the Christmases you have back in Wales.'

Tom told her about a typical Christmas and how, although his parents didn't have much money, they always gave him and his brother a magical time.

'I can still taste Mam's Christmas cake now. She used to let Glyn and me cover it with thick white icing. Even during the war, she saved up her sugar rations so we could have an iced cake. It looked like snow, and then we'd take turns putting miniature snowmen and Father Christmases on top. And tiny Christmas trees. Do you hang up stockings in Greece? We'd always have an apple and an orange in there with some nuts. Oh, and a sugar mouse and some chocolate coins. At the top of the stocking, or really one of my dad's socks, there would be some toy cars or a few colouring pencils.'

Cassia laughed at his enthusiasm. 'You'll have to wait and see what a Greek Christmas is like. Just less than a month to go.'

Tom stopped walking. 'What do you mean? December twenty-fifth is less than three weeks away surely.'

'Yes, that's when *Christoúgenna* is, but we also celebrate St Basil's Day on the first of January. New Year's Day is when we also exchange presents.'

Tom's face dropped. 'But I'll be back in Malta by then. I leave on the twenty-ninth.'

CHAPTER FIFTEEN

Michaíl stayed in the bar to serve several older men with their tots of local raki. Between them, they had celebrated many 6 December days, so instead they preferred to sit drinking, smoking their strong tobacco and playing Tavlí. He handed Eléni a small wooden boat he'd made for her. It was filled with sweets and, underneath, he'd hidden a drachma for her to find. Eléni's face broke into a huge smile as she examined every detail.

'I think her smile tells you everything you need to know, Michaíl. *Efcharistó* a hundred times.' Cassia hugged the old man, whose eyes were red-rimmed with unshed tears.

'You are so clever,' said Tom. 'Where did you learn to carve like that?'

'My pappoú was a carpenter and I spent a lot of time with him. You go now and get a good spot on the quayside. I've got customers to serve.'

The light was fading fast as Cassia, Tom and Eléni made their way down to the harbour. The sky had turned a deep apricot as the sun's orb sank further into the horizon and the lights on the small boats in the harbour gave the place a magical feel. Cassia had been right. There were fewer lights than in other years, but lots of fishermen had still made an effort, most likely because of the significance of the day.

Tom smiled at her, his hazel-green eyes crinkling at the edges.

'This is wonderful. I'm glad I didn't miss this.'

'You should feel at home here on this day. Remember me telling you it's to celebrate Saint Nikolaos. He is the patron saint of Greece and the protector of seamen and sailors like you. Today is the first day we start decorating our homes for *Christoúgenna* and soon you will see decorated boats in every home, not just with the children. Michaíl will set one up and light a candle in the middle of it by the time we return home.'

'So this is a Tom Day after all.'

They walked to the spot in front of the ship chandler's where Cassia had arranged to meet Eugenia and Maia.

They were both wrapped up warm for the crisp, clear evening and Maia held up her decorated boat with pride.

'You've arrived at just the right time.' Eugenia kissed her sister on each cheek and pointed to the harbour. 'Look, the lights are coming on in the boats.' The little girls watched in awe. The sun had now completely set and the harbour was transformed into an array of twinkling lights from tiny lamps.

'I think you can eat some of your sweets now.'

The two girls picked out one sweet at a time and compared what they had. Eléni's face altered when she found something strange at the bottom of her boat. She brought out Michaíl's drachma and held it up. Tom pretended to eat it, and everyone laughed.

'It's a very old tradition here on the island,' said Eugenia. 'Remember how we used to squabble about who would find the drachma each year. We didn't realise if one of us had it one year, it would be the other one's turn the next year. Why Mamá didn't put a coin in each boat, I'll never know.'

The girls resumed eating their sweets.

'Would you like one, Mamá?' asked Maia.

Eléni did the same. Cassia noticed it was Tom who got the first pick.

The crowd dispersed, so they walked back to Taverna Zervas, glad to leave the cold outside. Michaíl was playing the board game he loved and called over to them.

'It was a good sight, eh? Did you like it?'

'They did, *efcharistó*, Michaíl. And the sweets in the boats.'

He turned to his playing friends and pointed at Eléni as they all left the bar to sit in the kitchen. 'You should see that one playing Tavlí.'

'Would you like a coffee to warm you before you go?' asked Cassia.

'No, thank you,' said Eugenia. 'I must get this one off to bed. We'll see you soon.'

Cassia walked them to the door. They said their good-byes, then Cassia turned to Eléni.

'And you, *agápi mou*.'

Eléni nodded and hugged Tom. 'To-o . . .'

Cassia gasped. 'Did you try to say "Tom"? Good girl. I knew you could.'

Tom smiled at Eléni. He pointed at her, then himself, and clapped his hands.

'I'd leave it for tonight,' he whispered to Cassia as Eléni made her way to the door. 'Let's see if there's any more tomorrow.'

Without thinking, she kissed him and went to get Eléni ready for bed. When she rejoined him, Tom had made two coffees.

'I'm surprised you know how to make Greek coffee.' She eyed the copper *briki* on the stove. 'But I'm very pleased you do. Thank you.' She sipped the strong, sweet liquid, cupping her hands around the tiny cup.

'My brother is married to a Greek woman and the last time I was home, she showed me how. I thought I'd told you I had a Greek sister-in-law. Katerina. That's how I know a bit of the language. They have two boys, Antonios, known as Tony, and Filippos, who we call Philip or Phil.'

There was a lot she didn't know about the handsome man sitting next to her, and yet she seemed to have known him for ever. There was no doubt in her mind he would be the one who would get Eléni talking if anyone could. Eléni adored him.

'I can't believe she almost spoke your name. It wasn't me imagining it, was it?'

'No, it's the first time I've heard her try to say anything. It's why I don't think we should put pressure on her. Maybe after doing things that she loves, like tonight, it will relax her and she'll try more words. "Mamá", for instance.' Tom took Cassia's hand and brought it up to his lips. A tingle surged through her. 'You'd love that, wouldn't you?'

'More than anything. I still can't refer to myself as Mamá, though. Eugenia does all the time.'

'Then you should, too. You're all she's got. You *are* her mamá now.'

They sat, still holding hands.

'*Efcharistó* for today. I have loved every minute of being back with you both. I've hated being away from you. And Eléni,' he quickly added.

She'd missed him too, more than she dared to admit. There was no point in allowing herself to think of being more than a friend to him. In no time at all, he'd be back to Malta and it would be just her and Eléni again.

He took her hand to his lips again. 'Cassia, I have to tell you something.'

Cassia's heart raced, anticipating what he was going to say.

'You must have guessed . . . I've fallen in love with you. You're all I think about.' He put his hand to her cheek and gently stroked it.

Cassia didn't pull away. She didn't say anything at first. Her insides flipped. She'd been in denial, not admitting what Sophia and Michaíl had seen. 'I thought you were being a very dear friend. I bet you have a girl to love in every port. Isn't it what they say about sailors?'

She realised she was being flippant and Tom waited to hear what she really thought.

'I'm very touched. I think of you all the time too, but not in that way. I do love you, but I am not *in love* with you. Does that sound cruel to say?' She hesitated, knowing her feelings for him had changed. Perhaps she was falling in love with him after all, but, with Tom's ship leaving soon, a future together was impossible. 'I don't want you to think the holding hands and kisses on cheeks can mean anything more. I shouldn't have kissed you on the lips earlier, even if it was brief. I was just so thrilled by Eléni attempting to say your name. I'm sorry if that prompted you to say this.'

Tom placed her hand back on the table.

'I'd hoped you'd feel the same. I'm glad you've been honest about your feelings, but your kiss had nothing to do with it. I almost told you before I left back in September.' He paused and sucked in a deep breath. 'The main thing is we stay as we are. Good friends. I'll have to be happy with that. And, hey, we'll get our little girl talking whatever it takes. Friends?'

He raised his hand for her to clap.

'Friends.'

He stood to go. They embraced and as her heart beat faster, Cassia wondered if she'd just made the biggest mistake of her life. No man could replace Nikos, her first love. But he wouldn't want her to be lonely. She was convinced Nikos would have liked Tom. In many ways they were alike — kind, caring, loved children, and there was another thing binding the two men together. Each had been and was in love with her.

'*Kalinýchta*, Cassia. I shall see you tomorrow. That little girl upstairs is going to give you the best Christmas present by starting to talk.'

They walked into the bar where Michaíl was clearing up and washing glasses. All the elderly drinkers had gone.

'Will we see you tomorrow, Tom?' He smiled at Cassia again. 'This young lady has had a spring in her step and a sparkle in those lovely brown eyes since you arrived. Is there something you're not telling me?'

Cassia blushed. 'No, we just like each other's company, don't we, Tom? Just friends.'

Tom nodded in agreement, putting his arm around her shoulders. He'd got the gist of what Michaíl had said. 'We go through a lot in the earthquake, eh? We save Eléni. We do not forget it. Yes, we are just good friends.' Cassia was close enough to hear him whisper under his breath in English, 'More's the pity.'

'*Kalinýchta*, Michaíl.'

Cassia walked Tom to the door and watched him walk away. The sky was an inky indigo and dotted with diamond-like stars. She looked heavenwards.

Nikos, what have I done? He's a good man. Why can't I love him the way I loved you?

CHAPTER SIXTEEN

Tom didn't mention their conversation about his love for her again. As each day passed, the awkwardness between them lessened, and they fell back into their easy friendship. Tom would call by each morning and spend time with Eléni. He would tell her fairy stories or stories about Welsh dragons while she drew them. When Cassia returned from the market, she would often find them laughing together. Sometimes she would stand and watch if they were unaware she was there. One such morning, neither of them heard her enter the kitchen; they were so engrossed in Eléni's latest drawing. *They could so easily be father and daughter,* thought Cassia.

'M-am-á.' Tom pointed at a figure Eléni had drawn. He took the little girl's pencil and wrote the letter *m* on her paper.

What she heard next made her gulp.

'Mmm-a,' said Eléni.

Cassia held her chest, savouring the moment as happiness filled her.

'Mmm-a,' said Eléni again. 'Mmma-mmm-a.'

Tom hugged the little girl.

He looked up and realised Cassia was there to witness it. 'She is clever, eh, Mamá?'

Cassia nodded through a blur of tears.

The little girl picked up her paper and rushed to Cassia. She pointed at the drawing. 'Mma-mma.'

'Is that me? You are so clever.'

Eléni went back to her drawing and then pointed in the bar area as if to tell them she was going to show it to Michaíl.

Cassia sat by Tom. 'You really do have a way with her. You're the one she responds to. How do you do it?'

'Plenty of practice with Tony and Phil, I suppose. Each time I get home on leave, I can spend all day with them, playing the big uncle.' He grinned, remembering. 'Katerina says I have all the best bits and then when they're getting a bit out of hand, I just sail off into the sunset.'

Cassia laughed as she imagined the chaos he left behind. 'Eléni went back into her shell when you left in September, you know. She couldn't tell me, of course, but I knew she thought it was my fault you'd left us behind. You should have seen the scowls she gave me. I'm dreading you going back.'

He was gracious enough not to remind her that if they became lovers, she'd be able to promise Eléni he'd be coming back to them as soon as he could. She'd be able to tell her it was just his job. Being a mere friend, however, he might find another woman to love, and his obligation would be to go to her every time he was on leave. Did she want him to be happy — to find someone else to love and who loved him back? She felt she was being selfish by wanting him to keep coming back to her and Eléni.

'If you send me some of her drawings, perhaps it will help her understand I want to stay in touch and be part of her life. I'll write back to her — I mean it. You too, even though it's as a friend.'

Cassia hugged him. What could she do to fall in love properly with this beautiful man?

* * *

Cassia opened her eyes. A shaft of light crept into the bedroom through the thin curtains. *25 December. Christoúgenna.* Cassia, Eugenia and Michaíl had decided to make it the main day of celebrations for Tom as he would have left by the time they swapped their presents on New Year's Day, the day of Agios Vasilios. Everyone was invited to Eugenia's house later to let Tom sample a little of a Greek Christmas.

Cassia looked out of her bedroom window across the harbour. It was a crisp, clear day and the shape of Ithaca was visible on the horizon. She looked at Eléni, who was snug and still asleep under her blankets. She thought back to the Christmas service they'd all attended the day before, remembering the times her parents had taken her and Eugenia to the same church as children. It had been the first time she'd been inside any church since she'd lost Nikos, but she knew it meant a lot to Michaíl. She wanted Eléni and Tom to experience what Christmas was like on the island, too. They'd met Eugenia and Maia there. Sensing Cassia's unease, Eugenia had whispered, 'It's all right. Mamá is going to the early-morning service tomorrow.'

'Wake up, sleepyhead.' Cassia gently lifted Eléni out of her bed. 'We're going to have a special day showing Tom what a Christmas in Kefalonia would be like. We'll give him the gifts we've made for him, shall we? Come on, let's get dressed and have breakfast before we collect him.'

Eléni wriggled out of Cassia's arms and retrieved the gift she'd wrapped for Tom before leaving the room. Excitement shone from her face. Once they'd had a breakfast of fresh fruit and yoghurt drizzled with honey, and packed Michaíl's old car with their contributions to the day, Michaíl drove to pick up Tom from Kýria Galanos's house. Most of the houses in the street had decorated boats on display in their windows. He beeped the horn. When a beaming Tom descended the few steps onto the road, Cassia noticed the front-window net curtains twitch. She turned away, hoping the old woman would not have recognised her. 'I hope she didn't see it was me,' she told Michaíl. 'She will not approve of poor Tom being in the same car as a communist sympathiser, as she thinks of me.'

'Nor a communist chauffeur, either.'

The two of them were still laughing when Tom got in the back seat by Eléni.

'What are those two chuckling about?' he asked the little girl. She pointed at the house from where he'd just emerged. She formed her hands into circles and brought them up to her eyes. Then pointed at Cassia and Michaíl.

'She was spying? On these two?'

The little girl dissolved into fits of laughter.

A mere few minutes into the journey, a wave of nausea washed over Cassia. She wasn't a good passenger at the best of times, but Michaíl's driving didn't help. He seemed to hit every bump and every pothole in the road's surface. The road out of Fiscardo that led to Eugenia's house snaked along the spectacular white cliffs, and Cassia tried to focus on the vibrant turquoises and teals of the sea below rather than anticipate the bumps in the road — of which there were many. When she walked there, there was a shortcut through open land and away from the road.

Finally, they arrived. Michaíl parked alongside Eugenia's truck and Maia was out to greet them in no time, dragging Eléni away by the hand to play with Calix and Callista. They unpacked the car, and when they entered the house, the delicious smell of cooked lamb hit them.

'*Kalá Christoúgenna*, Eugenia,' said Cassia.

'We say Happy Christmas, and it's today!' Tom placed a box of drinks from Michaíl's bar on the table. 'Or in Wales, the Welsh speakers would say *Nadolig Llawen*.'

'Just a few bottles of retsina and *ouzo* for after the meal.' Michaíl looked over at the roasting pan just out of the oven.

'Thank you, all of you. It's small, I'm afraid, but we'll have to fill ourselves up with vegetables, and I've made olive bread.'

'But we're a lot better off than those poor people around Argostoli. No wonder people are leaving in droves.' Cassia picked up a newspaper from the sideboard. 'Look at this. People queuing for food and when they get there, it says there's not enough to go around. That'll be us up here in Fiscardo soon.'

Eugenia looked at her and frowned. 'Don't say that. It won't come to that.'

'Now, now, ladies. No more talk about people leaving Kefalonia. It's Christmas Day. Who wants a drink?' said Tom.

It struck Cassia as ironic that Tom was the one to stop the talk about emigrating, yet he was the one who would be leaving them all in two days' time. She had a sinking feeling in the pit of her stomach.

Eugenia brought in her tins of sweet desserts. As well as more melomakarona, she had baked kourabiedes, the traditional sweets for Christmas. The delicious aroma of the almonds filled the air when she lifted the lid of the tin.

'Let's sprinkle some of the icing sugar on the top of the table and draw some tiny footmarks.' Eugenia picked up some of the powdered sugar between her thumb and forefinger, spreading and sprinkling it around. Using the edge of a teaspoon, she drew little lines to represent feet.

Cassia laughed. 'I remember Mamá telling us it was the goblins playing pranks on us, making a complete mess in the kitchen.'

'And we believed her!'

Her thoughts were interrupted by a young voice. 'Who's made that mess?' Maia asked.

Eugenia looked at Cassia. 'It's the goblins. They play tricks on the adults and make a mess in the kitchen. Look, they've left footprints. Can you see, Eléni?' The little girl nodded.

Michaíl joined them and went along with the legend that had been handed down for generations. Cassia cleared up the mess while Eugenia went out to Michaíl's car to bring in the centrepiece of any Greek Christmas Day table, the special Christmas bread. The smell of cinnamon, oranges and cloves soon hung in the warm air next to the oven where the Christmas dinner was cooking.

* * *

Eugenia's meal of lamb kleftiko, slow-roasted on a bed of her homegrown root vegetables — stored after the summer and seasoned with oregano that she'd grown herself — was a huge success.

'It was a beautiful meal. Thank you.' Tom patted his stomach, and the girls giggled.

'Now you must taste something else we'll be having at our Christmas meal in January. The desserts.' While Eugenia cleared away the dinner plates, Cassia brought a large platter of baklavá, shredded filo kataífi and honey pastries. In the centre of the table, she placed the Christopsomo flavoured with cinnamon, oranges and cloves. The top was decorated with a cross.

'Christmas in Greece would not be Christmas without the Christopsomo. It is "Christ's bread" or "Christmas bread". A bit different from your mother's Christmas cake, I think.'

Tom held up his plate for a piece. 'You've all shown me a real Greek Christmas. I shall always remember this. *Efcharistó.*'

Michaíl handed round some small glasses of ouzo. 'Oh, it's not finished yet, Tom. Knock this back and while the women clear up, we'll sit outside and have a smoke. It's warm enough now the sun is out.'

'No. I'll help.' Tom started collecting plates and glasses. 'They've done all the hard work already.'

The look on Michaíl Pavlis's face told him it wasn't what usually happened. The two sisters smiled at each other. Once the three of them had finished the cleaning up, they called Michaíl and the girls inside.

CHAPTER SEVENTEEN

It was present-giving time. They'd only give theirs to Tom, and Cassia knew he'd brought gifts for the girls. The main Christmas presents would remain hidden until the first of January.

'Eléni, would you like to give your present to Tom?' Cassia handed her the gift Eléni had helped wrap.

Eléni stood and watched as Tom opened his gift.

'I wonder what this is.' Tom took his time to build up the excitement for the girls. He peeked inside the box. 'Oh, it is just what I want.'

'What is it? What is it?' Maia jumped up and down.

Tom pulled out a slim silver-coloured cigarette case. 'Oh, *efcharistó*. It is lovely. I think your mamá helps to choose.' He looked up at Cassia and beamed at her.

Eléni tugged on his trousers and pointed inside the packaging.

'There is more?'

Eléni nodded and pointed at her chest.

Cassia brought out some drawings that had been placed between two pieces of card to prevent them from creasing. They were Eléni's drawings Cassia had labelled. He held them up one by one for everyone to see. Cassia watched his face as he held up the final one — it was of her and Tom on either side of Eléni, all holding hands. She remembered the effect it had had on her when she'd seen it for the first time. One happy family. Tom was clearly affected by it too.

Eugenia gave Maia a little box to hand to Tom. 'I helped Mamá make these for you.' Inside were some little oval biscuits, smelling of orange, spices and honey. They were topped with nuts.

'Maia, these look so good.'

The little girl smiled.

Eugenia explained. 'They're *melomakarona* and it is traditional to give them as gifts at Christmas. Mind, I had to make sure Maia didn't eat them all.'

'Thank you, girls. I'll always remember this Christmas. Shall I go next? There are two special gifts for two special little girls in here.' Eléni and Maia clapped their hands as Tom put his hand in a bag and pulled out two identical parcels.

'*Efcharistó*,' said Maia.

Eléni pointed at Tom, then back at herself and then clapped. 'To . . .'

Tom smiled and hugged them both.

Eugenia looked shocked. 'When has that happened?' she whispered to Cassia.

'It's all down to Tom.' Her eyes shone as she saw her sister's mutual delight.

'You'll need some help from your mamás to help you get started,' he said.

Everyone watched as Eléni and Maia tore off the wrapping paper.

'It's a picture of a girl!' Maia held up a pack of cardboard sheets, on which were pictures of children surrounded by different styles of clothes.

Eléni clapped, her eyes wide with delight. 'To . . .' she said again.

'They're paper dolls. We used to have these, didn't we? *Efcharistó*, Tom, they're going to love playing with these.'

'Yes. *Efcharistó*, Tom. Come here, girls.' Maia and Eléni stood by Eugenia, and Maia handed her pack to her mother, who took out the sheets of dolls with care. 'I'll help you cut out the dolls and see this dotted line. We bend it back so the dolls can stand. Then we'll cut out the clothes, and see these little tags — we fold those back and then you can choose which clothes you'd like to dress your dolly in.'

'Can we do it now?' said Maia, excitedly. By her side, Eléni nodded in agreement.

Eugenia went to find pairs of scissors while the girls got their sheets of dolls ready.

'You men don't mind while we do this, do you? They'll be so engrossed in dressing their new dolls, we won't be disturbed. Thank you. It was such a good idea.'

Michaíl poured Tom an ouzo. 'Do you want some water with it? Or do you want it as it comes, like a true Kefalonian.' He laughed as he added water at Tom's request, watching the liquid turn milky. 'Let's leave them to it.'

Cassia wondered how Michaíl would have spent his Christmas if she and Eléni had not been staying with him. All she knew about him was that his wife had died and he'd been a staunch partisan. He'd never mentioned any family, and she didn't want to pry.

Eugenia returned and handed a pair of scissors to her sister. They cut out the dolls and then the selection of clothes, while both little girls watched intently.

'We must be careful not to cut across the tags,' said Cassia. 'You'll need those when you come to dress the dollies.'

'There. That's the first one done.' Eugenia held up a doll and proceeded to show them how to add the clothes.

The rest of the afternoon was spent talking while the girls played with their dolls. More ouzo was drunk and Eugenia made coffee before bringing out more melomakarona. 'We couldn't let Tom have them all, could we?'

They all laughed.

'I don't know how you've managed all of this with the shortages, Eugenia.' Michaíl savoured his pastry.

She told them how she'd been saving as many ingredients as she could, anticipating how much more she would need at Christmastime. 'I wanted to make it special for Maia since her baba came and went so suddenly, and for Cassia and Eléni who were caught up in the terrible earthquake. I had plenty of olive oil and flour, so that helped.'

'I hope by having a special day for me you still have enough for your second celebration in a week's time. I cannot thank you enough.' Tom stood and went to kiss Eugenia on the cheek.

'It's so good to have you all here today.' Eugenia's voice cracked. 'I was dreading Christmas. Maia asks for Georgios every night. How do I explain to a three-year-old her father is a womaniser and I was a fool to have had him back? He was so charming I believed him when he told me he would never stray again. He's gone back to her in Ithaca, you know.'

Cassia checked that Maia wasn't watching her mother get upset. 'We'll celebrate with you, won't we, Michaíl? You and Maia must come to Taverna Zervas for Saint Basil's Day. It will be me cooking and using up our rations. You've done more than enough for us today.'

* * *

Later that evening, with Eléni fast asleep upstairs at the end of such a long and exciting day, and Michaíl in the bar, Cassia and Tom went for a walk along the quayside. They found a bench at the far end of the harbour. A few people wandered past, but it was mostly quiet. The fine, clear day meant it was a cold and crisp evening. Moonlight bathed the water and the fishing boats in silver, so together with dotted lights from the bars and tavernas, the whole scene was magical. No one would believe what was happening to her beautiful island. Out of the blue, she remembered Rhodri Jones, the Welsh newspaper reporter, and how she'd yelled at him for benefiting from the islanders' misery. And yet, because of him, Eléni was alive. Having read about the hardship the islanders were going through in Eugenia's newspaper that morning and being shocked by how so many were emigrating for a better life, she wondered if he'd been right. Without news getting out to the rest of the world, they'd have had no help, no medical aid, no food supplies. She looked across at the man sitting beside her. *And no Tom.*

'Penny for your thoughts? Or should I say a drachma for them?' A cloud of white accompanied Tom's breath in the cold air as he spoke. Cassia looked at him, puzzled. 'It's what we say when we want to know what someone is thinking.'

'Oh, it's just the newspaper report this morning has had a real effect on me. I can't get the image of the queuing people out of my mind. And then to learn they would be turned away when the food ran out. They had queued in vain. I was shocked by the numbers who are leaving. I worry it will be as bad here soon.'

Tom placed his arm around her shoulders. 'Try not to worry. Didn't you say let's just think about Christmas for today? I haven't given you your present yet.'

Casia swivelled to face him. 'Tom, there was no need. I got you the cigarette case for Eléni to give you something after you dropped a hint you'd got something for the girls.'

He placed a finger on her lips. 'Shh.'

From his pocket, he took a square, flat box. 'Happy Christmas. *Nadolig Llawen.*'

Cassia's hand shook as she opened the box. Inside was a silver bracelet that shimmered in the moonlight. In the centre, the bangle widened to make room for a filigree Maltese cross.

'Tom, I can't accept this. It's beautiful . . . and expensive.'

'Think of it as a token of our friendship. Silver filigree is everywhere in the shops in Valletta. I thought if I hadn't been stationed in Malta we would never have met, and I'll be leaving there soon.'

He placed her wrist through the bangle. 'There, a perfect fit.'

He went to kiss the top of her head, but Cassia raised her face towards his. He stopped.

'Are you sure, Cassia? The bracelet is what I said it is. A gift for a friend. You mustn't feel obligated to show your appreciation this way if you don't want to be more than a friend. Isn't that what you want?'

'I'm sure. I want you to kiss me. Properly. Not as a friend but as . . .'

'Oh, Cassia.' Tom brushed his lips against hers, then pulled her closer. They kissed again, this time more urgently. Craving crept along Cassia's veins. She knew she was doing the right thing. Reawakened sensations tumbled inside her. They were not the fireworks she remembered always happening when she kissed Nikos, but Nikos was gone. She did love Tom Beynon, but in a different way. But it was still real love. She couldn't imagine him not being part of her and Eléni's life. She dreaded having to say goodbye to him in two days' time. What would happen after that she didn't know, but, at least, Tom now knew what he meant to her.

They walked back to Taverna Zervas with their arms around each other. Michaíl was still in the bar when they got in, but the regular drinkers had left.

'I was about to lock up. You two look pleased with yourselves.'

Nothing more was said. Tom left.

Cassia retired for the night, making sure she didn't disturb a sleeping Eléni. She lay awake for a while thinking of what had happened that evening. She'd convinced herself that because Tom wasn't Nikos, she couldn't be more than a friend to him. But once she'd allowed herself to kiss Tom and be kissed by him, her feelings had risen to the fore. Nikos would always be part of who she was. They'd been young and crazy when they'd fallen in love. But here was another man who loved her, and she loved him. A mature and caring man, and a different kind of love. When she closed her eyes, it was the handsome face of a fair-haired man that filled her head.

CHAPTER EIGHTEEN

The next four days leading up to Tom's departure flew by, and the anticipation of what his leaving would do filled Cassia with dread. They spent as much time together as they could, but Cassia still had to work at the market to bring in some money. Michaíl hadn't confided in her, but she suspected the diminishing numbers in the bar meant there was very little money coming in from there. Often she'd find him sitting in the corner, the rhythmic click of his kombolói alerting her to the fact that each worry bead represented his concerns. With the build up to Christmas, she remembered the tavernas and bars in Argostoli would normally be bustling and she suspected they would be the same here in Fiscardo. It had been when she was young. But this year, there were no bars left standing in the town she used to call home, and the few tavernas like Michaíl's were almost empty. Even his elderly friends, who might have made a tot of raki last all night, were not venturing out to play their beloved Tavlí.

Every morning, Michaíl went out to buy a newspaper.

'It's getting worse. There won't be any islanders left if it carries on like this. Look.' He spread out the paper on the table by the window for her to see. 'Look at those queues to get on the ship. Taking them away to a better life. If I was younger, I'd be first in the queue.'

The grainy image showed men, women and children waiting in a line to board a large ferry boat. 'Where do you think it's sailing to?' asked Cassia.

'Athens, I suspect.'

Tom had entered the bar. 'Tom! I didn't hear you come in.' Cassia wanted to rush over for one of his *cwtches*, as he called them, but was self-conscious to do so in front of Michaíl. As far as anyone else knew, they were still just friends. Apart from Eléni, who'd found them kissing outside a couple of nights ago. She'd smiled a big smile and pointed first at Cassia, and then Tom, and mimed kissing by pursing her lips.

'To-o . . . Mma-mma' she said, before making kissing noises.

They were half expecting her to repeat it all for Michaíl, but she didn't. Instead, she drew a picture of the two of them, close together with their lips touching.

'They can't all be going to Athens, surely,' Cassia said. 'It says here the majority are going to America, with others heading for Canada.'

'Many of them will have had all their documents destroyed in the quake. As long as a family member in those countries can vouch for them, they can enter the countries legally. I've been checking up on things for you before I leave on Thursday. Where's Eléni?'

'She's in the kitchen, dressing her paper dolls. What do you mean, "checking up on things" for me? What has it got to do with me?' Cassia called after him as he hurried off.

As she joined Tom and Eléni, they were already engrossed in placing the different outfits on the dolls. Cassia smiled as she watched a tall, fully grown man sitting on the floor by a tiny girl playing with dolls.

'Your sailor mates, as you call them, would never believe you like playing with dolls, Tom Beynon.'

'They won't know unless you tell them.' He looked at her and winked.

Cassia began packing up her baking to take to the market stall. 'You didn't answer me when I asked you what the information you've found out about Athens has to do with me.'

Tom stood and joined her by the range.

'You have to go to the market now, but I've been thinking. Why don't I stay here with Eléni and then when you get back, perhaps Michaíl will look after her so we have some time to talk.'

Cassia agreed, but was puzzled about what Tom wanted to talk to her about. It sounded serious. When she arrived at her stall, she was disappointed to see Rhea's was empty again. Eugenia had told her that she hadn't seen her friend recently either. Over the last few days, more and more stalls had closed and the number of customers had diminished. It should have been a busy time of year. She'd intended to bake baklavá along with the customary Vasilopita to sell ready for New Year's Day.

'Rhea still not coming in?' she asked the market owner.

'Haven't you heard? She's left.'

Cassia's heart sank. She was already missing her friend who used to make her laugh with stories of what her little one would say and get up to.

'What is she doing now? She told me she had to work.'

'I meant she's left the island. Emigrated. Canada, I think.'

Cassia thought back to the newspaper images. She imagined her friend as one of those queuing while holding her daughter's hand, about to board the ship and sail into the unknown. *How would Rhea be feeling? Scared of what lay ahead, excited, sad to be leaving Kefalonia, hopeful?* Cassia understood why the people of Argostoli were compelled to leave, but now people from Fiscardo where homes had been relatively untouched by the earthquake were emigrating too. It brought it home to her how serious things were.

She packed up early and returned home, having sold less than half her spanakopita and pastries. Before leaving, the market owner had told her he was reducing the opening hours of the market. Between them, she and Eugenia would just have one day each on which to make some money.

'It's not closing altogether. Once spring comes, there will be more fresh vegetables to sell and later the fruit.' Her face must have shown her disappointment. 'I'm sorry, but it's the same for all of us.'

She knew it was, but it didn't help lift the weight in her chest as she wondered how she was going to break the news to Michaíl. Everyone had been so cheerful on the day of Agios Nikolaos, so why had things got so bad in a matter of weeks?

Michaíl and Tom were sitting outside as she approached the taverna, Michaíl with worry beads in hand as always. The sun shone and Eléni played alongside them with Kynigós.

'Here comes the worker.' Tom flashed one of his smiles at her. 'But you're not usually home this early. Sold out, eh?'

His face dropped when he noticed the bag at her side, weighing her down.

'I wish I had. There's no money about. The owner is reducing the days the market will be open. One day each — that's all Eugenia and I will be working there.'

She hated seeing Michaíl's face become serious. He stood and entered the taverna.

'Michaíl. I'm sorry.'

Tom put an arm around her shoulders, pulling her close. 'Try not to worry. He just wishes things would improve so he doesn't have to rely on you so much.'

* * *

Later that afternoon, with just one day left before Tom had to return to his ship, he and Cassia walked out of Fiscardo hand in hand. She didn't mind who saw them now. They'd told Michaíl and Eugenia, who'd both wished them well. *If word gets back to Mamá. what can she do? I'm a free woman, and she disapproves of anything and everything I do.* She was convinced her mother deliberately made sure they would avoid each other, whereas Eugenia reported that on the days she ran the stall, their mother always came in to see her. When Eugenia had first admitted this, Cassia had felt a pang of envy, but she hadn't been surprised. Their encounter the first time she'd seen her mother since she'd returned to Fiscardo hadn't ended well.

On Cassia's suggestion, she and Tom walked to a pretty cove hidden from view not far from the village. They walked down the narrow track to where the turquoise water glowed in the sunlight. The creamy-white beach Cassia knew would be fine shingle when they got down there formed a half-moon shape, surrounded by rocks.

'I wanted to show you this. Isn't it beautiful? No desolate buildings, no people worrying about where the next meal is coming from, no queues of people leaving. Just look at it. How can anyone leave a place like this?' Tom didn't comment. 'Come on, it's quite a steep path to get down there.' A strong breeze blew Cassia's long black hair behind her as she led the way down to the cove.

Once they were there and sheltered by the cliffs, the air was much warmer for a December day. The wind had dropped.

Tom pulled Cassia in close and kissed her. Cassia's stomach flipped as her body responded to him. He took off his jacket and spread it on the fine shingle.

'This will have to do for a travel rug.' He patted the jacket. 'Come and sit by me. I want this day to be perfect, for you to forget all about the market and your worries.'

Cassia sat beside him and they fell back together with their arms entwined. Tom sought out her lips. 'I'm going to miss you.'

Her voice became scratchy. 'I don't want you to go. How will I manage without you? Eléni will miss you so much.' Her eyes filled with tears. 'No one can get her to open up like you do. Because of you, she's trying to say a few words. I'll always be grateful for that.'

He kissed her tenderly. 'When I left you both at Eugenia's last time, I was leaving a much-loved friend and her little girl. That was hard enough, not knowing if you wanted to see me again. But this time it's different. This time I know you love me too and all I can think about is that.' He sat up. 'You asked me why I looked into the people emigrating and I told you I found out for you. Well, I have something to put to you.'

Cassia's heart skipped a beat. Her mind whirred with ideas of what he was going to say.

CHAPTER NINETEEN

'What if I help you and Eléni leave Kefalonia for somewhere where you won't have to worry about money ever again? Where you could get help for Eléni?'

Cassia's mouth gaped open. 'No! No, I'll never leave — you know that.'

'Some of my mates on the ship carve out the insides of bars of soap and send money to their wives in there so they get the whole lot. I would do the same for you.'

Cassia shook her head. She didn't want to hear any more.

'But think about it. Michaíl told me even here, there will be no work — the economy is failing due to lack of resources. Things are not going to improve for a very long time. What if Eléni never learns to speak in that time? The longer she doesn't get help, the more likely she will never speak.'

Cassia stood and began pacing the beach. 'She will — I know she will.' Deep down, did she truly believe that? If Eléni did need professional help, would she be able to get it in Kefalonia? Would she be able to afford it? No! Using Eléni's problem as a way of trying to convince her to emigrate wasn't fair! Money wasn't everything, was it? She'd find a way of feeding her and her daughter if it was the last thing she'd do. But how was a different matter. And her little girl would learn to speak. Another thought entered her mind. What if someone worked out she wasn't Eléni's mother? She quickly dismissed it.

Tom stood up too. 'Don't get upset, please. I just want you to think about it. If you have a contact in the country you want to settle in—'

'I wouldn't even know which country to go to. I don't know anyone outside Kefalonia.'

'You could move to Wales. Like I told you, my brother is married to a Greek woman. You could use Katerina as your contact. She'd vouch for you, I'm sure. She would be your Greek connection. You'd like her. She'd help you settle in. In the little town where I'm from, there's a school for the deaf. The children are older, but we could find someone there to help Eléni, I'm sure of it.'

'I can't use a non-relative as my connection, and Eléni's not deaf!'

'I know, but they could help with signing and the methods they use when getting their pupils to speak.'

What Tom said next made Cassia freeze to the spot.

'You'd have a stronger connection if you were my wife, Cassia.' He took her hand and kissed it. 'Will you marry me? I love you so much.'

Her heart drumming inside her chest, Cassia stood openmouthed. She was happy for their relationship to move on past friendship. But marriage? Hadn't she told herself she would never marry again because of the depth of her love for Nikos? Yet, Nikos wouldn't expect her to remain single forever, would he? Where would they live? How could she uproot Eléni again? She was shocked at herself for even asking these questions. How could she tell Eugenia, Michaíl? Even though she was adamant she wouldn't leave the place of her birth, the questions kept coming. Cassia's mind was in turmoil. She was thinking of all the reasons she couldn't or shouldn't marry Tom, but she hadn't asked herself one important question. Did she love him and *want* to marry him?

'Oh, Tom. I don't know what to say. I know you said you loved me and I love you, too. But marriage? I wasn't expecting this. It's too soon. I'm flattered, but you'll be posted somewhere else and I won't see you for months. Isn't it better for us to stay here and wait for your visits?'

As much as he tried to cover it up, Cassia could tell by Tom's expression it was not the answer he'd been hoping for. But she had to be honest with both him and herself.

'Just think about it. The worse things get in Kefalonia, the more difficult it will be to visit you through the ports. I couldn't bear not to see you and Eléni.'

They sat back down, both deep in thought. The earlier moment for romance had been replaced with practicalities and serious decisions.

Tom looked at her. 'I know your love for me is not the same as your love for Nikos, but I'll be happy if you can learn to love me as a wife. We'll be a family for Eléni and give her the best life. She deserves that, doesn't she?'

Cassia wanted that above all else.

A cool breeze had sprung up, and the two of them decided to make their way back up the steep path to the road. The sun was lower in the sky now. The streaks of lemon and pale apricot against the blue-grey backdrop promised another spectacular sunset later. Cassia wondered what the sunsets were like in Wales and remonstrated with herself for considering the possibility of moving away from Kefalonia. *I have to stay. This is where I belong!*

'It's got to be your decision, *cariad*, but I truly believe we'd be doing the best for Eléni. And one last thing. I won't mention it again. We only have Sophia's word Eléni has no relatives.'

Goosebumps prickled the skin along Cassia's arms. All Tom was doing was expressing what she'd already thought herself.

That night, Cassia didn't sleep. Tom's face kept invading her mind.

The next morning, she and Eléni accompanied Tom to his waiting boat that would take him down to Argostoli to catch his ferry. It was a day Cassia had been dreading and now there was another reason why she was sad to see Tom leave. She'd promised she'd give him her answer, but she wasn't ready. Afraid he'd consider the delay as a rebuff, she was determined to put on a happy face so he would have no idea of the turmoil she was going through. Tom and Eléni seemed oblivious to her dilemma, and they laughed together as Tom scooped up the little girl, tickling her as he said a special goodbye.

'You be a good girl for your mamá. I come back to see you both soon.' Eléni nodded and wrapped her arms around his neck.

'Goodbye, Cassia. Please think about what I've had to say. You would make me the happiest man in the world if you said yes. One last *cwtch*?'

Cassia hugged him tight, the little girl between them, and tried to put all her feelings into that one embrace. Tom let go and put Eléni down, then ran up the gangway without a backward glance. Cassia knew his eyes would be full of tears like hers were.

Goodbye, Tom.

Hearing the hooter of the ship, they waited until the ship was manoeuvred away from the harbour wall. By this time, Tom was up on deck, waving.

Eléni spotted him first and pointed. 'To . . .' Then she burst into tears.

* * *

In the days after Tom left, Cassia felt empty inside. To make it worse, Eléni retreated into her shell and didn't utter a sound. Even Michaíl could not get a smile or reaction from her. New Year was approaching and yet, not one of them seemed in the mood to celebrate. Cassia went through the motions of making the melomakarona and Vasilopita to eat on St Basil's Day, and Michaíl even managed to get the promise of a small piece of pork from his butcher friend.

Cassia woke to the sound of sobbing. Eléni was hugging her Maltese doll, tears streaming down her face.

'What is it, *Elenáki mou?* She picked up the little girl, knowing the exact reason. 'You're missing Tom, aren't you? I am, too. Shall I give you an extra tight *cwtch* like he would do?'

Eléni nodded. 'Tom, Tom gone.'

It was the first time she'd spoken Tom's whole name and the first time she'd said the word *gone*. The first time she'd uttered anything since he'd left. It was Cassia's turn to become tearful. How she wished she could tell him what had just happened. Could she marry Tom and leave all ties with Kefalonia behind? The little girl in front of her would benefit and hopefully learn to speak with specialist help. She did love him not just because he would make Eléni happy but because it would make her happy to become his wife. It was Tom who filled her waking thoughts, and she missed him terribly. Cassia stifled a sob. She'd made a huge mistake. Why, oh why, hadn't she accepted his wedding proposal before he left on the ship?

'Eléni . . . Would you like it if Mamá and Tom got married, and he became your baba?'

Eléni pulled away from Cassia. She nodded and pointed at her heart. There was no going back now. She'd write and tell Tom she would love to become Kýria Tom Beynon. All she had to do now was tell Eugenia and Michaíl of her decision.

CHAPTER TWENTY

Unable to sleep that night, Cassia began to write the most important letter she'd ever written. She tried several times, but each attempt was screwed up into a ball and thrown on the bedroom floor. She wanted to get her love across to Tom, not sound as if she was accepting his proposal for Eléni's sake. She'd told him she loved him before he left, so why were the words so hard to write?

Taverna Zervas
Fiscardo
Kefalonia

My dear Tom,

By now, you will be back on board your ship. Life here is not the same without you. I miss our talks, how you make me laugh, the way you are with Eléni. Above all, I miss you. I know you were disappointed I didn't say yes to marrying you straight away and yet even then, you still wanted me. Since you left, I have not been able to think of anything else but you. Yours is the first face I see every morning when I wake up and the last at night when I close my eyes. I made the biggest mistake of my life by letting you leave without my answer.

If you still want to marry me, then, yes, I accept. Yes! I promise to be the best wife I can to you. I know we can't see each other until your next leave, but please write back and tell me you still want to marry me. I look at the beautiful bracelet you gave me and it isn't a friendship bracelet to me. In my eyes it is a gift from the man I want to marry.

Please write back as soon as you can.

With my love,

Cassia Xx

She folded the letter and tucked it into an envelope. Licking along the seal, she imagined how Tom would react as he read the words.

Once she and Eléni were dressed and had breakfast, they went to post Tom's letter.

'We're just popping out, Michaíl.'

He sat in his usual seat in the bar, Kynigós lying at his feet. A newspaper was spread out in front of him and his face was serious. Cassia hoped he wouldn't stop them and start complaining about the awful state of affairs in Kefalonia. She was on a happy mission, accepting a proposal of marriage, and nothing was going to spoil it.

As she got out into the street, she felt guilty. The old man was not just worried for himself, but for her and Eléni too. A shiver ran through her. How was she going to break the news to him that she intended to marry Tom and they were emigrating to Wales? By the time they reached the post office, she'd made a decision. She'd tell both Michaíl and Eugenia after the New Year's Day meal the following day. The woman behind the counter took the letter, making note of the address.

'Ah, Kýrios Beynon. He told me he will miss you. He will be pleased to get this, eh?'

'I hope so.' Cassia looked at Eléni and smiled.

When they got back to the taverna, Michaíl was outside in the yard chopping the meagre amount of wood left to heat the oven and the fire in the living room tomorrow. The wood from Eugenia had lasted a while, but after tomorrow she would have to ask her sister for help again. Eléni settled down to do some drawing while Cassia prepared food for the next day.

She cut the pork into small pieces and let it marinate in some of Eugenia's olive oil. Making sure she had all the ingredients for the morning, she placed everything in the small, cool pantry just off the kitchen. She wanted this to be a celebratory meal. It dawned on her it was going to be her last in Kefalonia, her last in Greece, so she wanted the meal to be typically Greek. This was the recipe her mamá had made when she was a child. But back then the piece of meat had been huge, with any spices readily available and no shortages. This was having to be her version 1953-style.

Eléni tugged at Cassia's skirt, dragging her to the front of the bar where the door was open. From the outside came the sound of singing.

'Ah, it's the carol singers.' Cassia held Eléni's hand and took her outside. 'Look, they have little boats like yours.'

One small boy stepped forward asking if Cassia and Eléni would like them to sing. By that time, Michaíl had joined them.

Once they agreed, the singing started. Some of the children held triangles or drums to accompany the singing.

'*Kalanta*. Our Greek carols.' Michaíl's face had softened. Gone were the earlier worry lines that had been etched on his face. 'If you listen, the *Kalanda* song will be wishing me, as head of the household, a long life and prosperity. I don't think it will happen, eh, Cassia?'

Cassia squeezed his arm.

'Come, Eléni. We must find something to give the singers.'

They went into the kitchen where Cassia had made some koulouri. She'd cut the dough of the sweet rolls into tiny bite-sized pieces for the carol singers to fit in their boats. Eléni helped Cassia carry the tray of breads back to the singers and then handed them around. Michaíl had a handful of drachmae to share and placed them in the little boats.

The three of them sat in the living room where the low table was laid with two glasses and an already opened bottle of retsina. In another glass was orange juice for Eléni. Michaíl poured and handed Cassia a glass of the pine-resin flavoured wine.

'*Yamas, agápi mou.*'

Eléni raised her glass, too, laughing at the chink of the glasses.

Michaíl went into the bar in the hope of some custom, and Cassia and Eléni got more things ready for the next day. Eugenia and Maia would be arriving in the morning.

* * *

Eugenia arrived right on time.

'*Kalí chroniá,*' she called out to them as she opened the back of her old truck. Her gift for Michaíl was a load of logs, piled into the back.

'*Kalí chroniá,* Eugenia. Ah, the best gift. *Efcharistó.*' The old man helped Eugenia take the logs to the outhouse. 'Come in, come in. I think Maia has already gone to join Eléni.'

Cassia greeted her sister, kissing her on both cheeks. '*Kalí chroniá, agápi mou.* Yes, Maia and Eléni immediately disappeared upstairs to play.'

Cassia brought out the marinated meat from the pantry. She cut up the peppers and other vegetables and sautéed them until they were golden brown. Next, she heated a deep pan on a high heat before adding the pieces of pork, which were cooked until they too got some colour. The vegetables were added and mixed.

'Now comes the best bit,' Cassia said.

With care, she added a dash of Metaxa brandy, some of the retsina from the previous day, honey, spices, cinnamon and cloves, then a little water and orange juice.

'Do you want to mix it for luck and make a wish?' she asked her sister. Eugenia smiled and took the large spoon.

'What shall I wish for? I can wish everyone left on Kefalonia good luck, but I mustn't say my wish out loud or it won't come true.'

Cassia took the pan from Eugenia when she'd finished and placed it in the oven, where it would bake for the next two hours. She thought about what Eugenia had said. Wishing everyone good luck was easy, but she wouldn't let anyone know she wished for Tom to write back immediately. She wished she were on a ferry to Athens to become his wife. She wished she'd accepted his proposal and told him face to face she wanted to be his wife.

Unexpectedly, Cassia's eyes misted. Even in times of hardship like this, the traditions of a Greek Christmas and Saint Basil's Day were being upheld thanks to her sister and Michaíl. The three of them were all working together to make sure Eléni and Maia had the same happy memories she and Eugenia had.

'Shall we open the presents while the food is cooking? Can you give the girls a shout?'

They handed around the small pile of gifts. 'I think Agios Vasilios has been,' said Cassia. 'This one is for you, Eléni.'

Watching the little girl's face as she opened the soft teddies, dressed in colourful clothes Cassia had made for her, was magical. Cassia wished Tom could have been there to share the moment.

When Michaíl handed Eléni and Maia his presents, the girls both felt all around them first and got even more excited, ripping off the paper as quickly as they could.

'I wonder what they could be,' said Cassia.

As Eléni unwrapped each wooden animal, her eyes widened further and her smile filled the whole of her face. She stood up and hugged Michaíl, who by then had tears in his eyes.

Maia squealed, 'Look, Mamá. A spinning top! I've always wanted one. *Efcharistó, efcharistó.*' She joined Eléni in Michaíl's arms.

'You've made two little girls very happy,' said Eugenia.

'They're beautiful, Michaíl.' Cassia's voice filled with emotion. 'You are clever.' She was about to take this kind man's surrogate granddaughter away from him.

'Girls, would you like to give these to Michaíl?' Cassia handed them each a wrapped gift.

The old man opened them one by one — a scarf from Eléni and Cassia, and a pair of gloves from Maia and Eugenia. His eyes lit up. 'These will keep me nice and warm. *Efcharistó.* Your mamás have been very busy, eh?'

'We hope they will keep the cold out when we get short of logs again,' said Cassia.

'Just two more now.' Maia jumped up and down as she handed the small gifts to Cassia and Eugenia, who opened them simultaneously. 'What have you got, Mamá?'

The sisters laughed and held up identical bars of olive oil soap.

'Exactly the same as we've given to Theía Cassia.'

'Great minds, I think. *Efcharistó polý*, Eugenia and Maia.'

CHAPTER TWENTY-ONE

Cassia and Eugenia cleared away the plates after they'd finished the main part of the meal.

'That was delicious, wasn't it, girls?' Eugenia turned to Michaíl. 'You'll have to tell your butcher friend it was a delicious piece of pork.'

'*Efcharistó*, Theía Cassia.'

Eléni smiled and rubbed her tummy.

'I hope you've got room for some Vasilopita now.' Cassia stood and fetched the cake from the kitchen.

'It smells of oranges.' Maia clapped her hands.

'Yes, it does,' said Michaíl. 'And St Basil's cake is very special. Inside is a drachma coin and whoever gets that piece will get good fortune for the next year.'

Cassia cut the cake, remembering where she'd put the coins with the help of the two almonds she'd placed on top of the mixture before baking the cake.

'A slice for you, Maia, and one for you, Eléni. Be careful how hard you bite, in case you're the lucky one with a coin.'

Eugenia passed a piece to Michaíl.

There was a shout from Maia: 'I've got it!' She held up the drachma.

Eléni hung her head. Her bottom lip quivered.

'Have you tried yours, Eléni?' Eugenia was in on the secret. 'Let me cut it for you.' Inside was another coin. 'There you are! You're going to be lucky, too.'

The little girl grinned and ate her cake.

The meal had been a big success and everyone was in a jovial mood. The girls played with their new toys and the adults agreed they couldn't eat another thing after devouring the Vasilopita.

'It's been a great day, hasn't it?' Cassia sat back in her chair.

'The best. *Efcharistó.*' Her sister reached across and patted her arm.

Michaíl was the perfect host and kept filling up their glasses with tots of ouzo.

'I have to drive home, Michaíl. You'll have me drunk.' Eugenia winked at the old man.

He smiled and then his expression turned serious. 'I have something to tell you both.' Michaíl paused. 'I wanted today to be a happy day because what I'm going to tell you makes me very sad.'

Concerned, the women looked at each other.

'A few weeks ago, I found out I haven't got long on this earth.'

Both Cassia and Eugenia gasped.

'My chest has been giving me a lot of pain and my cough, it does not go. I visited the Dr Alexatos, here in Fiscardo. He is sure I have lung cancer. It is what is causing my breathing problems and my cough. He blames my strong Karelia cigarettes. From what I've told him about the coughing up blood, the loss of weight, the pain, he says this is the end.'

'Oh, no! I'm so, so sorry, Michaíl.' Cassia's eyes brimmed with tears. She went and put her arms around the man who had given her a home and had become a father figure to her.

'You mustn't fret. I've had a good life. I mustn't be greedy. I'm ready to meet my maker.' His red-rimmed eyes told of his true feelings and a different story.

Eugenia sat quietly with sadness in her eyes. 'I haven't known you long, Michaíl. But you're a good man. The girls adore you.'

The old man's face was wet with tears. 'I cannot manage the taverna anymore. My sister lives in Patras. I visited her a few weeks ago to say goodbye, but she says I must go to her to be looked after. I'm sorry. Taverna Zervas will close.'

No one felt like celebrating after Michaíl's bombshell news. Eugenia and Maia got ready to leave not long afterwards.

'Come on, Maia. Let's get you home to bed. Say goodbye to everyone. What do you say to Michaíl for your spinning top?'

'*Efcharistó*, Kýrios Michaíl.'

Maia hugged the old man. 'You are very welcome, *agápi mou.*' His voice cracked.

Cassia walked with them to the door of the taverna.

'I'll call and see you tomorrow, Eugenia. Thank you for everything you brought today. Your melomakarona is the best around.' The sisters hugged. 'I'm sorry it ended like this, but poor Michaíl must have been desperate to tell us while we were all together.'

'I know. Poor man. What will you and Eléni do? You can always come back and live with us.'

Cassia bent down to kiss her niece goodbye and didn't give Eugenia an answer. Her plan to tell both her sister and Michaíl her news would have to wait. Now was not the right time.

* * *

It was a clear, sunny day when Cassia and Eléni set off the next morning. Cassia decided to walk to Eugenia's and take advantage of the crisp, cold air to give her time to think. On the way there, Eléni spotted a large boat in the bay. 'Tom.' She pointed. 'Baba.'

'No, *agápi mou*. Not yet. But I expect he will arrive on a boat like that soon.'

Tom may not have received her letter yet and in any case, Michaíl's news had changed things. She wouldn't leave the island until he'd left for his sister's, dreading how emotional leaving was going to be for him. Cassia would have to see someone she cared about decline and get weaker as the disease took hold. How would she explain to Eléni that Michaíl was very ill and was going to die? She brushed away her tears, cold on her cheek from the breeze coming in from the sea.

As they walked down to the smallholding, Eléni ran on when she saw Maia playing with the cats near where Eugenia was milking the goats. Calix and Callista had grown now. They spent most of their time outdoors catching mice at night and sleeping in the sun during the day. Eléni picked up the little tabby and began stroking her.

'*Kaliméra*. What a beautiful morning.' Cassia caught up with Eléni and stood chatting to her sister as Eugenia finished with the last goat. *Eugenia will be all right*, thought Cassia. *It's hard for her at the moment, but things will get better. She'll make the best of what she has here on the smallholding.*

They walked into the house, leaving the girls to play. 'Did you get any sleep after listening to Michaíl's news?'

'Not much.' Cassia's tone grew serious. 'I can't imagine him not being around . . . not — you know — but when he leaves the island to move to his sister's.' Before last night, her main worry had been how she would break the news that she and Eléni would be leaving him, but he'd beaten her to it. She couldn't tell him now. She'd write another letter to Tom and tell him she had to stay until Michaíl had joined his sister.

'I meant it. About you and Eléni moving back here. We'd manage between the two of us. The girls get on well now.'

'No, it's not fair on you. Two more mouths to feed. It's hard enough anyway.' Guilt overwhelmed her. If Michaíl hadn't broken his news, she would have told both of them hers. But there was no reason not to tell Eugenia. The sooner it was out in the open, the better. Her stomach churned in anticipation of how her sister would react.

'Come and sit down. I planned to tell you yesterday, but Michaíl's news came out first. I didn't have the heart to tell you then.'

'Now you're worrying me. What's happened? You're not pregnant, are you?'

'No!' Cassia was shocked her sister would think such a thing. 'Whatever makes you think that?'

'Don't think I don't know about Tom. He's besotted with you. And you have been looking tired and pale lately.'

'You've got it all wrong. I admit we are more than friends now, but that's only very recent. Nothing like that has happened. But what I have to say does concern Tom.'

Eugenia waited for her sister to continue.

'The night before he left to return to Malta. He proposed to me.'

Eugenia gasped and hugged her. 'That's wonderful news. Isn't it?'

'He thinks if we emigrate to Wales, we could get help for Eléni. There's a school for the deaf in his hometown.'

'But she isn't deaf!' The implication that Tom and Cassia would not be staying in Kefalonia dawned on Eugenia. 'Cassia. You can't go! I can't lose you for a second time. Damned men! It was Nikos the first time and now some Welsh sailor.'

She paced the floor, her eyes reddening.

'Stop it. I need to tell you everything. I didn't accept at first. I couldn't imagine leaving Kefalonia, leaving you and Maia, leaving Michaíl — that was before I knew his news. Tom was disappointed, but accepted my decision and we left as friends.'

'So what changed?'

'I missed him. I missed him so much and realised I'd made a big mistake. Eléni was distraught. She withdrew back into her shell. I knew she blamed me. The only way is to get married — Tom says it would give me a stronger case for emigrating to Wales, plus the fact that his brother is married to a Greek woman. Katerina. Tom says she's really nice and so are their two boys. They speak Greek as well. I wrote to him and told him I'd changed my mind. I hope he hasn't changed his.'

Her sister shook her head in disbelief as she sat back down and took Cassia's hands. 'So he doesn't know you've changed your mind yet? Then please don't tell him. All you've just told me is that you are willing to go through with a marriage of convenience for the sake of a little girl who isn't even yours.'

Cassia pulled her hands away. 'But I love him. He's a good man and I know I can make him happy.'

'But can he make *you* happy?'

'Yes, I know he can.'

'But what if you get there and you realise you've made a huge mistake. Away from your country, knowing no one apart from some Greek woman you haven't even met. Surrounded by people who don't speak your language. Tom will be away for months at sea. And what if Eléni never learns to speak? It will all have been for nothing.'

'I think I'd better go.'

With that, there was a crash and shards of bright blue glass shattered onto the tiles. The wind had sprung up and sent the *mati* that hung from the door frame hurtling to the floor.

Eugenia grabbed her sister's arm. 'The *mati*! I'm telling you. It's a sign.'

'You don't believe that rubbish about a glass ornament protecting you from the evil eye, do you?' Cassia shrugged herself out of her sister's grasp, but it didn't stop her from wondering what was to come.

'Why can't you be happy for me? I love Tom and nothing you say is going to stop me marrying him.' Cassia's voice rose and the two little girls came into the house after hearing the shouting. 'You're only jealous!'

If her sister couldn't support her, then she couldn't stay in the same room as her.

'Come on, Eléni. We're going.'

CHAPTER TWENTY-TWO

Cassia didn't see her sister for several weeks after their argument. She knew Eugenia would be thinking about her and Eléni, as well as what it would mean to lose her sister. But her words still hurt. Of course, Eléni was going to talk. If Tom had still been with them, Cassia was certain she would be saying more words now. She had to pin her hopes on a specialist doctor being able to speed along Eléni's recovery.

Eugenia was still in contact with their mother so she wouldn't be abandoning her. They'd managed perfectly well when Cassia lived in Argostoli. Although her mother and sister were not close, they still saw each other, and she'd heard Maia talking about Yiayiá to Eléni. If things got tough before they got better, she knew her sister could turn to their mother for help. Perhaps she had already done this and not told Cassia. If she hadn't, the reason would have been her pride — not wanting to admit her marriage to Georgios was a failure.

Cassia had written a second letter to Tom, telling him about poor Michaíl. Now she knew about his condition, she'd noticed tell-tale signs of how poorly he'd become. He found it difficult to eat. He'd asked her to attend to the few customers who came in to drink in the taverna when he was not up to standing for long periods.

'The man is not so good, eh?' said one old friend of his. 'I told him to get some food down him. He's wasting away. Tell him *yamas* from me.'

'Not as easy with all these shortages,' said another.

There was still no reply to either letter from Tom. Cassia began to think she'd been too late accepting his proposal, and he had moved on. How much longer he had in Malta, she didn't know. All he'd told her was he'd be getting another posting, but she didn't know where or when. She started planning what she could do to survive in Kefalonia when Michaíl moved to his sister's and when she had no money coming in to live on. She hadn't ventured anywhere near the market after her argument with Eugenia. She continued making her lace and embroidery in the hope that one day, visitors would return to the island to buy them as souvenirs or people would buy them for the bottom drawer of a bride-to-be. But it wasn't going to happen any day soon if the accounts of what was happening in the worst affected areas were to be believed. It had now been six months since that fateful day in August.

Michaíl was sleeping in his chair when Cassia and Eléni wandered outside for a walk. She locked the bar door so he wouldn't be disturbed and put the key under the stone urn by the window. There were so few people calling in for a drink in the daytime now, she knew they would not be losing much, if any, custom. Word had got round that old Michaíl was failing. Each evening she had to stave off enquiries about what was actually wrong with him.

The view over the harbour was as spectacular as ever. The sun reflecting on the aquamarine water never failed to lift her mood. It was here she'd waved goodbye to Tom. Had she also waved goodbye to a chance of a better life with him? *Tom, why haven't you written back?*

'Come on, *Elenáki mou*. Let's see if Mamá can find any work.'

Eléni pulled her back to the edge of the harbour wall. She pointed out to sea. 'Tom . . . Baba.'

I wish more than anything it could be Tom's boat. 'No, Tom's in Malta.'

They walked along the street and stopped outside the post office. The window where she'd seen Michaíl's advert displayed a board of notices. She remembered how adamant he'd been that he didn't want anyone taking the room if they had a child, and how he'd changed his mind once he'd assumed the child in question belonged to Nikos. To think how he adored Eléni now! She'd become the granddaughter he never had. Tears burned along her eyelids when she thought how soon that relationship was going to be severed. Eléni would be heartbroken.

Most of the notices were about items for sale. Islanders appeared to be selling everything they could to raise any amount of cash, no matter how small. She looked down at the beautiful silver bangle on her wrist. In future, would times get so tough she'd even contemplate selling Tom's gift to her? Just as Cassia was about to leave, she spotted another notice.

Dr Hector Alexatos seeks help for his wife with two children, a girl aged four years of age and a baby (boy) of ten months. Terms and wages to be discussed. Contact 4, Koutavos Street, Fiscardo.

Cassia went inside the post office to ask about the advertised post. Before she could say anything, the woman behind the counter smiled and handed her a letter.

'I hoped you'd be in,' she said. 'This came for you. It doesn't have a Greek stamp. Must be from that British sailor of yours.'

Ignoring the inquisitiveness of the woman, Cassia took it from her, her heart pounding.

'*Efcharistó.*' So anxious to read what Tom had to say, she forgot all about asking about the doctor's advert. 'Come on, Eléni.'

Once outside, her hand shook as she opened the letter. Would Tom still want to marry her? What would he say about Michaíl's news?

My dear Cassia,

Work here on HMS Daring is done. We will all be posted elsewhere at the end of the month. I have not heard from you so I have to assume . . .

'No!' Tears blurred Cassia's eyes and prevented her from reading further. She'd been too late. Eléni looked up at her expecting an explanation, but, not wanting to make a scene in the street, Cassia grabbed her hand and rushed back to the taverna where she could read the whole letter in the privacy of her room.

When they arrived, there was a car outside and the taverna door was ajar. Who could have let themselves in?

'I wonder who's calling on Michaíl?' Cassia was sure she'd locked the door.

'Tom.'

'No, *agápi mou*. Tom's not coming back.' It was going to be hard convincing the little girl they would not be seeing him again. She should never have told her that she and Tom were going to get married. She looked back at the car and noticed a red cross on the windscreen. Why would the doctor be calling on Michaíl? He'd seemed fine when she and Eléni had left.

'*Kaliméra?*' she called. Eléni left to play with Kynigós in the kitchen as a distinguished-looking man emerged from the living room.

'I'm Dr Alexatos. I told Kýrios Pavlis I would call on him today. Didn't he tell you? You are the young woman who is looking after him, I take it.'

'Cassia Makris. I have a room here in return for cooking and cleaning for Kýrios Pavlis, but we have become friends. Now I know how ill he is, yes, I suppose I am looking after him.'

The doctor's face became very serious. 'I'm afraid he is very ill. It is most urgent he gets to Patras. He says his sister will nurse him there. Are you able to help him organise it?'

Cassia was taken aback by the urgency of what the doctor had asked her. She knew Michaíl was getting worse, but how could she prepare him for the inevitable?

'I will do my best, Dr Giatrós. Do you know if he will have a doctor in Patras who will be able to see him?'

The doctor took a letter from his pocket. 'Kýrios Pavlis has just given me this. His sister has made all the arrangements. There is also a ferry ticket for him, and she will meet him on the other side. All I need you to do is to make sure he has all his personal belongings and to get him onto the ferry. I will call back tomorrow.' He took Cassia's hand. 'He thinks of you as a daughter, Kýria Makris. He is going to find this very hard to do. *Efcharistó.*'

As will I. For the second time that morning, emotion washed over Cassia. For different reasons. There was no point in regretting something that was her fault. She'd lost her chance of happiness with Tom. There was no going back. All she could do now was do the best for Michaíl.

After the doctor left, Cassia braced herself to join Michaíl. The living-room door was open and she could see Eléni had joined him. For a few moments, she stood at the doorway and watched them — two friends with over eighty years between them, but not one of those years mattered. Michaíl was making Eléni laugh, and she mimed what she had to say back to him. How the little girl was going to miss her surrogate pappoú.

'Someone's having fun.' Cassia drew in a deep breath and she went to sit beside Michaíl. Eléni looked up at her and grinned.

'He told you then?' Michaíl's eyes shone. 'All I want is a bit of help collecting my things. I haven't got much to take with me. Just my photographs. The rest can stay. They're merely *things*. And I won't be needing them for long, will I?'

Cassia squeezed his hand. 'Oh, Michaíl.'

It was then his tears began to fall along with hers. Even though Eléni did not understand why they were both upset, she hugged Michaíl and then Cassia. Both of them remained silent with their thoughts for a few moments. Cassia knew the best way to support her friend was to get everything he needed ready for his journey to Patras.

CHAPTER TWENTY-THREE

Cassia spent the rest of the morning packing Michaíl's case. He sat at the kitchen table sorting through his precious photographs, calling her over every now and then to show her a favourite that meant so much to him.

'Look at this one. 1910 in Ithaca. You didn't know I was young once, did you?' He held up a photo of a young couple, arms around each other and smiling. 'I'd just met her. I couldn't believe such a beautiful woman would even look at me.'

Cassia took the photo from him. 'Cora *was* beautiful, but why wouldn't she look at you? You were very handsome.'

And so it went on. Michaíl spread out his whole life in pictures, moments of milestones and important events captured through the eye of a camera. The quality of the photographs was often poor, but to the old man, the memories meant so much. The only photos of his childhood were formal, taken by a photographer. One was of his parents and Michaíl with the sister who was now going to nurse her big brother to the end. They were all dressed in dark clothes, the two children like mini adults, their faces serious and unsmiling. But it was the photographs of his beloved Cora that brought him the most joy and caused him to be overcome with emotion.

'We were never blessed with children. A reason for much sadness, but we had each other until . . .' His voice broke. 'Seven years ago.'

He placed the photographs into date order and gathered them into a neat pile. Then he stood and shuffled over to the cabinet where a picture of him and Cora on their wedding day took pride of place. *How things turn full circle*, thought Cassia. *A black-and-white image of a smiling young couple with their lives ahead of them would be a source of comfort to an old man looking back on his.* He handed it to Cassia. 'Make sure this is packed in the case, *parakaló*, as well as the others that I've picked out. They're all I need now.'

'Of course, I will.' She sensed Michaíl was on the verge of breaking down. 'I'll take them up now. You'll just need to check I've got everything you want to take.'

As soon as she was away from Michaíl in the hallway leading to the bar, she broke down in tears. It was heartbreaking to see her friend trying to put on such a brave face. Not only would he be leaving the island of Kefalonia and its people for whom he'd fought so bravely as a partisan, but he'd be leaving behind his home of many years and endless memories. Most poignant of all, he'd be leaving behind the place where his dear Cora was buried.

* * *

Later that evening, when Eléni was fast asleep upstairs, Cassia found the bar was busier than usual. Everyone was enquiring after Michaíl. *How did they know he was ill?*

He seemed to read her thoughts. 'Because I told them.'

The old man appeared at the doorway and found a seat with his friends. He soon became animated at the prospect of being with them again and the reminiscences being shared. 'Let's get the ouzo flowing!'

Cassia recognised pain etched on his face, but was determined not to fuss. This was what he wanted. 'Who's for another drink?' she asked, watching as the clear liquid changed to milky white as she added water to the first glass.

It didn't seem long before Michaíl's friends drifted away. All bid him a safe journey to Patras. Whether they knew how serious his illness was or not, they all said they'd look forward to his return in the spring. *It's something people do, isn't it? Nobody states the obvious.* Nobody admitted it would be the last time they'd see him . . . ever.

When the bar was empty at last, Michaíl sank back into his chair.

'That's another thing done. It was harder than I thought. I'm off to sleep now. The last in my own bed.' He took a deep breath. '*Kalinýchta*, lovely Cassia.'

'*Kalinýchta*, Michaíl.' The significance of her saying that for the last time caused her insides to churn with grief. She watched the hunched figure of her friend leave and go upstairs.

She busied herself by clearing away the glasses and was wiping down the tables when there was a knock at the door.

Who can this be at this time of night?

She slid back the bolt and opened the door a fraction.

'Cassia, it's me. Let me in.'

Her heart pounded as she recognised the voice. *It couldn't be, could it?* Maybe Eléni was right after all when she'd seen the big ship in the bay.

She opened the door and looked at the person she'd wanted to see most in the world. 'Tom! What are you doing here?'

'I wrote to say I was coming today. Didn't you get my letter?'

The letter was still in her pocket! Most of it had been left unread since the doctor had shocked her with Michaíl's imminent departure the next day.

'Come here.' He pulled her into his arms and hugged her tight. 'My time on the ship has ended early so we are free until we hear where the next posting is going to be. When I read about poor Michaíl, I came straight here to help you.'

Cassia didn't know if he'd received her first letter where she agreed to marry him.

'*Efcharistó.* He's going on the ferry in the morning. Leaving Kefalonia for Patras. I've been helping him pack. All he wants to take are his photos. It's so sad.'

He took her in his arms and kissed the top of her head. 'It must be very difficult for him, but he's enjoyed having you and Eléni living with him.'

'That's what he says. Can I get you something to eat or drink? You must be tired after your long journey.' Cassia couldn't believe Tom was back. But had he returned just as a friend to help her, or did he know she had agreed to marry him? There was nothing in what he had said or done yet to suggest he was doing anything more than helping out a friend in a difficult situation.

'A coffee would be good, thank you.'

Before she started to make the coffee, she dashed to her coat hanging in the hall to retrieve Tom's letter.

Agapití *Cassia,*

> *Work here on HMS Daring, it is over. We are posted to other places at the end of the month. I do not hear from you so still you do not marry me. I am your friend. I hope one day you love me like a wife. I wait for ever.*

February 1st

> *Your letter arrives with the sad news about Michaíl. I come to Kefalonia to help. I catch today's ferry.*
>
> *Yours,*
>
> *Tom xx*

Cassia's hand shook. Tom had not received her first letter! As far as he knew, they were still just friends with no prospect of marriage.

She returned to the living room empty-handed.

'I've just read your letter. You didn't receive the one I sent a few days after you left!'

Tom looked puzzled. 'No. Just a short letter telling me about Michaíl. That's why I came back here.'

Cassia took a deep breath.

'Do you still want to marry me, and take me and Eléni back to Wales?'

'Of course, I do. You shouldn't have to ask.'

'Please ask me again, Tom.'

Tom's face broke into a wide grin. 'Really?'

'Really.'

Tom got down on one knee and took her hand. 'Cassia Makris, will you please do me the honour of becoming my wife?'

'Yes, I will. I love you, Tom. In my first letter, I told you what a big mistake I'd made and if you still wanted to marry me, the answer was yes.'

His lips were suddenly on hers and they kissed for what seemed an eternity. Her insides somersaulted as familiar sensations coursed through her body.

'Oh, I never thought I'd hear those words. You've made me the happiest man in Kefalonia.'

She kissed him once more. 'I'd better go and get that coffee, I think.'

They laughed, and in spite of the sad situation that brought Tom back, Cassia hoped beyond hope she was doing the right thing.

Over coffee, they talked about their plans for the future. Cassia would contact Sophia in Athens to see if she and her daughter would be witnesses for their marriage.

'It will be better that we have someone we know and Sophia knows both of us. She's the one who told me you'd fallen in love with me all those months ago!'

'At least we'll have the marriage certificate to prove you will be Mrs Tom Beynon. I will try to get a letter sent from Katerina stating she will act on your behalf as the family contact in Wales.'

In such a short time, it all started to sound very real. They lay back in each other's arms on the sofa and kissed. Feelings Cassia hadn't experienced for a long time surfaced and she wanted nothing more than for them to make love there and then. But they stopped in time.

'I'll make a bed for you down here. It won't do for Eléni or Michaíl to find us in bed together. It will be all the sweeter for waiting.'

Tom nodded, but he didn't look convinced. Deep down she didn't believe it either.

'I'm meeting the doctor in the morning with instructions for what Michaíl needs on the journey. His ticket is here.' She got up to get it from the shelf and showed it to Tom.

'It's happening that soon, then.' He paused for a moment. 'I think one of us should go with him. Just travelling that distance is going to be an ordeal when you're not well, never mind the emotional toll of leaving your home for ever.'

Cassia hugged her husband-to-be. He was such a thoughtful man. 'That's such a good idea. I've been so worried about putting him on the ferry, all on his own. Maybe . . . No, it doesn't matter.'

Eléni would be perfectly happy to stay with Tom. What she was doing was avoiding a situation she'd been dreading since the doctor had given her Michaíl's ferry ticket.

'I'll go,' said Tom. 'I know it would be a hard trip for both of you and there's Eléni to look after. He does know me, but not as much as he knows you. I think he'd find it very emotional to say goodbye to you in Patras. Here will be bad enough, but at least I'll be able to talk about you and Eléni on the journey. I'll reassure him I will look after you both.'

'Are you sure? You've just had such a long trip.' They kissed again. '*Efcharistó*. Eléni and I will be waiting for you when you get back.'

CHAPTER TWENTY-FOUR

Cassia hardly slept a wink that night. Her head was full of what she and Tom had talked about earlier. She tried to imagine Eléni's face when she found out Tom had come back and contrasted that to when the little girl would have to say goodbye to Michaíl. What would Cassia's wedding day be like? Her first wedding had been a secret affair in Argostoli with just a handful of their partisan friends present.

In the darkness of the bedroom, she remembered Nikos's face as he'd turned to watch her join him at the altar. His shoulder-length black hair had framed his handsome bronzed face and his ebony eyes had sparkled with love.

'You look stunningly beautiful,' he'd whispered when she reached his side. '*Ekpliktiká ómorfi.*'

Tears trickled onto her pillow. It had been so different from the lavish Greek Orthodox three-day wedding her parents had apparently put on for Eugenia. If only they'd known then what Georgios was like! Cassia's wedding to Tom was also going to be a modest affair and another perfect day. Running alongside these thoughts was the farewell to Michaíl, one she was dreading.

She went to Eléni's bed and the little girl's eyes fluttered open.

'*Kaliméra, agápi mou.*' Eléni stretched. 'There's a surprise waiting for you downstairs.'

It didn't take long for Eléni to jump out of bed and make her way to the kitchen. She opened her arms wide as if to ask, *What?*

'Try the living room.'

Cassia followed the little girl, only to hear a shriek. 'Tom . . . Baba.'

Tom sat holding Eléni, who had a smile as wide as her face.

'*Kaliméra.* I've missed you, *cariad.*'

'You said it was Tom's boat out in the bay. You were right.' Cassia smiled at her daughter.

It wasn't long before they were joined by Michaíl. Deep shadows under his eyes suggested he hadn't slept either.

'Well, this is a surprise to find you here.' He embraced his sailor friend.

'*Kaliméra.* I have some time off and I thought I'd come to see you. I'd like to accompany you on the ferry journey, if that's all right?'

Cassia watched as the two men fell into conversation, completely at ease with one another. She went to cook breakfast and make coffee when she heard Tom's voice calling her back.

'We've got something to tell you both.'

Before he could continue, Eléni pointed at them in turn. 'Ma-má, Tom.' She then pointed at her heart, followed by kissing noises.

Tom laughed. 'You already know! What Eléni is saying is Cassia and I love each other, and I've asked her to marry me. What do you think was her answer, Eléni?'

The little girl nodded her head.

'That's right. She said yes.' Tom put his arm around Cassia.

Michaíl had tears in his eyes. 'I'm so pleased. Anyone could see you were in love. I just hoped when you left, Tom, you'd be back to marry her. I hope you will both be as happy as me and Cora were.'

* * *

Before Tom and Michaíl left, Dr Alexatos arrived as he'd promised.

'I am very pleased you have someone to accompany you on the journey.' He turned to Tom. 'He should be fine, but please don't let him exert himself. Once you find a seat for him, it's best not to let him move round too much.'

He took the old man's hand and shook it. '*Antío*. Goodbye, Kýrios Pavlis. Safe journey.'

The motorboat taking them to the ferry in Sami was due to leave at eleven o'clock. It was a short distance from Taverna Zervas to where it was moored. For Michaíl's sake, Cassia was glad no one else knew of the actual day he was leaving. It was difficult enough for the old man to leave his home and say farewell to her and Eléni.

Hugging them both, Michaíl whispered, '*Antío sas.*' His eyes were glassy with unshed tears, but his stoicism did not allow them to fall. Tom led him onto the boat.

The hooter sounded. Cassia and Eléni watched as the motorboat manoeuvred out into the open Ionian Sea. *God bless you, Michaíl. I will never forget you.* Cassia squeezed Eléni's hand. 'Tom will look after him on his journey.'

They walked back to the taverna in silence. In spite of her young age, Eléni seemed to sense the serious nature of the occasion and kept looking at Cassia with concern. In her short life, she'd experienced more tragedy and heartache than any three-year-old should have to deal with. *What will she remember when she's older?* wondered Cassia.

* * *

It was late when Tom arrived back from Patras.

Cassia rushed into his arms. '*Efcharistó*. Thank you for what you did for Michaíl today. Was he all right on the journey? What was his sister like?'

'Slow down. Let me get in through the door first.'

Cassia poured him a drink. They went into the living room and Tom recounted everything about the day.

'Once he'd said goodbye to you and Eléni, he relaxed. In some ways, I think it did him good before all the emotion of seeing his sister again. We had a long chat about *our* future. I understood a lot of what he was saying now that I've learned more Greek, thank goodness. How I was to do my best by you. It was just like a talk with the bride's father I've heard my mates talk about.' Tom paused to sip his beer. 'When we docked in Patras, his sister and his nephew were waiting for him. It was obvious she was shocked by his appearance, even though it had only been a matter of weeks since he'd last seen her.'

Michaíl's poor sister was going to have to watch her brother waste away. Yes, it had been a shock when Nikos died. There was no time for preparation — one minute he was there, and wiped out the next. But Cassia didn't have to see him suffer and could remember him as the healthy young man he'd been.

'As I left, Michaíl handed me this. It's addressed to you.'

Cassia took the letter and not knowing what it could be about, she opened it, her heart racing. She began reading aloud.

Agapití *Cassia*,
I want to thank you for making my last days happy ones. Seeing you and your little one every day has made this old man very happy.

Tavernas are kept within families and I am leaving Taverna Zervas to my nephew, Milos. But in a very short time, I've come to think of you and Eléni as family too, so I have made arrangements for you to have a home here for as long as you need it. Times are hard in Kefalonia at the moment but it will get better, I am sure of it. When I visited Patras last time, I told Milos of my plans. He has no

145

*intention of coming to live in Taverna Zervas and is happy
for you and Eléni to continue living here as you are doing.*
 Me agápi,
 Michaíl

Her eyes misted. 'What a lovely thing to do. Look, the letter was dated a few weeks ago. Before he knew we were getting married.'

'He never mentioned anything about this to me. He certainly didn't mention us emigrating to Wales. He must have thought a lot about how you were going to manage on your own.' He placed an arm around Cassia and they sat in silence remembering Michaíl.

* * *

Later that night, Eléni woke screaming. She hadn't had a nightmare since the one in Eugenia's house when Georgios had been so unkind. She shuddered and cowered under her blanket, her arms covering her head.

Cassia soothed and calmed her, but it was a reminder that the slightest change in circumstances could unsettle the little girl. Tom appeared at the door.

'Is she all right?' he whispered.

Cassia nodded and was pleased when he left her to comfort Eléni alone. She carried Eléni to her own bed and she went back to sleep as Cassia lay down. In the darkness, Cassia reflected on what had just happened. It was clearly a reaction to Michaíl leaving and sensing the emotions associated with that. *What is she going to be like when we move away from here? What if she reverts to her nightmares when we get to Wales? Was it fair to uproot her again?* Eléni was clearly very happy to know Tom and Cassia were going to get married, but wouldn't be able to grasp the implications of emigrating thousands of miles away. She would sense if Cassia was unhappy, and she wondered if moving to Wales was the right thing. Tom would be at sea for such long periods — could she manage on her own in a foreign country? Michaíl's letter had changed things. What if they got married and stayed in Fiscardo? Her problem at the moment was a lack of money, but she could apply for the job advertised by Dr Alexatos. She and Tom could start up the taverna in their name, even start providing food again. Eléni could start at the school she and Eugenia had attended. She'd perhaps be in the same class as Maia. Tom could send her money in the bars of soap, as he'd told her. They would manage — they could make a life for themselves in Fiscardo, couldn't they? Wondering how she was going to break it to Tom, she drifted off to sleep.

CHAPTER TWENTY-FIVE

The next morning, Cassia found Tom already up and dressed, making coffee.

'Is Eléni all right this morning? I didn't hear her again. She sounded terrified.'

Cassia sat down at the kitchen table while he poured the coffee from the copper *briki*.

'Efcharistó. I took her into my bed and she went back to sleep. She hasn't had one for ages. It was like going back six months. Poor little thing.'

She decided this was a good way to begin telling Tom her thoughts about staying. 'I'm worried even more upheaval — leaving everything she knows here — is going to set Eléni back to square one. She'll be having nightmares like that every night.'

His face became serious. 'What do you mean? She'll have both of us with her.'

'But she won't, will she? You'll be at sea for long periods of time. Michaíl's letter has given us another option. We can still get married, but make our home here in Fiscardo. Instead of waiting for you to come home to somewhere new, we'd be waiting here among people and the language we know.'

She waited for Tom to say something. 'I'm sorry, Cassia, but there is no future for us here. You've said it yourself. Everyone's emigrating as there is no work, no food, no . . .'

He stopped as Eléni joined them. Her face was serious. She'd obviously heard the conversation.

'No smiles for us this morning.' The little girl shook her head. 'I think we'll carry on with this later,' he whispered to Cassia.

Disappointment shone on Tom's face. He'd been so happy when Cassia had told him she'd marry him and move to Wales. Now all she could think about was how she could make things work by staying. She imagined what Eugenia would say. 'I was right. If you truly loved him, you wouldn't even be considering staying here. A marriage of convenience was all it was going to be to get away from the hardships of the island. Now you've got a permanent home, you don't have to move away.' *Is Tom thinking the same? That I only agreed to marry him as a way of getting away from the desperate state of the island?*

The subject was not mentioned again. Cassia set about making up a bed in Michaíl's room for Tom while he took Eléni out for a walk. The little girl was still subdued, but he did raise a smile from her when he suggested they walk down to the beach.

Cassia hoped things would soon be back to how they were.

While they were out, Eugenia arrived at the taverna. It was the first time the sisters had seen each other since their row.

'Where's Maia?'

Her sister hesitated. 'Umm, she's spending time with Mamá so I thought I'd come to see how you're getting on. I understand Tom is here. I was sorry to hear Michaíl has left. I would have liked to have said goodbye. It all seems so sudden.'

Cassia's throat constricted. 'Yes, his sister sent a ferry ticket for him, and Dr Alexatos thought it was better to go now before . . .' — she inhaled deeply — '. . . it was too late.

Tom went with him. I don't think he could have managed on his own.'

Eugenia reached across and held her hand. 'I'm so sorry. You're going to miss him . . . but then again you would have missed him when you leave for Wales anyway.'

Cassia pulled her hand away and retrieved Michaíl's letter. 'Read this.'

Her sister gasped as Michaíl's words sank in. 'So, you don't have to leave. You can live here permanently. What did Tom say?'

'That's the problem. When I suggested we make this our home and he leaves for his spells at sea from here, he wasn't very pleased. He came with several reasons why and then Eléni came in, obviously having heard us. She had another nightmare last night with all the upset. What is she going to be like when I uproot her again? I'm not even sure what I'll be like in a foreign country, not knowing anybody, having to speak English all the time and Tom away for months on end.' Tears fell. Eugenia pulled her close in a sisterly hug. All thoughts about their row forgotten.

'You know my feelings. But you must be really sure it's what you want. If there's any doubt, you must tell Tom.'

Cassia nodded. 'I know.' He deserved the truth. Was her love for him strong enough to take a risk for both her and Eléni? 'Anyway, how is our dear mother? Come into the kitchen with me and tell me.'

'As judgemental as ever. It's why I came to see you and to make it up with you after our row. Apparently, she's heard rumours I've been having visits from a man — it's obvious she means Tom — and she is concerned they'll get back to Georgios. I haven't told her he's gone again. A bit ironic when he's the one who's been unfaithful, eh? She invited us over with the excuse she wanted to play with Maia. Really it was to find out what I had to say about the rumours. Also, she wanted to know about you. I didn't let on the truth about Eléni.'

'*Efcharistó*. I couldn't bear it if she knew the real story. At least in Wales, no one would question if Eléni was mine.'

Cassia poured the coffee and the sisters sat deep in thought while warming their hands on the cups. 'I'm so pleased you called round, Eugenia. I've hated all this time not being friends. I was too stubborn to give in. I've got to decide whether it's worth me being stubborn about staying here when we get married or risk losing Tom for ever.'

Eugenia put down her cup and stood to go, kissing her sister on both cheeks.

'Only you can do that. Say hello to Tom and Eléni for me. I'd better go.'

* * *

Both Tom and Eléni came back from their walk in a better mood.

'We had a great time, didn't we, Eléni? We had a nice paddle in the sea.'

She beamed and couldn't wait to get her coat off before rushing to get her pencils and paper. Her drawings were becoming more and more detailed. She'd learned to write the first letter of her name and each drawing was always signed with an *E*.

While Eléni was preoccupied, Cassia and Tom sat and talked. She told him about Eugenia's visit and the rumours surrounding her male visitor.

Tom laughed. 'I've only been to her house a few times. This town and its spies.' Cassia didn't react, but wondered if he wanted to add, *The sooner we get away from here the better.*

Eléni came back with her drawing. She'd taken care to colour the sea blue with a creamy-white beach. In the water were several swimmers, with two figures near the edge of the water. This was the family life Cassia yearned for, so why didn't she have faith in Tom's judgement that emigrating would give her and Eléni just that?

Friends of Michaíl's came into the bar that night enquiring after him. Word had got round he'd left for good.

'Listen to them reminiscing about the times they had in here with him.' Tom watched from behind the bar. It struck Cassia that Tom was already taking Michaíl's place, even if it was for a short time.

After Eugenia had left that afternoon, Cassia had made a tray of spanakopita and that night she handed around the spinach-and-feta pies in Michaíl's honour. The old men raised their glasses of ouzo, knocked the drinks back and slammed them on the bar.

'*Yamas!* To Michaíl.'

One of the men took out his bouzouki from a battered leather case. He began to strum the steel strings with a plectrum. Soon the haunting metallic sounds of a traditional Greek folk song filled the bar. It was as if he was playing a musical homage to an old friend who had started his final journey. A lump formed in Cassia's throat and Tom's eyes glistened with tears. A few of Michaíl's friends brushed away tears.

There were cries of, '*Bràvo.* Excellent.'

Many came up and slapped Tom on his back. '*Efcharistó.* He was a good friend.'

When the last customer had left and Cassia had bolted the door, she and Tom cleared up. They retired to the living room with a glass of retsina.

'I think we did dear Michaíl proud tonight. I didn't realise how important a role this old taverna played in the past. I heard some of them talk about how it was the hiding place for the partisans during the war. I know now why it's called Taverna Zervas. After the leader of the Greek resistance, Napoleon Zervas.'

'And after the war, too. It's where I met Nikos. Michaíl let me and Eléni have the room once he knew I was Nikos's widow. He admired him for what he'd done for the ordinary people.' She took a deep breath, not knowing what reaction she'd get from Tom. 'After tonight, don't you see, Tom?

Taverna Zervas can't be left empty, only occasionally lived in by Michaíl's nephew. Its history surely shows it needs to remain the heart of Fiscardo's community. Please.'

Tom didn't say a word. For the second time that day, disappointment drew a veil across his face. She had no idea what he was going to say, but she knew she was fighting a losing battle. If she was determined to stay and run Michaíl's taverna, it looked as if she would be doing it alone.

CHAPTER TWENTY-SIX

That night they parted without kissing. Cassia lay in bed, knowing her fiancé was probably awake in the next room too. She remembered the earlier conversation that afternoon with Eugenia, when she'd admitted she had a stubborn streak. Now it seemed that Tom was the same.

Why was she wasting precious time that could be spent with the man she loved? She *did* love him. She crept out of her bed, taking care not to wake Eléni. Closing the door behind her, she crossed the landing. 'Tom,' she whispered. 'Can I come in?''

She heard footsteps on the floorboards behind the door. When it opened, she was greeted by a smiling Tom who enveloped her in his arms. Her heartbeat raced as he led her to the wide bed, and they fell back onto the soft feather mattress, kissing each other with pent-up passion. Their kisses became urgent, their tongues exploring. Tom planted kisses along her neck and shoulder, but when he slipped down the strap of her nightgown, he stopped. 'Is this what you want?'

She gave him her answer by pulling down both straps to reveal her breasts. He resumed kissing the rest of her. She moaned as they caressed each other's bodies. When they finally made love, she knew this was not merely a release of sexual frustration between them, but real love. She *would* marry Tom. If it meant following him to a land she didn't know, where she would be the outsider, then so be it.

'I've wanted to make love to you since the first time I saw you. I was so scared I'd lose you. But I think tonight you wanted me too.' Tom looked at Cassia and smiled. 'We'll work it out. I promise.'

A single tear trickled down her cheek. She was overcome with emotion about how beautiful their lovemaking was. They lay in each other's arms, just savouring their closeness.

He got out of bed and drew back the curtains. Moonlight bathed the room. 'Before we go to sleep, let me look at you.' He gazed down at her while his hands gently caressed her breasts. Surprisingly, she became shy. It was an intimate moment between them that was very special.

She raised her chin towards him for a goodnight kiss. 'I do love you, Tom. Really love you.'

They fell asleep entwined with each other. Their first night together.

* * *

The next morning, Cassia felt as if a heavy load had been lifted from her heart. A decision had finally been made. She would be sad to leave the taverna, but, after talking with Tom about it, he suggested they could contact Milos to see if he would like them to find a barman to run the taverna for him. Before he could do that, they received bad news. Dr Alexatos arrived with a message from Patras.

'My friend who has been seeing Kýrios Pavlis in Patras just phoned to say he passed away last night. His sister and nephew were both with him. I am so sorry. It was good you accompanied him there, I think.'

They stood silently in shock and hastily thanked the doctor. As soon as he'd left, Cassia broke down in tears. 'Poor Michaíl. To think when we were . . .'

'Don't. He doesn't want you to be sad.' Tom held her tightly. 'He told me he has had a long life, and he wants you and Eléni to be happy.'

'I know, but how can I not be sad? We must get a message to his sister to say how sorry we are. Maybe wait a while before telling Milos about our plans.'

'I agree. But I can contact someone about the all-important booking of a marriage ceremony in Athens.'

Cassia hugged him back. Neither of them noticed a little person enter the room until Eléni pushed in between them.

'Ma-má. Ba-ba.'

Cassia smiled, knowing she'd made the right choice. She'd let her sister know. Although there was plenty of time yet, she ought to pay her mother a visit and introduce her to Eléni. Once they left Kefalonia, Cassia knew they would not be coming back. As long as she got to Eugenia before the news she was leaving to become Tom's wife got out, she didn't care who knew.

'Come on, *Elenáki mou*. We're going to see Theía Eugenia and Maia.'

The sun shone brightly and there wasn't a cloud in the sky. It was cold and fresh as they walked the coast road to Eugenia's smallholding. Nearing the house, Cassia spotted a vehicle she didn't recognise next to her sister's old truck. The red car looked new with its chrome gleaming.

Eléni ran on in search of the cats and Maia.

Maia came running out from the house. All Cassia caught was, 'Yiayiá,' before her niece dragged Eléni with her as she went back inside.

Cassia's heart thumped. Her mother! *What's she doing here so early in the day?*

She entered through the back door to find Eugenia and their mother sitting at the kitchen table. 'Cassia. This is a nice surprise.'

Their mother glowered. 'Cassia. So this is my other granddaughter, then.'

CHAPTER TWENTY-SEVEN

ELÉNI

Rural Mid-Wales, March 1973

Eléni barged into her parents' room. 'Mamá, I'm slipping out to do some sketching down at Rock Park.'

Her mother sat on the edge of the bed, looking down at an open book. Flustered, she slammed the pages shut and pushed it behind her. Her face drained of colour. 'Haven't you heard of knocking?' Cassia's voice was unusually sharp.

'Sorry. Bronwen said you were up here getting some peace and quiet after she nagged you to take her shopping to Credenford for shoes. Again.'

'That's fine, but you could have just shouted you were going out. Peace and quiet? There's never any of that with you two.'

Without looking Eléni in the eye, her mother stood to put her book away in the drawer under the wardrobe. When she turned away, Eléni spotted a blue envelope left on the bedspread. She snatched it and put it in her pocket. *Just what's so serious you've got to hide it away, Mamá?*

Still puzzled at her mother's reaction, Eléni left the house and walked down the hill and under the stone arch into the park. They'd been living in Porth Gwyn for almost a year now. Before that, the family had lived with her elderly great-aunt, Gwladys, in a smart area of Cardiff until she died just over two years ago. It was her aunt who was given the credit for getting Eléni to speak as a little girl. Eléni didn't know why she hadn't been able to speak — she wasn't deaf, even though she'd had all the tests going. When they'd lived in Porth Gwyn originally before Bronwen was born, she had vague memories of being taken to see the principal of the school for the deaf in the town. Her mother had got a job there and they'd taught her to sign. Another memory came back to her. She remembered her mother bursting into tears one evening when she'd collected her from Aunt Katerina, who'd looked after Eléni while Cassia had worked. Whatever Katerina had told her, Eléni still remembered her mother's words: 'We can't stay. We'll have to leave. Again.'

Bronwen was seventeen now and it had been a long time ago. Eléni had been too young at the time to know why they'd had to leave Porth Gwyn in such a hurry, but, judging from the way her mother had tried to hide the book earlier, it suggested she still might have secrets to hide. Eléni found a bench and sat down. She felt for the paper in her pocket and opened the pale blue, translucent envelope edged in blue-and-red diagonals. It was stamped *Par Avion*. She began to read the letter, which was written in Greek.

Fiscardo, Kefalonia
4 May 1955

Agapití *Cassia,*

It is as I feared. Yesterday I received a visit from a man who is looking for his niece. Didn't I ask you to be absolutely sure no one from her family had survived? I told you it was wrong. He had been working in Australia when the earthquake happened and had to wait before he could return to

his homeland. Since he arrived back on the island, he has
searched everywhere. Someone in Argostoli told them a small
girl was pulled from the rubble of the house where his parents
and sister and brother-in-law lived. He's being helped by . . .

Eléni couldn't work out the rest of the sentence, so kept
reading.

> *The reporter told him she was found barely alive but*
> *once she was released by the Red Cross, no one knows where*
> *she went or who she was with.*
> *I don't know how he knew to call here, but I think I*
> *have put him off with my lies. But it is just a matter of time*
> *before he comes to find her. Please, Cassia. Be careful.*
> *Your loving sister,*
> *Eugenia*

Eléni's pulse raced and she felt sick. So, her mother had
a sister — her aunt. She knew nothing about an earthquake,
but could the little girl mentioned in the letter be her? Why
else would this Greek aunt write to her mother about it? *It was
wrong*, the woman said in the letter. Cassia must have taken
her away from Kefalonia without permission. Stolen her. Eléni
couldn't believe what she was reading. She was glad she could
get the gist of the letter even though it was written in Greek
lettering, but there was a part in the middle she wasn't quite
sure of. Aargh! It was so frustrating! She wished she'd paid
more attention to her reading and writing of Greek. In view
of the fact she hadn't talked for so many years, her mother had
always been so proud of her spoken Greek.

If this was true, it meant one thing — Cassia and Tom
Beynon were not her birth parents. Her birth parents had
died in some earthquake or other on the Greek island of
Kefalonia. No wonder her mother never wanted to talk about
her Greek background or wanted to visit Greece now that
holidays abroad were becoming more common. Why hadn't

they told her? Being adopted was nothing to be ashamed of. Patsy Barnham was adopted. She'd known from the time she was a little girl. *Chosen*, she'd said. Eléni stifled a sob. 'But mine! They've let me live a lie for almost twenty years. What have they got to hide?' As she spoke aloud, tears spilled over and streamed down her cheeks.

'Are you all right, *bach*?' A voice she recognised caused her to quickly wipe her cheeks on her sleeve.

'Yes, thank you, Mr Morgan. Just some dust in my eyes. I'm off to do some sketching now.'

The fact she was crying and talking out loud to herself would get back to her parents, for sure. Reg Morgan was a big mate of her father's. She could just imagine what he'd tell him: 'Saw your lass down the park. Upset she was. Denied it, mind.'

Bidding the older man goodbye, she gathered up her sketchbook and made her way down to the part of the park near the river called Lovers' Leap. She sat on a rock overlooking the deep drop into the Ithon and wondered how many lovers had leaped to their deaths from that spot. She'd never been in love. She'd had a couple of boyfriends in college, but no one she'd jump off a cliff for if it didn't work out!

Eléni took out the letter from her pocket and read it again, trying hard to work out the section she'd missed the first time. Could the one word be *reporter?* She made a guess. *He's being helped by a reporter from* . . . She thought hard about what the next Greek letters were. W-A-L-E-S. Yes, that was it, she was sure. The reporter who helped him was from Wales. She checked the date on the letter — May 1955. Bronwen wasn't born until 1956, so could the man turning up have been a reporter and that's what had caused her mother to leave Porth Gwyn? Or perhaps a relative had come looking for her. Yet her parents had never told her and had kept the secret all this time. How could they? She was never going to forgive them. She'd been living a lie for twenty years! It was no good. Eléni wasn't in the mood for sketching. She would return home and have it out with her mother. Her real parents may be dead, but she was determined to find out everything she could about who she really was. Cassia and Tom Beynon owed her that much.

* * *

The walk through Porth Gwyn to her parents' house on the outskirts of the market town helped to calm Eléni down. It gave her time to reflect on her memories of the happy years growing up in Cardiff. Her mother had kept house for Great Auntie Gwladys, and Eléni and the old lady had become firm friends. She remembered the delight on her father's face when he'd arrived home on leave from the Navy and she had spoken full sentences to him for the first time.

'All down to Auntie Gwladys,' her mamá had said. 'They're inseparable.'

Her father had retired from the Navy, and Eléni remembered how keen he'd been for the family to return to Mid-Wales. 'It's where I truly belong, *cariad*,' he'd told her. 'And now I'll have my three best girls with me.'

By that time, Great Auntie Gwladys had died and Eléni had finished her college course, so according to her father there'd been nothing to keep them in the smoke and bustle of the city. The fact her sister had been uprooted at a vital time from her grammar school hadn't seemed to bother anybody, including Bronwen herself. She would have hated it, but Bronwen had just taken it in her stride. Her sister had made new friends and seemed to be out all the time, whereas Eléni was happy to spend time with one good friend, Gabriella.

Her mother's pale grey Morris Marina wasn't in the drive when she arrived home. Eléni let herself into the house, empty apart from the presence of Lady, the family's corgi.

She bent down to stroke her. 'Hello, girl. That's a good welcome for me, at least. I don't suppose you'll mind who I am.'

There was a note left for her on the kitchen table.

Eléni,

    Have taken Bronwen to buy the platform shoes she wanted in Credenford. Yes, I know I've given in to her nagging. I've warned her if she falls and breaks an ankle, I'm not going to be the one taking her to Credenford Hospital.

    Just heat up the corned beef hash for you and your baba if we're not back before you want to eat.

    Mamá x

    P.S. Sorry about snapping earlier. Just tired.

The showdown Eléni had planned would have to wait. Tipping a spoonful of instant Nescafé into her favourite mug, she made herself a coffee and took it up to her bedroom. She couldn't get the contents of the letter out of her head. Sitting in front of the mirror on her dressing table, she wondered whether the face gazing back at her looked anything like one of her real parents. They weren't around to tell her, but she had an uncle. Perhaps he could tell her. *I may even look like him. Is he still in Kefalonia? Is he still alive? I have to know.* She had so many questions.

It all started to make sense. She'd seen photos of Bronwen as a baby, but there were none of her. She'd always wondered why she and Bronwen looked so different. But it was the case in lots of families, wasn't it? She took after her mother with her Greek colouring — the olive skin and black glossy hair — whereas Bronwen looked so much like their father and his family. 'Typical Celts,' her auntie Gwladys had always said. 'Fair skin, freckles and the blonde or copper-coloured hair.' Yet it was more than that. She'd always felt different. She'd reasoned it was because she didn't — no, couldn't — speak for all those years. Bronwen was five years younger, yet had raced past her as far as speech was concerned. In fact, she'd become Eléni's spokesperson. When they'd got older, Eléni had been known as the silent sister and Bronwen had been the 'chopsy' one. Even when the words had come, Eléni had let her sister carry on, happy to remain in the background and just converse with a few close friends and within the family. *Now I find out we're not even sisters. The silent sister who isn't a sister at all!*

Once she'd drunk her coffee, she slipped into her parents' room with the intention of returning the letter. She reasoned her mamá and sister would not be back for hours. Bronwen could never make up her mind when she was out shopping, and her father was never home before six.

Eléni pulled out the drawer at the base of their wardrobe, expecting to see the book her mother had replaced. It wasn't there! More proof Cassia had secrets to hide. Although she felt uncomfortable going through her mamá's things, she had to find out more. There was nothing in the chest of drawers, the rest of the wardrobe or the bedside cabinets. *I wonder,* she thought. After moving the sheepskin rug away from the side of her parents' bed, Eléni knelt down on the cushioned vinyl and placed her hand under the divan. She slid the book out from under the bed. It was a hardback journal. The words *Cassia Beynon. Wales 1954 onwards* were written on the first page in her mother's handwriting.

With her hands trembling, she returned to her own bedroom with the notebook. What secrets would she find inside?

CHAPTER TWENTY-EIGHT

Eléni sat on her bed and opened the book. First, she flicked through the pages and saw that her mother had kept a record of the time she'd arrived in Wales. There were newspaper cuttings, letters, photographs and diary entries. The last thing she'd done had been to stick in the estate agents' brochure of their present house. She'd labelled it: *Our own home.*

Eléni turned back to the first page.

> *19 May 1954*
>
> *What have I done? I never want to travel by sea again. How Tom spends his working life on board ship for months on end, I will never know. Spent most of the time up on deck being seasick. Thank God Tom was there to take care of Eléni. Felt guilty for uprooting her again. More change, more nightmares.*

Eléni vaguely remembered those awful times when she'd woken up in the dark bedroom after feeling trapped inside a black cave, as if something heavy were weighing her down. She'd panicked, thinking she was being pressed further and further down into an abyss. It was always the same bad dream.

Her mother had soothed her and held her tightly until she'd become calm again. After reading the letter earlier and wondering if she was the little girl pulled from the rubble of the earthquake, perhaps it wasn't a black cave and she was reliving being buried when the earthquake had struck her house. She shuddered.

Arrived in a place called Tiger Bay, the name for Cardiff Docks. There were so many houses all joined together, rows and rows of narrow streets. Even our street in Argostoli was wider than those. I have not seen any blue sky yet. It's done nothing but rain, and in another month it will be summer. It's so cold.

Underneath she'd stuck a postcard depicting a scene of Porth Gwyn Lake and boathouse. Eléni thought how idyllic it looked. It was where she liked to walk and sketch, now she was living back in the town. The swans were always eager to eat the stale bread she took along for them on her walks.

Her mother had described meeting her baba's brother, Glyn, his wife, Katerina, and their two boys, Tony and Phil, and the warm welcome they'd all given her and Eléni. On the next page was a newspaper cutting. Apparently, Katerina had given it to her. It was dated some days after the earthquake had struck. *Kefalonia, 15 August 1953*. It gave the facts and figures of the devastation caused by the earthquake. It had been written by a reporter from Wales, named Rhodri Jones. The report detailed the harrowing scenes of bodies being pulled from the wreckage and how the seamen from rescue boats were working tirelessly to bring aid to the people who had been injured and lost their homes. Eléni wondered if this was how she'd survived. It mentioned a British ship being one of the first on the scene. Could one of the sailors who'd pulled her out be her father? She looked down at the main accompanying picture. Although the photograph was unclear, she was convinced the woman standing in a line of men passing back bags of provisions was her mamá. The article mentioned how the earthquake had affected the island. So many inhabitants were homeless, and so many emigrated in search of a better life.

More diary entries followed. It all seemed to be going well until Tom had to return to sea. Tears formed in Eléni's eyes as she read how desperate her mamá had been, dreading months of not seeing him. Yet one sentence jumped out at her.

In capitals, Cassia had added _A MARRIAGE OF CONVENIENCE!_ and underlined it. _Perhaps Eugenia was right_, she'd written.

No! Her parents' marriage had always appeared rock solid. She and Bronwen often found them with their arms around each other. They used to call them the lovebirds. So, was that a lie, too? Had her mother pretended to love her father all these years? It was obvious she was a good liar. Her pulse raced. Perhaps she shouldn't read on. She was intruding into her mother's personal space. She went to close the journal, but the need to know everything was too strong.

She read on. There was another letter from Aunt Eugenia, dated before the one she'd read in the park. It seemed odd to call her 'aunt' when she'd learned of her existence a mere few hours ago. It was clear it had been written in answer to one her mother had sent.

Agapití _Cassia,_

I'm sorry to hear how unhappy you are. Back here, you had convinced yourself you truly loved Tom. I'm so sorry the doubts appeared when you'd left the island. I just wish you'd stayed and run Taverna Zervas as dear Michaíl wanted you to. You'd have more than a two-ringed gas stove there to cook your spanakopita, and I don't expect you can get lovely, salty feta in Wales. Remember the big range at the taverna? I do miss you. But it's too late now.

Who was Michaíl? Was her mother running away from him, too?

Try to make the best of it. For Eléni's sake, if nothing else. It makes me sad to know her nightmares are no better and you've had complaints from the people living in the next flat. Give her a hug from me and Maia. Katerina sounds like a good Greek friend and I'm pleased you have someone you can speak to in your own language. It's a shame the boys are not kinder to Eléni. No wonder she doesn't want to stay with Katerina when you go to work. How long is it before Tom comes home on leave?

Eléni placed the letter on her lap and racked her brain to think back to those times. Their first home in Porth Gwyn had been a flat in a tall building near the crossroads in the middle of the town. Theirs had been on the top floor, and from the bay window in the living room, she could look across to the red-brick building where her mamá had worked as a cleaner. Mamá had told her the principal of the school there had been helping her learn sign language, and, in the evenings, Cassia would teach Eléni how to sign. *But I preferred to draw and mime*, she remembered. It was hard for her to remember not being able to speak, but she did recall the boys making fun of her. The worst was Tony. He'd pretend to talk by mouthing the words at her, and his brother would dissolve into fits of laughter. She had found the best way was to turn her back on them, but then they would turn her around and around so fast she'd get dizzy and fall over. Auntie Katerina would come in and tell them off but as soon as her back had been turned, they'd be playing pranks on Eléni again. Although her family had left Porth Gwyn in a hurry, she was not sorry to leave behind the taunts of her cousins.

There was another newspaper cutting, folded between the next two pages.

IS MISSING GREEK GIRL IN WALES?
Rhodri Jones — 12 June 1955
    Almost two years on from the devastating earthquake that decimated the island, Kefalonia is being rebuilt and island-ers are returning home. One such man is Kostas Koulouris,

38, an engineer who had been working in Australia at the time of the earthquake. He returned to find all his family had perished — his parents, his sister and her husband all died when the earthquake flattened their house. However, a year on from his return, he has found out his five-year-old niece, Ióánna, may have survived. After extensive research, he believes she was taken out of Kefalonia without permission from the authorities in Greece and brought to Wales.

Can you help? Has a Greek woman and a little girl who answers to the name of Ióánna settled in your town or village in the last two years?

If so, please contact Rhodri Jones, Chief Reporter, on Cardiff 3421. Help Kostas Koulouris be reunited with his niece.

Eléni gasped and put her hands to her mouth. Her throat constricted. There was no mistaking who the little girl in the cutting was. She'd never seen a photograph of herself that young, but there was no doubt. She wasn't five — or was she? — and her name wasn't Ióánna, but the large brown eyes and thick black hair, the shape of the face . . . She took a deep breath. *It has to be me!* It had to be the reason she and her mother had left in such a hurry. When they'd gone to live in Cardiff with Great-Aunt Gwladys, everything had improved. She'd had no more nightmares and she'd begun to speak. Perhaps her mother had thought they could remain anonymous in a large city. There were lots of different nationalities and their communities in Cardiff, whereas in Porth Gwyn they'd stood out. Hot tears pricked along her eyelids as she thought of the wonderful old lady whose plump arms would envelop her every night as she'd told her a Welsh folk story before bedtime. Eléni remembered the first time her father had come home on leave when they'd just moved to the Cardiff house. Her mamá had taken her to Tiger Bay where his ship had docked. He'd scooped her up in his arms and squeezed her tight. She'd been practising saying, 'Welcome home, Baba,' with the help of Auntie Gwladys and he'd given her the widest smile she'd ever seen when she'd said it. Her mamá had been happy too. On that first leave of her father's since they'd been in Cardiff, her great-aunt had often looked after her, taking her down to the boating lake and nearby park 'to give your mam and dada time on their own'. It was strange how she'd always referred to them as 'mam and dada' not 'mamá and baba'.

On the next page was another letter from Aunt Eugenia.

Agapití *Cassia,*

I was so pleased to receive your letter. I have been worried thinking you and Eléni were unhappy and I could do nothing about it. You were right to leave the small town. Could it be the reporter you told me about? Be careful. You may still be found out.

Eléni thought back to the newspaper advertisement. The head offices of Rhodri Jones's newspaper were in Cardiff, so her mother had been taking a chance on staying anonymous.

Theía Gwladys sounds as if she is a good woman. Does she know Eléni isn't yours? Try not to keep any secrets from her. With Tom away, you need her.

You sound so happy in this latest letter. Perhaps Tom being at sea for so long was what made you realise you had indeed fallen in love with him after all and the feelings you had for him in Fiscardo were genuine ones. I am pleased to be wrong. Treasure him. You are lucky to have a man who loves you back.

I am so pleased there is to be a new baby. Eléni is going to love her new baby brother or sister. You do not love Tom like a friend now, eh?

As she read the words, Eléni was taken back to the day her mother had told her she was expecting. They'd been sitting with Auntie Gwladys in the sitting room.

'I've got some exciting news, Eléni.' Her mother had smiled. 'What if I tell you that in a few months' time you're going to have a new baby brother or sister?'

Eléni squealed and clapped her hands. 'Really? I am going to be big sister!' She mimed rocking a baby.

'You are and you're going to be such a help to your mam, *cariad*,' said her auntie.

Bronwen's arrival had been a happy time, Eléni remembered.

This letter was proof her concerns after earlier reading about a so-called marriage of convenience were for nothing. So her mother *didn't* live a lie. Her parents *did* love each other as she thought. There was only one person who had been made to live a lie. And it wasn't her fault.

There were photographs of baby Bronwen and one of Eléni holding her baby sister. She found the newspaper cutting and compared the photographs. She *was* the missing five-year-old Iôánna!

Conscious of the time, Eléni flicked through the rest of the book. Her mother had pasted in certificates from events in Eléni and Bronwen's childhoods — swimming events at the Empire Pool, ballet exams — even though she would never be a ballerina — and Brownie badges that had once adorned their sleeves on the tan-coloured uniforms. A whole page was given to an Eisteddfod certificate, where Eléni had won first prize in a drawing section. Underneath was written: *My lovely Eléni, who learned to draw so well when she couldn't talk*. In capitals, Cassia had added: *WE ARE SO PROUD OF HER!*

Tears ran down Eléni's face. She wanted so much to rant and rave at her parents, but if she hadn't read the dropped letter they would still be the close, loving family her friends envied, in spite of the annoying little sister.

She heard her father's truck pull up outside. She gathered up the journal and replaced it under the bed. There was one thing she kept back. The newspaper cutting with her photo on the front. She would decide what to do with it later.

'Anybody home?' her baba's mellow voice echoed in the hallway. Eléni went to the top of the stairs.

'Just me, Baba. Be prepared for Madam Bronwen to swan in on high platforms. Got her own way with Mamá as usual. They've gone to Credenford.'

'Now, now. Your mother wouldn't have gone if she didn't want to. Have you had a good day?'

'It was . . . interesting.' Eléni hoped and prayed he hadn't seen Reg Morgan.

CHAPTER TWENTY-NINE

Eléni found that time passed painfully slowly as she waited for her mother and sister to return. But at the same time, her stomach performed somersaults as she tried to decide what to do. *You'd best come straight out with it,* she told herself. *You won't be able to carry on as normal after what you've found out. You'd just be perpetuating the lie.*

Did it make a difference? Eléni or Ióánna, a twenty-three-year-old, or was she twenty-five? She was still the same person, so did it matter?

Yes! shouted a voice in her head. *It matters a lot! They have been lying to you and letting you think they are your real parents.*

Eléni read the newspaper advert again. *IS MISSING GREEK GIRL IN WALES?* The man looking for her would have given up now after almost twenty years. She imagined how distraught he must have been to find out his family had been wiped out in the earthquake and then to learn his niece had survived only to be stolen by strangers. She, little Ióánna, or Eléni as her parents had named her, would have given her uncle some hope that not all was lost. Cassia and Tom Beynon had denied him that.

She heard the front door open and Bronwen shouting for her to come downstairs.

'We're back. Come and see what we've bought.'

She'd let her sister have her moment of glory and then she'd confront them. Her stomach churned and her heartbeat raced as she went downstairs. Bronwen pulled out her new shoes from the box, scattering the tissue paper they were wrapped in over the floor as she hurried to put them on and model them for Eléni.

'Very nice.' Her voice sounded flat and disinterested. Eléni didn't take her eyes off her mother, who stood behind Bronwen.

'Don't sound so impressed then.' Her sister glared at her. 'You could have come with us if you wanted a pair.' Her voice rose. 'It's always about you. You're never happy for me, are you?'

Eléni clenched her fists so hard her nails dug into her palms. She didn't even notice the pain as she yelled at her sister. 'I've had other things to deal with. More important than a trashy pair of shoes.' She was close to tears.

'Stop it, both of you.' Her mother looked confused. 'I don't know what this is all about. Eléni, all she did was show you her new shoes.'

By this time, Tom Beynon had come into the kitchen.

'You two. Squabbling again. What's it all about this time? I could hear you from the garage. Shut it, both of you!'

Now she was able to talk with fluency and put her thoughts into words, the squabbles between the sisters had become worse.

Cassia didn't take her eyes off Eléni, but Bronwen wouldn't let things lie.

'Go on, then, sister, dear. What other things have you had to deal with, poor thing?'

Eléni snapped. 'This!' She waved the newspaper cutting in front of her sister who took the piece of paper from her and began to read aloud. '*Is missing Greek girl in Wales?* This Greek man whose name I can't pronounce . . . *has found out that his five-year-old niece, Ióánna, may have survived the earthquake. After extensive research, he believes she was taken out of Kefalonia without permission from the authorities in Greece and brought to Wales.'*

Eléni watched as her mother's face drained of colour and she grabbed the back of a chair.

'Aw, look at the little girl. She's so cute. She reminds me of someone.'

Her father's face was like thunder. 'Here, let me see. Where did you get this, Eléni?' He looked at her mother. 'Cassia, do you know anything about this?'

Tears poured down Cassia's face. She nodded. 'You had no right to go through my things, Eléni.'

'What things, Mamá? said Bronwen.

'She's been keeping a journal of her life since she came to Wales. If you've never seen this, Baba, then she's been keeping secrets from you, too. And there's a huge secret you've both been keeping from me, isn't there? Does Bronwen know?' Eléni's voice rose to a screech.

'What do I know? Will someone tell me what's going on? Is the little girl you? Oh, my God, it is!'

Tom put his arm around Cassia. She dissolved further into tears.

'Why didn't you tell me?' Eléni's voice cracked. The look on the faces of the two people facing her told her she was right. They were not her real parents. 'When were you going to tell me? Ever? You kidnapped me — no stole me, forged my birth certificate and got me a fake passport just so you wouldn't be found out. No wonder I've always been the odd one out in this family!' Eléni's voice reverberated throughout the house.

Her father's face became red with anger. 'Stop it at once, my girl! Although I know we were wrong not to tell you, we did it to give you a better start in life. You had no one left, so don't you dare start throwing around words like "kidnap", "forgery" and "fake passports". If you knew the lengths we went to to get you here. Apologise to your mother.'

'No, I won't. It should be you two apologising to me!'

174

Eléni had never seen her father so angry. She knew she'd gone too far. Her mother's face remained ashen and her eyes were red with tears.

'I thought you knew Mamá and Baba are not your real parents. The boys told me when we came to live in Porth Gwyn. So, yes, I did know. The reason you and Mamá had to leave the first time was because a reporter came looking for you.' Bronwen looked at Eléni and then her parents' shocked expressions. 'What? It's no big deal, is it? Loads of people are adopted. You treat us both the same. In fact, I think you treat her better.' Eléni went to push her sister. 'Just joking.' Bronwen ducked out of the way.

Eléni glared at her. 'Well, I don't think it's funny.'

She placed the newspaper cutting on the table and went to leave the room. 'If you haven't seen this before, Baba, you should read the journal. It makes for very interesting reading.'

Her mother got up from the kitchen table and tried to put her arms around Eléni who stood in the doorway, her dark eyes blazing. She shrugged her away.

Cassia looked at her husband, who had calmed down by then.

'Come and sit down, Eléni. You're right. We should have told you. Years ago.' Her father patted a seat beside him. 'It's my fault. Your mother always said this would happen. But I was . . .' His voice broke. 'Afraid. I didn't want you to go back into your shell and stop speaking again. You've done so well.'

Her mother went to him and clutched his arm. 'Don't get upset, Tom.' She turned to Eléni. 'You deserve to know everything. You, too, Bronwen.'

'No,' shouted Eléni. 'I've read all I need to know. You've deceived me for almost twenty years and I'm going to find out everything about who I really am. For a start, I'm going to find my uncle. My real uncle and my real family, that is.'

She left the room, slamming the door behind her with such force it shook on its hinges.

'Eléni.' Her mother's wail followed her into the hallway.

CHAPTER THIRTY

CASSIA

'Don't cry, Mamá. She'll calm down. She's had a big shock.' Bronwen got up and held her mother in her arms while she sobbed.

'Let me talk to your mother alone. You go and see if Eléni is all right.' Tom wrapped his arms around his wife as Bronwen left. 'I'm sorry, Cassia. You said we should have told her when she was a little girl, and she would have just accepted it. This would never have happened if I'd just listened to you.' He paused. 'I didn't know you were keeping a journal. I've never seen the newspaper cutting.'

How could she tell her husband how she'd felt in the early days when they'd first arrived in Wales? Instead, she'd poured her heart out into that book by writing diary entries every day. She'd written them in her own language of Greek, never dreaming that anyone would read it.

'I'm sorry. I didn't want to worry you. You were so far away and you couldn't have done anything. Glyn arranged for us to move in with Auntie Gwladys and it was the best thing that could have happened. You already know that. Both of us were so happy with her.'

Cassia looked at the concerned face of her husband. Eléni was right about one thing. She had kept things from Tom too. If he'd had a normal job coming home every night after work, perhaps she could have confided in him. But when she'd first been on her own, she'd not wanted him to worry about how homesick she'd felt, alongside squabbles with nephews and reporters calling. She'd used the journal as a way of getting things out of her system. She'd used it as a diary to record her true feelings. She'd told Eugenia things in her letters she hadn't wanted to worry Tom about in the ones she'd written to him.

'I thought it was just because my aunt needed help in the house and you'd be near the docks whenever I came home on leave. You should have told me. But let's forget about the row for now. When Eléni has calmed down, we'll tell her all about her Kefalonian heritage and deal with any questions she has. How about a cup of sweet tea? I'll make it. It all seems quiet upstairs, anyway.'

'What would I do without you? Thank you.' Cassia sat up straight and watched her husband. Hand on heart, she knew she'd always loved him as a wife should love her husband. Her mind went back to the first time he'd arrived home on leave. They'd been living with Aunt Gwladys in Cardiff by then and she'd been counting the days. All her previous doubts about only marrying him for Eléni's sake had only been because she'd felt so lonely and unhappy when she'd first arrived in Wales.

Why, oh, why, had she got the book out today? Eléni would have been none the wiser and the family's easy, contented lifestyle could have continued. But perhaps it was for the best Eléni had found out. Tom was right. Their beautiful girl would calm down. Cassia had always felt guilty about not telling Eléni the truth. The longer it had gone on, the less it had ever seemed there was a right time. She knew why she'd looked at the book that morning, though. It was always going to be an emotional day. It was every year. Twenty-three years ago today, she'd given birth to baby Angelika. Memories flooded back as she relived that awful time. The panic, the pain, the grief.

'No! It's too early.' Cassia's startled cries had echoed through the empty house. Her stomach had tightened in another contraction. Pain had seared through her body. 'Not yet! I need you to stay where you are.' She grabbed the back of a kitchen chair, her knuckles whitening as another excruciating contraction cut through her like a knife. Warm liquid trickled down her thighs. There was no going back. She needed to push.

It'd happened ten days after her beloved Nikos had been murdered. She'd known it had been too early to give birth. The image of the lifeless body of her tiny daughter had never left her.

Cassia's heart had shattered. Sobbing, she'd clutched Angelika to her. 'My beautiful girl, my last link to your baba. How am I going to live without you both?'

She remembered being comforted by the words of her dear neighbour, Sophia, who'd called at the house after hearing her screams. Sophia had found her rocking back and forth with the baby in her arms. 'It's the stress, *agápi mou*. But she's gone to be with her baba. They will be together for ever.'

The book helped to remind Cassia of why it was important that Eléni should have a loving family. She could give her all the love she would have showered on Angelika.

* * *

Cassia heated up the corned beef hash and laid the table. She called everyone to come once she'd dished up the steaming stew into the bowls.

'Eléni's not joining us,' Bronwen said. 'She's not speaking to me either, so you're not alone. Best to leave her. She'll soon come to join us when she gets hungry.'

'Tom,' Cassia called to him from the doorway, before taking her seat at the table by Bronwen. 'She'll never forgive us. Those were her words and I believe her.'

Tom entered the kitchen. 'What's this?'

'Mamá thinks Eléni won't forgive us for keeping her in the dark.' Bronwen rolled her eyes.

'Now then, Bronwen. We have to appreciate what a shock it was for her.' He patted Cassia's hand. 'She'll come round eventually.'

Cassia looked at the empty place set at the table. Was this how it was going to be now? Her eyes pricked with tears. She hardly ever looked at her journal now. She'd even been tempted to bin it when they'd packed up for the move back to Mid-Wales. She'd had one last read through before putting it in the bin, but had retrieved it, not able to throw away part of her life. It's how she viewed it — a part of her life. And now, because of that decision, her life was about to change for ever. She didn't feel like eating.

She walked upstairs and knocked on Eléni's bedroom door. 'Come on. You've got to eat. Why don't you come down and we can talk about it?'

'No. Go away! I don't want to talk about it. And certainly not with you. First thing in the morning, I'm going to find out everything about Kefalonia and I'm going out there as soon as I can. You can't do a thing to stop me. I'm overage and you won't ever see me again.'

Cassia could tell from the pitch of Eléni's voice that she was still very angry and upset. She was at a loss as to how to deal with her daughter when she was in such a state. She turned and retraced her steps downstairs.

Tom waited in the hall. 'No luck, I presume. I think we've just got to let her take it all in and wait for her to want to talk about it when she's ready.'

Cassia nodded.

As they were standing at the foot of the stairs, Eléni's bedroom door opened. She stomped down the stairs, barged past them to grab her coat and left the house.

'Where are you going?' Tom called after her.

'Out! Away from you lot,' came the answer.

'Oh, Tom. What have I done? She's never spoken to you like that before. She said she's going to Kefalonia tomorrow and that we can't stop her. I can't lose her. After everything we've been through, we can't let her go.'

CHAPTER THIRTY-ONE

ELÉNI

The slam of the front door echoed in Eléni's ears. She couldn't bear to be in the same house as her parents and sister anymore. There was only one person she wanted to see. She made for Gabriella's house. The two of them had met when they'd shared, and sometimes overlapped, shifts at the Welsh craft shop opposite the large Victorian hotel that faced the main street running through Porth Gwyn. Like Eléni, Gabriella thought of herself as an outsider, too. Her father was also a local man, but her mother was Italian rather than Greek. Steve Collins had been a British prisoner of war who'd been captured in Italy. He'd fallen for her mother, married her when the war ended and brought his Italian bride back to Wales. Gabriella had always felt different but, unlike Eléni, she visited her Italian family every year. The girls had soon become friends and enjoyed spending time together.

Hot tears stung Eléni's eyes as she broke into a run. Gabriella's house was in the same avenue as her aunt and uncle's house, and she hoped she wouldn't see them as she passed.

She opened the gate and walked the short distance to the house. She hammered on the front door until her knuckles hurt, fearing no one was in.

Eventually, the door opened. Gabriella's mouth gaped as Eléni burst into tears.

'Eléni, it's you. What on earth's happened?' It felt good when Gabriella hugged her and invited her in.

'I've left home, Gabbie. I want nothing to do with them. Not after what they've done. They've been lying to me. Everyone else knows. I bet you do, too. Why didn't you tell me?' Eléni's body was wracked with sobs.

'I don't know what you're talking about, but slow down and tell me everything. We'll go upstairs. My mum is in there.' She pointed to the door at the back of the hallway. As she did so, Isabella Collins opened the door.

'Who was at the . . . ? Oh, it's you, Eléni. Are you all right, *mia cara*?'

'She's a bit upset, Mamma. I'm taking her upstairs and she's going to tell me what's happened.'

Gabriella and her mother exchanged glances. Nothing more was said.

Gabriella's bedroom overlooked the swings and children's playground opposite.

'Here, you sit on the chair. Now what's happened to make you like this? What have they done that's so bad you want to leave home?'

Eléni took a deep breath and related to her friend everything she'd found out.

'They stole me, Gabbie. Took me away and forged my papers, got me a fake passport. I don't even know what my real name is.'

Gabriella's expression was one of shock. 'But if you were an orphan . . .' She leaned over and patted Eléni's arm. 'I'm so sorry. What a terrible thing to have happened. But you survived! Perhaps they thought what they were doing was for the best. You've had a happy childhood, haven't you? Your mum and dad worship you.'

'They keep saying I would have ended up in an orphanage and they were doing it to give me the best chance. But, Gabbie, why didn't they tell me instead of letting me live a lie? Everyone else knows.' Eléni wiped her cheeks on her sleeve. 'Anyway. I want to forget about them now. Do you think your mother will let me stay tonight and then I'll find a room somewhere tomorrow? Oh, tomorrow's Sunday. Well, two nights then.'

'I'm sure she will say yes, but I know she'll only agree if you let your parents know where you are.'

Eléni shook her head. 'No, let them stew. I'm going to Kefalonia. With a one-way ticket. I don't care what they say. I'm over twenty-one, don't forget?' She stood and paced the bedroom floor.

'And acting like a ten-year-old. I'm surprised at you.' Gabriella frowned.

Eléni knew if she didn't have her friend's support, life would be even harder.

'Please, Gabbie. Let's see what your mother says. And then let's decide what we're going to do tonight.'

Isabella Collins agreed to Eléni staying and did ask her if she'd let her parents know where she was. Eléni didn't lie, but she evaded giving a straight answer.

'What about the dance down at Rock Park? Come on,' said Eléni. 'It'll be fun. I've been the silent sister, the quiet one, for too long. I want to be the rebel sister, the wild one.'

As she spoke the words she doubted whether she would ever be a rebel, but it was a good feeling to say it out loud. At least she was thinking about something else apart from her parents' betrayal.

Gabriella didn't need much persuading. She laughed. 'I can't wait to see that.'

'Oh, no, I can't.' Eléni looked forlorn. 'I've just got the clothes I'm wearing. I can't go to a disco in these tatty jeans.'

She didn't dare return home to change.

Gabriella opened her large pine wardrobe stuffed with clothes. 'Take your pick.'

'Wow. Are you sure?'

Eléni's eyes widened. She'd been in Gabriella's bedroom many times, but hadn't seen inside her wardrobe before. She was amazed by not just the number of outfits, but the array of colours. Eléni had always dressed conservatively in blues and greys, the hemline of her skirts and dresses not venturing far above the knee. But in front of her were fabrics of orange and lime green, patterned into swirled shapes, black-and-white op art and tie-dye. Gabriella wore colours to work, but Eléni didn't realise how adventurous a dresser her friend was.

Gabriella held up a purple-and-cerise maxi-dress split to the waist, to be worn over matching hotpants.

'Here. Try this,' she said. 'We're the same size, I think. You can wear these platforms with it.'

Eléni undressed and tried the outfit on. Would she have the courage to wear it? She admired herself in the full-length mirror on the inside of the wardrobe door.

'I don't know. It's fab, but I don't think it's me. If it was just a maxi-dress, I'd love to wear it but . . . the split is a bit daring for me.'

'Nonsense. Didn't you tell me when you arrived about an hour ago you wanted to live a bit? I think we both need to spread our wings. You look fab. Even Handy Andy will notice you in that.'

'Oh, not again.' Eléni's face reddened. Just because she'd once admitted to Gabriella she thought Andrew Smith was good-looking, her friend had never let her forget it. 'All right then, but I may have to dance with my hands over the split so no one notices.'

They both laughed and for the first time since the shouting match with her mother and father, Eléni relaxed and enjoyed some girl time with her friend. 'What are you going to wear? You've got plenty of choice.'

Gabriella held up a pair of white crimplene flares and an orange skinny-rib top. 'What about this? I got them in Credenford last week. I haven't worn them yet.'

Eléni nodded. 'I love them.'

'I told you I go every week on the bus once I get paid, didn't I? There's a great little boutique not far from the bus station. They've got all the latest Chelsea Girl stuff in there.' Gabriella tried on the new clothes for Eléni to see.

'Oh, Gabbie. Those flares fit you like a glove. They show all your curves off.'

'Thanks. If you've got it, flaunt it, I say. I hope Handy Andy's friend, Dave, is going to be there.' Gabriella took off her outfit and laid it on the bed, ready for later. 'Let's work on our hair and make-up now, shall we? You can hang the dress up on the hanger on the side of the wardrobe.'

* * *

The girls heard strains of Slade's 'Cum on Feel the Noize' belting out into the night air before the lights of Rock Park Pavilion came into sight as they walked through the stone gates. Bill Baker's Beats resident disc jockey was renowned for turning up the records to maximum volume.

Gabriella grabbed Eléni's arm as they neared the single-storey building.

'Look who's here.' She pointed at a red Mini with a cream-painted roof parked under a streetlamp a little way from the entrance doors. 'Handy Andy couldn't get any closer if he tried.'

'He's got a grey minivan, hasn't he?' Eléni's heart raced. The thought of watching him on the dance floor was something she couldn't wait to see and view from afar. That's what she'd do. He'd most likely have a trail of girls following him around, anyway. Apart from thinking he was so good-looking, she hadn't even admitted it to herself — but she realised then she did fancy him. Not that he'd give her a second look. She wasn't streetwise enough for him. She wondered how old he was.

'He must have changed it for this. He was driving round town in the red Mini yesterday. The chrome work gleamed in the bright sun and he kept revving when he was at the halt sign so everyone would look his way. I didn't give him the satisfaction. He's *so* pompous. I don't know what you see in him. Now, his friend, Dave, is a different matter . . .' Gabriella was still talking as they entered the pavilion. 'I hope he's here too.'

After paying, they went to the cloakroom where they were each given a raffle ticket with a number to reclaim their jackets at the end of the night.

'Put it in your shoe . . . or your bra,' said Gabriella, laughing. 'So you don't lose it.'

CHAPTER THIRTY-TWO

Eléni and Gabriella walked through the double doors, letting their eyes grow accustomed to the darkness. A glitter ball was suspended from the high ceiling and as it rotated, moving rays of coloured lights cast jewel-like circles on the dance floor. A large crowd of dancers filled the space to practise the latest dance moves Eléni had seen on *Top of the Pops* and never imagined doing herself. What had she let herself in for?

'Let's get a drink,' shouted Gabriella, attempting to be heard above the noise. 'Bacardi and Coke?'

'I'll try one. How much do you want?' Eléni went to unzip her handbag for her purse.

'No, I'll get these.'

Standing at the bar with a pint of beer in one hand and a cigarette in the other was Andy Smith. His friend, Dave, who Gabriella was so keen on, faced away from them.

'Hey, Dave. This is a cool surprise. We didn't expect to see these two stunners here, did we? The night's looking up.'

Dave swivelled around. 'You could say that. What are you two ladies drinking?'

Eléni went to refuse but Gabriella smiled at Dave. 'Two Bacardi and Cokes, please.'

Eléni knew her cheeks were beetroot red as she felt her face and neck burning. She wanted the floor to swallow her up. It would look too obvious if she pulled the split in her maxi-dress together. Andy looked her up and down. She looked at the floor.

'Eléni Beynon, isn't it? Bronwen's sister. I don't think she's here tonight. Couldn't compete with her big sister in the fashion stakes, I bet. Agreed, Dave?' His friend had returned with the drinks and handed them to the girls. 'I got another two in for us, too. So knock it back.'

'Thank you.' When the boys drank back their beers, Gabriella nudged Eléni and whispered, 'I think we're in.'

Eléni had never been so uncomfortable in her life. She'd been out on dates with a couple of boys in college, but they were not in the same league as Andy Smith. They'd gone for walks or for the odd meal, more as friends getting to know each other. He exuded self-confidence and sexual tension hung in the air. She didn't know whether she liked it. She'd never even spoken to him until tonight. She'd have one drink and then make an excuse to leave.

'Let's go in and dance,' said Andy. 'We can put our drinks on the windowsill.' He held her arm and led her through the crowd of dancers. Electricity fizzled along her skin. She couldn't tell if it was fear or excitement.

A glance behind them told her Gabriella had no such concerns about Dave. She hung on his arm and looked up intently at his face as he spoke. 'By the way, girls, I got you doubles to save queuing up again at the bar.'

Gabriella giggled. The four of them returned to the side of the dance floor.

The lights changed. Gone were the shafts of coloured light and in their place was ultraviolet light. Everyone squealed and pointed at those whose white underwear shone through their dark clothes. Even Eléni laughed as Gabriella tried to cover her glowing white bra. It was as if her orange skinny-rib had disappeared. Eléni looked down at her dress and hotpants, relieved she'd worn dark undies. More luck than judgement!

'Oh. My. God. How embarrassing!' Gabriella drank her Bacardi quickly. 'Do they have those lights every week? It's our first time tonight.' She added, 'We've been meaning to come for ages, haven't we, Eléni?'

Eléni didn't answer. It was because of her own suggestion they were there at all and she had a strong feeling they wouldn't go again. She'd have to ask Bronwen. A look around told her the dancers were mainly sixth formers trying to look cool. She felt decidedly old. Andy Smith wasn't in school either. He had to be about her age.

The music changed to a slow number and the lights dimmed further.

'This is more like it.' Andy took Eléni's drink and put it on the windowsill with his. He held Eléni's hand and led her into the middle of the dance floor. The haunting melody of Procol Harum's 'A Whiter Shade of Pale' filled the room and Eléni's heart drummed in her chest. Andy held her tightly and swayed to the music. She'd never been held like that before.

'You look amazing tonight,' he whispered. His lips and warm breath on her earlobe sent fizzles of excitement through her. Why had she spent so long shying away from having a good time? She wanted to rebel, didn't she? But now she was, she didn't know how to react. Instead, she looked down and moved in time to the music.

The DJ's voice broke into her thoughts.

'Enough of the smooching, you lot. Let's have some Slade.'

The tempo changed, and Eléni and Andy broke apart to dance in time to the music. When they went back to retrieve their drinks, Gabriella and Dave had been joined by another couple. Eléni knew the girl vaguely, but had never seen the boy before.

'Marie and Paul.' Dave introduced them.

'Hi,' said Eléni, taking her glass from Andy.

'The place is full of bloody kids.' He pointed to the teenage dancers who were now letting their hair down, laughing and screaming at the top of their voices to strains of 'Mama We're All Crazee Now'. 'Too right. You're all bloody crazy,' he shouted. Everyone laughed. 'Anyone fancy a spin over to Nant Melin? There's a Young Farmers' do on tonight. At least they won't all be in school. Come on, drink up.'

Eléni did as she was told, but as she walked with Gabriella to retrieve their jackets her head started to swim. 'I feel a bit wobbly, Gabbie. I don't think we should go with them. Andy's had loads to drink. I think I'll go home.'

'You'll be fine once you're out in the fresh air. Besides, you can't go home — if you mean my house — because I've got the key. We'll be fine. Dave says Andy's a good driver.'

Left with no other choice, Eléni followed the others, piling into the Mini.

'Eléni, you and Marie are the smallest so you sit in the front. And, Gabbie, I know you don't want to be parted from Dishy Dave here, so you two and Paul sit in the back. It's not far.' Andy lifted the front seat for them to get into the back. Eléni sat on Marie's lap reaching for the handle above the door. Andy started the car and revved the engine. 'Isn't she a beaut?'

He drove out of the park and soon they were out on the open road leading from Porth Gwyn. 'Go on, Smithie. Show us what she can do.' Dave egged his friend on.

'Everyone want some music?' Andy handed Marie his box of cassettes. 'She's even got a cassette player. Cool, eh?'

Marie chose the Stones. Very soon everyone, except for Eléni, was singing 'Can't You Hear Me Knocking' at the top of their voices.

Eléni's pulse raced as Andy drove faster and faster.

'Andy, please slow down. Please.' She gripped the handle until her hands hurt. She was sick with fear. Why hadn't she stuck to what she wanted to do?

The car approached the bend just before the old mill at the entrance of Nant Melin when Andy yanked the wheel to the right. The tyres screeched along the road into a skid as Andy tried to brake. 'Jeez! I've bloody lost it.'

The singing abruptly stopped. Screams filled the car as the Mini left the road and rolled over onto its side into the hedge. Eléni shot forward, banging her head on the wind-screen and her arm snapped free of the handle. For a few seconds, she heard the others yelling and scrambling over each other to get out.

'Run to the phone box and call an ambulance. Eléni's in a bad way.' It was Gabriella's voice.

'Oh, my God. Is she still breathing?' Marie shouted at Andy. 'Andy, do something. Don't just bloody stand there like a zombie.'

Excruciating pain shot down her left arm and then it all went black.

CHAPTER THIRTY-THREE

CASSIA

Tom led Cassia into the sitting room. 'She's right. We can't stop her, but how is she going to get there? She has no money to speak of. She's never even travelled to Cardiff on her own. She'll have to organise flights, a place to stay and how would she start looking for a man whose name appeared in a newspaper article and who may or may not even be her uncle? We'll ride this storm, Cassia, and you mustn't worry. All families have rows, don't they?' He pulled Cassia in close and kissed her forehead.

After all the upset of the earlier row with Eléni, Cassia and Tom were spending a quiet evening together. Quiet apart from the thump, thump, thump of rock music blasting out from Bronwen's record player in the bedroom above. Tom was following the TV highlights of a football game where his beloved Bluebirds had struggled against their arch-rivals, the Swansea Jacks. Cassia sat reading, smiling at the expletives coming out of her husband's mouth that continued long after the match had finished, as well as after the pundits had completed their post-mortems.

'I take it they lost, then?'

'Bloody ref. The last goal was clearly offside.'

Normally Cassia would have been so engrossed in her book that she wouldn't have been interrupted, but tonight she was going through the motions. Her mind was on Eléni. She looked at her watch again. It wasn't like Eléni to be out late.

'Why don't you go up? I'll wait up for her.'

'I hope she's all right.' Cassia stood and kissed her husband. 'I'll tell Bronwen to turn the music down.'

She went upstairs and knocked on her younger daughter's door. 'I'm turning in now, Bron. Baba's waiting up for your sister. Turn the music down a little, will you? *Kalinýchta.*'

Bronwen opened the door and hugged her mother. '*Nos da*, Mamá. She'll come round. I know she will.'

Although both her daughters were bilingual and she'd taught Bronwen Greek as she'd done Eléni, Bronwen always answered her in snippets of Welsh she'd learned at school in Cardiff. Bronwen was proud to be Welsh as well as half-Greek. Cassia reflected on the change of circumstances the day had brought. Usually, it would be sensible Eléni reassuring her that her extrovert sister would not come to any harm and that she was having so much fun she'd lost track of the time.

But Cassia shivered as a sense of foreboding washed over her. A feeling that all was not well. She opened her bedroom door as the telephone in the hall rang.

Tom answered. 'Yes, I'm her father. I'll come straight away. Is she badly hurt?'

* * *

Cassia's heart thumped as she and Tom were led to the ward where their daughter lay in bed and looked to be asleep. She'd been involved in a car accident and because her injuries were serious, she'd been transferred from Porth Gwyn Cottage Hospital to the larger one in Credenford. Tom had raced along the roads in order to cut down the journey time that normally took at least an hour. Cassia had gripped the handle above the car door until her knuckles were white, begging him to slow down.

'Tom, please. At this rate, we'll be in hospital beds with injuries of our own, or worse . . .'

Ward Sister Evans, who accompanied them to Eléni's bedside, explained that although they'd given her something to help her sleep, she was conscious. Now almost midnight, the lights in the ward were dimmed.

'She's sustained a bad head injury and has broken her arm. She's a very lucky young lady,' she said.

Cassia sat beside the bed and took Eléni's hand. 'Oh, what have you done, *agápi mou*?' Her head was bandaged so none of her beautiful black hair framed her face. Her left arm had been set in a splint and she was propped up on several large pillows. Cassia was back in the Red Cross hospital in Argostoli where, as a three-year old, her daughter had worn a similar bandage that had been encrusted with blood and her tiny arm had been secured to Sophia's walking stick acting as a splint. She looked across at her husband. Tom's face was the colour of milk.

Eléni's eyes flickered and in the dim light looked from Cassia to Tom. It was as if she was turning the clock back twenty years. Her huge brown eyes widened and she looked terrified.

'Oh, no.' Her father looked horrified. 'She can't go back there.'

'It's all right, *agápi mou*,' Cassia spoke softly in Greek to her. 'You've been in an accident. Mamá and Baba are here, now.'

Eléni gripped her hand.

Tom stood and paced the area at the end of the bed. Cassia knew what he was thinking. What if Eléni reverted to her silent world?

The ward sister returned and asked Cassia and Tom to leave.

'Can't I stay with her? Please. She's terrified to be left here alone. You can see that,' Cassia pleaded with her. Eléni gripped her hand so tightly Cassia had to stop herself crying out in pain.

The nurse shook her head. 'Hospital rules, I'm afraid. It's all the time we can allow you. Your daughter hasn't spoken since she arrived.'

Cassia pulled herself away from Eléni. '*Kalinýchta, agápi mou.* We'll be back tomorrow. You're safe now, in the best place.'

Eléni's eyes brimmed with tears and she tossed her head from one side to the other. Tom went to his daughter and kissed her forehead. '*Nos da.* Now get some sleep, *cariad.*'

He squeezed Cassia's hand as they walked away with the nurse.

'Can you come with me so I can take some details? Your daughter, Eléni, I think that's right, arrived in an ambulance from Porth Gwyn, over the border in Wales. I presume that's where you're from?'

'Yes,' said Tom. 'We came as soon as we could, once we got the phone call from the police.'

As they walked the length of the ward, Sister Evans continued talking in an officious manner. 'The ambulance driver told us the police had called 999 from the village near the site of the accident. The other five teenagers got out of the crash almost unharmed, but your daughter took the full force of the collision. She was a passenger in the front and wasn't wearing a seat belt.'

Five others! What was she thinking? It was so out of character for Eléni. Apart from Gabriella, she'd never mentioned any other friends. Cassia knew it wasn't compulsory to wear a seat belt, but Tom had always taught them all to do so.

'They wouldn't be fitted on the cars if there wasn't a good reason to wear them,' he'd nagged them every time they went on a journey.

The sister took them to a small office near the entrance and took down details about Eléni.

'Normally we would have got this from the patient herself as she was conscious when she came in, but I'm afraid she refuses to speak. All we have is what the ambulance personnel were told by the police at the site of the crash. They got the information from the other passengers.'

Tom looked at Cassia. 'Eléni didn't speak for several years. She was traumatised when she was trapped in the rubble of a house when we lived in Kefalonia.'

'I see. Was it the earthquake? I remember reading about it. How terrible for you.' The sister became serious. 'And you think this is maybe what's happened again now. I'm sorry to say we thought she was just being awkward, not wanting to cooperate because she thought she was already in a lot of trouble. The ambulance driver reported the police were shocked at how many young people were crammed into the vehicle. It was a Mini, of all things. And they could smell alcohol.'

Cassia looked surprised. 'Eléni doesn't drink.'

'But we never even knew she had that many friends.' Tom turned to Sister Evans. 'Our daughter has always been a bit of a loner, see. Just one best friend since we moved to Porth Gwyn from Cardiff, we know of. This is all so out of character. But thank you, Sister. We'll be back to see her at visiting times tomorrow. Two o'clock, is it?'

Yes, out of character and we both know why. It's all my fault. That blasted journal.

Cassia thanked the sister as they left the hospital, then they made their way in silence to the space where they'd parked the car. Tom was the first to speak.

'I hope and pray she won't revert to not speaking permanently, Cass. I couldn't bear it if we go back to square one.'

Cassia linked arms with her husband. 'Don't go there. Let's hope now we've been in to see her she gets some sleep and feels more like talking tomorrow. By the time we get here in the afternoon, they will have checked the seriousness of the head injury. It's more worrying than the broken arm.'

She sounded more positive than she was feeling. Deep down, she knew the terrified look in Eléni's huge eyes could mean just one thing — her words had been locked away again.

Tom smiled. 'I'm sure you're right. Let's get on the road.'

CHAPTER THIRTY-FOUR

It was almost 1 a.m. when Cassia and Tom arrived home in Porth Gwyn. Cassia was about to put the key in the door when a concerned Bronwen opened it.

'Is she all right? I've been thinking all sorts of things. Awful things. Gabriella rang after you left. She was crying so I don't know what happened.'

Cassia pulled her younger daughter into a hug. 'She's going to be fine, Bron. She's got a broken arm, which will heal. And a nasty bump and cut on her head, which they'll check again in the morning.'

By this time, Tom had joined them, and they went into the sitting room. 'Her injuries are the least of our worries. She was in a Mini with five others, all squashed in like sardines in a tin. Gabriella was one of them, but what was Eléni thinking? She was lucky her injuries were not more serious. They could all have been killed. You know the bend going into Nant Felin? Whoever was driving came off the road there. Ended up in the hedge.'

Cassia's eyes filled with tears. 'I can't believe she'd act like that. She got into a car with a driver who'd been drinking!'

'The nurse didn't say Eléni had been drinking. She said the police could smell alcohol in the car. She's overage anyway, but it's all so unlike her. I've never known her to have a drink even here in the house. The worst bit, Bron, is that she hasn't spoken since it happened.'

'Oh, no. Auntie Gwladys isn't here to help her now.' Although she was too young to remember all the details of what it had been like for her sister, it was talked about so Bronwen knew the struggle the whole family had gone through. 'I remember Auntie Gwladys sitting side by side with her and coaxing her to say more words, and then giving her tight *cwtches* if she got it right. I couldn't have been very old but I was quite jealous of her.'

Cassia remembered. For a time, Bronwen had pretended she couldn't talk either just so she could get extra hugs from their great-aunt, even though she'd always got plenty anyway. It had brought it home to her and Auntie Gwladys that little Bronwen had been feeling a bit left out. After that, one of them would play with Bronwen while the other had helped Eléni practise her speech.

'Come here.' Cassia pulled her daughter into her arms. 'We're all going to make sure she doesn't stop speaking again. Come with us to visit her tomorrow. We need to let her know we understand how upset she was about us not telling her the truth about who she is. She needs time to take it all in. I'm afraid the crash has just made things worse, so the sooner we're all together again under one roof, the better. Now, back to bed. What would Auntie Gwladys say? *Tomorrow's another day.*'

It took Cassia a long time to drift off to sleep. Every time her eyelids started getting heavy, an image of Eléni in bandages roused her with a start. *What if?* questions whirred in her brain. What if the bump and cut on her head led to a brain injury? What if Eléni never spoke again? What if she *did* go to Kefalonia and shunned the Welsh side of her family? What if she did find her uncle and he reported Cassia and Tom for illegally taking his niece out of the island? Tom lay awake beside her.

'Can't sleep either?' Tom squeezed her hand. 'I think we've got to make it up to Eléni somehow. This sorry business tonight is all a reaction to her finding out the truth. We should take her out to Kefalonia. Go as a family. Find this uncle with her.'

Cassia sat up in bed. Her pulse raced. She'd vowed she'd never go back.

'No. No! We must persuade Eléni that her place is here. We don't even know if there is an uncle now. It's been almost twenty years since he looked for her. Perhaps he left Kefalonia when he didn't find her and thought there was nothing left of his family. No. I refuse!'

She began to sob. Tom pulled her close and they fell back onto the bed in each other's arms.

'Shh. I didn't mean to upset you. Eléni's going to go anyway. She's twenty-three, so we can't stop her. I just thought if we all went together, Bronwen as well, it would be like a family holiday and would make up for keeping her in the dark. I still feel I'm to blame.'

Cassia felt the warmth of her husband's chest beneath her. His heart raced alongside hers. What he said made sense, but the panic she'd tried to suppress ever since reading the missing-child advert in the *Celtic Chronicle* all those years before loomed close to the surface. She couldn't risk it. What if they were prosecuted for taking her illegally? Maybe the uncle had married and had children of his own now, and would welcome his lost niece back to live with them. It would be tempting for Eléni to be the Kefalonian Greek girl she and Tom had denied her becoming. Cassia had often wondered why she'd been so keen that Eléni learned to speak the Greek language and yet she hadn't shared anything about her Greek homeland or heritage with her. *If you were so keen on denying her that, why didn't you keep to English or even help her learn Welsh?* She couldn't answer. All she knew was the pleasure she felt hearing her once-silent daughter speak in her home language and converse with her Theía Katerina and her half-Greek cousins. *I've done the same with Bronwen*, she reasoned, yet deep down she knew she might not have bothered if Bronwen had been her only daughter.

'We'll talk about it in the morning. *Nos da.*'

Cassia turned away from Tom in her usual position in the bed. '*Kalinýchta.*' She knew there would be no sleep coming. Her mind was too busy with images of Eléni emerging from a crashed car, and being carried out of the earthquake rubble by Tom as a three-year-old.

Once she heard the gentle breathing that told her Tom was fast asleep, Cassia crept out of bed and felt under the divan for her precious journal. She tiptoed out of the room and went downstairs to the sitting room. She turned on the floor lamp and sat on the chair beside it. The book had been her only lifeline when she'd been so unhappy the first time they'd lived in Porth Gwyn. She'd even doubted her love for Tom and had berated herself for doing what her sister had accused her of — marrying him for Eléni's sake. She flicked through the pages, stopping every now and then to read a letter from Eugenia or a diary entry. One dated ten years ago was from her sister telling her their mother had died and how she'd asked for Cassia before she'd passed. Cassia's throat tightened. As her daughter, she knew that she should have gone to make amends for the rift between them. But she hadn't even told Tom about what was in Eugenia's letter. She'd replied to her sister, explaining she couldn't go and she'd not heard from her since. That decision had caused a falling-out with the sister who'd been so good to her and Eléni. Her eyes burned with unshed tears.

She found the newspaper cutting she was looking for. It was one that had caused her to flee to the anonymity of a big city. A beautiful child stared up at her from the page. The large black-and-white photo Rhodri Jones had used in the missing-child advert was striking and there was no mistaking that the little girl was Eléni. Cassia remembered cutting her long black curls to try to change her looks, but her huge dark eyes would still identify her. She'd even worked out an explanation if anyone in the neighbourhood where Aunt Gwladys lived had challenged her. No, her daughter's name was Eléni, she was three, not five, and, yes, she was half-Greek, but they'd find lots of little girls from Greece with black hair and dark eyes. However, in those early days, not a day had gone by when she'd not been constantly afraid the charismatic reporter would knock on the door and find her and Eléni.

She read the appeal in the advert again. The uncle's name was Kostas Koulouris. But perhaps he was the brother of Eléni's mother, so her married name would be different. *If Eléni did go to Kefalonia, where would she start looking?* Cassia tried to imagine what Eléni's uncle would look like. She'd never met Eléni's parents before they'd died, so she had no idea. Her thoughts were filled with devastating images of the piles of rubble that had been all that remained of Eléni's house on that awful August day. Argostoli had been razed to the ground by the force of the earthquake. Now, almost twenty years later, buildings would have been erected, but it would be unrecognisable as the town she'd once lived in.

I have to stop her from going. I can't lose her after all we've been through.

CHAPTER THIRTY-FIVE

Cassia, Bronwen and Tom stood in a queue of hospital visitors, all with their eyes on the clock, watching the minute hand move towards two o'clock. Cassia's stomach churned as she wondered about the state they would find Eléni in. Tom had called the hospital to see how their daughter was, but all he'd been told was she'd had a comfortable night.

'You'll have to speak to the doctor,' was all the person on the other end of the line had said.

At dead on two o'clock, a young nurse opened the double doors, and the visitors streamed into the women's ward. Cassia noticed a sign on the wall saying, *STRICTLY ONLY TWO VISITORS TO A BED*.

'You go in with your baba, Bronwen. Eléni will be pleased to see you.'

'No,' said Tom. 'I'll wait. I'll try to find someone who can tell us how things are.'

Eléni was propped up on two plump pillows, her broken arm supported by another pillow on the bed. The bandage around her head had been removed and part of her hairline had been shaved to reveal a line of stitches where she'd cut her head. Violet bruising ran from the head wound down her left cheekbone. Cassia leaned over to kiss her daughter. Eléni smiled, but did not say anything. She seemed a lot calmer than when they'd left her the night before, but Cassia would not relax until she heard her daughter speak.

Bronwen sat on the chair beside the bed opposite her mother.

'Well, you certainly put the wind up us lot,' Bronwen told her. 'Getting in the car with Handy Andy driving! You must have taken leave of your senses.'

Eléni shook her head, but crinkles appeared at the corners of her eyes as if amused. But Cassia wasn't amused. She knew the boy to whom Bronwen was referring. Andrew Smith was the town's tearaway and even though they'd only been living back in Porth Gwyn for a year, they already knew of his unsavoury reputation. What on earth was her sensible, level-headed daughter doing getting mixed up with the likes of him? Her heart pounded. She'd hoped that Eléni would start to speak but she remained silent, just responding to Bronwen with the familiar nods and facial expressions she'd relied upon all those years ago.

'You look a lot better than you did last night, *agápi mou*. You've got a bit more colour in your cheeks.' Cassia patted Eléni's hand. 'Has the doctor been round this morning? Baba's gone to see if he can find out more.'

Eléni pointed at the wound on her head with her free arm. She put her good arm across the one in plaster to form an X shape. Cassia was puzzled.

'You've been for an X-ray,' said Bronwen. Her sister nodded in agreement and made a thumbs-up sign. 'Everything is all right?' Eléni nodded again. 'See, Mam. I'm getting good at this. Here's Baba, now. I'll wait outside. We'd better stick to Sister's orders.'

Cassia watched Bronwen walk the length of the ward as Tom approached the bed. She tried to read his expression, hoping for good news from the doctor.

Tom's face broke into a wide grin as he got closer. He kissed Eléni before taking the chair vacated by Bronwen.

'Well, you're looking better today. You didn't half give us a fright, didn't she, Mamá?'

Cassia nodded. 'But what did the doctor say? Did you manage to speak to anyone? Eléni says she's been for an X-ray on her head and it's all right.' Tom turned to Eléni and took her hand. 'You've been speaking. That's great news.'

Eléni shook her head.

'She mimed it to Bronwen and gave the thumbs-up sign,' said Cassia.

'Ah. Well, it's still good because that's what they told me.' Tom turned to Eléni. 'The sister on duty today said they've checked you over and they're happy there's no lasting damage to your head. The cut will heal now they've stitched it and the bruising will go. We have to bring you back in a week to check the bones in your arm have knitted back together properly.'

Cassia breathed a sigh of relief. 'Oh, that's such good news, isn't it?'

Eléni's eyes sparkled as she nodded. She opened her mouth to say something, but no sound came out. Her eyes filled with tears.

Cassia stood and put her arms around her daughter. 'Don't get upset. The words will come back. I'm sure of it.' Eléni snuggled into her mother's neck. For the first time since the blazing row they'd had, it looked like things might be all right after all. Cassia sat back down. She looked across at Tom. 'So can we take her home with us this afternoon, then?'

'No, we've got to ring in the morning to check the doctor has been to the ward on his rounds and if he's happy, we can pick her up sometime in the afternoon.' Tom smiled at Eléni. 'We'll soon have you back in your own bed. You can put this behind you then. Your arm will soon mend, a young girl like you. You're lucky it's your left hand so you can get back to those amazing drawings you do.'

Eléni again went to speak, but the words just wouldn't come. Cassia cast a concerned glance at her husband. She tried to hide her worries by changing the subject and looked up at the clock on the wall above the door. 'I'll let Bronwen have the last ten minutes with you. Lady's missing you. She keeps going to the back door as if you'll be there soon.'

Eléni smiled and nodded. She moved her free hand back and forth to indicate the dog's wagging tail.

Cassia hugged her daughter, and they waved to each other as she walked away.

* * *

The next day, after getting confirmation she was fit to be discharged, Tom and Bronwen left Porth Gwyn to fetch Eléni from the hospital. Cassia stayed behind to make her daughter's favourite treat, baklavá, to welcome her home. After all the years of living in Wales and even though Aunt Gwladys had taught her to make the most amazing Welsh cakes, Cassia always returned to her Greek recipes for special occasions. Living in Wales meant she'd had to make some adjustments, but with practice her sweet pastries were now almost as good as those she'd made in Kefalonia. In Porth Gwyn, it seemed olive oil was only available in small bottles from the chemist to treat blocked ears. Instead, she melted half a block of butter to mix with the strong white flour. She rolled out the dough, getting it thinner and thinner to make the layers for the pie. Her mind wandered back to her time in Fiscardo when she would do this each day before taking the baklavá to sell at the market. She had not heard from her sister in years so she didn't know if she still ran her stall at the town's market. What would Eugenia think about her refusing to contemplate a return to Kefalonia as Tom had suggested? But she would not give in over this. Cassia had vowed she would never set foot on the island again. She filled the layers with a mixture of chopped nuts and brushed the final layer with melted butter before cutting the dough into diamond shapes.

Cassia heard the tyres of Tom's truck crunch on the gravel drive. She finished drizzling honey over the tray of pastries when Bronwen opened the front door. 'She's home, Mamá.'

Cassia brushed her hands on her apron and rushed to greet them. Lady beat her to it and barked with excitement as Tom helped Eléni from the passenger seat of the car. Her plastered arm was now supported with a sling, and she'd combed her hair towards her forehead so her wound was less obvious. She leaned over to stroke Lady who rolled onto her back, inviting Eléni to tickle her tummy. Eléni looked up at her mother and beamed.

'She's been pining for you. Let's go in. I've made your favourites.' Bronwen appeared in the hallway with her mouth full.

'And mine!'

'Don't talk with your mouth full,' Cassia and Tom spoke in unison, laughing. Eléni rolled her eyes and chuckled too.

CHAPTER THIRTY-SIX

ELÉNI

Later that night when she lay upstairs in bed, Eléni thought back over the last few days and how much everything had changed. She was pleased to be back, but also frustrated. Just three days before, she'd left home in such a temper she'd told herself she was leaving for good, never wanting to see her parents or her sister ever again. She knew now that wasn't going to happen. She'd wanted to break free from her quiet goody-goody image — well, she'd done that. According to her parents, who'd had to pass the crashed car on the way to see her in hospital, she was lucky to be alive. All they kept saying was it was so unlike her, so out of character. They'd let her live a lie, so what was her true character? She was so confused she didn't know herself. The last thing she remembered on Saturday night was the Mini speeding towards the hedge, the noise of the skidding crash and the car rolling over into the field. Every time she closed her eyes, her head filled with her own blood-curdling scream and panicked voices of the others. Then no images. Just blackness.

What had she done? She'd put her parents and sister through hell all because she didn't have the courage to do the right thing. She didn't want a second double Bacardi and Coke. And yet she'd drunk it. She knew Andy had been drinking and still got in the car with him. Did she really think it was worth trying to impress Andy Smith and show him she was one of the trendy girls? It was obvious he only thought of himself. She was sure there would already be someone else to show off to by now. How could someone as weak as her even contemplate travelling to Kefalonia on her own and trying to find a long-lost relative? She knew her parents had been overprotective of her because of her mutism. She'd always shied away from social situations because of it, but she was a grown woman now!

She tried to turn over and pain shot through her arm. She had to remember how restricted she was with her arm in the splint. In a week's time, she'd return to have it replaced with a plaster cast once the swelling had gone down. Her quickly made plans as she'd rushed to Gabriella's house after the row were dashed. She'd planned to get the money for the Kefalonia trip by asking for extra shifts at the Welsh craft shop and trying to get work at the large hotel in the evenings. They were always advertising for waitresses to do evening shifts. *But how could she manage waitressing with a broken arm?* Tears prickled along her eyelids. She'd ruined everything!

Eléni heard what sounded like a tap on the window. Then several more. Slowly, she got out of bed and drew the curtain back a fraction. Standing below, about to throw more chippings up at the window, was Andy Smith. Eléni gasped and closed the curtain. He continued to throw the tiny stones until she drew back the curtain again and managed to open the window with her uninjured hand.

'Eléni, I've come to see if you're all right,' Andy said in a loud whisper.

Eléni went to answer him, but it was as if a door slammed shut at the top of her voice box. No words would come out. Her pulse raced. She'd hoped her speech would come back now she was home and sleeping in her own bed. The ordeal of the crash was over, so why couldn't she get her words out? All she could do was give Andy the thumbs-up. *Yes, I'm all right.*

In a louder voice, he said, 'That's good. I want to say I'm sorry.'

The outside light flashed on, and her father marched across to where Andy stood looking up at her.

'What the hell are you doing here, Smith? You've caused enough trouble so GO!'

She thought her father was going to hit him. Andy put up his hands in protest.

'Okay, I'm going. I just came to see if your daughter is all right and to apologise. If you must know, she was begging me to slow down and I was too pig-headed to listen. Showing off, see.' He looked up at her window and waved as he slunk away.

The next morning, PC Cooper arrived at the house to speak to Eléni. Her mother called her down from her room and they went into the sitting room.

'I'm afraid my daughter won't be able to answer you, constable.' Tom placed a hand on Eléni's shoulder.

The young man frowned. 'Well, I'm afraid she'll have to, otherwise she will be obstructing the police with our enquiries.'

'No, what my husband means is she is physically unable to answer you. She has lost the ability to speak . . . since the accident. It's happened before. But I think she'll be able to write her answers down, won't you, *agápi mou*?'

Eléni nodded. Cassia went to the bureau and took out a writing pad and pen. She handed it to Eléni.

'Oh, I see. Sorry.' The policeman faced Eléni. 'Now, Miss Beynon, all I want to know is everything you can remember before the accident. The six of you who were travelling in the red Mini had just left the dance at the Rock Park Pavilion, is that right?'

She nodded.

'Can you tell me why you left the dance and whose idea it was to get into the car?'

Eléni paused before beginning to write, her left arm propped on a cushion. She knew she would be incriminating Andy Smith, but he did seem genuinely sorry by calling last night to see if she was all right.

Everybody thought the dance was full of sixth formers. We'd all left school and were working. Somebody said there was a Young Farmers' dance in Nant Melin, so we left to go there. She still hadn't mentioned Andy's name.

PC Cooper read what she'd written and handed the pad back to her.

'Whose suggestion was it?'

She wrote, *I can't remember.*

'Think. I put it to you it was Andy Smith who suggested you go to Nant Melin as he wanted to show you all his new motor.'

Eléni's face burned. *Yes, I think it was Andy.*

Her parents exchanged glances. 'Why are you shielding that yobbo? He's a waste of space.'

Eléni's eyes blazed. *No, he's not,* she wrote. *He told me he's sorry.*

'Anyway, let's get back to Saturday night,' said the police constable. 'We know Mr Smith was driving. He was seen racing out of Porth Gwyn, and it seems he lost control on the bend before the mill. Was anyone egging him on before the impact? Anyone telling him to increase his speed, for instance.'

Eléni decided not to tell the policeman that, led by Dave, everyone had laughed and shouted, 'Faster, Smithie', 'Put your foot down', 'Woo-hoo' . . . except for her. She remembered her terror. Perhaps that's what had locked in her words again.

She shook her head. She didn't want to get them into any more trouble. The accident had happened, and that was it.

PC Cooper made a note of her answer. 'Now one more thing and then I'll leave you all in peace for now. The police officers who arrived on the scene reported a distinct smell of alcohol on the driver and indeed on the passengers. Can you verify this, please? How much had everyone had to drink at the Rock Park? I must stress this is very important because if Mr Smith drove while under the influence of alcohol, the people in the next accident he has may not be as lucky as you were. He would not cooperate and refused to be breathalysed, so he's in trouble for that anyway. Do you understand?'

It was the constable's last statement that made Eléni realise the seriousness of what had happened. She had no doubt Andy shouldn't have been driving so she had to tell the truth.

She picked up her pen again. *Gabbie and I had two Bacardi and Cokes. They were doubles. Dave and Andy had a beer each time and they'd already had drinks before we arrived. I don't know how many. Does that make him over the limit? I don't know how many drinks Paul and Marie had.*

She handed her pad to PC Cooper.

'Thank you, Miss Beynon. May I tear out these pages and keep them as evidence of our conversation today? In due time, I'd like you to come down to the station and make a formal statement. I hope your arm heals quickly.' He turned to Tom and Cassia. 'Thank you, both. If there's anything else your daughter remembers, please don't hesitate to call me. I'll see myself out.'

Eléni ran back upstairs to her bedroom.

* * *

Eléni had another visitor the next day. Gabriella arrived with the clothes she'd left at her house and a bunch of flowers.

'Come in, Gabriella. Eléni will be pleased to see you.' Eléni heard her mother invite her friend into the hallway and approached them. In a low voice, her mother told her, 'I'm afraid she can't speak so she may mime or draw things in answer to you. See if she'll talk to you. I'm not going to say anything about what you both did on Saturday. I'm sure you've had all that from your mother. We're just so pleased her injuries weren't more serious.'

Gabriella looked contrite and nodded. When she noticed Eléni halfway down the stairs, her face broke into a smile. 'Hiya.

211

I came to see how you are. You gave us all a fright. These are from Mr Williams at the Welsh craft shop to get well soon.'

Cassia led the girls into the living room. 'I'll let you girls have a chat while I make us all a cuppa and put those beautiful flowers in water.'

'Thank you, Mrs Beynon.' Gabriella handed Cassia the bouquet. She turned back to Eléni. 'He says once you can work the till with your good hand, you can come back to work and we'll manage the other jobs between us.'

Eléni nodded but knew that until the words flowed again, serving at the till in a shop would be impossible if she couldn't converse with the customers.

Gabriella took her hand. 'We're all so sorry about what happened. When you were lying on the ground when the car door flung open, I thought you were dead. I couldn't bear it if we were the cause of you losing your life.' Her voice became scratchy. 'I've finished with Dave. Well, I didn't really get started, did I? He was the one egging Andy on to go faster. We had this almighty row.' She paused. 'No, we were all doing it. We were all to blame.'

Eléni stood and got her pad and pen. *I'm going to be fine. Once this arm heals, I can forget about it. The police came by. Have you had to give a statement?*

'Yes. I told the truth as we all had to. We'd be found out if we didn't. My mamma heard Andy has been charged with drink-driving and refusing to take a breath test. He'll probably be banned from driving for a year, she says.' Gabriella became thoughtful. 'But why can't you talk? You told me all about when you were a little girl, but because you've been talking for all these years, I don't understand it happening again now.'

Eléni held her arms open wide to indicate she didn't know either. She began to write. *It's horrible. I try to speak and it's as if the words get stuck at the back of my throat. How can I get back to the craft shop if I can't speak with the customers. I was going to see if I could get some shifts waitressing at the Metropole, but no one will want a silent waitress, will they?*

For the first time since the accident, her whole body dissolved into racking sobs.

'Aww. Come here.' Gabriella stood and pulled her friend into a tight hug. 'I'm sure it won't last long. It won't be like before.'

Cassia entered the room carrying a tray of tea and pastries. Eléni dried her eyes on her sleeve, but not before her mother noticed.

'Oh, don't cry.' She placed the tray down on the coffee table and hugged her daughter.

'She's worried about not being able to speak. I've told her it won't be like last time, will it? She was so little, she didn't know how to speak then. This is temporary, I'm sure of it,' said Gabriella.

Her mother smiled and agreed, but Eléni wasn't sure either of them actually believed it.

'Come on, let's have some tea and some of Eléni's favourite baklavá. Sugar, Gabriella?'

CHAPTER THIRTY-SEVEN

While Eléni recuperated at home, Gabriella's prediction she would soon be able to speak again came true. There was no more tension in the house regarding the row she'd had with her parents before the car accident. She and Bronwen spent a lot of time looking at her sister's teenage magazines and watching television together. The more Eléni relaxed, the more the words flowed. Not many to start with, but once she was able to converse with her family, she knew it had been just a temporary setback. She thought back to when she was a little girl and how frustrated she'd been, dreading going to school, enduring the name calling, seeing the annoyance on the teachers' faces just like the expression she'd seen on the ward sister's face in the hospital.

Gabriella was a frequent visitor too. She kept Eléni up to date with all the gossip of the town, mainly about who was going out with whom. One afternoon, the conversation turned to Andy Smith and the fact he'd been seen riding around Porth Gwyn on a pushbike.

'Getting used to it before he gets banned, I suppose. My mother heard the Mini was a write-off.' Gabriella smiled as the two of them chatted away. 'Oh, it's so good to have the old Eléni back. Mr Williams told me to tell you he's looking forward to having you back in the shop on Monday. Nine o'clock sharp. You know what he's like.'

They both laughed. Eléni's boss was a stickler for punctuality but, as he'd proved during the last few weeks, he was very kind and thoughtful. He came into the shop to cover Eléni's absences himself, even though he was supposed to be semi-retired now and left the running of the shop in their capable hands.

'I thought I'd go into town this afternoon and see him.' Eléni stood and brought over her sketchbook to show her friend her latest pen-and-ink drawings. 'At least having this time on my hands means I've been busy with these. Thank goodness I hadn't broken my drawing hand. What do you think?'

'Oh, these are fab, Eléni. The detail is amazing. I'm sure Mr Williams will be interested once these are framed. The more local to Porth Gwyn the subject is, the better. I love this one of the Rock Park Pavilion. Look at all the scrollwork under the roof.'

'Thanks. I've been building up a portfolio of them and concentrating on local scenes. I've been experimenting with coloured inks too, but I'm not sure.' Eléni held up a drawing of the boathouse at the lake she'd drawn in green and blue inks, as well as her usual use of traditional black.

Gabriella's mouth gaped open. 'Oh, I love it. You know me and colour.'

Eléni smiled as she thought back to the kaleidoscope of colours in Gabriella's wardrobe. She gathered up her sketchbook and placed it in a canvas bag. 'Come on, I'll get my coat and walk back into town with you. You'll have to help me get it on and button it for me, if you don't mind. And could you carry the bag for me, please? Thanks.'

The two friends walked into the hallway and Eléni handed Gabriella her coat from the bentwood coat stand. After Eléni had slipped her good arm into its sleeve, with some manoeuvring, Gabriella fastened her friend's coat over her sling.

'I'm counting the days until this bloomin' cast can come off. It's itchy as hell, too.'

The two continued chatting as they walked into town from Eléni's house. They passed a terrace of red-brick houses with neat, narrow front gardens. Most of them were illuminated with clumps of vibrant daffodils and crocuses that showed spring had finally arrived. This was further evidenced when they passed a wide sloping field where a few baby lambs gambolled around their mothers, their tiny tails wriggling as they sought milk.

'I love this time of year,' said Gabriella. 'All the awful grey of winter has gone.'

It was true, thought Eléni. Now the cloud of not being able to speak had lifted, her monotone mood had faded too. Seeing the vibrant spring colours seemed to reflect her frame of mind. She hadn't told a soul, not even Gabriella, but she was more determined than ever to travel to the country of her birth and find her uncle. She would make plans and when she was ready, she would tell everyone then. Before long, they were walking along the main street into Porth Gwyn. Opposite the late Victorian hotel where Eléni was hoping to get work, they turned into a road to the left. *Siop Crefft*, the Welsh craft shop, with its large picture bay windows gleaming on either side of a wide glass door, was situated a little way up from the halt sign.

'I'll come with you to carry the bag in and then I'll leave you to it. After my shift tomorrow, perhaps we can go to Smoky Joe's for a coffee?'

The bell rang as they opened the door. Mr Williams looked up from behind the counter and when he noticed Eléni, he smiled. 'Oh, it's so good to see you, *bach*. Your good friend here has been keeping me up to date with what's going on.'

'I'll put the bag here. I'll be off, Mr Williams. See you for a coffee tomorrow, Eléni.'

'Okay, Gabriella. There's nothing to report. I'm expecting a new delivery of the Welsh love spoons tomorrow, so if you've got time to unpack them and price them, that would be fine. Trade's been very slow today, but it would appear there's a coach tour due in across the road tomorrow, so we should get more customers in then.'

'Bye, and thanks, Gabbie. I'll see you then.'

Eléni enjoyed the days when the shop was busy. Talking to the customers about the Welsh crafts on sale was what she loved most about the job. She made it her business to find out as much as she could about the artists and craftspeople who exhibited there.

Mr Williams brought a fold-up chair from the stockroom for Eléni to sit down.

'Now, then, *bach*. Are you sure you're ready to come back to work?'

'I am. I can't wait to get back.'

The look on the elderly man's face was one of relief. 'Well. If you're sure, how about you just work a few hours in the morning this week and I take over from you in the afternoons? There are no coach tours booked in for next week so you shouldn't be too busy. How does that sound?'

Eléni beamed. 'Perfect, Mr Williams.'

Together they looked at her new drawings and, as Gabriella had predicted, he was very interested.

'These are your best yet, *bach*. All the local scenes will sell. The visitors can't seem to get enough of the lake and the Rock Park, so I'll buy these six from you.'

'Oh, thank you. That's wonderful! I haven't wasted my time at home then.'

It would all help with building up her savings ready for her trip to Kefalonia.

After her shift, Eléni made her way across to Porth Gwyn Library. The solid red-brick building was set back from the street in the immaculate town grounds, which were set out in lawns and gardens. The focal point was the war memorial on which were the names of those who had lost their lives in the two world wars. Eléni's baba had never missed an armistice parade each November if he'd been home on leave when they'd lived in Cardiff and did the same in Porth Gwyn, remembering men like himself who had been members of the armed forces protecting their country.

She entered the quiet building and approached the desk where a grey-haired woman was busy sorting the books from a shelf marked *returns*.

'Excuse me. Where would I find a section with old newspapers, please? 1953 to be precise.'

The woman stopped what she was doing and turned to Eléni.

'If you go through the double glass doors on your right, you'll find the archive section in there. They're arranged in year order. The *Celtic Chronicle*, the Welsh daily paper, is in the centre of the room along with the main British dailies. All are displayed alphabetically. If you have a particular date in mind, I can take it to a table for you to examine. Of course, if you want a wider search, you can use the microfiche on the screens there. I'll come with you.'

Eléni now knew the woman as Margaret Harris. *Mrs*, from reading her name badge.

'Thank you, Mrs Harris. You've been very helpful. As it happens, I do know the exact date. It's the twelfth of August 1953 and maybe a few from the days following.'

The librarian retrieved the *Celtic Chronicle* from that date and some from the days after. She placed them on a large table and invited Eléni to sit down. 'I'll give you these to start and maybe a couple of nationals as well. *The Times* and maybe this tabloid. Just be careful as you handle them, please.'

'Thank you. That's great.' Eléni looked at each front page and it was the *Celtic Chronicle* alone that ran the story as a lead. It was dated 13 August, the day after the earthquake had happened. The name of the reporter was Rhodri Jones. She'd heard that name before. Yes, it was the reporter's name that had accompanied the missing-child advert, with what she believed was a photo of her. The same reporter who'd written the article dated 15 August that she'd found in her mother's journal, with the photo of a woman she believed to be her mother. She read the article carefully.

A day after the devastating earthquake razed most of this beautiful island to the ground, help is at last getting through. The British Royal Navy vessel HMS Daring arrived this morning from Malta and already essential food and medical supplies are reaching the homeless and injured. Across the bay, the town of Lixouri is now being referred to as 'The Death Town'. I spoke to one woman waiting outside a pile of rubble that had once been her home. She told me, 'I won't leave him. Until he comes out. Dead or alive. I wait.' She couldn't say any more. Her sobs took away her heartfelt words. I didn't ask who 'he' was. Husband, father, son, grandson. There is so much heartache and so much grief here on these hot streets.

A Greek Earthquake Appeal has been set up. Please give what you can, no matter how small. You may donate via your local branch of the Midland Bank.

Eléni sat back in her chair. *I lived through that!* The emotion was overwhelming when she realised how close she had been to dying along with her birth parents and grandparents. If it hadn't been for her father and his fellow sailors, she wouldn't be alive.

It wasn't a long article but it was accompanied by several photographs, including mounds of rubble in the streets, damaged buildings and lines of people handing along boxes of supplies. At the end of the line nearest to the camera was a lone woman. This photograph was clearer than the one in the newspaper cutting from her mother's journal. Eléni knew then that she'd been right. The woman was her mamá. Seeing the images as evidence of the disaster was far more powerful than a full page of text. Eléni was drained. She'd known some things about what had happened from what her parents had felt obliged to tell her after she'd confronted them, but seeing the evidence for herself in picture form made her sick to her stomach. Her mother had also experienced the terror of it and her father had been the one to rescue her. No wonder they wanted to forget and protect her from the horror of what had happened. In her head, she heard her angry words again and saw the hurt look on her mother's face. She felt ashamed.

She took out a small writing pad from her bag and rifled through the rest of the contents to find her pen. She made a note of what she could see in the photos. She would return with her sketchbook and record what she saw in pen and ink. The other national papers had shorter reports on their inside pages, but it was Rhodri Jones's report that had made headline news. She was still going to travel to Kefalonia. She had to. But now she would talk to her parents and try to make them realise why — she needed to find out her true identity. She would not be betraying or rejecting them. *I know Baba will understand. I just hope I can go with my mother's blessing, too.*

CHAPTER THIRTY-EIGHT

Two months later, May 1973

It was the day Eléni had been waiting for. Her mother was taking her to Porth Gwyn Hospital to have the cast taken off her arm. She'd managed to return to work as planned and, as Mr Williams had promised, she'd been working on the till where she'd become proficient at using just her right arm while the other was supported in a sling. Her plans to get a waitressing job would have to wait.

'Ready? I bet you can't wait to get that old thing off.'

'I can't wait. It's so heavy as well as itchy.' Eléni remembered being told by the nurse on the first check-up that on no account was she to poke anything down inside the plaster cast to relieve the itching. She didn't dare admit she had been doing just that with a knitting needle!

Cassia parked her car in the spaces along the front of the hospital. Once inside, they were led to a waiting room and it wasn't long before Eléni was called in to have the cast removed.

She looked down at her arm and wriggled her fingers as if to prove to herself everything was working. The skin was wrinkled and shiny where it had been covered in plaster for the last eight weeks. Had it really been that long since the accident?

The nurse smiled at her. 'Yes, it all works. Just make sure you treat it with a bit of care to begin with. Here's a sheet with some exercises to help build up your strength again.'

After thanking her, Eléni joined her mother outside in the waiting room.

'All done?' said her mother. 'Why don't we go and have an ice cream up at the lake? It's a nice day and it's not often it's just the two of us, is it?'

Eléni smiled. The row hadn't been mentioned again and Eléni had been putting off mentioning a trip to Kefalonia. Instead, she'd enjoyed feeling close to her mother again. The visit to the library had brought home to her how terrible it must have been for Cassia living through the trauma of the earthquake. Eléni had been back to the archives several times and Margaret Harris had gone out of her way to be helpful. She'd found books about Kefalonia's varied history and its geological past. Eléni had learned that because of its position, major earthquakes were commonplace. She'd also borrowed more modern books that told her how tourism had been picking back up after the restoration of the towns around Argostoli and the photographs had showed her what to expect when she visited the island. What would her mother's reaction be if she could persuade her to return, she wondered. How would the new town appear to her mamá, who had lived there before the earthquake had ruined everything?

Ice creams in hand, they found a bench overlooking the lake. Several swans, their white feathers gleaming in the sunlight, swam past them. Their long necks gave them an air of importance as they were followed by the smaller ducks.

'You used to love to bring bread for the ducks when we first arrived in Porth Gwyn.' Cassia smiled.

'Why did we have to move to Cardiff?' Eléni watched her mother's eyes darken.

'Oh, it seemed better to be nearer to the docks when your father came home on leave.' Cassia paused and then added, 'Uncle Glyn was worried about Auntie Gwladys being on her own. She'd had a fall, see. It worked out well, didn't it? And of course, Bronwen arrived soon after.'

Nothing to do with a reporter turning up, then. Could the reporter have been Rhodri Jones? 'You must have missed Porth Gwyn, though. It's so much better than a big city.'

Her mother nodded. 'Yes, but I'm happy here now. I wasn't back then but I knew when your baba left the Navy, we'd always come back. I want you and Bronwen to be happy here too. Shall we have a walk around the lake before going home? It's exactly a mile, so your father says.'

* * *

Her next day off from the craft shop was her birthday and Eléni called in the Metropole to see if there was any work going. She'd waited tables in a café in Cardiff and at Smoky Joe's coffee bar since she'd returned to Porth Gwyn, only leaving to work in the craft shop. The waitressing job was going to be in addition to the hours she worked for Mr Williams. She had to start earning more money.

The young woman behind reception took down Eléni's details.

'I'll pass this on to the manager and he'll be in touch. I'm afraid I don't think they need any more waitresses at the moment, but I may be wrong. Of course, with summer coming up, it's always a busier time of the year for visitors then, isn't it?'

Eléni's heart sank. She'd set her sights on getting an evening job.

'What about positions for chambermaids? I could always work on my days off.' She knew she sounded desperate. 'And some weekends.'

The woman shook her head. 'I'm sorry, but it would be daytime and most of our ladies work every day.'

Eléni thanked the receptionist and left the hotel foyer.

Porth Gwyn was a spa town and full of large hotels built at the height of the time when visitors had come to take the waters. Eléni smiled to herself when she remembered how she and Bronwen had tasted the water from the chalybeate fountain in Rock Park.

'Ugh!' Bronwen had grimaced. 'It's foul. How can that awful taste be good for you?'

Yet many people in the nineteenth century had believed it was and had paid handsomely to stay in the town.

Eléni walked through the gardens opposite and tried her luck at the hotel on the side street. The receptionist there told her the same thing — the manager would be in touch.

'What's your telephone number?'

'Porth Gwyn 2419. Thank you.' All Eléni could do was hope.

She strolled back to call on Gabriella in the craft shop.

'I came in to tell you I've had no luck getting the waitressing job. Mind, it was only the receptionist saying she doubted there were any vacancies. It looks as if I won't be going anywhere soon.'

Gabriella was the only person she'd told about her Kefalonia plans. 'Sorry to hear that. But didn't you say you got some money from your great-aunt after she died? And what about the money your parents gave you for your twenty-first?'

Eléni had totted up all the money she had in her building society book and, yes, she might just have enough for a plane ticket, but she had no idea what it would cost to live in Kefalonia for a few months. 'I'm not expecting to find my uncle in a few weeks, so I have to allow for a longer stay and it's going to cost money if I stay in a hotel or lodging house. My next day off is Thursday so I'm going to go to Credenford on the bus. There's a travel agent on the main street. I hope to figure out the cost then.'

'It's so exciting.' Gabriella rubbed her hands together. 'I just know you're going to find him . . . and maybe a handsome Greek Adonis too.' The doorbell chimed as a group of women entered the shop. 'I'd better go. See you later.'

On her walk back home, Eléni thought back to what Gabriella had said. Her excitement about her forthcoming trip would not be matched by her mother. Things were good between them at the moment, so Eléni didn't want to spoil it until it was necessary to tell her.

As she opened the door, she heard her mother on the phone.

'Thank you, I'll tell my daughter.' Cassia turned to Eléni. 'That was The Crown. Something about a waitressing job. The girl said she'd spoken to the manager and they don't have any vacancies at the moment, but will keep your details on file. I didn't know you were leaving the craft shop.'

Eléni took off her coat and hung it on the hall stand.

'I'm not. I love working for Mr Williams. I'm just trying to get more work to boost my wages. You know I'm saving.' Her heart pounded as she waited for her mother to ask what she was saving for, but the question didn't come.

CHAPTER THIRTY-NINE

'Before I work on some more drawings, I'm going to make a cup of tea. Do you want one? Slice of lemon with it?'

Her mother nodded. 'Yes, please. I know you'd love me to drink it with milk like you, but I can't break a habit of a lifetime, can I?'

They both laughed as Cassia followed Eléni into the kitchen. For as long as she could remember, there were certain traditions her mother had brought from Greece that she always followed, even though most of the time she'd embraced Welsh culture. Auntie Gwladys had taught her to bake the best Welsh cakes, and her bara brith was legendary. Her baba said her mother's lamb cawl was even better than Granny Megan's. His mother had died when he was a young boy and it was the reason he and Uncle Glyn had been so close to Great Auntie Gwladys. She'd practically brought them up.

After serving the tea and taking a couple of pastries from the tin, Eléni excused herself and went up to her bedroom, which faced the back garden. She marvelled at the straight lines of mown grass marking the long lawn, her baba's pride and joy. From a life at sea, he'd now settled into being the perfect gardener for this detached house on the outskirts of Porth

Gwyn. Two neat rows of standard roses edged the wide path by the patio. They would soon be laden with tresses of pale-peach blooms with the most marvellous perfume. They were most fragrant on a balmy June evening, wafting up through her open window. It was one of the first things she'd noticed when she'd moved to Porth Gwyn from Cardiff. Her great-aunt's house had had a courtyard concreted with crazy paving at the back, rather than a garden.

She pulled out her sketchbook from her desk under the window. She selected the six drawings Mr Williams had thought would appeal to customers most and removed them from the pad with great care. Placing them between two sheets of stiff card, she put them aside to take for Mr Williams to get framed.

She took out the pile of borrowed library books about Kefalonia that she'd hidden in the long drawer under her wardrobe. Selecting one about the 1953 earthquake, she flicked through the pages to find images of the destroyed buildings. One showed a house with one wall and the contents of a bedroom still intact. She began to sketch it, first in soft pencil to map out the correct proportions and perspective, and then worked over the markings in pen and ink. The building slowly became real on the page and Eléni sucked in a deep breath to prevent tears from forming. It was as if she was there, witnessing the terror of what had happened to the family who had once called this place their home. Again, she thought of what her mother had experienced and wondered if, like her, she would want to lock it away in a hidden compartment in her mind. Her thoughts were interrupted by Bronwen knocking at the door.

'Eléni, can I come in?' Eléni covered her drawing with the sheet of blotting paper she always kept to hand when working in ink and closed her sketchpad.

Bronwen breezed in before Eléni could answer.

She spotted the books on Eléni's desk and picked one up.

'What's this? I thought you'd given up the idea of going to Kefalonia. Well, you haven't mentioned it since, anyway.'

Eléni shook her head. 'No, but you must promise not to tell Mamá and Baba. Since the accident, they've been fantastic. But I *have* to go, Bron. It was such a shock to find out I'm not who I thought I was, but I do understand why they didn't tell me. I've been reading all I can about the earthquake and what Mamá went through. No wonder she doesn't want to talk about it. But I may have blood relatives out there. I need to find out. It won't make any difference to how I feel about Mamá and Baba or you, I promise.'

'But why keep it a secret, then?'

'Because Mamá is afraid of losing me to my real family. And she and Baba broke the law. I'm saving up everything I can and when it's all settled, I'll tell them and ask for their blessing. At the moment, I want to keep enjoying how close we all are. So, please, Bron. Please don't say anything yet.'

'All right. But I don't think they're going to be happy you've been planning everything behind their backs. Remember how you felt when you were the last to know about not being theirs. I'll see you later.'

Eléni thought about what Bronwen had said. Being the last to know was what had hurt her most, but she was still a long way off from booking her trip. If she didn't get another job, it would be next year before she could afford to go.

* * *

The following Thursday, Eléni travelled to Credenford as she'd planned. At first, her mother had talked about joining her, but to Eléni's relief, she remembered she'd promised to have coffee with a friend.

Eléni knew it would have been difficult not to explain why she needed to slip away on her own if her mother had accompanied her. The hour-long journey to Credenford gave Eléni time to think. She shuddered as they rounded the bend where Andy had misjudged the speed of his Mini and they'd travelled much faster than the bus was currently going. The ambulance with its blue lights flashing had got her there as fast as it could.

Looking out of the window, she noticed how the landscape had changed. The soil was now a rich red-brown and she remembered her father telling her it was good for growing hops that produced his beloved beer. Soon the bus was travelling through villages filled with picturesque black-and-white houses that lined up on either side of the road. Most had steps up to the front doors. Some had thatched roofs and she imagined the climbing roses that would soon trail over arches in the gardens and maybe even over some front doors. The scene resembled the colourful images she'd seen on tins of chocolates, but here was proof the idyll did exist. It was a stark contrast from the pictures of what was left of the houses in Argostoli. Perhaps when she arrived there, the new town would have regained some of its former glory but, even then, it would not be anything like the villages here.

It wasn't long before the coach pulled into the bus station. The main street was only a short walk away and Get Away Travel was found about halfway down. The large front window was covered in posters that advertised the holidays and travel destinations on offer. Inside the office there were stands with brochures organised in alphabetical order. Eléni pulled out one for Greece. There were lots of Greek islands mentioned in addition to mainland Greece, but nothing about Kefalonia. Her heart sank.

Eléni waited for an assistant to become free and then sat in front of their desk.

'I'd like to travel to Kefalonia. But it seems to be the one island not advertised in here.' She pointed to the brochure.

The young woman opposite was dressed in a smart navy-blue suit with a red-and-blue neckerchief.

'It's a beautiful island, but, of course, it was devastated by the 1953 earthquake. Although it's been almost twenty years, tourism is just starting to grow again there. So many islanders left. Of course, with the twentieth anniversary coming up, everyone's hoping this will be a bumper year for them. Apart from one small area in the north, everywhere had to be rebuilt. The new hotels are more in a villa style than the sixties tower blocks of say, Spain. It's very pretty. The airport opened last year. You'll need to fly to Athens and then to Kefalonia from there.'

'Oh. What about hotels or lodging houses? Is it easy to book accommodation? I need to visit there.' Eléni's voice cracked. She was surprised at the magnitude of emotion pent up inside her and how important the visit had become.

The assistant reached behind her and retrieved a brochure with a general heading, *Travelling to Greece*.

'Let's have look in here. I can see this means a lot to you.'

'Thank you.'

'In here, it's not package holidays but visits in general. You have a section on flights and then a separate one on hotels and places to stay. So, for instance, if you just need a flight and are staying with relatives or have a home there, you pick a flight from the flight timetable, and it may be all you need. Here, look. Flights from Heathrow to Athens.'

It was more than Eléni was expecting. In her head, she totted up everything she had in her account. 'Thank you. This looks like what I need.' She took the brochure from the assistant and left the shop.

On the coach journey home, she scoured the pages of the brochure for the best prices and any low-cost accommodation in Argostoli itself. As long as it was clean and central, she didn't need to stay in a fancy hotel that was going to eat into her money. In spite of not being able to fly direct from Britain, Eléni was more determined than ever to get to the country of her birth. The coloured photographs of the turquoise sea and busy fishing harbours, together with the vibrancy of the fresh fruit, vegetables and cheeses made her dead set on making the visit happen. She put the brochure in the bottom of her bag and walked up the hill from the bus station to her house. She couldn't wait to tell Gabriella her plans.

Her mother was already back and Eléni could hear music blaring from Bronwen's room.

'Hiya, Mamá. I'm back.'

Her mother was in the kitchen preparing their evening meal. 'How did you get on?' Eléni went to tell her about what she'd found out and just stopped herself in time. Her mother knew nothing of her visit to the travel agents.

'Get anything nice in the shops? I don't see any bags apart from your handbag. Not like your sister.' She laughed. 'She'd buy up the whole of Chelsea Girl if she could. By the way, someone from the Metropole called. You need to call in tomorrow and they'll talk to you about a waitressing job. I told them you'll be working, but maybe you can slip over in your lunch hour. They said that would be fine.'

'Oh, really. That's great. Thank you, Mamá. No, I just had a browse around. I bought some new sketching pencils from the art shop next to the cathedral.'

'I still don't know what you want more work for. It's not as if you spend much, is it?'

CHAPTER FORTY

CASSIA

Cassia continued peeling the potatoes. Smiling, she knew she was lucky to have both her girls still living at home. This time next year, Bronwen would be at university. Now the awful row with Eléni was all forgotten, she enjoyed the feeling of them being a tight family unit again. An image of her handsome first husband entered her head. She'd been younger than Eléni when she'd married Nikos after the terrible argument with her father. After his death, she'd had to survive on her own in a town where she'd known no one. She still thought of Eléni as being a child. The sound of her daughters chatting and laughing together made her happy. *No longer the silent sister, eh, Eléni?*

Cassia filled a saucepan with water and put the potatoes on the electric stove to boil. She was relieved Eléni had forgotten all about her threat to go to Kefalonia. She hadn't mentioned it again. Cassia knew there was nothing she could have done to stop her daughter. She was over twenty-one and officially an adult. Her heart racing, Cassia gripped the edge of the table. But what if that was what she needed the second job for? She could be saving up to go. But surely, she wouldn't plan it in secret . . . would she?

She heard Tom's car pull up outside. The row had not been mentioned by Tom or Bronwen either. It was as if it was all a bad dream and had never happened. But what if that was what Eléni wanted them to think?

'Hi, *cariad*.' His voice carried along the hallway. 'Something smells nice. I'm starving.'

He entered the kitchen and kissed her on the cheek.

'Shepherd's pie. Just for you. A change from moussaka, eh?'

They both laughed. Not being able to get aubergines in Porth Gwyn, Cassia's moussaka was nothing like the authentic Greek dish — she had to use slices of potato in between the meat layers instead. She'd switched from attempting Greek dishes with the ingredients she could find available to Welsh ones. Today was one of Tom's favourites. Just like Auntie Gwladys used to make, in his opinion.

'It won't be long. I've just got to mash the potatoes for the topping and put it back in the oven to brown.'

'Had a good day? I fancy a cuppa. Do you want one?' Tom took two mugs from the pine mug tree and filled the kettle.

'Yes, I met up with Pam. She needed a shoulder to cry on. Her mother's very ill and not expected to last much longer. Poor thing. I would have gone to Credenford with Eléni, but I didn't like to let Pam down.' Cassia thought back to Eugenia's letter from a few years ago, begging her to return to Kefalonia to see their mother before she passed. She'd always regret her refusal had caused the rift between them.

Tom was talking. 'Cass? I said, did Eléni enjoy her day off?'

'Sorry. I think so. She didn't buy much. The Met rang while she was out and asked her to call in about a waitressing job tomorrow. She's serious about getting more work, you know. Don't you think it's odd? She won't have any free time.

Do you know why she wants this extra job? She says she's saving, but she hasn't said for what. You don't think . . .'

Tom reached across the kitchen table and took Cassia's hand. 'I know no more than you, Cass. But I do think we have to let her do what she wants. She's a grown woman and if it hadn't been for her being so shy and those years when she didn't speak, she'd have left home years ago. She'll tell us when she's ready.'

'Who'll tell us what when she's ready?' Bronwen entered the room.

Cassia and Tom exchanged glances. 'Your mamá can't understand why Eléni needs another job and wonders what she's saving up for.'

'Maybe she's planning to elope with Andy Smith and be the breadwinner because he's lost his job again.' Bronwen laughed.

'It's not funny. Anyway, I thought she wanted nothing more to do with him.'

'I'm just teasing you. I know how much you can't stand him, Baba.'

Cassia stood up to take the shepherd's pie out from the oven.

'Will you call your sister down?'

Bronwen went out into the hallway.

'Why did you say that?' Cassia whispered to her husband. 'She'll tell Eléni now.'

'And what if she does? You should ask her yourself.' Tom sighed. Cassia knew better than to mention it again.

* * *

Eléni got the job at the Met. After receiving training in 'silver service', she was given three shifts a week serving dinner to the guests.

Cassia listened as she recounted what she'd had to do.

'They're so strict, Mamá. My uniform must be neatly pressed and my hair pinned back under the cap. Oh, and my skirt mustn't be too short either.' Excitement showed in her voice. 'I'm used to that after waiting at table in the Louis in Cardiff, though.'

'You'll have no trouble looking smart. But it was afternoon teas you served at the Louis, wasn't it? So how did you get on with the "silver service"? I'd be all fingers and thumbs.'

'I got the hang of it in the end, and carrying two plates along one arm, too. I'll let you know after my first shift tonight. Wish me luck.'

Eléni left the living room to get ready. It was good to see her daughter so animated. She was back to the old Eléni.

* * *

Over the next few weeks Eléni came home exhausted after each shift at the hotel, but she was full of stories about the guests and what had been on the menu each night. She didn't work on the day off she had from the craft shop so she had a full day with no work. Each week she handed over some of her wages to Cassia towards her keep.

'There's no need. But thank you. I thought you were saving?' said Cassia.

'I am, but if I wasn't living here with you and Baba I'd be paying rent somewhere, wouldn't I? It's only fair. Did I tell you Mr Williams had my drawings framed and four have sold already?'

Cassia beamed at her daughter. 'I'm not surprised. They are stunning.'

'Thank you, Mamá. You'll never guess, the manager at the Metropole bought one of them and as you walk along the corridor from the foyer, there's one of my drawings among the other Welsh artists' work. It's the one of the waterfall in Rock Park.'

'Oh, I love that one.' Cassia was pleased to see her daughter so happy. If Eléni continued to sell her drawings, she could see her fulfilling her dream of renting a space for a small gallery of her own. Then, she would need every penny she earned to finance it so perhaps Cassia would put the money aside each week and hand it back to her when the time came.

On one day off, Eléni went to Credenford again.

'Was it busy?' Cassia asked her when she came in.

'Not too bad. The sun was out so I expect that's why. Do you know if Bronwen's in tonight? You and Baba will be here, won't you?'

Cassia was puzzled. Her face creased into a frown. 'Yes, and as far as I know about Bron. She's not going out much now her exams are approaching. Why do you ask?'

'I just want to tell you something and I'd prefer to tell you all together.'

Cassia's heart raced. What could be so important that her daughter needed them all together? What did she have to tell them? Her mind went back to what she'd found in Eléni's room earlier.

Eléni hugged her mother. 'Don't look so worried, Mamá. It's nothing to fret about.'

But Cassia knew it was.

CHAPTER FORTY-ONE

ELÉNI

The time had come for Eléni to share her plans with her parents and sister. She'd booked and paid for her plane ticket to Athens and from there to Kefalonia. She'd made another visit to Get Away Travel in Credenford. The assistant had found the best route for her journey and appeared to be as excited as Eléni herself. In one of the brochures she'd been given, Eléni found a small family-run hotel situated in the main square of Argostoli. It looked quite basic, but reports were it was clean and the family who ran it were friendly and welcoming. The main attraction for her was the price. It was a lot cheaper than the larger hotels with more amenities. All she wanted was a base and to make her money last as long as it could.

Her stomach churned as she flicked through the books, a map of the island and the travel brochure she was going to show everyone. Her mother's worried face earlier told Eléni it was she who needed to be persuaded that the trip to Kefalonia was a good idea. She was prepared for resistance from her. She was sure her baba and Bronwen would wish her well.

She left everything on the chest of drawers and went downstairs after hearing her mother call everyone for their evening meal. Once they were seated, her mother dished out the steaming lamb cawl into large bowls. Her mother had prepared it before going to her typing classes. She'd never worked while the girls were small but with Bronwen going away next year, she'd talked about getting a job as she'd have more time on her hands.

Eléni didn't have much of an appetite as she rehearsed what she was going to say later. In the end, her mother's announcement paved the way for her.

'Eléni's got something to tell us after dinner, but I've got some news, too. I've got a job!'

Everyone looked at Cassia in amazement. She'd always said she wouldn't work as looking after the house and family was a full-time job. When she'd started her typing classes at the beginning of the term, she'd said she'd get a job at the end of it but Eléni wasn't sure she'd go through with it.

'Where?' the three of them said in unison.

'This morning, before my typing class, I went for an interview at the clerk's office in County Hall. I had to show my typing speed and they seemed to like I could do shorthand, too. They don't need to wait to see if I pass my exams. I can start a week Monday.'

Tom got up from his side of the table and kissed her cheek. 'Well done, *cariad*. If that's what you want.'

'Yes,' said Bronwen. 'It will be good for you.'

Eléni could feel her mother's eyes on her.

'Eléni, what do you think?'

'I'm just surprised. I thought you didn't agree with working mothers after having to work when I was young. You never said a thing.' Why did she say that? She wouldn't be here anyway.

Her mother got up and took a booklet from the magazine rack next to Tom's wooden armchair in the kitchen.

'Well, it seems it's not just me who doesn't say a thing.' It was a brochure on Greek holidays that Eléni had taken when she'd visited Get Away Travel for the first time. 'Planning

238

something?' Cassia's face was blotchy. 'When were you going to tell us?'

Eléni's face and neck reddened. 'Where did you get that?'

'Too much time on my hands. When I stripped your bed, I spotted the corner peeping out from under it.' She held up the brochure. 'Oh, look. The page on Kefalonia has been turned down.'

Eléni didn't like the sarcasm in her mother's voice. She was desperate not to rise to the bait. She'd planned to tell them in a calm manner, but her mother had just scuppered it. Her father began to clear away the crockery and pile it near the sink.

Eléni went upstairs to fetch the books, brochures and the all-important map.

They all sat around the table. Her mother's face was like thunder.

Eléni spread the map over the table.

'When I found out you were not my real parents, I was angry you hadn't told me and said some awful things. I'm sorry. I do understand why you took me away from the island. I'll always be grateful for that. Since then, I've been trying to find out everything about the island and what happened. The more I read, the more I understood why you did what you did.' She reached across and squeezed her mother's hand. 'You will always be my parents. Always.'

Cassia's eyes had welled with unshed tears. 'We couldn't leave you. You had no one . . . or so we thought. We really believed that.'

'I've been spending time in the library and reading about the earthquake. I think I found you in one photo, Mamá. Talking to a reporter. Remember the article appealing for people who may have seen a child who looks like me? It means I have an uncle who looked for me, doesn't it? So you see, I have to go to Kefalonia and see if I can find my uncle. He may have children, so I could have cousins too. It won't mean I love you both or Bron any less.'

'Loads of people go travelling these days. I want to go after uni.' *Thank you, sister dear.* 'I think it's exciting. Especially if I can join you after A levels.'

Eléni proceeded to tell them about how she was going to get to Kefalonia and the hotel she'd booked into. 'I think it was Argostoli where Baba brought me out from the house. So I chose a place there.'

Her mother nodded, but didn't comment.

'Please say something, Mamá. Just think of me going travelling. I'll be back, I promise.'

'I don't want you to go. Go to another Greek island if you have to travel, but when we left Kefalonia to come here I vowed I'd never return. I didn't even go back to see my mother when she was dying or go to her funeral.' Cassia's voice cracked with emotion.

She stood and dashed from the room.

'Leave her. She'll come round. She'll have to,' said Tom.

'I don't understand why she's so against me going. I know it was wrong to keep all the planning to myself, but I didn't want to upset her until I knew I was definitely going. I knew she'd be like this.'

'Yes, why *is* Mamá so upset? It's been almost twenty years since she left. Eléni is a grown woman.' Bronwen was as puzzled as Eléni.

Their father sighed. 'She's afraid. Afraid, if you find your uncle, he will want to make up for all the years he hasn't had you in his life. For all we know, you may be the sole blood relative he has left. He could put pressure on you to stay. When he came looking for you, your mother didn't even tell *me* until the day you found the letter and confronted us about not being your birth parents. In her eyes, we broke the law by taking you. Her way of dealing with it is to shut out anything to do with her homeland.'

Cassia entered the kitchen, her eyes red-rimmed. 'Sorry. I just wish you'd told me what you were planning. I think it's a mistake, but, as your baba and sister say, you're a grown woman. I don't want your heart to be broken if you can't find your uncle or, worse still, he rejects you because of what me and your father did. Now, who wants some jam roly-poly?'

Eyebrows were raised and looks were exchanged by everyone around the table as Cassia poured the custard into a serving jug and spooned out dishes of their favourite pudding. The subject was closed . . . for now.

CHAPTER FORTY-TWO

Four weeks later

Early-morning light poured into Eléni's bedroom. Opening her eyes, her stomach knotted again as it had done repeatedly during the last few days. *This is it! I'm returning to the place of my birth.* The day she'd been planning and waiting for had arrived. She'd hardly slept a wink. Her mind whirled with thoughts of what was ahead. It was just going to be Eléni and her father going to the airport. Bronwen had said her goodbyes the night before because of their very early start.

'You will send loads of postcards, won't you?' she said. 'Let me know what the local talent's like.' The two girls laughed.

Eléni realised how much she was going to miss her sister.

There was a knock at the door. 'Can I come in, *agápi mou*? I thought you'd like a cup of tea.'

'Oh, thank you.' She sat up and took the cup from her mother. *You haven't slept much either, have you, Mamá?* 'You shouldn't have got up at this ungodly hour.'

'What and leave my girl to get ready on her own?' She smiled as she squeezed Eléni's hand. 'Your baba's in the bathroom now and will give you a shout when he's out.' Leaving her mother was going to be difficult. Eléni was torn between feeling she was letting her down and doing something she knew she had to do.

After a quick breakfast, it was time to leave.

'I'll be back before you know it, Mamá.' Her throat tightened and she willed herself not to cry.

Her mother's eyes shone with tears. 'I know. Stay safe, *agápi mou*. Here . . .' She thrust a sealed envelope into Eléni's hand. 'Open it on the plane.'

'Come on, you two. We don't want to be cutting it fine.' Her father got in the car and started the engine.

'Bye, Mamá.' When Eléni kissed her mother goodbye, her cheeks were wet with tears. Cassia brushed them away and pulled her into a tight embrace.

'One last *cwtch*. The Welsh word for hug is the best. Now you go.'

Before her father drove off, Eléni noticed her mother had already gone back inside the house, not able to watch her go.

* * *

It was Eléni's first time travelling by plane. She bit her lip as she looked around her at the crowds of people walking in the direction of the various departure gates. Her father had accompanied her as far as he could, but now it was all up to her.

She found her seat matching the number on her boarding card and sat down, only to be asked to stand again by the person whose seat was past hers.

'Hi, I'm Betsy. Are you travelling alone too?'

'Eléni. Yes, I've never flown before.'

The two young women began to chat and learned much about each other. It turned out Betsy was a seasoned traveller. This flight to Athens was the third leg of a flight that had begun in California. She'd travelled from there to New York and then on to London, where she'd spent a few weeks sight-seeing before boarding this plane.

'Once I get to Greece, I'm joining a group of friends to sail around some of the Greek islands. It's something I've always wanted to do.'

Eléni was very grateful to have Betsy's company on the first leg of her journey to Kefalonia. They touched down in Athens and parted company in the airport, with Betsy going through passport control and customs, and Eléni finding the boarding gate for her next plane. Her mouth was dry. She was travelling the last leg of her journey alone, to a place she'd never visited before and not knowing what she was going to find.

Once aboard the plane, Eléni looked down over the ancient city from her window seat. The panoramic view was impressive. From her mother's journal, she'd read her parents had brought her here on their way to Wales. Eléni had thought she'd been too young to remember much, but, suddenly, images of the old lady, Sophia, who she'd found out had played a part in saving her life, and Sophia's daughter, who'd lived in Athens, entered her head. Now a memory of her mother wearing a pretty dress for her wedding to her papa, and Sophia giving her a little bag tied with silky ribbon and full of pink-and-white sugar almonds, surfaced. The next day they'd sailed out of the port on a larger ship and on a much longer journey to get to Wales. The memories had been buried deep for all these years but as she'd looked down on the vanishing city, they had resurfaced.

It was then she remembered her mother's letter. She'd placed it in her bag to read on the plane, but this was the first opportunity she'd had to be alone to read it. Her mamá's distinctive cursive handwriting on the envelope brought a lump to her throat. She ran her finger along the seal and took out the folded letter.

Agapití *Eléni*,
By the time you read this, you will be well on your way to Kefalonia. Although I did not want you to go, I want you to know it is only because I love you with all my heart and

am so afraid of losing you. Like Baba says, you have every right to know who you are and I am the one in the wrong for not giving you my blessing earlier.

You will have a big task ahead of you to find your uncle as it's twenty years since the earthquake, so I am enclosing two addresses to help you. One is the address of your Aunt Eugenia. When your yiayiá died in 1963, she still lived at the smallholding just outside Fiscardo then. Because I refused to go to her, I have not heard from Eugenia since and I regret that. If she is still there, I know she would help you no matter what she thinks of me.

The other address is not so accurate. It's a street name, I'm afraid. Byron Street is where my neighbour, Sophia, and I lived. Our houses were 145 and 163. Your house was somewhere on the same side as ours, but it would have had a lower odd number.

Eléni's pulse raced and her skin prickled. If she could find the street, how would it feel to visit the actual spot where her parents and grandparents were killed? She read on.

Please stay safe. Write often and tell us how you are getting on. I would not recognise what you'll be seeing in Argostoli as my last memories of the island are ones of horror and destruction, but if you do manage to visit Fiscardo to see your aunt, Kefalonia was and I hope still is beautiful.

I'm sorry for everything I've put you through.
All my love,
Mamá xx

Eléni looked at the two addresses written on two separate pieces of card. She tucked them back inside the letter, folded it and returned it to the envelope. A warm feeling washed over her. *Oh, Mamá, I do love you and nothing will ever change that. Efcharistó.* To receive her mother's blessing meant everything to her.

CHAPTER FORTY-THREE

Kefalonia, June 1973

It was mid-afternoon when Eléni arrived in Argostoli. The sun was still high in the sky, so the intense heat reflected from the paved streets and pale-rendered buildings. She was glad to walk along the shady side of the road as she searched for the small hotel where she was to stay for her first two weeks. Eléni placed her suitcase down on the pavement to take a rest. Her stomach churned with both excitement and nervousness as it dawned on her what she was doing. She was in a foreign country, her first trip abroad and, more than that, her first trip on her own. Because she'd had her speech problems in the past, her parents had always protected her. Overprotected her, perhaps. She'd been happy to be a day student at Cardiff Art College rather than share a flat with other students. She thought of how different they'd been with Bronwen. Although she was younger, her sister had been to more places on her own and done more things than she'd ever done. But it wasn't their parents' fault — she hadn't wanted to be independent . . . until now. She smiled to herself. Bronwen had never travelled alone and she'd never been to Kefalonia.

The wide street emerged onto a large square surrounded by restaurants and bars. The smell of coffee wafted in Eléni's direction as she passed tavernas bustling with people sitting outside and chatting away. Vibrant clusters of magenta bougainvillea tumbled over wooden pergolas, and large earthenware pots full of white pelargoniums divided each bar area on the pavement. Her hotel was tucked up a side street. The glass doors were set back from the pavement under an arched overhang that provided shade to the reception area inside. *Hotel Athena*. The square reception area was flooded with light under its glass-domed ceiling.

Eléni approached the desk where a smartly dressed man attended to some paperwork. He looked up.

'May I help you?'

'*Nai*. I have a room booked in the name of Eléni Beynon.' She was glad of her command of the Greek language. All thanks to her mother.

After being told of the housekeeping rules and breakfast times, Eléni was handed her door key and given directions to the lift. Her room was on the second floor.

Eléni's hand shook as she put the key in the lock. *What am I going to discover about my birth family? What would have happened if I'd stayed and been sent to the orphanage?* She was filled with guilt as she thought back to the family row that had taken place when she'd just found out about Cassia and Tom taking her away from this island. They were convinced they'd done the right thing. And maybe they had. Eléni had been horrible to them all and the look of hurt on their faces as she'd flung her insults and accusations at them would stay with her for ever. She'd thought things would never be the same between them and it was all her fault, but after reading her mother's letter she hoped she could make it up to them.

The tiny room was dark and cool inside. Eléni opened the blue wooden shutters and the door onto the balcony. For a moment, she stood resting against the metal railings and drank in the view. Over the tops of the terracotta-tiled roofs stretching out before her, she had a view of Argostoli harbour in the distance. Even from that far away, Eléni could see the sea was a deep teal colour in the afternoon sun.

Well, this is it! It's what you've worked so hard for, every penny. Let's hope it will be worth it.

She walked back into the room. A hand-embroidered counterpane covered the bed that was pushed up against the wall opposite the double doors to the balcony. Clusters of silver-green olive leaves interspersed with blue-black olives had been meticulously stitched on the white linen coverlet edged with lace. It reminded Eléni of the tablecloth her mamá had embroidered that came out every time they had visitors.

She unpacked her case and filled the wardrobe and chest of drawers with her clothes and belongings. On the rattan bed-side cabinet, she placed the precious sketchpad she intended to fill while she was here. As well as pen-and-ink sketches, she would write accounts of what she did every day to share with her parents and sister on her return. And she *would* return. Her wild threat to leave home and never go back was an empty one.

After unpacking, Eléni left the hotel behind to walk through the square. All the buildings had been rebuilt since 1953. They were modern in design and most were just two storeys high. She'd read how they'd been constructed with certain specifications to strengthen them in the event of further earthquakes. Again, her thoughts went to her mother and what she would think of the new town. Following the street map she'd picked up at the hotel reception, Eléni made her way down to the harbour. At every turn, she looked up at the street signs in the hope of finding the one now imprinted on her brain. Byron Street. None matched the name her mother had written down.

She crossed the road and continued walking along the quayside. Gleaming white vessels of every shape and size were moored along the harbour wall, from luxury yachts to more modest sailing dinghies and painted wooden fishing boats.

The water stretching out in front of her glowed a deep aquamarine and was so clear she saw shoals of small fish wriggling around the hulls of the boats.

'Damsel fish,' said a voice. Eléni looked towards an elderly man whose thick white moustache starkly contrasted his tanned, weathered face. 'You should come back in the morning. Before ten. When the fishermen come back in. The loggerhead turtles meet here then.' He spoke to her in rapid Greek while hardly taking a breath, but Eléni managed to understand what he was saying.

'*Efcharistó*, I will.'

Eléni strolled along the quayside, stopping to browse the little souvenir shops displaying racks of colourful postcards. She picked out three — one displaying the harbour itself and two showing Argostoli's main square. After paying, she found a bar with tables outside. An ivory-coloured awning ran the whole length of the bar's front wall to protect customers from the hot sun. A middle-aged waiter dressed in black brought her a menu.

'*Kalispéra.*'

She knew exactly what to choose — something that her mamá cooked often.

'Éna *café kai* éna *baklavá, parakaló.*'

Greek coffee was something she'd never tried, as her mother wasn't able to buy it in Wales. Eléni had read the Greeks served little cups of the dark, sweet liquid after boiling it up in a small copper saucepan called a *briki*. She would have to remember not to drink it down to the layer of sludge settled at the bottom. While she waited for her order to arrive, Eléni took her postcards and a pen from her bag.

Choosing one with a view of the pristine square in the centre of Argostoli, she began to write to her parents.

Dear Mamá and Baba,

I've arrived safely after a long journey. I was lucky to meet a nice American girl who was good company on the

flight. The little hotel is spotless and situated on a street just
off this main square. I chose this postcard especially for you
both to show you how they have rebuilt it. I am down by the
harbour just about to try my first Greek coffee and a baklavá.
I wonder will it be as good as yours, Mamá.

   I will write again when I have more news.
   Your loving daughter, Eléni Xx

The waiter arrived with her coffee and pastry. The sweet
honey taste was just the same as her mother's, but she could
understand why Cassia always complained that the substitute
pastry she made with butter was not the same as the crisp,
flaky layers Eléni sampled now.

Eléni wrote cards to Bronwen and Gabriella, then sat
and people-watched. There were lots of families enjoying time
together. On the next table to her was a little girl with enor-
mous ebony eyes and glossy black curls framing her little face.
She reminded Eléni of the missing child in the *Celtic Chronicle*
newspaper cutting. She'd thought there could be no denying it
was a photo of her at five years old, but this little girl was identical. Perhaps the one in the newspaper wasn't her. Perhaps
the man looking for his niece was not her uncle after all. All
she could do was speculate.

Eléni called the waiter and paid her bill. Wandering along
the quayside, she browsed the little shops and then walked
back into the centre of Argostoli using her street map to find
her bearings. She'd planned to visit the museum and library
early on in her stay so she could find out as much as she could
about how Argostoli had looked before the disaster happened.
Walking up the white-tiled main street, she noticed a beautiful, blond-coloured building standing out from the rest. The
Greek Orthodox church had a separate bell tower at its side.
Eléni entered through the arched double doors. Once inside,
she gasped. Although her eyes took a few moments to get
accustomed to the change in light from the bright sun, she was
amazed by the beauty of the carved wooden screen dividing

the sanctuary and the nave. When the door opened as another person entered, the shaft of light showed the true magnificence of the colours and the gilding.

Eléni wandered around the church. A sign told her it had been reconstructed after it had been destroyed during the earthquake and it had been rebuilt across the street from where it had originally stood. Surprisingly, the bell tower had remained intact. Although she wasn't religious, the stillness and peace inside the church had a profound effect on her. She was drawn to an icon in front of which flickering red candles had been lit in memory of loved ones who had passed on. Putting drachmae in the slot of a small wooden box, she selected four candles and lit them in turn. She thought of her birth parents and grandparents who had perished in this very town and of whom she had no memory. Tears welled in her eyes. *Rest in peace, Mamá, Baba, Yiayiá and Pappoú.*

CHAPTER FORTY-FOUR

Despite being exhausted after her long journey, Eléni didn't sleep well the first night in Kefalonia. She tossed and turned thinking about all the things she planned to do in order to find her uncle. Every time she closed her eyes, she saw an image of a middle-aged man with a tanned complexion and dark hair streaked with silver at the temples. For some reason, it was the face of the waiter who'd served her at the bar where she'd had her coffee and baklavá earlier in the day. She'd eventually drifted off to sleep only to wake in a panic when she dreamed about the same man, but this time in a coffin in the church she'd visited. Along with other mourners she'd filed past the body, drawn towards unbodied images of her parents and grandparents lined along the altar steps and beckoning to him to join them. She'd been drenched in sweat, her heart pounding. Convinced it was her uncle in the dream, she wondered whether her visit to the island was worth it. What was the point if he was dead?

* * *

Eléni had forgotten to close the shutters and was woken a few hours later by a shaft of sunlight streaming into her bedroom at dawn. She yawned as she walked to the balcony to look out over the silent, peaceful town. The terracotta-tiled buildings gave a warm feeling in the pale sunlight and the strip of sea in the harbour glinted silver. The sky was brushed with pale lemon and coral that promised to turn to a vibrant blue once the sun rose fully. After she'd washed and dressed, Eléni made her way to the quayside where several fishermen were arriving with their hauls of fish.

'It's very early for the lady, I think,' called one. He stopped what he was doing to flash her a wide grin.

'The sun woke me up. I came to see people hard at work.' Eléni laughed. Even though there was blood and grime over his clothes and plastic apron, he was still very attractive. For the first time since she'd vowed she was no longer interested in men after the accident, her stomach tightened. For a split second, it reminded her of the effect Andy Smith had had on her.

'Hey, Christós. Back to work.' An older man pointed at his fishing boat.

Eléni watched as Christós heaved large plastic tubs of glistening fish from his fishing boat onto the quay. Other fishermen sat mending their nets. Further along the quayside, small trucks were parking up. Their drivers opened the double doors at the back of the vehicles and negotiated the prices of large trays of fish before loading them into the trucks.

'From the restaurants. They have to be early to get the freshest fish, eh?' A woman dressed head to toe in black stood by Eléni. She held an empty wicker basket over her arm. 'Like me. I go to the market early to get the freshest goods. *Kaliméra.*'

Eléni watched as the old lady walked towards the market, before strolling back to her hotel in the opposite direction. By then, breakfast had been laid out on long tables in the dining room for guests to help themselves. It consisted of fresh fruits, natural yoghurt and honey, along with a wide selection of pastries, baklavá and large jugs of fruit juices in every colour. She was led to a table in the window and gave her order for coffee. Not having realised how much the strong smell of the fish had affected her, the sweetness of the fruit and pastries was just what she needed to set her up for the day.

After a delicious breakfast, she walked the short distance to the museum, which was part of the town's library. The library could be found through metal gates and up a flight of stone steps to a modern building rendered in its now familiar pale-blond colour. Olive and oleander trees grew in the beautifully maintained gardens on either side of the steps. The museum building was accessed from the side. Eléni entered the cool interior and found a glass sign informing visitors where the different sections of the museum were housed. She would view the early history and folklore of the island at another time, but for her first visit Eléni wanted to view the extensive collection of photographs depicting the aftermath of the earthquake and what the island had looked like before.

A smartly dressed man sat behind the desk at the entrance to the museum. 'May I help you?' He stood and walked out from behind his desk to speak with Eléni. His name badge informed her he was Otis Petrakis, the curator of the museum.

'*Nai. Efcharistó.* My family came from Kefalonia, here in Argostoli, and I want to find out everything about what it was like before the earthquake.'

'You speak perfect Greek, but I think there is a hint of a British accent, eh?'

'I learned Greek from my mother, but my father is Welsh. I live in Wales. We left after the earthquake.' There was no point in explaining the full situation.

The man nodded and smiled. 'Now the island is getting back on its feet, we have so many Kefalonians returning. This summer is going to be very busy with people returning for the twentieth anniversary of the earthquake. Please follow me.'

Eléni was led into a small room off the main display area.

'The labels and explanations are in English as well as in Greek, but I don't think you will need them. If I can be of any more assistance, please let me know. I'm afraid I didn't catch your name?'

'Eléni. Eléni Beynon. *Efcharistó.*'

The photos were dated in order and the main difference was the style of the buildings. The tall and elegant Venetian-style houses had crumbled like packs of cards. They had been replaced by lower, sometimes just single-storey ones. She found a photograph of the original church she'd visited and lit candles in. While she looked, she made notes and annotated drawings in her sketchbook. She looked at each display, searching for one name. Byron Street.

She was about to move on to another part of the exhibition when she noticed a photograph of an elderly lady dressed in traditional black, with a headscarf covering her white hair. She was covering her face with her hands. The hairs on the back of Eléni's neck stood up and her pulse raced. The caption underneath the photo read, *Grief on Byron Street. A yiayiá awaits.* Whose yiayiá was it? Who was she waiting for? It was the street where Eléni had once lived. The devastation in the background was the scene Cassia and her friend Sophia would have experienced. Not for the first time, guilt washed over Eléni when she relived the row with her parents. Her eyes burned as tears formed along her eyelids. She would have perished in the rubble of that street if it hadn't been for them.

'Is everything all right?'

Eléni hadn't noticed the curator standing beside her. She brushed away her tears with her hand.

'*Nai, efcharistó.* It's a shock to see how horrific it was.'

'I know. So many people perished on that awful day twenty years ago. That street was hit particularly badly.'

Eléni brought out the card that the address was written on.

'I know,' she whispered. She showed the card to Kýrios Petrakis. 'It was my home. I survived. Everyone else was killed.'

Guilt consumed her again. This time it was guilt that she had survived and the rest of her family had been wiped out.

'Oh, my dear. I am so sorry. These photographs must be very harrowing for you to see.'

Tears spilled over, wetting her cheeks. At first all Eléni could do was nod. Then she took a deep breath. 'I was taken to Wales as I had no other family left. Before I came here, I was given this address, but I can find no street of that name on the map. I'd like to go there and see what it's like now.'

'Ah. Come with me.'

Kýrios Petrakis led Eléni back to the foyer and a large table topped with two detailed maps of Argostoli set under glass. They were titled *Before and After the Earthquake*. 'See here.' He pointed to a street on the first map. 'There's your street. Byron Street. But if you look for it on the second one, it's not there. See if you can find its equivalent.'

Eléni compared the two maps. 'Elpizō Street? *Elpizō* means "to hope", doesn't it? But why give it a new name? I don't understand.'

'Very few people living in that street survived and it was decided no one would want to live where so many had lost their lives. What if the street was doomed as the planners had said? So they renamed it Elpizō Street, and built shops and businesses there.'

Eléni could see that the long street led into the central square and was parallel to the one where her hotel was situated. She'd walked down there. Walked over the place where her parents and grandparents had lost their lives! She shivered.

'It isn't unusual to rename streets in a new town. In fact, we have one street named after the British ship that came to the rescue of the islanders so early on. HMS *Daring*.' He pointed to the map. 'Daring Street.'

Eléni was ready to leave. 'Thank you for your help.'

She felt drained from viewing the shocking images and strolled back into Argostoli in the sunshine. She walked to the harbour and found a table at the taverna she'd visited on her first day. There was no sign of the handsome Christós, as the fishermen had all long gone for the day. It was good to sit with a coffee and survey the boats coming and going, dropping off tourists or taking them on excursions around the island.

Taking her sketchbook from her bag, Eléni jotted down what she had seen and learned that morning. She sketched the scene in front of her, capturing the busyness of the moment with people milling round, stopping to look at the more expensive yachts and schooners moored along the quayside.

Afterwards she made the long walk to the lighthouse at the top end of the Argostoli peninsula. The gleaming white construction was a replica of the original that had been destroyed in 1953. She clambered over the rocks and found a place to sit and draw. After mapping out the construction of its circle of white columns, Eléni used coloured pens to finish the drawing.

'There you are, Gabbie. Is this enough colour for you?' She smiled as she spoke aloud and thought about her friend back home in Wales. The turquoise and blue inks glowed on the thick watercolour paper of her sketchpad and helped her forget about the harrowing scenes in the museum photographs for a little while.

CHAPTER FORTY-FIVE

The next day, Eléni visited the museum again. She was pleased to see it was Kýrios Petrakis sitting behind the desk in the foyer again.

'*Kaliméra*, Thespína Beynon. What can I help you with today?'

'*Kaliméra*, Kýrios Petrakis. I want to find out as much as I can about my family. Like I told you yesterday, my parents and grandparents were killed in the earthquake, but I want to know if I have any other relatives who survived. An uncle, maybe. Where would I go to find this, *parakaló*?'

The man picked up his pen and began to write down a name and address on the pad of paper on his desk.

'I think I know just the man. You will need to go to the archives department, which is behind this building. Obviously, there are many gaps in the records now before 1953, but you should ask for this person.' He handed her the sheet of paper. 'Simos Georgatos. He is in charge of the Archives Department and is making a name for himself with people like yourself searching for lost relatives. He's a young man, but already his reputation is very well respected.'

This was the first step in Eléni's search.

'*Efcharistó*, Kýrios Petrakis. You have been very helpful again.'

The office was easy to find. She'd noticed the blue-and-white Greek flag flying on top of the roof. Eléni entered and asked the receptionist if she would be able to see Simos Georgatos.

'I'm afraid he's not here today. May I ask what it's about and I will get him to contact you?' said the young woman.

'Yes. I understand he could be the person to help me trace a relative who may have survived the earthquake.'

The woman smiled and handed Eléni a notepad and pen. 'Kýrios Georgatos is always very busy. So many people are searching. Even after twenty years they search. Please write your name and address here.'

Eléni did as she was asked, hoping it wouldn't be too long before the archivist contacted her. All she could do was wait. She walked down to the taverna on the quayside to sketch out some plans for more pen-and-ink drawings.

When Eléni arrived back at the hotel later, there was a message waiting for her.

'Ah, Thespína Beynon. Kýrios Georgatos called to say he was sorry to have missed you this morning, but he is back at his office now and will be there all afternoon if you'd like to see him today.'

Eléni's heart raced. From what the man at the museum had told her, if anyone was going to help her find her uncle, Simos Georgatos would be the person to do so.

'*Efcharistó*. That is good news.'

She left the hotel and hurried along to the archive office. The streets were quieter now as most of the shops had closed for lunch. She ignored the growling in her stomach — right now. Seeing the archivist was more important than eating. Soon she was entering the cool interior of the building.

'I'm here to see Kýrios Georgatos. He is expecting me. Eléni Beynon,' she told the woman behind the desk in the entrance hall.

The woman smiled and picked up the phone. 'Kýrios Simos. There is a young lady here to see you. She says you are expecting her. Eléni Beynon.'

After replacing the telephone on its stand, the woman looked up at Eléni. 'He's coming down now. He won't be long.'

Eléni thanked her and wandered to the side wall to look at a display of pre-1953 photographs displayed there. How different the town looked now. Gone were the beautiful, elegant, tall buildings, labelled as Venetian in style. The town her mother remembered was gone. Eléni's thoughts were interrupted by a mellow, cultured voice.

'Thespína Beynon?'

She turned and her heart skipped a beat. Facing her was a young man immaculately dressed in a crisp white linen shirt and navy slacks. He held out his hand to introduce himself.

'Gerasimos Georgatos. Everyone calls me Simos.'

His hand was warm and smooth. Electricity fizzed throughout her body.

'Eléni Beynon. Eléni.'

He smiled as if it was expected of him, but he remained aloof.

'Would you like to come to my office and you can tell me how I may help you?'

They walked up the staircase to the first floor, where his office overlooked the street below. Large picture windows ensured the room was filled with natural light.

Eléni explained her situation and handed him the name of the street of her former home.

'I know it's been renamed, but I would like to know anything you can tell me about my family who lived there. You see, I was the sole survivor. Rather than let me be taken into an orphanage, I was brought up by a couple who took me back to Wales. They say they did it to give me a better life.'

Simos Georgatos stiffened. 'And they were right,' he said under his breath, frowning.

'Sorry?'

'Ignore me. Please go on.'

'They kept everything a secret. I wouldn't have known they weren't my real parents if I hadn't found my mother's old journal. In it was a newspaper cutting about a man who had been looking for his niece who had survived the earthquake and been taken off the island without permission. The little girl looked like me as a child, but her name was not Eléni and she was older than me.'

The young archivist leaned forward. 'And you'd like me to help you find him? Do you have his name?' His voice was now animated. 'After the disaster split so many families I do this all the time, but your story fascinates me. If this uncle still exists and lives in Kefalonia, I'm sure I can help you.'

Eléni's eyes misted with tears. She'd feared he would shut down her hopes and say this was impossible, but perhaps this man could help her find out her true identity. He listened.

'*Efcharistó.* The name in the newspaper was Kostas Koulouris.'

The young man made a note of this.

'Why don't you leave it with me for a few days and I will do some research? In the office here, all the records are post-1953 apart from a few things they were able to retrieve from the rubble. To be honest, many of those were items rather than documents, so I'm not holding out much hope for those. The other thing is that Koulouris is a very common name here, so perhaps it's not good to build your hopes up.' He stood and shook her hand. 'But I will try. I lived through the earthquake, too. In fact, my dissertation at university was about the 1953 earthquake and its effect on the Ionian islands afterwards.'

After thanking him, Eléni left the building feeling excited that Simos Georgatos was going to take on her case. She found the nearest taverna and ordered herself a simple lunch of a Greek salad drizzled with olive oil and a large slice of kreatopita, the famous Kefalonian three-meat pie she'd seen on all the taverna menus. She didn't have to wait long before the dishes arrived. The steaming phyllo pastry pie was delicious, full of meats, rice, cheese and spices.

'I'll definitely have that again.' Eléni laughed when the waiter came to take away her empty plate.

'Here, it is the best kreatopita in the whole of Argostoli. You must come again. Anything else?'

'*Nai*. I'll have a beer, *efcharistó.*' She rarely drank at home, but here on the island she'd found an ice-cold beer was always very refreshing.

She left the taverna and instead of strolling down to the quayside as she had been in the habit of doing, she walked in the opposite direction and found a park surrounded by cypress trees on one side. Large areas of the garden were filled with flowering bushes of pink oleander. Finding a wooden bench in the shade, she sat for a while and wondered if this was the park she'd read about in one of the books borrowed from Porth Gwyn Library. It was large enough to be the one where the town's homeless had erected temporary shelters after the earthquake. She looked on her map and found Maitland Square. That was where the Red Cross had erected its large grey bell tents to act as hospital wards and treatments rooms. Somewhere there she'd been looked after and her injuries attended to. When pressed for information, her mother had told her the details. No wonder both her parents had been worried about her similar injuries after the car accident. It was here they'd found out she couldn't speak when she'd regained consciousness.

She took out her sketchbook and recorded what was in front of her. A metal structure stood in the centre. A circle of steps led up to a space reminding her of the bandstand back home. Before leaving the park, she wandered over to a plaque and read a dedication to all the people of Argostoli who had lost their lives in 1953.

CHAPTER FORTY-SIX

It was a week until Eléni heard from Simos Georgatos again. He messaged the hotel to say he had some information for her and could she call by the archive office at 11 a.m.? She didn't know what the information would be and she became more and more nervous as she neared the town. He'd either drawn a blank and found nothing, or she was one step closer to finding out who she was.

'I'll let Kýrios Georgatos know you've arrived.' The receptionist smiled as she rang Simos. After speaking with him, she put the phone down. 'He's asked me to take you to the archive basement. He'll meet us there.'

They walked down a flight of wooden stairs and into a large windowless room where the lights came on automatically when the door opened. The walls were lined with varying depths of shelves with labelled files. In the centre was a huge wooden table where documents were spread out next to a green-painted metal box. It was crushed along one side and where the paint had chipped off, the underneath was rusty.

Simos Georgatos joined them. He turned to the receptionist. '*Efcharistó*. That will be all.' He nodded at Eléni. '*Kaliméra*, Thespína Beynon. I was being a bit presumptuous expecting you to be able to come here at the time I suggested. You could have had other arrangements, but I'm very pleased you are here.'

This was a different man from the sober, stuffy one she'd first met a week ago. His eyes sparkled as he led her to the table.

'I've made a breakthrough and I couldn't wait to tell you. Take a seat.'

Eléni's heart raced.

'A census was taken in 1951 and held centrally. Although census records are not available to the public, as an archivist, I was given permission to view them.'

He picked up one of the documents and placed it between them. 'This is a photocopy of the census record we need. Because you had part of the address in Byron Street, I looked at all the names of the people living there in the 1951 census, searching for a family of four adults. If you were three in 1953, there should be a baby listed too.'

Eléni followed Simos's finger as he traced down the list of handwritten words. He took a magnifying glass from his pocket and handed it to her.

'Here, look at number twenty-five. *Andreas Spyros Mouzakis, age twenty-seven.*'

'What does that mean?' Eléni pointed at the document.

'Head of household.'

Eléni gasped. *'Dimitra Maria Mouzakis, wife, age twenty-six. Theodore Kostas Koulouris, age fifty-eight. Iôánna Pelagia Koulouris, age fifty-seven.'*

Tears streamed down her cheeks. She placed her hands over her eyes. *Koulouris.* The same surname as the man who was searching for her.

'Eléni, are you all right? This must be so hard for you. We can stop to give you time to take it all in, but just let me read the last entry for number twenty-five. *Iôánna Eléni Mouzakis, age three.*'

Eléni opened her eyes to see for herself. 'So the newspaper cutting was right! If it is me, I was five at the time of the earthquake, not three, and my name *was* Iôánna not Eléni.'

She wanted to hug Simos Georgatos, but stopped herself. He was just doing the job he had trained for. But he did it for her.

Simos placed an arm around her shoulder and pulled her close. 'I'm so pleased for you!' Immediately, he sprang away from her. 'Oh, I'm sorry. That was unforgiveable! So unprofessional.'

'It's fine. You seem almost as excited as I am.' Eléni placed her hand on his arm. He didn't pull it away.

Simos looked directly at her with tears forming in his eyes.

'Perhaps I should have told you. I survived the earthquake like you. My family was all killed too. I'll tell you about it at another time. But I was shipped away from the island to a religious orphanage run by nuns in Patras. I didn't realise how much I'd bottled up over all these years until I started working on your case. I'm sorry about this.' His voice cracked. 'The orphanage was awful. If we cried for our parents, we got beaten. The way to survive was to become hard ourselves and pretend we did not care.'

'Oh, Simos.' She thought of how happy her childhood had been with her parents. 'If you'll let me, can we forget about you being professional and we just become fellow survivors? I think you need what we call in Wales a big *cwtch*.' Before he could object, she hugged him. The tears that had threatened trickled down his cheeks. Eléni didn't say a word. Ignoring his embarrassment, she just held him.

'Sorry about that.' Simos brushed his cheeks with the back of his hand. Pulling over the metal box, he clicked open the locks on either side that were positioned underneath the lid. 'If anything was found in the rubble, it was collected and labelled with details of where it was found. This box was found in Byron Street. It looks as if it was some sort of safe with important documents and keepsakes in. No one ever claimed it. When I started here, I found it pushed to the back of a cupboard and labelled with other finds from the street.'

He opened the lid. The box was full of paper documents and various items.

'I think some of this stuff is going to be of real interest to you. Take a look.'

Eléni's hands shook as she lifted out a buff-coloured folder. It was speckled with age and smelled musty. 'Is this a marriage certificate?' She read each column.

'Yes, if you look it has the same names as the census. Your parents, Andreas and Dimitra, were married here in Argostoli and the certificate lists what they did for a living. Your mother was a lacemaker and your father was an artist.'

Eléni gasps. 'I've followed my father, then. That's what I do, too. I thought it was because I had to use drawing as a means of communication when I couldn't speak. But is it possible to inherit a skill?'

'I don't know. Perhaps my father was curious about the past like me.' He laughed, then his expression became serious. 'I'll probably never know . . . But look at the name of one of the witnesses.'

Eléni read it aloud. 'Kostas Koulouris, the same name as my grandfather. It's got to be my uncle.' It all fitted. She had a true identity.

'This is your birth certificate. *Iôánna Eléni Mouzakis. Born thirtieth of July, 1948. Weight 2.49 kilos.* You were tiny!'

Eléni had no idea what that was in pounds and ounces.

Simos could see her trying to work it out mentally. 'I think it would be about five and a half pounds.'

'Yes, very small.'

'And my birthday is not on the seventh of May when I've always celebrated. I have a July birthday!'

Everything contained in the missing-child article in the *Celtic Chronicle* was accurate. She'd been five at the time of the earthquake and her name was Iôánna. 'My uncle got it right. I do hope we can find him.'

'I think I know why you were known as Eléni rather than your first name. It's a tradition here to name a girl after her grandmother. Remember on the census there was a woman called Iôánna Koulouris. By her age, she must have been your grandmother. I think they called you by your second name to avoid calling the two of you the same name as she lived in the house with you.'

Simos moved the folder to one side. 'Look at this.' He held up a tiny white bonnet, embroidered with little pink rosebuds and the initials *I.E.M.* edged in lace. Although the cotton had yellowed with age, the workmanship was exquisite.

'Do you think my mamá made it for me?' Eléni took it from Simos. 'You said I was tiny, as tiny as a doll, I think.' Emotion flooded through her. She had no idea what her mother had looked like, but she imagined a young dark-haired woman preparing for the birth, sitting and making beautiful clothes for her baby. Like any new mother, she would have had hopes and dreams for her little one's future, never imagining she would not see him or her grow up. Eléni stifled a sob.

Together, Eléni and Simos rummaged through the records and items in the box. There was a small icon of St Gerasimos, the patron saint of Kefalonia, and a tiny gold cross and chain that Simos explained would have been given to her by her godparents.

Towards the bottom of the box, Simos found a detailed pen-and-ink drawing of a reclining baby.

'Look at this.'

Eléni's skin prickled with goosebumps. The drawing was labelled *Ióánna Eléni, aged four months*. 'My baba has signed it. *A.S.M.* Not only was he an artist, but he drew this in pen and ink. It's so detailed. It's so much better than a photograph, don't you think? I can't quite believe it. Guess what my favourite medium is?' She didn't wait for Simos to answer. 'Pen and ink. I'm nowhere near as good as this, though.'

Simos reached across and patted Eléni's arm. 'I can see how much this means to you. But I think we should stop now and let you digest everything you've learned about your family. The next step is to find this uncle of yours. We now have his full name from the census. And it looks as if he was one of the witnesses at your parents' wedding, so it will narrow it down.'

Eléni stood. 'I can't thank you enough. Never in my wildest dreams did I think I'd find all this information about my birth family so soon. It's all down to you.'

'I'd love to just carry on with the search, but I do have other cases to work on. I've already heard comments that I'm spending all my time on yours.' He laughed, but then his face became serious. 'I think, as well as wanting to help you, I can just imagine what it must be like to find out your true identity. I still carry around this feeling I don't belong to anyone.' He inhaled deeply. 'Anyway, enough about me.'

'You are so good at your job. You must research your own family, even if it sounds impossible now. I'm sure there must be a way.'

'Perhaps.' He looked directly at her. 'Do you know I have told you more about myself than anyone else I know? I can't believe I became emotional in front of someone I've just met. In such a short time, I think of you as a good friend. Is that even possible?'

Eléni's insides did a flip. *Of course, it's possible, you gorgeous man. Friendship is fine.* From the time she'd set eyes on Simos Georgatos she'd wanted more, but seeing him so vulnerable and opening up about his feelings, she knew this was enough for him. And anyway, she would have to return home once her money ran out, so there was no hope of their relationship leading to anything serious.

Simos continued. 'If it's all right with you, I'd like to meet you for dinner tonight. Perhaps we can take a boat from the harbour to a bay where the view of the sunset is supposed to be one of the best. Shall we say seven o'clock in front of Taverna Xénia on the quayside?'

CHAPTER FORTY-SEVEN

That evening, Eléni approached the taverna where Simos waited for her. Her insides flipped when he turned to face her. In the early-evening sun, his face and arms were a deep bronze. Although he was more casually dressed than when he worked at the museum, he still looked immaculate in a short-sleeved pale blue linen shirt, worn with the top two buttons open, and cream-coloured slacks. She wondered if she was underdressed in her long cheesecloth skirt. Striped in shades of pink, purple and ecru, its unironed look was a stark contrast to Simos's expertly pressed clothes.

'Eléni.' Simos's face broke into a wide smile that reached his eyes. 'You look lovely.'

He kissed her on both cheeks. His lips were soft and warm on her skin and his musky cologne caused her stomach to tighten.

'I hope the restaurant isn't too posh. I feel a bit under-dressed. You look so smart.'

He looked puzzled. 'Posh?'

'Smart. Where rich people go.'

'No, you will see all kinds of people there, enjoying the views. They all wear what they want to.'

The motorboat was almost full by the time they went aboard. Eléni and Simos found two seats together on the left-hand side of the boat.

'It takes about fifteen minutes to get there. We should have a good view of the island from this side. The only access to some of these beaches and coves is down very steep lanes. It's much better to get to them by boat if you can,' said Simos.

The early-evening sun shone on the surface of the sea, making it sparkle and glisten. Shades of turquoise and aquamarine reached as far as the steep white cliffs. Eléni looked over the side of the boat and marvelled at the clarity of the water. She could see right to the bottom and watched shoals of fish swimming close to the boat.

'It's beautiful. The colour of the water is almost jewel-like.'

The boat passed several secluded beaches and little coves on the way. By one stood a whitewashed single-storey building. It looked deserted, yet a colourful rowing boat was moored to a small wooden jetty. There was no lane leading from the beach so it could only be reached by boat.

It wasn't long before they reached their destination. People were disembarking from motorboats, while others were lining up to join boats on the return journey. Bars and tavernas lined the quayside and already bustled with people trying to get the best tables.

'Don't worry.' Simos smiled. 'I phoned and booked us a good table for the view.'

The restaurant had a large eating area at the front but when Simos gave his name to the waiter on the door, they were led upstairs to the roof terrace. The one unoccupied table was right at the front with a magnificent view over the sea and the harbour. The reserved sign had the name *SIMOS GEORGATOS* written on it.

'Perfect, *efcharistó.*' The waiter pulled out a chair for Eléni and left them. Simos sat down opposite Eléni. 'This is a good position, eh?'

It was obvious Eléni that Simos came to the restaurant often — the waiters all knew him. An image of him bringing an elegant young woman here filled her head. With long black tresses tumbling over her slim tanned shoulders, she would also be dressed in immaculate designer clothes, and diners at the other tables would stop and watch as the couple was shown to their table — this table. She looked down and smoothed her skirt, which appeared more creased than usual. *Stop it, Eléni. Of course, he's had girlfriends, maybe still has. This is just an evening with a new friend. We have the earthquake in common and that's all.*

A waiter appeared at the table and handed them each a menu. 'We recommend the bakalàos.'

Simos explained. 'It's dried cod. Here it is always served with agliada, a sauce made of boiled potatoes ground with garlic, olive oil and lemons. It's delicious. I tell you what, why don't I ask Stephanos, here, to bring us a selection of the restaurant's speciality dishes for you to try? I want you to try real Kefalonian food. *Efcharistó*, Stephanos.'

'I understand. And you would like an aperitif?'

'*Nai*. Ouzo, *parakaló*. With lots of ice. And a bottle of Robola.'

The sky was now a deep coral, streaked with fiery orange. The glowing tangerine sphere slowly sank into the horizon.

Stephanos brought the ouzos and placed the wine in the ice bucket on the table. 'It's beautiful, eh?' He lit the candle in the glass lamp on the table. 'For later.'

'I love watching sunsets at home, but they're nothing like this. It's spectacular!' With that, the sun disappeared completely.

'The island is famous for its sunsets and now you can see why.' Simos swirled the ice cubes in his glass and the liquid became milky. 'What do you think of our ouzo?'

Eléni sipped the aniseed liqueur and let the burn travel down her throat. 'It's . . . different.'

Simos laughed. 'You will get used to it. Ah, here comes our food.'

Stephanos drew up a small table and put it beside theirs while another waiter brought an array of small dishes.

'Your starters. I will let Simos explain to you what the dishes are.' Stephanos opened the wine and poured a little for Simos to try.

'*Efcharistó*. Excellent as always.'

The waiter filled the wine glasses and left them to their meals.

Simos turned back to Eléni. 'I hope you will like what they have chosen for us. Maybe we'll start with the dolmades. They're stuffed vine leaves. Then, these are mini lamb souvlaki, which go well with the tzatziki, the cucumber and yoghurt dip. But I'll stop. Discover the tastes for yourself, *parakaló*.'

Eléni was amazed at the variety of foods to choose from and tried a little of everything, even the olives which she'd always said she hated!

'Well, what did you think?'

'I loved the variety. A bit different from the prawn cocktail I always choose back in Wales! I think my favourites were the vine leaves stuffed with rice and the lamb kebabs. The dish I wasn't keen on was that one.'

'Ah. It's octopus. Disguised in a tomato sauce.' Simos laughed. 'Perhaps it takes some getting used to.'

It was dark now and each restaurant was lit with twinkling fairy lights. Moonlight reflected on the sea to give the whole place a magical, romantic feel. Eléni looked across at Simos and her heart skipped a beat. The contours of his face were accentuated by the light from the lamp.

'I've told Stephanos to give us a few minutes before serving the main courses.' Simos smiled. 'You will have room, I promise. Let's plan the next steps in your search.'

He took out a folded piece of paper and passed it over to Eléni. 'From the 1971 census, I've made a list of all the men with the surname Koulouris living in Argostoli. So many went north to Fiscardo, as it was relatively untouched by the earthquake, so I've included a list from there too.'

Eléni unfolded the paper. 'There are so many! Where do we start?'

'It's a very common name here. But we can rule out lots of them. Look at the column with their dates of birth. Anyone born after 1953 is going to be a teenager or a child. You said your uncle was thirty-eight in the newspaper report written in 1955.'

Eléni worked out the maths in her head. 'So we're looking for anyone who's fifty-six now, fifty-four two years ago.'

She scanned the list. The long list was narrowed down to fourteen men of that age.

'But none of those fourteen have the name Kostas, I'm afraid,' said Simos. 'I know it's disappointing. Ah, here comes our main course. We'll look at it again later.'

He picked up the paper to make room for the food. '*Efcharistó*, Stephanos.'

'Enjoy what we have prepared for you.' The waiter placed two serving dishes on the table. 'This is our speciality — bakalàos, accompanied by some horta.'

Eléni noticed the strong smell of garlic as Simos spooned the fish onto her plate. The dark green leafy vegetable served alongside it reminded her of spinach, but it had been drizzled with lemon juice and olive oil.

They ate in silence for a little bit, just stopping now and then to sip the cool white wine.

'What do you think?' Simos could see Eléni had left the horta.

'Sorry, it's a bit strong for me.' She quickly added, 'But I like the fish. The sauce is delicious.'

He laughed. 'It's okay. You don't have to like everything. You will find horta everywhere in the fields. They say it is full of minerals and it grows like a weed. I think you like the wine, though?' Simos grinned at her.

Eléni's glass was empty again and she felt a little light-headed. She didn't want the evening to end.

After the plates and dishes were cleared away, Stephanos returned. 'With the compliments of the restaurant. Our man-tola liqueur and honeyed baklavá.'

'*Efcharistó*, Stephanos. The food has been exceptional, as always.'

'Yes, *efcharistó*. This has been a real experience for me,' said Eléni.

Simos took the piece of paper out from his pocket again. 'Let's get back to finding Kostas Koulouris. I think the next step is to put out a request in the local press to see if anyone knows him.'

'A bit like he did, to try to find me.'

'Yes. You never know. Some of these Koulouris families may be his relatives . . . and yours. In the meantime, we could go to Fiscardo and look up these men. There are three with the name of Kostas. Perhaps your uncle didn't want to settle back here in the place where he lost his family.'

Simos became quiet. Was he thinking of his own situation?

'It must have been hard for you to return to Kefalonia if you were taken to the orphanage on the mainland. Why did you come back?'

'You're right. There's no one in the world I belong to but when the position for an archivist came up in Argostoli, the pull was too much to resist. I can't explain why. It was the same at university. I chose to write my dissertation on the very disaster that wiped my whole family out. It was as if I had to know everything and yet I still know nothing.' He inhaled deeply. 'Apart from my name.' His eyes misted.

Eléni reached across and took his hand. 'I'm sure you can find out more . . . when you're ready. You can tell me anything you remember if it helps.'

'Perhaps. When I'm ready.'

CHAPTER FORTY-EIGHT

After their dinner watching the sunset, Eléni and Simos met most evenings. He would call for her at her hotel after he finished work. Usually, they went for a drink and something to eat in one of the tavernas along the harbourside. On other occasions, they went in the other direction to the central square, which was always buzzing with tourists and locals.

On one occasion, Eléni stopped about three quarters of the way along Elpizō Street. She looked up at the number etched in the glass panel over the door of the offices. Number twenty-five. She shivered. A strange sensation hit her. It was not quite a memory, but more a feeling of *déjà vu* that she couldn't explain. Yes, she had already walked down this street but that was before she'd known it had been the location of her family home.

'Eléni, you're shaking. What's wrong? You look as if you've seen a ghost.' Simos took Eléni's hand.

Her throat tightened when she tried to speak. 'I think I'm standing on the very spot where my parents and grandparents were killed. Where my baba rescued me.' She closed her eyes and saw an image of herself as a little girl sitting on an old lady's lap as she sang to her. Close by, a man with scant white

275

hair and a full drooping moustache accompanied her with a haunting melody on a mandolin.

'I can't imagine what it feels like. We will find your uncle. I'm sure of it. It will be okay.'

Eléni nodded and they continued the walk to the square where they found a taverna with spare tables. She didn't feel hungry — her mind kept returning to the image of the couple who she assumed were her grandparents and their song reverberated in her head.

'Sorry. Just a Greek salad for me tonight.'

'You've had a shock, I think. It is very understandable.'

After their meal, they took a different route to the harbour. Taverna Xénia was busy, but now they were regular customers the waiter led Eléni and Simos to the room upstairs where there was a free table on the wooden balcony above the quayside. Below them, three mandolin players played traditional Greek music.

'It's Wednesday, so there's always live music,' said Simos. 'They are good, eh?'

Although her grandfather's playing of the same instrument was like an earworm in her head, instead of sadness, Eléni was proud she'd had the good fortune of being loved by two families — her birth family and the one who'd brought her up in Wales. She would write to Cassia, Tom and Bronwen, and thank them. She looked across at Simos and realised they had spared her from the awful experiences he'd had as a child. Without thinking, she reached across the table and placed her hand on his. Instead of pulling it away, he turned his over so that they were holding hands. *Anyone watching will think we're a couple sitting listening to romantic music.*

When the song ended, they broke hands to applaud along with the other customers.

'I wondered if you were free to visit Fiscardo this weekend. I can't spend any more work time on your case, I'm afraid, but my weekends are my own.' Simos brought out the same piece of paper with the addresses of men with the name of Kostas Koulouris. 'We've got these three to check on. One lives just outside and the other two are in Fiscardo itself.'

'*Efcharistó.* That would be wonderful. Then if we don't find him there, I have to assume he's moved from Kefalonia or, worse, that he's passed away. I have my aunt's address just a short distance out of Fiscardo. If we have time, would you mind if we went there too?' The earlier melancholy that Eléni had felt as she'd stood by her former home had now completely lifted, first with the beautiful mandolin music and now with the prospect of spending a whole day with Simos.

'Of course. I'll pick you up at the hotel on Saturday morning. Say nine o'clock.'

* * *

The next few days dragged. She'd written to her parents and sister as she'd planned and had told them how she'd stood on the very spot where she'd once lived and how the street where Cassia had also lived had been renamed. She'd told them about Simos and how helpful he was being by assisting her in her search for her uncle Kostas.

> *. . . Simos helped me find my birth certificate. My name is Ióánna Eléni Mouzakis and I'm two years older than you thought I was. Like me, he was the only one of his family to survive the earthquake. But unlike me he was sent to an orphanage in mainland Greece. He had a terrible time there and cannot talk about what happened. You were right, Mamá! You saved me from what Simos went through by giving me a happy childhood. I'm so ashamed about how I've treated you and Baba. You, too, Bron. Thank you from the bottom of my heart. I hope you will forgive my bad behaviour. You risked so much to get me out of Kefalonia.*
>
> *We still haven't found Theíos Kostas, but Simos is sure we will. I'll write again soon. I'm missing you all and will be home before you know it.*
>
> *Love from Eléni Xx*

She'd been living at the hotel for over three weeks and her money was running out. On her way to post the letter, she called in at Xénia's. July was fast approaching and in August, the town would be overrun with tourists arriving for the twentieth anniversary of the earthquake. Because it was her and Simos's favourite taverna, they knew her by name.

'*Kaliméra*.'

'Ah, *Kaliméra*, Eléni. What can I do for you?' Kýrios Panas was all smiles when she entered the coolness of the bar. A couple of local men were playing cards at a table in the corner, surrounded by a fug of smoke from their strong cigarettes.

'I wondered if you could do with extra staff. I noticed how you seem to be getting busier and I'm going to extend my stay in Argostoli. If you have a room I could rent, it would be even better, *parakaló*.'

The bar owner nodded his head. 'It is true, we are getting short of staff. I was going to advertise so you read my mind, I think.' The man smiled. 'But do you have any experience of working in a taverna — waiting tables, pouring drinks, clearing up afterwards? The hours are long. And how many days or evenings were you thinking of?'

'Maybe four days and three evenings.' She couldn't believe she was being asked to choose her working hours. She told him how she'd worked at the Metropole before coming to Kefalonia, and was used to dealing with customers and money from her time at the craft shop. 'I can't do tomorrow as I've arranged to go to Fiscardo with Simos, sorry.'

'Picking your days and you haven't been offered the job yet.' The bar owner pretended to look cross. Eléni's cheeks burned. 'Eléni, I tease. Yes, I will give you a week's trial to see how you get on. How about evenings starting at six o'clock on Tuesday, Wednesday and Thursday, then all day Friday, Saturday and Sunday. Beginning this coming Sunday, starting at ten o'clock until six o'clock? But I'm afraid there is nothing here to rent. There is only one free room in the taverna and it must be kept for the tourists.'

'*Efcharistó*. That's good. I will look for a room to rent that's cheaper than the hotel.'

She wasn't surprised the full days were at the weekend when Simos didn't work, but at least she had four free evenings to meet up with him. Before she started working, she had the trip to Fiscardo to look forward to. She wondered what sort of reception she'd get from Theía Eugenia. Her mother had told her she'd not heard from her sister because she'd not returned to Kefalonia to visit their mother before she'd died. Would her aunt be happy to see Eléni? Now she knew they weren't related by blood, perhaps she should call her Eugenia or even Kýria Papadatos. That's what her mamá had written on the note with the address she'd given to her. But it seemed too formal somehow. She had vague recollections of a warm, smiling woman with her own little girl, who'd looked after her when her mother had worked at the market. She remembered the sweet honey smell of baklavá baking in her aunt's kitchen. The longer she'd been in Kefalonia, the more distant memories were surfacing.

CHAPTER FORTY-NINE

The sky was a perfect deep blue as Eléni and Simos set off for Fiscardo that Saturday. As they drove away from Argostoli, the coastal road became narrower. At one point, they came to a complete stop when they had to wait for a herd of brown-and-white goats to pass.

'I've never driven along this road without our friends here holding me up somewhere. Not usually as many as this.' Simos laughed. 'Still, we have to put up with them if we want our lovely, salty feta. They roam free on the island, even on the rocks by the sea.'

With all the windows down, Eléni loved the feeling of the wind in her hair. The smell of wild thyme was strong as they drove through the mountainous area dotted with yellow broom. They'd been driving for about half an hour admiring the views of the sea to the left and the mountains to the right when Simos pulled into a layby.

'No drive to Fiscardo is complete without stopping here. You'll need your camera.'

There were already three other cars parked nearby, and the occupants looked down on the most amazing sight Eléni had ever seen. A sapphire-and-deep-turquoise sea edged with frills of foam broke onto a pure white beach.

'Wow! The colours are just amazing!' Eléni took a photo with the Kodak Instamatic she'd bought especially for the trip, along with several film cartridges. 'I don't suppose this will capture how wonderful it is in real life, but at least I'll have something to remind me. Now a photo of you, Simos.'

He sat on the low stone wall, looking embarrassed as the people from the other cars watched.

'You have to say cheese.' Eléni pointed the camera in his direction.

'Feta!' His face broke into a wide grin and they both laughed.

Eléni asked one of the people nearby if he would take a photograph of them both.

'*Nai.*' The man invited them to stand in front of the wall with the view of the beautiful beach behind them. The warmth of Simos's skin as he pulled her close made her tingle.

'Smile, *parakaló.*'

The man handed the camera back to Eléni, who thanked him.

Once back in the car, Eléni and Simos chatted about what, if anything, she could remember about Fiscardo. One memory that surfaced immediately was of her playing with a tiny kitten.

She paused for a moment, trying to remember the kitten's name. 'Callista. Yes. That was her name. When I stroked her, she used to purr loudly. I used to purr back and she'd snuggle up to me.'

Eléni remembered being happy with Eugenia and Maia until Georgios returned.

'Who was *he*?' asked Simos.

'Maia's father and my aunt's husband. I don't know much about what happened, but we had to leave.' She remembered a lot of shouting. Much more was coming back to her. She hadn't thought about her life just after the earthquake before. 'We moved into Fiscardo and Mamá worked in a taverna. The old man who owned it was kind and looked after me when she was working. He made me wooden toys, I remember. I still couldn't talk, but I was happy and safe.'

As soon as she'd said the words, she regretted them. The orphanage had not been like that for Simos. She changed the subject and asked him how much further it was to Fiscardo.

'Here's the sign. This is the famous Fiscardo. If I'm right, there is a car park not far from the harbour.'

They walked from the car park to the quayside to have a coffee before knocking on the doors of the three Koulouris households. Eléni immediately recognised Taverna Zervas where she'd once lived, even though it had fallen into disrepair. The metal balcony that led from the bedroom she'd shared with her mother was now rusted and the wooden shutters of the windows and entrance door were rotten.

'That's it! The taverna where Mamá and I lived. I remember. The nice old man was called Michaíl.'

Simos read the plaque attached to the wall of the taverna.

Taverna Zervas. Famous for being the meeting place of Kefalonian partisans and communists during the Civil War, 1946–1949

'It only ended four years before the earthquake.' Eléni wondered what Michaíl's role had been when he'd allowed his taverna to be used in that way.

'In my studies, I read about the war. It split families. Everyone took sides. It's a pity we can't go there, for old time's sake.'

They found another taverna a few doors down. While waiting for their coffees and baklavá to be served, Simos spread out a map of Fiscardo on the table. 'Look, these are the houses where someone called Koulouris lived two years ago. I suggest we go to these first and then call on your aunt. Do you have her address?'

Eléni took out the piece of card and read it out to Simos.

'There's nothing of that name on the map. Can you remember anything about where it was?'

282

As she remembered playing with Callista, an image of a small beach came into her head. 'Is there a beach or a cove nearby?'

Simos pointed to an inlet on the map just outside Fiscardo. 'There's one here. We could try there.'

They left the taverna and walked further up into the town. What struck Eléni was how very different the buildings were from modern Argostoli. The beautiful houses were rendered in various pastel colours ranging from pale pink to a delicate ochre shade under terracotta-tiled roofs. The windows were accompanied by painted shutters that protected them from the intense sunshine.

The first house they visited was along a side street. Simos knocked on a door that had once been a vibrant turquoise blue, but now peeled back to bleached wood in places. They waited before knocking again. No answer. They went to leave when the neighbouring door opened.

'There's no one there.' An old lady dressed in black eyed them with suspicion.

'We'd like to speak with Kýrios Kostas Koulouris. Do you know when he'll be back?'

The woman placed her hand on her chest, looked up and then crossed herself. 'He is with God,' she said. 'An accident. Even at his age, he was a fisherman and he died at sea. His son lives here now.'

'Did he speak about looking for his niece after the earthquake?' asked Eléni.

'No, he arrived here only three years ago from Patras. Shall I tell his son you came to see him?'

'No,' said Simos. 'He isn't the Kostas Koulouris we want. *Efcharistó.*'

Two more to try. Eléni was disappointed, but not surprised. The next household they tried was further into the town. Set away from the street, it was a larger property and in better condition than the last house. Under the porch that ran the length of the house, four cats basked in the sunshine on the mosaic-tiled terrace. The door was opened by a young woman who looked about the same age as Eléni.

'We'd like to speak with Kostas Koulouris, *parakaló*.' Simos did the talking again.

The woman turned her head and shouted, 'Pappoú! Some people to see you. Go through — he's in the orchard. But I should warn you, he gets very confused. He forgets things. His memory is very poor now.'

Eléni was disappointed, but thanked the woman for warning them.

The passageway of the house was dark and cool, and led to a large square full of mature fruit trees. An elderly man sat in the shade of one of the fig trees.

'Pappoú. These people would like to talk to you. Please, sit down.'

'*Kaliméra*, Kýrios Koulouris. Do you remember the terrible earthquake? Lots of people were killed. Did you know anyone who died?' Simos looked at Kostas's granddaughter for reassurance that it was okay to ask. 'Did you try to find a little girl, your niece?'

There was no reaction from the old man. Eléni hoped he might remember this significant event from twenty years ago, even though his memory was poor.

'You weren't here when the earthquake happened were you, Pappoú?'

Eléni's heart raced. 'You weren't in Australia by any chance, were you?'

'No. My grandfather was born to Greek parents and lived in America for many years. He missed the big earthquake in the fifties. My yiayiá was his second wife. I call him Pappoú, though. She emigrated with our family and always longed to return once the island was back on its feet. We all only came here about ten years ago.'

There was disappointment in Eléni's heart for the second time that day.

Simos and Eléni stood and bade farewell to Kostas Koulouris.

His granddaughter saw them out.

'*Efcharistó.* We're sorry to have bothered your grandfather.'

'And I'm sorry he was not the Kostas Koulouris you wanted.' The woman turned to Eléni. 'From your reactions, it's important you find him, I think. Are you the niece?'

'Yes, I emigrated too. Everyone thought my whole family perished, but I found out later an uncle was looking for me.'

The three shook hands.

'Well, good luck. I hope you find him.'

CHAPTER FIFTY

The third contact turned out to be a false trail, too. That Kostas had left the island the previous year and the new tenants did not have a forwarding address for him.

'I'm sorry. It looks as if we are back at the beginning. Now our only hope of finding your uncle is the advert I put in the local paper. It is a weekly Saturday paper, so it should be in tonight's edition. Come on, let's go and get some lunch, and then we'll find your aunt.'

After their meal, they returned to the car again and travelled in the direction of the cove on the map. If Eléni had remembered correctly, her aunt's house would be close by.

'Stop! I think it's down there.' Eléni pointed to a narrow scree lane leading to the left. The sea glistened below them. As Simos drove slowly over the uneven surface, her pulse raced. She knew she was in the right place — memories were fast returning. Through the pine trees, the smallholding looked the same, apart from the fact that the olive trees behind it were noticeably larger and the house itself had been extended. She half expected to see Maia playing with the kittens by the barn.

'Is this the right place?' Simos parked outside the gate and they walked towards the house. 'It's a lovely spot with that view.'

A brown-and-white dog bounded up to greet them, barking and wagging its tail.

'Hello, boy. You seem pleased to see us.' Eléni bent to stroke him. 'Yes, this is it. Mamá used to take me and Maia to this beach to play.'

By the time they reached the house, a young woman with a curly-haired baby propped on her hip had come out to see what all the barking was about.

'Shh, Titan. Can I help you?'

'I'm looking for my aunt, Kýria Eugenia Papadatos.' Eléni's heart pounded. It was obvious the woman didn't recognise the name.

'I'm sorry, we moved here last year. We bought it from a family called Drakos, I'm afraid.'

'Thank you, anyway. I lived here for a few years when I was young, before I moved to Wales.' Eléni turned to leave before the woman could see the hot tears pricking her eyes, leaving Simos to say goodbye. Why had the letters between her mother and her sister stopped? Where had Eugenia moved to?

As they walked back to the car, Simos placed an arm around her. 'I'm so sorry, Eléni. I know how much you were looking forward to seeing your aunt again. I would normally recommend we go to the post office for a forwarding address, but there have been two owners since she left the house.'

'It's not turning out to be a very good day, is it?' said Eléni. 'But I've enjoyed seeing more of your lovely island. I just have to accept I'm not going to find my uncle or my Aunt Eugenia.'

They drove back in silence until Simos banged his hand on the steering wheel. 'Of course. Why didn't I think of it before? I know the person who has the same job as me here in Fiscardo and I could see if he'll do me a favour. I'd do the same for him. I'll ask to see the census records from 1971. If your aunt is still in Fiscardo, we'll find her address there.'

* * *

Eugenia Papadatos was indeed still living in Fiscardo. Eléni and Simos arrived at the locked wrought-iron gates of a large, detached house in a street where pink oleander trees in full bloom edged the wide pavement.

'This is a bit grander than the smallholding. Can you see a bell?' Eléni pressed the brass button set in the gate frame. They waited a while before she pressed again. Still no one answered. Just as they were about to go, a grey-haired woman emerged and walked towards the gate.

Eléni forgot all her worries about formality. 'It's me, Eléni.' Memories of how kind this lovely woman had been to her when they'd first arrived at her house came flooding back.

Her aunt gasped and peered through the metal bars as she unlocked the gate. 'Cassia's Eléni? I can't believe it! You have grown into a beautiful woman from the tiny girl you were when I last saw you. Come in, come in, please.'

The two women embraced and were overcome with emotion. 'Theía, this is my friend, Simos.'

'Welcome, Simos. It's good to meet a friend of Eléni's.'

'You, too, Kýria Papadatos.'

'Please call me Eugenia.'

The two shook hands.

'Eléni, why don't I leave you to catch up with your aunt and I'll call back for you — say, an hour? You'll have so much to talk about. I will be in the way, I'm sure.'

'You don't have to, but if you're sure, *efcharistó.*'

Eugenia saw Simos to the gate and locked it behind him.

Eléni's aunt led Eléni to the back of the garden where they sat in the shade under an ecru-coloured awning. In front of them was a paved area full of ornamental pots overflowing with colourful trailing plants. A bright cerise-pink bougainvillea tumbled over a wooden pergola at the end of the cultivated space that led into an orchard full of orange and fig trees laden with fruit.

'This is a beautiful house, Theía. What made you move here?'

'It was our family home, where Cassia and I were brought up. I moved here after our mother died. See the swing hanging from the ancient olive tree?' She pointed to the left of the pergola. 'Well, that's where we used to have hours of fun. Maia did too. It's had new ropes, but the seat is the one my baba made for us, and the branches have just grown thicker and stronger. How is Cassia?' Her face became serious.

Eléni knew there had been some sort of row between them. 'She's fine, but she didn't want me to come to Kefalonia. I've only just found out she's not my birth mother. A few months ago, I found a letter from you saying someone had come looking for us.'

Eugenia let Eléni talk. 'I know why she took me away and I've had a very happy life, but they should have told me. It's why I'm here. To find all I can about my birth family starting with the man who I think is my uncle.'

'I'll never forgive her for not coming back to see Mamá when she was dying.'

For a moment, neither spoke and there was an awkward distance between them. Eléni defended her mother. 'I'm sorry, but Mamá is terrified she will be prosecuted for taking me out of Kefalonia without permission from the authorities. It's the reason she doesn't want me to find my uncle. She said she broke the law, but what she did was in my best interest. After meeting Simos, I know it was. I just wish they'd told me so I didn't have to find out like I did.'

'But it's been nearly twenty years. So many people emigrated. I doubt they would be concerned about your mother doing what she did, even then. And what do you mean about Simos?'

'His family was wiped out like mine, but he didn't have anyone like Cassia. He was taken to an orphanage on the mainland where he suffered terrible abuse.'

Eugenia held Eléni's hand. 'Oh, poor man. One thing is for sure, I know my sister loved you very much. She was even willing to marry Tom to have a better chance of getting you away. Let's go inside and I'll make you a drink.'

Eléni thought the comment about her mother being willing to marry her father was strange. But she remembered being surprised that her mother had written *A MARRIAGE OF CONVENIENCE* over one of her diary entries and added, *Perhaps Eugenia was right.* Maybe that's what it had been at the start, but she knew without a shadow of a doubt that her parents loved each other very much.

The kitchen was much bigger than the previous one, but it was still a cook's kitchen. Well-used pots and pans of various shapes and sizes were displayed on an overhead clothes airer suspended from the ceiling. The copper *briki*, essential for making Greek coffee, took pride of place.

'Would you prefer an iced coffee, a frappé or a lemonade? The lemonade is freshly made.'

'Lemonade, *parakaló*.'

The large refrigerator doors were covered in children's drawings. Eléni thought back to the time when she'd used drawings to communicate with her aunt and Maia.

'Whose are these lovely drawings?'

'Ah, they are my granddaughter's. Eléni. She's five.'

Eléni gasped. 'My name!'

'Yes. Maia named her after you. We often talk about you. They live in Patras now so I don't see a lot of her, but Maia sends me lots of drawings. They remind me a lot of yours.' Eugenia pointed to a framed photograph displayed on the dark wooden dresser. 'That's her there.'

Eléni walked over to take a good look. 'She's beautiful. She looks like Maia.'

Eugenia agreed and they went back outside. The mid-afternoon sun was still intense and Eléni was glad to sit under the shade of the awning. 'I haven't found my uncle, but with Simos's help — him being an archivist — I have found out a lot about my birth parents. It was very sad to stand on the very spot where they and my grandparents were killed. My father was an artist. It's what I do too.'

'I'm not surprised,' said Eugenia. 'Your drawings were exceptional for a three-year-old.'

'Ah, but my birth certificate says I was five. My full name is Iôánna Eléni Mouzakis. Simos says it was a tradition for baby girls to be named after their yiayiás, so he thinks I was known by my second name. It's a bit more Greek than Beynon, eh?'

'Your Greek is excellent. Your mother did a great job teaching you.'

'Yes, I am very grateful for that. It's made getting around Kefalonia a lot easier. She insisted my sister, Bronwen, and I both learned. I'm not so good at writing it, though.'

They continued chatting and the hour flew by. The bell rang and Eugenia let Simos in.

'Have you both had a good catch-up? I visited my friend. It may not come to anything, but he's going to look up some records at the orphanage for me.'

Eléni stood and hugged him. 'That's the best news.' The fact he'd confided in his friend had to be a step in the right direction.

'Efcharistó, Theía. It's been so good to see you again. Please remember me to Maia. And I promise I'll come to see you before I go back home.'

The two women hugged each other, neither one of them wanting to pull away first. But it was Eugenia who abruptly stepped back. 'Did you say your surname was Mouzakis? It's not common here in Kefalonia, but I've been racking my brain to remember where I've heard it before. Your father's name wasn't Andreas, was it?'

Eléni's heart raced and she looked at Simos. 'Yes, Andreas Spyros Mouzakis. The names of both my birth parents are imprinted on my brain. Why?'

'In the school hall, artwork from well-known Kefalonian artists is displayed on the walls. I'm sure there is one by Andreas Mouzakis. It may not be him of course and I don't want to build up your hopes.'

CHAPTER FIFTY-ONE

Eléni couldn't believe what was happening. Was she about to see an exhibition featuring art painted or drawn by the father she had no recollection of? Eugenia had said 'well-known artists'. It was all Eléni could do not to break into a run.

The school would be closed as it was a Saturday, but her aunt had directed her to the caretaker's house nearby. She hoped she could persuade him to open the school up for her. At the top of a stepped street, they found the salmon-pink house situated on the edge of the school playground. The gate into the yard was open and a man was sweeping the paved area next to the main doors.

Eléni and Simos crossed the yard and approached the man. '*Kalispéra*. My name is Eléni Mouzakis. Some of my father's artwork is exhibited in the school hall, I believe.' The man rested on his broom handle.

'I do not look at the names. I do not look at the paintings. I have more important jobs to do around the school.'

He began sweeping again.

Eléni's heartbeat raced. 'My aunt, Eugenia Papadatos, wondered if you would let me see them, *parakaló*. You see he died in the earthquake, and I was too young to remember him.'

'I should not open the school at a weekend, I think.'

Eléni's skin prickled. *Can't you break the rules for once, you stupid man?* Simos held her arm as if knowing she was about to say something she shouldn't.

'We understand,' he said calmly. 'But Eléni has come to Kefalonia to find her family, and I'm sure your headteacher would forgive you if you just let her into the hall to see her father's work. *Efcharistó.*'

The caretaker took a bunch of keys from his pocket. 'Ten minutes.'

They walked through a hallway and entered a large, light and airy room. Eléni scanned the walls until her eyes rested on a plaque that made goosebumps form on her skin. *Andreas Spyros Mouzakis (1924–1953). Studied at the Athens School of Art.* The head-and-shoulders photograph was of a young, bearded man with black curly hair and large dark eyes. He appeared to be looking straight at her. *Oh, Baba. I wish I could remember you.*

'So that's your baba.' Simos took her hand as she began to weep. In silence, they walked slowly to look at each painting or drawing in turn. A few larger pictures were painted in oils and had a freedom of brushwork that suggested spontaneity. They reflected the vibrant colours of the island. Seascapes in a range of turquoise, aquamarine and teals, or mountain land-scapes with dark green cypresses, Aleppo pines and silver-grey olive trees, dotted with wildflowers and the occasional goat. But it was the smaller pen-and-ink drawings that fascinated her most. The style and attention to detail could be mistaken for her own. In her mind, there wasn't any doubt that this was the correct Andreas Spyros Mouzakis. She reprimanded herself for comparing her modest drawings with her famous father's when she was just starting out on her own art career.

'It has to be in the genes,' Simos voiced what she wondered herself.

Even though the purpose of the visit to Fiscardo had been to find her uncle and that had proved to be in vain, seeing her father's artwork displayed was more than Eléni could have hoped for. She'd made contact with Theía Eugenia again and hoped she'd built bridges between her aunt and her mother.

* * *

Eléni turned up for work at the taverna the following day. It took her a while to get used to the prices and making sure she served the tables in the order the customers had arrived. Even though she'd worked all day and had had several night shifts as a waitress before coming out to Kefalonia, Eléni was surprised how tired she was after being on her feet in the heat. It was at these times she wished she still had the deep bath at the hotel where she'd stayed when she'd first arrived to sink into. Instead, she'd managed to find a room at a shabby lodging house. At least it was clean and cheap, and it meant she could stay on in Kefalonia.

When Simos was working, she used her free time to get as much drawing done as she could. Inspired by her father's paintings, she started using coloured inks more and more. She kept her drawings of the buildings in her customary mono-chrome, but for any seascapes she used the transparency of blue, turquoise and emerald inks to create pictures glowing with Mediterranean colours. Normally Simos wouldn't visit the taverna until her evening shifts were almost over but, one Thursday evening, Eléni noticed him sitting at a table under the awning when she went outside to serve.

'Simos, I didn't expect to see you here until much later.'

His eyes sparkled. 'I've got some terrific news and I couldn't wait to tell you.'

'What is it?' Eléni's heart quickened in anticipation. It must be important if he couldn't wait for just a mere three hours. She checked there were no customers waiting to be served.

'The advert. You know the one asking for the where-abouts of your uncle?'

She nodded. That was weeks ago and there'd been no response. She had resigned herself to the fact that Kostas

Koulouris wasn't on the island. She'd have to be content with knowing who she was, but with no living relatives.

'Well, today I received a phone call from a man who said his name was Theo Koulouris. He lives in Argostoli with his wife and daughter. They've just got back from a holiday and he found the local paper in the mail that had built up. And his father is a Kostas Koulouris! He remembers his father telling him about returning to the island to find all his family had perished . . .'

'Eléni. You have people waiting to be served.' The owner glowered at her from the doorway of the taverna.

'I'll have to go. I'll see you at ten.' She rushed inside and attended to a family of four. Taking their order, all she could do was think about what Simos had just told her. *Don't get your hopes up. Don't get your hopes up.* They'd found countless men with the same name as her uncle. Many of them would have found they'd had no living family after the earthquake if they hadn't been living on the island at the time. She went through the motions of being the attentive waitress and ensuring the owner had no reason to reprimand her again, but all she could do was wish away the minutes and hours until ten o'clock. When she hung up her apron and left the taverna, she expected Simos to be outside but he had left. She sat on the harbour wall and it wasn't long before he joined her.

'I'm sorry about earlier. I hope you didn't get a hard time,' he said.

'No, nothing was mentioned. I made sure I didn't give him anything else to complain about. But tell me more about this Theo. Shall we stop at our usual bar for a drink?' Eléni pointed at a taverna that was popular with the locals, where she and Simos had started frequenting after she'd finished work.

'If you like,' said Simos. 'But I wondered if you'd like to come back to my flat. I've been doing some investigating and we won't be disturbed there.'

She'd never been to Simos's place and the invite surprised her. He was such a private person, but slowly he was opening up. At times, she felt guilty her family search took up so much of his time, but, on the other hand, perhaps it helped him to reflect on his.

'If you're sure. You'll have to finish what you were saying in the taverna, though. It's all I could think about.'

He took her arm and guided her along the streets into the large square.

'You got to the bit where this man told you his father had returned to find his whole family had perished.' Eléni's pulse quickened. Was there a 'but' to the story?

'He was devastated and his son said he turned to drink. One night in a bar, Kostas overheard a British man asking for personal family stories about the earthquake. It turned out he was a reporter who'd helped rescue a little girl from the rubble. He asked the question to people around him — how did they really know what had happened to their relatives when there were no death certificates or identification? It got Kostas thinking. Here we are.'

Simos's flat was on the second floor of a white-rendered building in a street parallel to the office where he worked.

'I don't have far to get to work.' He laughed as he opened the door. 'Come in.'

The narrow entrance hall led to a large square living space defying the style of the communal hallway. The white walls were bare. Sleek, modern Scandinavian furniture was kept to a minimum apart from a large corner sofa dominating the room. There were no ornaments and no photographs on display. Every surface was clear. Eléni thought how different it was from her own home back in Wales. Everything here looked expensive and classy, but it wasn't a home. It looked more like one of those show houses you saw in magazines.

'Sit down. What can I get you to drink?' Simos opened a door in the wooden cabinet positioned on the opposite wall from the sofa. 'I have all the usual spirits, ouzo and raki. There's wine and beer in the fridge, or perhaps you'd like a coffee.'

'I'll have a wine, please. This is a very smart place you have here.' He returned with the wine, a beer for himself and a dish of pistachio nuts and olives. 'How do you keep it so tidy?' Eléni thought of her cluttered bedroom back at the lodging house.

'I can't cope with things lying around or out of place. Force of habit after being in the orphanage. If we didn't pick up our things, they were thrown away. We soon learned . . . not that we had much. Anyway, let's talk about Kostas Koulouris. What do you think?'

Eléni sipped her wine. She recognised it as the same Robola one she'd enjoyed on their evening to see the sunset. 'It certainly sounds promising, doesn't it?'

'It does. And here's the best bit. He questioned the reporter for more information about the little girl and found out she was rescued in the street where his parents and sister lived. I think we have to pay Kýrios Koulouris a visit, don't you?'

Eléni's hand shook and she placed her wine down on the glass coffee table. She thought about the reporter who'd been the reason her mother had taken her from Porth Gwyn and moved to Cardiff. It was too much of a coincidence, surely. '*Nai, parakaló.* I know I mustn't get my hopes up. Does this Theo think his father will want to see us?'

'*Nai.* He'll take us there. I hope you don't mind me arranging it before checking with you first, but I said we could go on Monday. I can always cancel it if it's not convenient.' Simos looked so excited on her behalf. If only she could repay him and help to find his family.

'Of course I don't. *Efcharistó.* That's wonderful. I'd given up hope as it's been a few weeks since the advert.'

He brought a map of the island over from a drawer in the cabinet. He spread it on the coffee table in front of them. Leaning over to look at the map, Eléni felt the warmth of his thigh against hers. Fizzles of excitement shot through her, but she knew he was unaware of the effect his closeness had on her.

'He lives here. Just a few kilometres away. The town was badly hit by the earthquake and instead of building over the ruins, they built a new town close by. In Old Farsa, you will see parts of buildings and single walls left standing as they were left after the disaster. The new town is lower down and built to survive any new shocks . . . they hope. He'll pick us up by the museum at ten o'clock. Is that all right?'

CHAPTER FIFTY-TWO

Theo Koulouris arrived dead on time in his open-top silver BMW. Eléni thought he looked about the same age as her, maybe a few years younger. After morning greetings and introductions, they were soon leaving Argostoli behind, winding along the coast road and avoiding the occasional goat along the way.

Theo looked in the rear mirror. 'My father is looking forward to meeting you, Eléni. With just the little information we have, he is convinced you are his niece, Iôánna. It makes us cousins if you are! There's no one else. Mamá died several years ago.'

'I'm sorry to hear that. I can't wait to meet your baba either. But we mustn't build our hopes up. I'd almost resigned myself to never finding my uncle, hadn't I?'

Simos turned around from the passenger seat and smiled. 'I have a good feeling about this.'

For the rest of the journey, the two men chatted in the front of the car while Eléni drank in the magnificent views of the sea and the little coves below. It was good to feel the breeze on her face and her long hair blew out behind her.

In what seemed like no time at all, they arrived at their destination.

'Here we are,' said Theo. 'Baba moved to New Farsa after Mamá died. He couldn't bear to be in the house without her. Here there are no memories.'

Turning off the main road, he drew up into a street leading down a hill and parked halfway down. The sleek BMW seemed out of place. The one other vehicle parked nearby was an old Datsun Cherry, covered in thick dust and sporting several dents. Theo led them to his father's house and entered through a wooden beaded curtain.

'Baba, we've arrived.' He turned to Eléni and Simos. 'Come on through.'

Eléni clasped her hands together to stop them shaking. She found it difficult to breathe. The room at the back of the house was dark and cool. Kostas Koulouris got up from his chair in the corner and embraced his son.

'Baba, this is Eléni, the young woman I told you about, and her friend, Simos Georgatos.'

The man immediately broke down in tears. Theo wrapped his arms around his father to comfort him. 'Whatever's wrong?' he said. 'I haven't seen you like this since Mamá passed.'

His father moved towards Eléni and took her hands. 'This is my niece. There is not a shadow of doubt. It is like looking at my sister, your dear mamá, at the same age.' Tears still streaming down his cheeks, he pulled Eléni into his arms. '*Efcharistó, efcharistó*. I never thought I would see this day.'

Her uncle's body convulsed into sobs against her. She'd dreamed about this moment ever since she'd found her aunt's letter. She wept in silence with her arms around her uncle. Theo and Simos allowed the two of them time to savour their moment.

'Come with me, Simos. We'll take some drinks into the garden and let Baba and Eléni get to know each other.'

Kostas took Eléni to sit on the small sofa. He held her hand. 'You have to know, *agápi mou*. I tried so hard to find you. Once I heard you may be alive, I wanted to bring you up as my daughter, a sister for Theo. My wife, Philia, agreed. We were blessed with one son and you would have made our family complete. I was working away in Australia when the disaster happened. I couldn't get back here until almost two years after the earthquake and by then you had left Kefalonia.'

Eléni imagined what it would have been like being brought up here on the island. 'How did you find out I'd survived?'

Her uncle seemed to want to talk about that awful time. It was as if just seeing his niece had opened up all these horrible memories. 'Philia and Theo were still living in Athens. I'd come back here to find out who of my family had survived. I'm ashamed to say I was so shocked everyone in my family had died, I started to drink. Every night, too much raki. I got talking to a reporter who'd been here right after the earthquake and his paper had sent him back two years later to find out how the island was doing after so many had emigrated.'

Rhodri Jones! Eléni was convinced of it.

'He told me he'd seen a couple take a little girl away in a farmer's horse and trap with a doubtful explanation of going to visit the animals on the man's farm. He didn't believe them and found out they'd gone to Fiscardo to the woman's sister.'

'And you tracked my Theía Eugenia down and visited her there.'

Kostas sat back on the sofa. 'How do you know that?'

'Because my aunt warned my mother someone was looking for me.'

His face turned red as he stood and paced the floor, his voice rising. 'And she did nothing about it? How could she?' Her uncle spat the words out.

Eléni spoke in a whisper. 'Please don't be angry, Theíos Kostas. She just did what she thought was best for me. She *honestly* thought I had no one. She saved me from going into an orphanage. I had such a happy childhood. I've heard awful stories about cruelty if I'd been taken in by the authorities.' Eléni thought of Simos and the life he'd had.

Kostas's face remained serious. 'But she denied me finding the one member of my family who'd survived!' Calming down, he brushed away a tear and returned to sit beside his niece.

'Anyway, I sorted myself out and brought Philia and Theo to Argostoli. We made our life here on the island where I could be close to my sister and parents, and where I grew up.' He turned to Eléni and let out a big sigh. 'She had no right to do that, you know. But I can't change what happened. Let's see where the men are.'

Eléni noticed the framed photographs displayed on a dark wooden bureau. As well as a wedding photograph with a young-looking Kostas as the groom and a portrait of a baby that must be Theo, one stood out to Eléni. Her heart skipped a beat. It was like looking in a mirror. It had to be her mother. The same heart-shaped face, the huge dark eyes and the curly hair reaching below her shoulders. Her hands shaking and her eyes welling with tears, she asked, 'Is this my mamá?' She knew full well it was.

'*Nai.* Wasn't she beautiful? *You* are beautiful.'

For the first time since Eléni had found out, the feeling of not knowing who she really was lifted. She at last knew whose blood ran through her veins. First seeing her father's photograph in the school hall in Fiscardo, and now this one of her mother, had had such a profound effect on her. She had one person to thank. Simos Georgatos.

Her lip trembled. 'She was very beautiful. And who's this?' Cassia pointed to another photograph. One of a little girl about five, which was in colour.

'My granddaughter, Amara. Remind you of someone?'

'She looks like my mamá, I think.'

'And you!'

They joined Theo and Simos outside. The small court-yard was partially shaded by a wooden pergola, draped in a well-established magenta bougainvillea.

'Ah, good. You've got glasses for us, too. Help yourself to the lemonade, Eléni. Homemade, using the new-fangled juicer my posh son gave me, no doubt.'

Theo laughed. 'Well, someone has to use it, Baba. I found it still in the box!'

It was clear father and son got on well. Eléni felt a pang as she wondered what life would have been like for her if Kostas Koulouris had returned to the island earlier and then berated herself for her disloyalty.

It was soon time to leave. The old man disappeared into the house and brought out a handful of small black-and-white photographs.

'Here, you must have these, Eléni. To remind you of your real family.' His voice became scratchy.

Eléni's heart raced. There were photos of a baby at different ages, some of a toddler with black curls and others of a young couple she recognised as her parents. Her eyes pricked with tears. She turned over each one to see they had been labelled and dated. The baby and young child was her. Her uncle pulled her into a hug.

'This is a special one,' he said, handing her a bigger photograph of an older woman dressed in black with her hair pulled back from her face. She held a young child who looked up at her with a wide smile on her face. 'I took this on your fourth birthday before I left to work in Australia. Mamá adored you. Her first grandchild.' His eyes misted with tears. 'It was the last time I saw her.'

Eléni hugged him tighter. '*Efcharistó*, Theíos Kostas. I shall treasure them. And thank you for looking for me. I'll come and see you again before I leave. Perhaps on a Monday. It's my day off.'

CHAPTER FIFTY-THREE

She'd been working at the taverna for several weeks. It now wasn't long until the anniversary of the earthquake and Argostoli was growing busier with holidaymakers. Eléni worked some longer shifts but managed to keep her Mondays free and not work any more evenings. She saw Simos whenever she could and spent her free time drawing. Before visiting her uncle again, she'd wanted to finish a drawing of the church with the bell tower so she could present it to him as a gift to remember her by.

She took the ten o'clock bus to Farsa. There were few seats left and even in the morning, it was stiflingly hot. She smiled to herself when she compared the bumpy, uncomfortable ride with the luxury of the one in Theo's sleek convertible. Once at her uncle's cottage, she called through the beaded curtain. 'Theíos Kostas. It's me, Eléni!'

The old man greeted her with a beaming smile and kissed her on both cheeks. After making frappés, they sat outside under the pergola and chatted.

'Your mamá was a talented embroiderer and lacemaker, you know.'

Eléni gasped. 'Cassia did that, too. It's such a coincidence, don't you think? And I don't know one end of a needle from another.'

They both laughed.

'People use to come to her for handmade table linen to give as wedding presents and layettes for their babies. She even made her own wedding dress.' Kostas stood and went back inside the house. He brought out a large photograph in a cardboard cover, yellowed with age. 'Doesn't she look wonderful?'

A lump formed in Eléni's throat. 'Nai. So beautiful. Did she make the long train?'

Her uncle nodded, then laughed. 'She was stitching it for months.'

'Is that you, standing by Baba?'

'It is. I was — how do you say? — their best man. I won't give you that one as it is the only picture I have of the three of us together.' He took a deep breath. Eléni could see how difficult it was for her uncle to deal with his loss even after all that time.

'And Baba was an artist. I went to see his work in Fiscardo.' Eléni brought out the drawing from her bag. 'Much as I loved his large oil paintings, it was the pen-and-ink drawings that fascinated me. It's the medium I work in.' She showed her uncle her drawing of the church.

Kostas Koulouris gasped. 'You drew this? It's the church in Argostoli. The bell tower survived. A miracle! You are so talented just like your baba. Even as a tiny girl, you would draw all the time. He was so proud of you.'

Eléni swallowed, afraid of letting the tears fall. 'Thank you for telling me that. He must have passed his love of drawing on to me. I'd love to make a living from my art. Eventually get a workshop and gallery. But that is a long time in the future.'

Her uncle took both of her hands and looked into her eyes. 'After everything that has happened, follow your dreams. Follow in your father's footsteps. Carry on the Mouzakis name in the field of art.'

Was she talented enough to do that? An image of her birth father entered Eléni's head as if to give her his approval. But she couldn't drop the name of Beynon and become a Mouzakis, could she?

'Now, before you need to catch the bus back, I think it's time for lunch. Will Greek salad and olive bread do you?'

Kostas entered the kitchen and brought the food outside. 'The tomatoes are my own,' he said, pointing beyond the paved area to where staked plants laden with juicy red tomatoes continued to ripen in the hot sun among a variety of herbs and courgettes.

Eléni drizzled more olive oil and sprinkled oregano over the slab of feta Kostas had served in a rustic terracotta bowl for her. 'This is delicious, Theíos Kostas. The tomatoes are so sweet compared to the ones we have back home.'

When it was time to leave, Eléni handed her drawing to her uncle. 'I want you to have this to remind you of me when I go back to Wales. I can't thank you enough for trying to find me all those years ago and especially today for telling me more about my mamá and baba. I just wish I could remember them. Now you've told me about Baba encouraging me to draw, I do seem to have a recollection of sitting at a big table and someone putting cushions underneath me on the chair so I was high enough to draw. Perhaps it was him.'

Her uncle hugged Eléni. 'They would be so proud of the young woman you've become, *agápi mou*. It's down to the people who brought you up. I'm no longer angry and I'm sorry about how I behaved last time. I'd like your parents' address so I can write to them.'

Eléni smiled. She had some serious apologising to do too. Taking the pen and paper from her uncle, she wrote down her parents' name and address. '*Efcharistó*. It will mean so much to them, to my mother in particular.'

Kostas walked her to the door where they embraced for the final time. '*Antío*. Keep in touch. Maybe come to Kefalonia often. This is your home, don't forget.'

'*Antío*, Theíos Kostas.'

* * *

That evening, Eléni and Simos met at the taverna along from the one where she worked. They ordered beers and two portions of kreatopita, with salad. Simos moved his food around the plate as if he wasn't hungry, so Eléni finished well before he did. She was so excited to tell him everything about her visit to see her uncle that she didn't notice how quiet Simos was at first. After a while she became aware he hadn't commented at all on her news. Eléni worried something had happened at work. She took his hand. 'Is everything all right? You're very quiet tonight.'

He pulled his hand away, not able to make eye contact. 'Yes, I'm fine.' Sounding unconvincing, he continued, 'I'm pleased you found out more about your family. But that's my job done, isn't it? You'll be going home now.' He paused. 'I'm going to miss you. I've never been as close as this to anyone before. The very few relationships I've had have all been disastrous. The girls accused me of being — how do you say? — a cold fish. But with you . . .'

Eléni took his face in her hands and turned it to hers. His eyes were shiny with unshed tears.

'I'm not going anywhere yet. I'm staying until at least the anniversary celebrations are over and afterwards, who knows? Yes, I will go back to see my parents and sister. But I feel at home here in Kefalonia. Theíos Kostas has told me to come back often so this isn't the end.'

The way Simos looked at her was different somehow. There was an intensity in his gaze as if he was locking the vision of her into his mind, never to let her go. Eléni hadn't realised how close their faces had become. She could feel his breath on her cheeks. Leaning across, she kissed the handsome man sitting opposite her. His lips were warm and soft. When he responded, her insides somersaulted.

'I've been wanting to do that since I first met you,' she said. 'I had to wait until you were ready.'

Simos stood and moved to sit on the same side of the table as her. He pulled her towards him, whispering, 'I'm ready.'

He kissed her again, this time with more urgency. When they broke free, a cheer went up from the surrounding diners. They both grinned.

'Come on, let's go.' Simos grabbed her hand.

Arms around each other as they walked down the streets, Eléni felt the relationship between her and Simos had turned just a corner. Her heartbeat raced. She'd known for a while he liked her as a friend and enjoyed her company, but he'd responded the way a lover would to her kiss. Could love have a future when two people were thousands of miles apart?

They reached Simos's apartment block and he led the way up to his flat. They resumed kissing as soon as the door shut behind them. Electricity fizzed through her veins. It was as if all the longing and not knowing if there was any hope of him feeling the same had built up and was about to explode. They fell back onto the sofa with their arms and legs entwined.

'Oh, why have I wasted so much time?' Simos planted butterfly kisses down her cheek and along her shoulder. His hot breath on her earlobe made her shiver with pleasure.

'Shh,' she whispered. 'We can make up for it now.'

Taking their time, they caressed and undressed each other. Simos took Eléni's hand and led her to the bedroom. And make up for lost time they did.

CHAPTER FIFTY-FOUR

Throughout July, Eléni and Simos spent more time at his apartment now their relationship had moved to a different level. She often thought back to the evening when they'd made love for the first time. In spite of them both being so inexperienced, it was as if they were learning together. Very soon Simos became a passionate and skilful lover who made sure Eléni reached new heights of pleasure she could have only imagined.

One night, they were lying in each other's arms in the afterglow of making love. Moonlight bathed the bedroom in silver. Without warning, Eléni was overcome with sadness. A single tear trickled onto the pillow as she caressed Simos's cheek. 'I'm going to miss this so much. Miss *you* so much. I don't want this night to end.'

Simos sat up. 'Then don't go. Why not stay and make your home here? Become another famous Mouzakis artist.'

Before she could answer, he lay back down and kissed her.

'I can't. Although I've extended my stay, I've promised my family I'll go home after the anniversary. But I've promised *myself* I'll be back here soon. I'll be here for my actual birthday and you can help me celebrate on the real day for the first time in my life.'

Eléni needed to tell her parents everything she'd found out. It didn't seem fair to write it down in a letter, but, once she'd been to see them, could she make Kefalonia her home? Simos had given her an idea. What better place with all the magnificent scenes, both seascapes and landscapes, to concentrate on her artwork? She'd always dreamed about having a studio, so why not here? Many girls had left home by the time they were her age, she reasoned. It was easy now to get to the island by aeroplane and it would be a good way of getting her mother to keep in touch not just with her, but with Theía Eugenia too. Perhaps Cassia would be prepared meet her uncle, and she knew Bronwen would be a frequent visitor. Eléni and Simos got dressed and returned to the sitting room.

'You know, you've given me an idea. Do you think I would be able to sell my drawings and paintings? And would there be a market for them, do you think?'

Simos smiled. 'Of course, there is. I'd buy them anyway!'

'And spoil those pristine white walls?' She teased him, but the difference between the gorgeous man sitting beside her and the reserved, aloof person whom she'd first met at the archive office was remarkable. They were like two completely opposite men. She held his hand. Seeing how Simos had opened up and not been afraid to show his feelings in such a short time was something she would never forget. She'd fallen in love with him almost straight away. Could there be such a thing as love at first sight?

'So I've got to be prepared to lose you for a little while and then you'll be back. Promise? Because if you don't, I'll come looking for you. It means we have to decide how to make the most of the time we've got left. When is your plane ticket booked for?'

'I extended it until after the actual anniversary and the feast day of St Gerasimos. Someone told me it's quite a spectacle when everyone attends his monastery.'

'It is. The sixteenth of August, four days after, and it's also my name day. Not that I ever celebrate.' Simos became pensive. Eléni knew he had no one to celebrate with.

'Well, you will this year. I'll make sure it's a special day for you before I catch my plane the next day.'

Eléni rested her head on Simos's shoulder and they sat, holding hands, together with their thoughts. She thought back to how her parents had made birthdays happy and fun for her and Bronwen, and yet Simos had no memories to reflect on. There must be something she could do to help him find his true identity as he'd done for her. She made a vow to herself there and then that, when she returned to the island, she would do everything she could to help him. He'd made a start by talking to the archivist when they'd visited Fiscardo, but nothing more had been mentioned. Perhaps he still wasn't ready. Because of his research, she could return home knowing a lot about her birth family that she could tell the parents and sister who loved her.

'Come on. Let's go for a walk.' Simos pulled her up from the settee.

The balmy night air was a complete contrast to the air conditioning in the apartment. Apart from the chatter of diners as they passed a taverna, it was quiet when they walked in the direction of the harbour under the moonlight. Instead of turning left towards the quayside where boats were moored, they made their way to the edge of a park overlooking the sea and found a bench. The noise of cicadas pierced the silence.

'The moonlight is tricking the tzitzikas it's daytime,' said Simos. 'They are very loud tonight.'

'I'd never heard of them until I came to Kefalonia and certainly had never heard them.' Eléni snuggled up to Simos. 'There are so many things I'd never seen or heard before I came here.' She added with a grin, 'Or felt.'

He turned her head and sought her lips, kissing them softly.

'And you have made me see how much I was missing. I don't just mean the sex. That's been wonderful. But it's more than that. You've put me in touch with my emotions again. From the little boy in the orphanage when I'd shut everything down, I feel alive now. And it's all down to you.'

'Oh, Simos.'

The moonlight sprinkled its magic on the water in front of them and as they kissed, Eléni marvelled at being in such a romantic setting with the man she loved. And she did love Simos. She would do everything she could to make this long-distance relationship work. She had a feeling he wanted that, too.

CHAPTER FIFTY-FIVE

The hotels were now full. Although there was not going to be a formal event on the actual day of the anniversary, when Eléni spoke to customers during her shifts in the taverna, they all said they wanted to come and pay their respects to those who had died. Many were Greeks who had emigrated to America in the aftermath of the disaster. Most had married local men and women and were bringing them and their children to the island for the first time, as part of their Greek–American heritage. All were staying on to observe the spectacle of the annual pilgrimage to the church of St Gerasimos, when hundreds would arrive to pay their respects to the island's patron saint.

One evening, after finishing her shift, Simos surprised Eléni by taking her to a restaurant she hadn't visited before. With its prime position overlooking the harbour in the distance, away from the bustle of the tavernas and bars, Ta Elaiódentra was a pale-pink building set in its own grounds surrounded by mature olive trees from which it took its name. Oleander bushes with blooms the same colour as the rendered walls of the restaurant lined the short walkway from the street to the glass-covered outside seating area.

'I thought we could try this place tonight,' he said. 'You deserve to be wined and dined after being kept so busy now at the taverna.' He took Eléni's hand and kissed it. 'If you like it, perhaps we could come here the evening before the anniversary. I expect every restaurant and taverna will be overflowing with diners on the night of the twelfth. And, besides, do we really want to celebrate the day both of us became orphans? Acknowledge it and remember it, yes, but I want the evening to be special for you.'

Eléni smiled and took his hand as he led her into the restaurant. 'Every meal out with you is special, Simos Georgatos. Especially when you pick amazing places like this.'

'Ah, but this is going to be *extra* special. You'll have to wait and see.'

The restaurant was full and Eléni was pleased when the waiter took them to the table on the upstairs verandah that Simos had booked for them. The food was superb. Eléni had the sea bream and Simos chose his favourite lamb souvlaki. After they'd drunk their coffees and were sipping the complimentary ouzos, Simos took Eléni's hand.

'Do you remember me saying my friend, the archivist in Fiscardo, was going to help me with a bit of research about my family?'

'Yes, have you heard from him?'

Simos became animated. 'Yes, Lysander rang the office today. All I'd given him to go on was my name and the name of the orphanage.' He inhaled deeply. 'I haven't mentioned anything to you but since talking to him, I've been letting myself think about the day of the earthquake more. I remember I had two brothers who were much younger than me, babies perhaps. My mother was beautiful and kind. She had a sweet singing voice.' Bringing his fist to his mouth, he stifled a sob. 'As well as my parents and grandparents, my aunt, uncle and cousins lived in the house next door. Everyone was wiped out while I played in the garden.'

Eléni stroked his hands with hers. 'Helping me find my family must have been so hard for you. I'm so sorry.'

314

'No, not at all. It's what I needed! Anyway, he's found out I was from Old Farsa. I could have done this myself years ago, of course, but hadn't been able to face it. The best news is he's visited the area, and, better than that, he's found someone who lived through the earthquake. Kýria Lourdata. She is willing to see me!'

* * *

On her day off, Simos picked up Eléni in a hired truck that would be more suitable than his car to reach the ruined village of Old Farsa up in the mountains. Lysander had told Simos that, at first, Kýria Lourdata had refused to be rehoused in New Farsa when her home had been destroyed in 1953, but had relented in the end as long as she could be at the nearest point in the new village to her original home.

'I told Kýria Lourdata we'd arrive about eleven o'clock, so I thought we could go to Old Farsa first and see what's left of it. Perhaps more memories will come back to me. I was a bit older than you were, don't forget?' Simos looked across at Eléni. 'It's strange, but I'm feeling quite nervous.'

Eléni squeezed his thigh. 'You're at the stage I was when we came to visit my uncle. I know how you feel.'

The car climbed its way up to the ruined village. Eventually, they had to get out and make the last part of the journey on foot.

'I'm glad you warned me to wear strong shoes,' said Eléni. The narrow gravel path clung to the edge of a steep cliff and it would be so easy for them to lose their footing. Below them, halfway down the mountain and nearer the sea, the orange-red roof tiles of the houses in New Farsa glowed brightly in the sun.

Reaching the ruins, there was still plenty of evidence of the houses that had once stood there in the old village. The paths were now covered in grass and they could make out the shape of the village square.

They came to a ruin where one wall stood with its wooden door still attached to the masonry. Behind it was a plot of land in which there was what looked like an olive press and several squat olive trees, their trunks gnarled and twisted. All the colour drained from Simos's face.

'Are you all right? What is it?'

He shivered.

'I think this could be where I used to live. See the old tree at the farthest point from the house? I had a treehouse there and that's what saved me.' He walked across to where the tree stood, forlorn and gnarled. 'Look, there are still some rotting planks of wood underneath. They must have fallen from the fork in the branches where the floor was.' He pointed to the heap of rubble beside the standing wall. 'Everyone else was in there.' He put his hands over his ears. 'There was an ear-splitting, huge bang. I heard everyone's screams and the crack from the wall shattering threw up so much dust I couldn't even see the house.'

He steadied himself against the solitary wall. 'I've never allowed myself to remember until now. Oh, Eléni.' She held him until he'd cried twenty years of tears. 'I'm sorry.'

'Shh. If it's too much, we don't have to do it all today.'

'No, I'll be fine. It's long overdue.'

They wandered around the old, ruined buildings. It was eerily silent apart from the sound of birdsong and an accompaniment from the cicadas. A welcome light breeze sprang up and wafted the smells of wild thyme and a neglected jasmine bush.

'It must have been a beautiful place to grow up before . . .' Eléni's voice was barely audible. She was living the emotions Simos must have been feeling inside.

From the colour of the stone and the size of the buildings, Eléni tried to imagine what it had been before the fateful day when Simos's life had changed for ever. He'd carried his burden around for twenty years. She'd only known about being an orphan for five months.

He looked at his watch.

'Come on. Let's go and meet Kýria Lourdata.'

CHAPTER FIFTY-SIX

They found the single-storey house that belonged to Kýria Lourdata. It was situated at the top of a steep hill leading from the main road of New Farsa, whitewashed and with a pristine terracotta-tiled roof. Eléni could imagine how difficult the old lady would have found it to settle here when she'd been part of the community in the original village, with its hundreds of years of history high above her, for all her life. The path up to the door was edged with stone pots where trailing scarlet geraniums tumbled over the sides. Before they had a chance to pull the rope bell, the door was opened by an elderly woman leaning heavily on a stick. Her snow-white hair was scraped back into a tight bun, giving her face a pinched expression. Her caramel, weathered skin suggested she'd spent much of her life outdoors.

'Kýria Lourdata?'

'I've been waiting for you.' Her wrinkles then softened. 'Call me Kýria Delia. Come through.'

Simos checked his watch. They weren't late.

Walking into the tiny house, Eléni noticed how tidy everything was. It was a little like Simos's apartment but in miniature, and so unusual for an old lady's home. She thought of all the ornaments, photographs and mementos on display at Auntie Gwladys's house. But of course, Kýria Delia had lost all hers. Maybe they couldn't be replaced.

She took them to the back of the house where the outside space was as immaculate as the inside. Again, there were lots of pots and an abundance of colour.

'This is so lovely. Do you do all this yourself?' Eléni looked around at the courtyard before sitting on the bench offered by Kýria Delia.

'*Nai.* I have got to keep going, you know. This is nothing compared to my house up there.' She nodded in the direction of Old Farsa. 'Twenty years since it happened. Pah! This isn't my home. It's just somewhere they told me I had to live. They should have rebuilt up there. It broke my heart.' The old lady's eyes shone with tears. 'Now, what do you want to know?'

Simos was taken aback by her abrupt tone. 'I've just found out from Lysander Favata I'm from Old Farsa. After all my family was killed, I was taken to an orphanage in Patras and my memory of what happened is very sketchy. Almost non-existent. He said you may be able to help me.'

'Everyone left the village, mostly to live with relatives in the north where they'd escaped the worst of it. The children who were orphaned like you were rounded up and taken to the orphanage outside Argostoli, but soon it was so full they started sending the orphans to the mainland orphanages.' Kýria Delia got up from her wooden chair opposite to look intently at Simos. 'You remind me of someone. My old brain isn't what it was but, when I saw you at the door, I thought it then too. What did you say your name was?'

He looked at Eléni. 'Simos Georgatos.'

'That's it! Gerasimos Georgatos. The headmaster of the school. He looked just like you!'

Eléni hugged Simos. 'He must be your baba.'

'When it happened, he had a little boy about six — I remember he'd just started school the year before — and they also had twin boys who were about two. The family was well known in the village. Every one of them was wiped out apart from the little boy. So sad. Living next door to them was his sister and all of her family, if I remember rightly.'

'Theía María.' Simos closed his eyes. 'She often looked after me and I played with her girls. My cousins. More is coming back. So the wall still standing with the large wooden door, was it where I lived?'

Delia nodded. 'I haven't been up there for years but if it's the one I think you mean, yes. It was the old schoolhouse, and next to it would have been the school itself, and the yard, but there's nothing to see of it now. It was lucky the school was closed for the summer.' Her voice cracked. 'All those children . . .'

The old lady sat back in her chair.

Simos looked again at Eléni, as if for reassurance. 'One more thing, Kýria Delia. I can see this has been so hard for you and I'm very grateful. But do you know where my family is buried?'

'In the cemetery in New Farsa. Everyone was.'

Eléni stood and went to the old lady. It was obvious she was exhausted by all the talk. '*Efcharistó*, Kýria Delia. Please don't get up. You've helped Simos such a lot.'

'Yes, Eléni's right. I've shut away all that happened on that awful day. We can pay our respects to my family now.'

In spite of their protests, Delia Lourdata struggled to get up again with the help of her stick. 'I offered to look after you and another boy who was orphaned, you know.'

Simos's mouth gaped open.

'I didn't know either of you well, but I wanted to do something to help. They told me I was too old and you had to be taken away. Pah! I was only sixty then and a lot fitter than this.'

'That was so kind of you, Kýria Delia.' Eléni wondered what would have happened if the authorities had allowed Delia Lourdata to raise Simos. It would have been no different to the many orphans who'd been raised by their grandparents.

She allowed Simos and Eléni to hug her before they left to drive further into the village. They parked the car and walked into the cemetery where there were row upon row of stone memorials. Several of the newer gravestones had inscriptions with full names, dates all post-1953, and messages. On some were enamelled colour portraits of the family members lying beneath the soil. However, the vast majority were plain, square headstones of white marble, simply inscribed with a name and the date of the earthquake.

Simos and Eléni split up to try to find his parents' resting place. After searching for some time, Simos found three headstones touching each other in a line.

'I've found them! Come and see, Eléni.' She found him kneeling on the ground in front of the first one, his hand outstretched on the top of the stone.

Gerasimos Christós Georgatos
Pelagia Darnia Georgatos
Alexander Christós Georgatos
Andreas Christós Georgatos
12 August 1953

Simos stood and bowed his head. 'At least I have proof they existed. Alexander and Andreas, my little brothers.'

'I'm so pleased you've found them. Do you think the next grave could belong to your yiayiá and pappoú? They have the Georgatos name, so they could be your baba's parents.'

Simos agreed and read their names aloud. '*Gerasimos Constantine Georgatos, Daphne Gaia Georgatos, Yiayiá and Pappoú.* Another Gerasimos. Perhaps they were very religious. Especially as my twin brothers had Christós as their middle names. I do remember having to go to church a lot. Why haven't I had these memories before?'

Eléni squeezed his hand. 'Because you were afraid to remember and you buried it deep inside you. I expect the next grave belongs to your auntie. *Demosthenes Stavros Pandis, Maria Eléni Pandis, Daphne Zena Pandis, Cora Maria Pandis.*'

'I can't explain, but, after coming here, I feel different. Being reminded of everyone's names and knowing they are lying at rest together has somehow lifted the heaviness in my chest that always weighed me down.' Tears wetted his cheeks as he pulled Eléni into a hug.

'Thank you,' he whispered. 'I couldn't have done this without you.'

Eléni didn't suggest calling in on her uncle. She could see Simos was emotionally drained. She would visit Kostas Koulouris once more before she left.

Instead, they headed back to Argostoli and returned the hire truck. They ate a light meal in their usual taverna.

'I shall be looking like a Greek salad before long.' Eléni laughed. She was going to miss the creamy feta and sweet tomatoes when she returned home.

'And you'll remember me as the one full of spanakopita!' He patted his stomach.

It was good to see him relaxed after the intensity of the morning, thought Eléni.

'I think we need a treat. How about a swim? If you go and get your swimsuit, I'll see if I can hire a boat. How does that sound?'

Her heart skipped a beat. 'Perfect.'

* * *

Simos was already in a small motorboat when she got back to the quayside after changing at the lodging house.

'We were lucky. Just one left. Welcome aboard, *agápi mou.*'

He took her hand and she sat down in the middle of the boat while he guided them out of the harbour. Soon they were out on the open sea, with the wind cooling Eléni's face as the boat picked up speed. The aquamarine water sparkled in the sun and splashes of white foam came over the side as the boat hit the waves.

Simos turned off the engine and came to sit beside Eléni as the boat slowed down. 'Just look down into the water and see how clear it is.'

She leaned over and watched a shoal of silver-white fish in the turquoise water below her. They were marked with black bands. 'There are loads of fish and I can see right down to the rocks at the bottom.' Eléni was mesmerised.

'I bet they're a silvery colour with black bands near the neck and the tail. Two-banded sea bream. You know the fish you ate at the restaurant the other night? Well, this stretch here is where they catch them.'

Simos started up the engine again and took the boat into a secluded cove. The beach was backed by steep white cliffs curving around to form a horseshoe shape. Sparse dark green shrubs grew on the side of the rocky surface. He dropped the anchor a short distance from the marble-white beach. It was deserted and there were parts of it that would not be able to be seen by other passing boats.

'There's no one around, but you can change inside the helm if you like,' said Simos. 'I'm going to swim to shore and pull her in.'

He stripped off and dived into the water. The toned muscles on his abdomen caused Eléni's insides to melt. There was no white line where his swimming trunks would have been. There were no other boats in sight so she did the same. The feeling of the cool water on her body was exhilarating. By the time she reached the shore, Simos had dragged the motorboat onto the beach and had spread beach towels on the fine white pebbles. He came to meet her and pulled her towards him. The feeling of their wet skin touching sent fizzles of longing through her. They lay down on the towels and kissed. Taking their time to explore each other's bodies made the ultimate pleasure they eventually reached even more intense than usual.

Simos planted gentle, tender kisses along Eléni's cheek and neck. 'Thank you for today, *agápi mou*. I'm a completely different person because of you. You've put me in touch with my feelings for the first time I can remember.' He kissed her again.

'Oh, Simos. I can only imagine how much better you feel. And you helped me, too, don't forget.' How could this come to an end? Again she was torn between returning home and staying with Simos.

'I hope you can tell I've fallen in love with you. I've never had feelings like this for anyone before. I can't imagine a future without you.'

Eléni's pulse raced. This was all she'd dreamed about since she'd first met him.

'I love you, too . . . And you won't have to.'

She sat astride him and brought her mouth to his.

CHAPTER FIFTY-SEVEN

CASSIA

Three weeks earlier

'An airmail letter addressed to you, Mamá. Strange Eléni has sent it to you and not to me and Baba, as well. Doesn't look like her handwriting, mind.' Bronwen handed her mother the translucent blue envelope. 'I'm off out. See you later.'

It was the second letter with a Greek stamp that had arrived in the past week. Eugenia had written to tell her sister all about Eléni's visit. It was the olive branch that Cassia herself should have made, but she had been afraid to. She noticed from the return address that Eugenia was back living in their family home and wondered how Eléni had found her, since the address she'd given her daughter was for the smallholding just outside Fiscardo. Her sister also told her that Maia was married with a little girl, and was living in Patras now.

Cassia's hand shook as she slid her nail under the seal of the new letter and unfolded the paper. The address was from a house in New Farsa, wherever that was. She knew where Farsa was — it was a small village just outside Argostoli, where she and Nikos had first looked for somewhere to live when they'd left Fiscardo.

Agapití *Kyría Beynon,*
    My name is Kostas Koulouris, the uncle of Ióánna Mouzakis, the young woman you know as Eléni.

'No!' Cassia threw the letter on the table, not able to read any more. Her pulse raced. It was the moment she'd dreaded for the last twenty years.

Tom rushed into the kitchen. 'Whatever's happened?' Cassia, unable to get her words out, pointed at the letter. He picked it up. 'I can't understand this. You know I can't read Greek.' His face turned ashen and his voice broke. 'It's not Eléni, is it?' He sat beside his wife. 'Cassia, tell me. What's happened? Has she been in an accident?'

'No, it's from *him*, the uncle. I can't read it.'

Tom let out a big sigh. 'Thank God. You panicked me then. I had visions of Eléni being in another accident or worse.' He picked up the letter and handed it to Cassia. 'I can't read it for you, but I can be here with you as you read it. There's not going to be anything he can do from over two thousand miles away, is there?'

He pulled up a chair to sit beside her.

'I'm sorry I frightened you about Eléni, but him catching up with us is what I've always dreaded.'

She started to read, translating each line to Tom.

Dear Mrs Beynon,
    My name is Kostas Koulouris, the uncle of Ióánna Mouzakis, the young woman you know as Eléni. I returned to Kefalonia early in 1955 to find my whole family had perished in the earthquake. Or so I thought. I learned my young niece may have survived and so I made a promise to my sister that if she was alive, I would find her and bring her up as my own.

Cassia stopped reading. She was afraid of what would be written next. Tom patted her hand. 'Go on, *cariad.*'

I heard from a reporter that she may have been taken to Fiscardo, where I tracked down your sister. But then you know that. You were already in Wales by then. The reporter even put an advert for her as a missing child in his newspaper. You did a good job at hiding her. But I never gave up hope.

'Rhodri Jones. Remember he questioned us when we were leaving for Fiscardo and we told him we were taking her to the farm to look at the animals,' said Tom.

Cassia's skin prickled with goosebumps, afraid to turn the next page. She read on.

How could someone do that?

Cassia's eyes blurred with guilty tears. Her throat tightened.

But last week a miracle happened. My lovely niece found me. She is the image of her mamá, my sister, Dimitra. At first, I was angry you and your husband had denied me almost twenty years of knowing her. You took her away from her homeland, away from where her mamá and baba, her yiayiá and pappoú lie in their resting places.

'This was what I feared when I heard he was looking for us. This is why I didn't want Eléni to go there.'

Tom pulled Cassia into a tight hug. 'Maybe you should have told me . . . So Eléni's done what she set out to do. I wonder how she tracked him down. I can't wait for her to come home and to hear all about her trip.'

But my feelings have changed. There is no point in being bitter. This letter is to thank you. Eléni told me what a happy childhood you gave her. I believe her when she explained you

genuinely thought there was no one left to look after her and
you stopped her from being sent to an orphanage. By the time
I could get back to Kefalonia, she would probably not have
been on the island anyway, but in a children's home on the
mainland. Eléni has made me see that.

'There you are. All our lovely Eléni wanted was to find
out about her birth family. She doesn't love us any less.'

Your daughter has grown into a wonderful young woman
and it is down to you and your husband. I have been able to
give her photographs of the family. She may look like her
mamá, but she takes after her baba with her artistic talents.
I understand from Eléni you have never been back to
the island. You would not recognise it! I would very much like
to meet you and thank you in person, so I hope one day you
will return for a holiday.
Thank you again from the bottom of my heart.
Me ektímisi. *Yours sincerely,*
Kostas Koulouris

Cassia sat back in her chair with tears streaming down her
cheeks. Tom took his wife in his arms and held her while she
sobbed. All the fears about losing their daughter that she'd carried deep inside for so long fell away. 'It's okay. Let it all out.'

'Oh, Tom. I wish I could see Eléni and tell her face to face
how much I love her. And thank her.'

Tom squeezed her hand. 'She's done what she went to
Kefalonia to do and our girl will be home before you know it,
Cass. In her last letter, didn't she say if she hadn't found her
uncle by the time of the twentieth anniversary of the earthquake, she'd be coming home? That's just a few weeks away.'

Cassia folded the letter, knowing she would never part
with it. 'It will be a long few weeks,' she whispered.

* * *

Later that afternoon, Tom reminded Cassia of what she'd said. 'I've been thinking. If you can't wait to see Eléni, why don't we surprise her and go to Kefalonia for the anniversary? You will get to thank her face to face much sooner and we can have a much-needed family holiday. Bron's been missing her terribly and has always wanted to go to Greece. And Eugenia said she'd love you to be there for the anniversary, too, didn't she? It would be good for you two to spend some time together. What do you think?'

Cassia thought back to the words in her sister's letter. It was obvious that the visit from Eléni had thawed Eugenia's feelings towards her. She had, as Tom said, suggested visiting the island for the anniversary. Twenty years! The catastrophic event had mapped out the rest of her life. She'd never have met Tom, or their lovely Eléni. She'd never have had Bronwen. Cassia had vowed she'd never set foot on Kefalonia again but . . .

'I don't know. There isn't time to organise it, is there? Where will we stay? The hotels will be full by now. And what about work? I'll have just started there.'

'If you'd like to go, I'll organise it. Didn't Eugenia say we must stay with her if we ever visit? Anyway, *I'd* like to go back. To remember all those poor people who perished. Pay my respects to them. So please say yes. I think Eugenia gave you a telephone number — a letter will take too long to get there.'

Cassia nodded.

'All right. I'll ring her. If you're sure we can organise it in time.'

She was surprised she'd agreed so quickly. When she saw the wide grin on Tom's face, Cassia knew she was doing the right thing. She was going home! She went to get the other airmail letter that had arrived a week before the one from Kostas Koulouris. Her hand shook as she dialled the number. 'Eugenia? Yes, it's me, Cassia.'

CHAPTER FIFTY-EIGHT

Cassia looked across at Bronwen, who was sitting next to the plane window and looking down on Kefalonia.

'The sea is bright turquoise, Mamá. A bit different from Borth, eh?'

They both laughed. 'Just a bit. And warmer.'

Tom squeezed Cassia's hand as the plane descended, landing smoothly on the runway. The pilot's voice came over the tannoy to welcome them to Kefalonia and inform them that the temperature outside was thirty-four degrees. He then repeated the message in English.

'Oh. No. My poor freckly white skin. Over ninety Fahrenheit.'

'You and Bron will have to be careful.' Cassia thought how different it was for her and Eléni. They had to use suncream, but their olive skin was far better suited to the hot sun. Who in their right mind would go to Greece in August?

Her stomach churned when she thought of what lay ahead. Just treat it like a holiday, Tom had said. Bron's face when they'd told her about the visit had been a picture. She'd kissed them both and told them she'd love them for ever.

'I should hope so,' Tom had told her.

Nearly twenty years was a long time to have stayed away. The island was no longer in ruins. It was slowly building up its tourist industry and Eugenia had told her many people were returning to their homeland from abroad, often with husbands or wives and families to start again. For the first time in ages, she thought about Nikos and baby Angelika both buried in the cemetery in Argostoli.

Once through passport control and arrivals, Tom led the way to the car rental desk to pick up the keys for the car, a red Toyota Corolla. Even to Cassia, it seemed strange to be sitting in a left-hand drive car after the years spent in Wales.

She was the navigator for the journey to Fiscardo. When they passed the town of Argostoli just a few kilometres into the journey, Cassia's skin prickled as she thought about the last time they'd been in the capital city with their eldest daughter, and how awful it had been. It had been rebuilt, with structural specifications to prevent such devastation again, but the threat of seismic activity was always present. She was glad when they were out on the coastal road away from her memories, and she was able to point out the views of the coast on one side and the mountains on the other.

'It's so beautiful, Mamá. I can't see Eléni wanting to leave this. I know I wouldn't and I haven't got a handsome boyfriend like she has.'

Cassia's heart raced. 'What do you mean? I know she'd got a friend who helped her find her uncle. But that's all he is. He was with her when they called on Eugenia. A nice young man, but she just said they'd become friends. And of course she'll be coming home. She's got her ticket.'

Nothing more was mentioned until Tom slammed on the brakes as the car came round a bend. Three goats were in the middle of the road.

'Bloody things.'

Cassia jerked forward in her seat. 'Take your time. They roam everywhere.'

Cassia thought back to the first telephone call she'd made to her sister. Eugenia had been thrilled. She'd been sworn to secrecy and now it was just Eléni who knew nothing about their visit. Cassia thought back to what Bronwen had said. She knew the girls were writing to each other and Bronwen had promised to keep it a surprise, too. When she'd last spoken to Eugenia, her sister had told her Eléni's friend had booked a meal in a restaurant supposedly just for the two of them and he wanted her family there as a surprise. Tomorrow they would see their daughter again.

It wasn't long before they were entering the beautiful village of Fiscardo. She remembered how apprehensive she'd been when she'd left for Athens to marry Tom, before emigrating to Wales. In her head, she was back at Eugenia's smallholding one last time, intending to tell her sister her plans, but instead facing her mother, introducing Eléni to her for the first time. Eléni had clung to Cassia's skirts as if she'd sensed disapproval from her grandmother.

'Doesn't she have anything to say for herself, then? A bit different to her cousin here. You always have plenty to say to Yiayiá, don't you, Maia?' Her mother had pulled the little girl onto her lap and stared at Eléni.

'She's just shy.' Annoyed at herself for making an excuse, Cassia gathered up Eléni and left without telling Eugenia her plans. Now, here she was, returning not as a Greek citizen but as a visitor, just like the many others who would be coming to commemorate the twenty years since the island had been decimated.

Eugenia rushed out to unlock the gates and enveloped Cassia in the tightest hug.

Both women had tears streaming down their faces. 'I'm sorry, Cass. We should never have left it so long.'

'I'm sorry too. It's as much my fault as yours. If Mamá hadn't been there, I would have told you I was leaving face to face. That's why I came.'

'I know. But it was a shock to find out from your letter. But let's forget about that now.'

Cassia turned to see Bronwen standing there while Tom unpacked the car. 'This is our lovely daughter, Bronwen. Bron.'

'There's no doubt who you are, *agápi mou*. You are the image of your baba. And Tom. *Efcharistó*. It was you who persuaded my sister to return, I think.'

Entering the house was like going back in time. Cassia could see her sister had recently decorated the rooms. It was bright and fresh, but it was still the family home. She chose to remember the happy times when she and Eugenia were children, and suppress the heartache of the last time she'd been there after her father had found out about Nikos and banished her from the family. She shuddered.

'I've put you and Tom in your old room, and Bronwen in Maia's. Do you remember the view from the back of the house? You can see the sea in the distance. I always envied you.'

There was an awkwardness between the sisters despite their apologies. How could Cassia make Eugenia realise she was sorry? 'Thanks, Eugenia. It feels strange to be back, but I'm so glad Tom and Bron persuaded me. We can talk face to face now.'

* * *

After their meal, Tom and Bronwen left them to it. They walked into Fiscardo and he took her down to the pretty harbour where they looked at the variety of boats and yachts before stopping for a drink in one of the tavernas.

'We didn't order any olives or pistachios, did we, Baba? Perhaps they're not for us.'

Tom laughed. 'You'll find the Greeks always serve little snacks with drinks. My beer, your orange juice and something to nibble on. What do you think about the place?'

Bronwen speared another two olives on a cocktail stick. 'It's so beautiful. I'm glad I know where Mamá is from. I know she doesn't like the idea, but I mean it when I say I don't think Eléni will leave it.'

Tom's face became serious. 'Has she said anything, then?'

'Not in so many words, but I think things between her and this Simos are getting serious.'

'Well, as much as I don't want her to, many daughters her age have left home and are married with children. After the upset earlier this year, I just want her to be happy. And you'll be off to uni soon, so it will just be Mamá and me.'

'So you can visit Eléni as often as you want.'

'You mean you want free Greek holidays. Come on, drink up. I'll get the bill.'

* * *

When they got back to Eugenia's house, the two sisters were sitting out on the terrace, chatting. 'We're out here,' said Cassia. 'Come and see this amazing sunset.'

Tom and Bronwen joined them. By then the sky was a deep apricot, streaked with scarlet and coral. They all watched in awed silence as the fiery orange ball sank behind the silhouette of Ithaca and disappeared.

Bronwen turned to her mother. 'Wow! I've never seen anything so spectacular. Aren't you glad Baba persuaded you to come now if only to see that?'

Cassia laughed. 'Yes, Bron. I'm so pleased I came.' She turned and took Eugenia's hand. 'We've had a great time catching up, haven't we?'

'We have.' Eugenia grinned at her sister. 'After all the years apart and our silly rows, we've realised that nothing can break the bond between us.'

Cassia felt the long-held guilt inside her finally leave. She may not have had her mother's blessing or made up with her, but she knew that she had her sister's love and that meant far more to her. Determined not to cry in front of Bronwen and Tom, she smiled warmly at Eugenia and changed the subject.

'Right. What shall we do tomorrow?'

'As long as we go to the beach, I don't care. Please,' Bronwen said. 'I can't wait to swim in a turquoise sea.'

'That's settled then. We all have to do what Madam says,' Tom said.

'Great. I'll go and unpack my bikini now.'

They all laughed. *Dear Bron, always so enthusiastic about everything*, thought Cassia.

Later that night, she lay awake thinking back to the same time twenty years before. The warning signs had all been there. The whole summer had had more seismic activity than usual and, in the weeks building up to that fateful day, more frequent tremors had warned of a disaster coming. She tossed and turned, not able to get the images of devastation out of her mind.

'Not able to sleep, *cariad*?' It seemed Tom was awake too. 'It will be better once the day actually comes. On the morning of the twelfth, we should go down to Argostoli and pay our respects. We'll have seen Eléni tomorrow night, so let's hope she'll join us. I'm sure there will be something organised for us to attend. Now, it's been a long day. Try to get some sleep.'

He kissed the top of her head and held her close until she finally drifted off to sleep.

CHAPTER FIFTY-NINE

The next morning, Eugenia took them to a small beach a short way out of Fiscardo. It was just along from the one overlooked by the smallholding where she'd once lived. They followed a narrow stony path down through the trees to the sea which was, in Bronwen's words, a deep turquoise. The smell of the wild herbs growing over the path was strong as their legs brushed against them. Cassia bent and picked one, rubbing the leaves between her fingers. As they got closer to the beach, the hint of saltiness in the air deepened and they could hear the gentle waves breaking onto the tiny white pebbles.

Several families were already there, so they found an isolated spot near the edge of the cliff to spread out their towels. Bronwen stripped down to her bikini and ran into the sea, before diving into the water and swimming away from the beach. She turned round and shouted to them, 'It's like bathwater! You should have brought your bathers.'

Tom laughed. 'I think you can tell she loves Greece, Eugenia. Thanks for bringing us here.'

'I used to bring Maia here. And now we bring baby Eléni.' Her face grew pensive. 'I just wish they didn't live so far away. I do miss them.'

Cassia patted her hand. Eléni had been away a mere few months and she'd found it hard enough. She couldn't imagine what it must be like for her sister.

The rest of the morning was spent looking around Fiscardo. To Cassia, it seemed very little had changed, apart from Taverna Zervas where she'd once worked and lived with Eléni. Poor Michaíl would turn in his grave if he saw its present dilapidated state. There were more tavernas and restaurants now as tourism was bringing more visitors to the island. They walked to the little market, which was just as she remembered it.

* * *

The table at Ta Elaiódentra was booked for seven o'clock. Eléni's friend had rung Eugenia to ask if everyone could be seated upstairs by that time, then he and Eléni would arrive at seven fifteen. Cassia couldn't wait to see her and wondered what she would make of the surprise.

'This is beautiful,' said Cassia, as they approached the restaurant. She turned and looked out to sea. 'What a view!'

'It will be even better from our table. Simos told me he'd booked one upstairs on the verandah.' Eugenia led the way through the outside terrace.

'It's a bit posh,' whispered Bronwen.

'We're with the party booked by Kýrios Georgatos. Efcharistó.'

'Ah, yes. Follow me, parakaló. Some people have already arrived.'

Cassia's stomach churned as they walked up the stairs. Perhaps they were late, and Eléni and her friend were already there. She looked at her watch. No, it was ten to seven.

The waiter took them onto the verandah. Sitting at the long table was a young couple and a middle-aged gentleman, who was engrossed in pointing out things to look at with a little girl. The young man stood to greet them.

'You must be here for Eléni too.' He held out a hand. 'I'm Theo Koulouris, her cousin.' Cassia caught her breath. Her head started to spin. *No. Eugenia hadn't mentioned anything about others being there.* 'And this is my wife, Irida.'

Tom was the first to shake his hand. 'My wife, Cassia. Our daughter, Bronwen and my sister-in-law, Eugenia.'

The little girl joined them. Cassia nearly gasped and had to blink away tears. The same huge dark eyes. The same black curls. It was like turning the clock back twenty years.

'And this is our daughter, Amara.'

Cassia knelt down and took the little girl's hand. '*Kalispéra*, Amara. You are beautiful, aren't you?'

Amara held her head down and clung to her father's legs. Her shyness reminded her of another little girl at a similar age.

'You must be Kyriá Beynon.' The older man had been waiting patiently to shake everyone's hand. 'Kostas Koulouris. It's very good to meet you in person. You know who I am. You've met our beautiful Amara and I can tell from your reaction who she reminds you of.'

Cassia nodded as her eyes blurred with tears once more. 'The spitting image.'

Theo looked at his watch. 'I think we should all take our seats. They'll be here soon. If we leave the two middle ones free, Eléni and Simos can talk with us all. Those were his instructions to me anyway.'

Cassia warmed to the young man. To him and the Koulouris family, everything seemed completely natural — a family meal together — but to her, it had much more significance. Her stomach still churned. Her eyes were fixed on the top of the stairs in anticipation of Eléni's arrival. As always, she knew Tom sensed her turmoil. He squeezed her hand.

'Here they are!' Bronwen squealed. Pushing back her chair, she rushed to give her sister a bear hug.

Eléni's mouth fell open. Her eyes were wide, as if she didn't believe what she was seeing. 'Bron! What on . . .'

Spotting everyone else, she rushed over and hugged her mother. 'Mamá! Baba! What are you all doing here? I had no idea.'

Both mother and daughter had tears pouring down their cheeks.

'Come here, *cariad*. Time for a big *cwtch* from your old baba, I think.'

Cassia watched as her daughter greeted everyone, kissing them on both cheeks the Greek way with such excitement. She knew she'd done the right thing by returning to Kefalonia.

'I think I'd better introduce myself as your daughter has neglected to do so. Simos Georgatos.' He beamed at them.

Cassia shook his hand. 'Pleased to meet you, Simos. I understand from my sister this is all down to you. *Efcharistó.*' Bronwen stood behind him with her eyes full of admiration for this handsome young Greek. She was clearly dying to be introduced. 'And this is Bronwen, our other daughter.'

Surprisingly, Bron appeared tongue-tied and answered a simple, 'Hiya.'

They all found their seats again. Eléni sat between Kostas and Bronwen, facing Simos who'd placed himself by Cassia and Theo.

The waiter took their orders and the conversation flowed. Eléni sparkled. From the adoring looks her daughter gave Simos, Cassia knew straight away he was much more than a friend. They were completely at ease with one another. Cassia's heart raced. It was clear to her Eléni had fallen in love, not only with a beautiful Greek man but with Kefalonia itself and, from the look of it, her birth family too. Halfway through the main course, Cassia excused herself and went to the cloakroom.

Bronwen followed her. 'Everything all right, Mamá?'

Cassia brushed away the tears. 'Yes. You go back. I'll follow you soon.'

'He's gorgeous, isn't he? Eléni's got a catch there. I wonder if he's got some younger brothers.' Cassia smiled at her

338

younger daughter who was oblivious to why she'd had to leave the table. *I hope not. I couldn't lose another daughter.*

Bronwen left Cassia to splash cold water on her eyes and return to the others soon afterwards. Everyone was deep in conversation and it was only Tom who looked in her direction and mouthed, 'You okay?'

Cassia nodded. She relaxed and enjoyed the rest of the meal. It felt good to be back doing what Greeks did best — eating and drinking together as a family. Eléni's birth family side by side with the one who had brought her up. While the night went on and the wine flowed, the laughter and noise level rose. Finishing the meal with her favourite baklavá and a strong coffee, followed by a mantola liqueur, Cassia regretted her earlier panic.

The restaurant slowly emptied with groups of people drifting away until their party was the only one left. Lights twinkled along the edge of the wooden verandah and glowed below them in each of the oleander trees lining the pathway up to the restaurant. Cassia thought how perfect the setting was and whatever the future held for Eléni and Simos, she knew she would never stay away from her beautiful island for as long again.

Simos had insisted on paying for everyone despite Tom's offer to share the bill. 'No. It's not the Greek way. My treat for Eléni. Bringing her two families together has been my pleasure.'

Kostas took Cassia's hand. 'You may have helped my dear niece find us, but it's this wonderful couple who we have to thank for looking after her.'

Cassia whispered, '*Efcharistó*, Kostas.' Apart from little Amara asleep in her father's arms, there was hardly a dry eye among them.

They left after making arrangements to meet the next day for the thanksgiving service at a church in Argostoli. Eléni had managed to get the Sunday off work by swapping it with her usual shift on Monday. Simos was going to Old Farsa to have some private time remembering his family, too.

Eléni pulled her mother to one side, away from the others. She hugged Cassia. '*Efcharistó*, Mamá. Thank you for coming to see me here. It means so much. I know how hard it must have been. I'm so, so sorry for all the hurt I caused when I found out.'

Cassia buried her head in Eléni's chest. 'I'm sorry, too. I've been far too protective of you. Tonight has been proof you had every right to find your family, *Elenáki mou*. It's lovely to see you so happy.'

'And I'm so pleased you've met Simos, too. Isn't he wonderful?'

She knew then her daughter's future was there in Kefalonia with the man she loved. Cassia thought of the love she'd had for Nikos and how she'd have followed him anywhere. And hadn't she followed her gorgeous Tom to Wales? It was Eléni's turn now.

CHAPTER SIXTY

The next morning, the little church was full as they filed into their seats. Kostas and his family sat two rows in front. Cassia admired the gilded screen displaying paintings of saints and scenes from the Bible. She looked up at the huge ornate chandelier above her and remembered the old church that had been destroyed. Dressed in black, the orthodox priest entered and before stepping up into the sanctuary, he crossed himself. Although it was a Sunday and the usual religious services would take place throughout the day, this was not going to be a formal service. It seemed appropriate to commemorate the anniversary in a church. Cassia's faith had lapsed — she told herself it was because she couldn't find a Greek Orthodox church in which to worship in Wales, but she knew it was an excuse. There'd been Greek churches in Cardiff when she'd lived there.

'Today we are here to remember the six hundred men, women and children who lost their lives on the fateful day twenty years ago today. At exactly twenty-four minutes past eleven, the exact time the earthquake struck, let us take a minute's silence to remember those who perished. Will you please all stand?'

Cassia and Tom, standing either side of Eléni, held their daughter's hands. Eléni sucked in a deep breath. Kostas's head was bowed and Cassia realised, like Eléni, he had lost his parents that day too.

A bell from the outside belltower struck eleven times and the church became eerily silent apart from a single sob that came from the row behind them.

'*Efcharistó*. Please be seated.'

The priest ended the service by reading an account of how the island had progressed, starting to rebuild and recover over the last twenty years.

'Let us depart in peace.'

The congregation left the solemnity of the church for bright sunshine. Families were milling around — some were reuniting with people they hadn't seen for years.

'Let's catch up with Theíos Kostas,' said Eléni. 'He's going to take us to the memorial he's had erected for . . . um . . .' She paused.

'It's all right. You can say it. Your mamá and baba, eh?'

Eléni nodded.

Together, both families made their way down to the harbour and walked across the long bridge to the municipal cemetery. They walked through the large metal gates into what seemed like a sea of white marble. Large family tombs stood alongside single gravestones, memorial plaques, crosses and obelisks. They followed Kostas until they came to a simple slab of white marble inscribed with four names and the date of the earthquake.

'Here it is. They died together so they are remembered together.' Kostas stood with his head bowed and his hands clasped together.

Tom placed an arm around Eléni as she too bowed her head. 'Rest in peace, Mamá and Baba,' she whispered.

After some quiet reflection, they walked away and left the cemetery.

Eléni was the first to speak. '*Efcharistó*, Theíos Kostas. It means a lot that I can come here and pay my respects. I'll see you again before I leave. I'm going to spend the rest of the day with everyone up in Fiscardo now. Bye, Theo. Irida. Can I have a hug, Amara?'

The little girl ran into Eléni's arms. 'Ooh.' Eléni picked her up and rubbed her head into Amara's tummy, making her squeal.

On the journey back to Fiscardo, Cassia smiled as she listened to Eléni and Bronwen talking non-stop in the back of the car to catch up on what they'd missed while they'd been apart.

'You're not going to leave all this behind, are you? Break the divine Simos's heart?' Bronwen whispered.

Cassia strained to hear.

'I promised, Bron. In any case, lots of people have relationships with hundreds of miles between them. It makes the heart grow fonder, doesn't it? Look at Mamá and Baba when he was in the Navy. Simos understands. I'll come over as often as I can and he'll come to Wales.'

'If you say so,' said Bronwen. She didn't sound convinced.

It was good to reach Eugenia's house. It had been a solemn morning, but it had meant so much to Cassia. To them all. Looking around the sitting room, she focused on the photographs on the sideboard and wondered what the couple whose picture was central to the display would have thought. Would they have accepted Eléni as their granddaughter? And what about bubbly, excitable Bron? Could she have thawed her pappoú's heart?

CHAPTER SIXTY-ONE

ELÉNI

After a light lunch of bread, cheese and olives, they all walked into Fiscardo, admiring and comparing the range of luxury yachts to more modest motor launches. In some of the colourful fishing boats, fishermen sat mending nets and taking out the small fish caught in the nets. They all called for a drink in one of the new tavernas along from Taverna Zervas.

'You won't remember this, Eléni,' said Cassia. 'But you and I lived in the dilapidated taverna over there for a while. With a kind old gentleman called Michaíl. He loved you. The little granddaughter he never had, according to him.'

'I do remember bits of it. More is coming back to me.' Eléni smiled at the memory.

'He came to us for the first Christmas after the quake, didn't he? He made Maia a spinning top and you some wooden animals,' said Eugenia. 'Lovely man.'

They found a table outside and ordered their drinks, 'A beer for me and a bottle of house red for the ladies, *parakaló*. What about you girls?'

Bronwen nudged her sister. She read the menu. 'A beer for me, too, and my sister will have a tsípouro, *parakaló.*'

'No,' said Cassia. 'Tell her Tom. You'll have a soft drink. Eléni can have what she wants. You're underage.'

'Only just. Eighteen days and six hours to go.' Bronwen pretended to pout.

Eléni giggled. 'I'd better have a soft drink with Bron, then. Two Cokes, *parakaló.*'

She looked over at the boats moored along the quayside. There was a long queue for a motorboat advertising trips over to coves and beaches along the coast. She thought of the time she and Simos had taken one and made love on the white beach. How she was going to miss him!

'Penny for them?' Her father's voice interrupted her thoughts.

She felt her cheeks redden. 'Oh, I was looking at all those people queuing for their boat trip. You should do that before you leave. The little coves are beautiful.' She knew her sister would love it.

After leaving the taverna, they browsed the pretty souvenir shops. The two sisters entered one while the others waited outside. Eléni bought a silver bracelet with the Greek key design for Gabriella.

'She's missed you a lot.' Cassia admired the gift. 'She'll love it. What have you bought, Bron?'

Bronwen took her purchase from its wrapping and held it up for the others to see. It was a stunning polished-glass pendant. The colour was a vibrant sea-green that glowed and sparkled as it caught the sun.

'It's so you, Bron. Bold and sparkly.' Her father and all the others laughed.

'It's gorgeous.' Cassia took the necklace from her for a better look.

They slowly walked back to Eugenia's house, where they spent a lovely afternoon in the garden.

'What time are you meeting lover boy?' asked Bronwen. 'Hasn't he got any dishy friends he can introduce me to?'

Cassia rolled her eyes. 'Eugenia, it's all she thinks about.'

Eléni agreed. 'In answer to both questions, seven o'clock and no. In any case, if he had, I'd need to warn them what you were like.'

Bronwen nudged her sister.

* * *

'Thank you for driving me back, Baba. There are very few buses on a Sunday.' But she wondered if there was another reason why he was keen to take her back to Argostoli himself. From the way he had persuaded her sister to stay behind, Eléni suspected he wanted to speak with her alone.

'There's no way I'd have let you do that. I wanted to speak to you anyway. Find out what your real plans are.'

Eléni shifted in her seat. 'Plans?'

'You've done what you came out here to do. You've found your uncle. Mamá and I are so pleased for you.'

'Mamá, too?'

Tom looked across. 'Yes. She changed after she received the letter from Kostas and it's all down to you, Eléni. She was nervous about meeting him and even Eugenia, too, if I'm honest, but since yesterday she's relaxed. No, I mean your plans for you and Simos. You seem to be very close, yet you haven't known him long. How is it going to work with you two being over two thousand miles apart?'

Eléni's pulse quickened. What did her father want her to say? 'Sorry, Baba. I'm not coming home after all'? She and Simos had talked about it. She *would* go home and they'd keep in touch through letters and phone calls. If they'd have her back, she'd go back to working at the Welsh craft shop and the Met to save every penny she could. But should she tell him everything?

Eléni took a deep breath. 'I knew from the first time I met Simos he was the one.' Warmth spread up from her neck. It seemed strange talking to her father about love. 'I know it was love at first sight. It was the same for you with Mamá, wasn't it? For Simos, it took longer. But now we both know this is for ever. And as for the distance, look how long you were away for when you were in the Navy. We will make it work, Baba.' She decided it was enough for now.

'We both want you to be happy, *cariad.*'

They spent the rest of the journey planning their visit to the monastery of St Gerasimos in four days' time and before their return home the following day.

'Just drop me here, please, Baba.' Tom parked in the street across from Simos's apartment. Eléni leaned across and kissed her father on his cheek. 'Bye. See you soon.'

She hurried to the apartment block and waited for Simos to open the door. Before she was through the door, they began kissing and fell onto the sofa in each other's arms.

'How was it?' asked Eléni. 'I kept thinking I should have been with you. I can't remember my parents, but the minute's silence in the church and the visit to the cemetery were both very moving. I was lucky to be with people who loved me. Are you sure you're all right?'

'I was fine. I *wanted* to be alone if you can understand that. There were several people in the cemetery doing the same thing. I even met someone who recognised me from when I was a small boy. A friend of my mother's, who told me how my mother was a brilliant pianist and used to sing to us all the time. A certain song came into my head. On the way back here, I turned on the radio and the folk song was playing. Can you believe it?'

Eléni hugged him. 'More and more is coming back to you. I'm pleased everything went well.'

* * *

The next four days flew by. Eléni managed to work her final shifts at the taverna, spend time with her family and be with

Simos every evening. Time was precious, and they never talked about Eléni leaving.

The feast day arrived. She'd stayed over at Simos's apartment, as she did most nights. She sat on the side of the bed and watched him sleep. *How I'm going to miss waking up beside you, gorgeous Simos!* His eyelids flickered as if he knew Eléni was watching him. 'Happy name day.' Eléni leaned across and kissed him. Simos pulled her back into bed. Resisting, she said, 'We should get going. We'll keep our kisses for later. I told Baba to arrive early, as you said it will be chaotic to park.'

They travelled the fifteen kilometres to the monastery and church of Agios Gerasimos, and Simos was proved right. Cars were parked in every available spot on the hard, stony ground. Crowds of people filled the steps up to the beautiful church with vineyards on either side that had been built after the earthquake.

'There's your father.' Simos had spotted them waiting at the side of the steps.

'Shall we go in?' said Eugenia.

They all began to file in with the other worshippers who had been waiting and the nearer they got to the entrance doors, the louder the choral chant from within became. Many of the congregation had canes to aid their walking or were disabled. They were there in the hope that their patron saint would protect and heal them of their illnesses on this 'day of miracles' as it was called.

Whether religious or not, Eléni defied anyone not to be moved by the spectacle they were witnessing. Once inside the church, Simos pointed out the carved silver-and-glass case that held the patron saint's relics. She stood on tiptoe to see above the crowd. The ceremony was conducted by clergy, nuns and many officials, but it was the haunting music, both beautiful and sad, that summed up the meaning of the occasion.

At the end of the service, young men dressed in white shirts and deep-blue velvet waistcoats and trousers lifted the relic case and went outside where many people were lying, face up on the ground, for the body of Saint Gerasimos to travel over them. A brass band struck up and the musicians began to march.

After the cool interior of the church, walking into the heat of the sun was intense. Tom led everyone to stand in some shade to watch the procession.

Even the normally lively Bronwen was subdued.

'It brought some memories back. Do you remember Father insisting we attended every year?' said Eugenia.

Cassia nodded. 'Yes. It didn't mean much to us then, but today, whether it's because of the service commemorating the earthquake being so close, I found it quite moving . . . in spite of all the hordes of people.'

Before going back to their cars, they said their goodbyes.

'We're going to head off now. I'm going to spend my last afternoon with Simos and he's going to take me up to see Theíos Kostas.' Eléni embraced her aunt. 'I won't see you before we leave. *Efcharistó* for everything.' She turned to her parents and sister. 'I'll see you all at the airport in the morning.'

After visiting her uncle in New Farsa for the last time, Eléni and Simos were alone. She took a present she'd wrapped from her bag.

'I want you to have this as a reminder of me. Think of it as a name day present.'

He took the gift and opened it. His eyes widened as he realised what it was. 'Our cove where we made love on the beach! It's beautiful. I love it, Eléni! The colours of the inks. The colours of the sea.' He stood and positioned it on the blank white wall opposite them. 'It will go there so I can look at it whenever I feel lonely . . . which will be often. *Efcharistó*, Eléni. I'm going to miss you so much.' Simos pulled her to him as he sat back down next to her on the sofa. 'I'm sorry I was so frosty towards you when you first came to me for help.'

Eléni kissed him on the lips. 'I'm glad you like it. Anyway, you're far from frosty now, Simos Georgatos!' Giggling, she said, 'In fact, you could be described as a red-hot lover . . .' He slipped a hand under her T-shirt.

'I can get hotter if you like.' Laughing, he stood and pulled her by the hands into the bedroom.

Lying in Simos's arms before she had to leave to go back to the lodging house and pack, Eléni wondered what the future held. Would their secret plans work out? Dare she dream they would? Whatever happened, she knew she had found a man who truly loved her as she did him.

EPILOGUE

Argostoli, Kefalonia, 30 April 1974

'This is the last one to hang. How about here?'

Simos stretched on the stepladder to show where he thought the ink drawing could go. It was the largest and most colourful of Eléni's pictures.

'Just a tad to the right.' She watched him adjust the position. 'Perfect.'

'That's it! Ready for tomorrow morning. May the first. The opening of the summer season in Argostoli and the opening of the Eléni Mouzakis Gallery. How does it feel? Your very own gallery and studio with your name over the door.'

Her face shone with excitement. 'Fantastic! I couldn't have done it without you. Come here.' She pulled Simos into a tight hug and kissed him.

'You've done all the hard work. Look at all these paintings and drawings. The tourists are going to love them.'

Butterflies fluttered in her stomach. There was no guarantee her work would sell, but hadn't this always been her dream?

She remembered her and Simos's tearful goodbye at Argostoli Airport eight months ago. He'd insisted on taking her there, even though it would have been easier for everyone if her father had picked her up from the lodging house. She'd kept her promise of returning home, but she hadn't told her parents what she and Simos had planned. It was for the best, she'd told herself. Rather than spring it on her parents while they'd been in Kefalonia, she'd waited until she'd been back home working and saving, before telling them of her dream to own a gallery. Over the winter months, Eléni and Simos had proved their commitment to one another through several visits to Kefalonia and Wales, almost daily phone calls and many, many letters.

In the end, it was her cousin, Theo, who'd made her dream a reality. During one visit to her uncle, Theo had been there. He'd asked her about her idea of opening a gallery.

'I've spotted a vacant premises in Elpizō Street that may be suitable. It has a small flat above it that's included in the rental.'

Goosebumps formed on her arms.

'It's an omen, *agápi mou*.' Theíos Kostas smiled at her.

'But I can't afford anything in Argostoli. I thought of something small in a village.'

'You've made my father a very happy man by finding him, hasn't she, Baba? So how about I invest in your business until you start making a profit?'

Eléni gasped and hugged them both.

As she looked up at the picture, Eléni then thought back to the moment she'd broken the news to her family about her plans to settle in Kefalonia. Remembering how quiet her mother had been to start with, it had been down to her father and sister that she had come round.

'Just think, *cariad*. We'll have no ties once Bron goes off to uni. We can go to visit as often as we like.' Her father was always the diplomat, not mentioning that her mother now had a job.

'And I can spend every holiday out there trying to add some colour to my pasty skin. I may even find the love of my life out there like Eléni.' Bronwen laughed.

Perhaps not the best thing to say when trying to persuade our mother, sister dear.

To everyone's surprise, it didn't take long for Cassia to accept Eléni was leaving. Her mother's words meant so much to her.

'Follow your heart, *Elenáki mou*. I did when I came to Wales. You and Simos make the perfect couple.'

Her mother also handed over the savings from Eléni's rent money. It was now for a gallery a bit further from home than expected, but the money was given willingly. Her mamá accompanied her father to come and decorate the gallery in preparation for fitting it out and hanging all the pictures. And now they were both arriving in time for the opening the next day.

Simos opened the bottle of Robola chilling in the ice bucket on the reception desk and poured two glasses.

'*Yamas!* To my beautiful and talented Eléni. Every success.'

'*Yamas!*

It's all down to me now, she thought.

'*You're a Mouzakis. You'll be fine,*' whispered a voice Eléni imagined to be from another artist with the same surname.

THE END

ACKNOWLEDGEMENTS

The publication of any novel does not happen without the help of so many people. Firstly, I want to thank my husband, Alan, for his unwavering support and faith in me as a writer, all the meals cooked and endless cups of tea and coffee. You're a star! Thank you, as well, to other members of my family who are forever spreading news about my books, far and wide.

A research trip to Kefalonia in May 2024 would not have been as successful or enjoyable without the invaluable help of my daughter, Joanna. Huge thanks go to her not only for her great company but also for acting as my travel agent, tour guide and chauffeur as she negotiated the hazardous mountain roads of the island with aplomb! We stayed in the capital, Argostoli, where the earthquake did so much damage. It was good to feel we were walking in the footsteps of my characters.

As with my debut novel, also set on a Greek island, I am indebted to Jo's friend, Vicky Æ Nicolaou, for her help with the incidental Greek used in the novel. Any missed errors — and accents! — are entirely my own.

Special thanks are due to Theotocoula Moulinos (Theo), a member of staff at Korgialenio Historic and Cultural Museum, Argostoli, who gave me so much of her time and a great deal of helpful information about not only the earthquake but also what island life was like in the 1950s.

Thanks are also due to others in the writing community for their encouragement and generous support, especially members of the wonderful Cariad Chapter, and many more writers online. Of those, special thanks must go to my beta readers, Judith Barrow and Luisa A. Jones, for reading an early full draft of the novel and for their insightful, helpful feedback.

I'm grateful, too, to Zumrut Edwards for our chat about her family's experience of the earthquake in Turkey in 2023 and to Sally Hodges for our talk about selective mutism and how it differs from how it would have been judged as elective mutism at the time Eléni was unable to talk in 1953. Thank you both.

Finally, last but not least, thank you to my publisher, Joffe Books/Choc Lit Publishing. I was delighted to be working with my wonderful editor, Jasmine. It's been great to work with you! Thank you, as well, to Jarmila Takač for another stunning cover.

Thank you all!

THANK YOU

Dear Reader

Thank you for reading my fifth novel, *The Silent Sister*. I hope you enjoyed reading the novel as much as I enjoyed writing it. Through Eléni's eyes, I've tried to capture what it must have been like to find out about her Greek heritage and visit Kefalonia for the first time, sampling its colours, its beauty, culture and foods. If, through my words, you were able to accompany her on her travels to that beautiful island, I shall be happy.

Just as with every novel, it's both exciting and nerve-wracking to introduce you to characters I now know very well. They've become my friends. I'd love to hear how you enjoyed *The Silent Sister* and would be thrilled if you could take the time to leave a review in order for the book to reach more readers. Reviews are very much appreciated. Thank you.

My contact details appear at the end of my author profile. I'd love to hear from you and learn what you think. Please look out for the final 'sister' story about another family and its secret in 2026.

Love Jan x

ABOUT THE AUTHOR

After retiring from a career in teaching and advisory education, Jan joined a small writing group in a local library where she wrote her first piece of fiction. From then on, she was hooked! She soon went on to take a writing class at the local university and began to submit short stories for publication to a wider audience. Her stories and flash fiction pieces have been longlisted and shortlisted in competitions and several appear in anthologies both online and in print. In October 2019, her first collection of shorts was published. Her stories started getting longer and longer so that, following a novel-writing course, she began to write her first full-length novel. She loves being able to explore her characters in further depth and delve into their stories.

Fascinated by family secrets and 'skeletons lurking in cupboards', Jan's dual narrative, dual timeline novels explore how decisions and actions made by family members from one generation impact the lives of the next. Setting and a sense of place play an important part in all Jan's stories, and as well as her native Mid-Wales, there is always a contrasting location in sunnier climes. *The Secret Sister*, partially set in Sicily, was shortlisted for the Romantic Novelists' Association's Romantic Saga Award in 2024.

Originally from Mid-Wales, Jan lives in Cardiff with her husband. Having joined the RNA in 2016, she values the friendship and support from other members and regularly attends conferences, workshops, talks and get togethers. She is an active member of her local chapter, *Cariad*.

You may find out more about Jan here:

X/Twitter: @JanBaynham
Facebook: Jan Baynham Writer
Instagram: janbaynham
BlueSky: Jan Baynham
Blog: www.janbaynham.blogspot.com

THE CHOC LIT STORY

Established in 2009, Choc Lit is an independent, award-winning publisher dedicated to creating a delicious selection of quality women's fiction.

We have won 18 awards, including Publisher of the Year and the Romantic Novel of the Year, and have been shortlisted for countless others. In 2023, we were shortlisted for Publisher of the Year by the Romantic Novelists' Association.

All our novels are selected by genuine readers. We are proud to publish talented first-time authors, as well as established writers whose books we love introducing to a new generation of readers.

In 2023, we became a Joffe Books company. Best known for publishing a wide range of commercial fiction, Joffe Books has its roots in women's fiction. Today it is one of the largest independent publishers in the UK.

We love to hear from you, so please email us about absolutely anything bookish at choc-lit@joffebooks.com.

If you want to receive free books every Friday and hear about all our new releases, join our mailing list here: www.joffebooks.com/freebooks.